You
Were
Here

You
Were
Here

GIAN SARDAR

G. P. PUTNAM'S SONS

NEW YORK

PUTNAM

G. P. PUTNAM'S SONS
Publishers Since 1838
An imprint of Penguin Random House LLC
375 Hudson Street
New York, New York 10014

Library of Congress Cataloging-in-Publication Data

Names: Sardar, Gian, author.
Title: You were here / Gian Sardar.
Description: New York : G. P. Putnam's Sons, 2017.
Identifiers: LCCN 2016036567 | ISBN 9780399575006 (hardcover)
Subjects:
LCSH: Family secrets—Fiction. |
BISAC: FICTION / Psychological. | FICTION / Romance / Gothic. |
   FICTION / Romance / Contemporary. |
GSAFD: Romantic suspense fiction.
Classification: LCC PS3619.A7235 Y68 2017 | DDC 813/.6—dc23
LC record available at https://lccn.loc.gov/2016036567.
p.   cm.
International edition ISBN: 9780735215719

Printed in the United States of America
10 9 8 7 6 5 4 3 2 1

Book design by Michelle McMillian

For my son, Maximiliaen,
a little boy with a big name.
You have my heart.

Turquoise, magenta, lime, bright bursts of red and gold; flashes of irony from a stone deemed colorless. A wave good-bye could cast a rainbow, a bolt of brilliance from a hand drawing shut a door. A ring that shines with such fire should not be stifled, tucked away in darkness and extinguished, and yet it has been for decades. First placed in a safe by shaking hands, then hidden in a drawer by someone who no longer believed in romance or diamonds or promises.

Until now. Now a little girl has the ring and holds it in her small, hot hand. The door to the bathroom is shut; her mother is at work and her grandmother asleep. Carefully the girl places the ring on her thumb, and with each turn of the stone, each reflected color, a moment flashes in her mind—a moonlit dinner by a river, a kiss among vines and white flowers, a breathless confession as footsteps draw closer.

But then the door swings open. Her grandmother is standing there, and immediately her eyes find the ring, that ring she'd never wanted to see again.

Get it off. <u>Get it off now.</u>

1

Now

THAT DEEP BLUE OF SUMMER, endless and brilliant. The heat seems to come with a noise like insects, a noise that shimmers. Coolers hold down blankets and bees are gathered at trash cans. Abby is lying in the sand, happy, but when she turns the ocean is gone, replaced by a dark meadow, the waves now undulations of tall, dry grass. The sky's gone gray, a storm churning, gathering. This was the noise she heard, the storm's approach. In a flash she sees it, the giant oak tree, black limbs snaking into an ashen sky. At its base is a table set for two, always set for two. A crystal chandelier quivers on the branch above.

It's been years since she's been here, and understanding bangs her heart into a furious rhythm as suddenly she's sinking, unable to move, the sand that had been so soft a moment before now dirt that spills into her mouth. At once she's choking, gasping, waking to a bed soaked with sun, sheets shoved to the floor.

Outside, a dove's cry turns to a demand: *who-ooo, who, who, who.*

The dark meadow. The nightmare that started in high school and recurred once or twice a month until she left Minnesota. An ending that's always the same—suffocation, desperate gasps for breath. The one time she'd gone home during college, brave with longing and rested from a year of unplagued sleep, the dream had returned like a waiting, loyal friend. Never again has she been back, never again has she had the dream. Until now.

"It's been fourteen years," she tells Robert later, in the car. He was asleep when she left, and she's waited to tell him in person. Though her voice holds striations of panic, he doesn't understand—words are a pale shadow of meaning. "Fourteen years since I've had the dream."

"One nightmare," he says, "is one nightmare. Try not to worry, okay?"

The air-conditioning blasts, her toes chilled. The entrance to the freeway is in an old residential neighborhood, and the once-proud houses are faded, pockmarked with missing siding. Glass shimmers in the gutter.

"Anxiety," she says. "That's what they used to say. But it never made sense. They stopped when I left for college—if anything I was more stressed."

"You had an estate visit today?"

An attempt to change the subject, to loosen her mind's grip. She tries to let him, to take herself from the meadow and join him in a re-cap of her day, her work at the antique jewelry store and the estate trips it involves, crowds of family photos on shelves, paintings darkened with time, marriages that last longer than most lifetimes or end faster than the turn of a season. A screenwriter, Robert loves the stories Abby collects. *Tell me more*, a constant refrain in their relationship, a request made as they fall asleep at night or while walking down boulevards flanked with magnolia trees, flowers as wide as saucers. "Forty-eight years they'd been married," she says, though she still sees the tremor in the oak tree's leaves, feels the dirt that fell into her mouth. "The wedding ring was her mother's. Once sewn into the hem of a dress in Poland."

Then they're on the freeway, the oldest in Southern California. *Made for horses*, she tells people. *You enter from a stop sign. Zero to sixty in the time it takes to change the radio station.* Robert changes lanes to pass a car, and out of the corner of her eye she feels another driver doing the same. She looks away. Think pretty—one of the rings from today, an aquamarine the same pale blue as a pool's shallow end, a welcome glimmer in a June light. Still the freeway's energy pulses, gathers for impact, and her legs push against the floor.

Death, accidental and early, has always been her preoccupation. Horrible images exist behind Abby's eyes—pretty eyes, eyes that laugh, eyes that should not look for such things. *Girls who wear pink should not think your thoughts*, she was once told by an ex-boyfriend who did not understand that she chose these colors, these bright soft colors, precisely because of what exists in her mind.

"Did I ever tell you I didn't get my license till I left Minnesota?" she says. "All those one-lane highways. The accidents. That and my mom tried teaching me on a stick." A three-point turn, the car rolling forward, angled into the street, other drivers patient but waiting. Abby'd simply thrown it into park, gotten out, and run to the passenger side. Her mother had no choice but to take over.

"I was at the DMV on my birthday," Robert says.

Robert at his core is logic, a calm voice, a man who highlights when he reads, straight hair and ironed shirts. Abby is always, without fail and from the start, a few decibels too loud, chaos, the person who drops the book in the bathtub, curly hair that tends to knot and nail polish that's always chipped. All reasons he loves her, she knows—she's his voice when he wants to scream, the mess he longs to make.

He flicks on the blinker, then glances over his shoulder. "Wine?"

"I had it—" but even as she's saying this, she's looking in the back-seat and not seeing it, that bottle with its graceful lettering, better than they normally drink, more expensive than they normally allow. Chosen especially for the evening, for her best friend Hannah's first dinner at her first house. Left on the kitchen counter.

"We get lucky then," Robert says. "Tomorrow night. In-N-Out. Burgers and Bordeaux. You sent them those cheese knives, right?"

"Last week. But we can't show up empty-handed."

As they exit, Abby sees their only hope will be some convenience store bottle best suited for cooking. *Here, to put in the pasta,* she'll say when Hannah—a wine rep, long red hair and an impeccable palate— answers the door. Somehow it seems fitting that Abby's failed in this, the simple ability to bring a bottle of wine to dinner. Left behind, that's how she feels. The thirty-three-year-old trapped in an apartment, in a relationship without a ring. Marriage? A house? Children? That's for everyone but her, everyone else who hurtles along while she tries to enter from a stop sign. And now she'll show up to dinner, a frazzled guest with Gallo jug wine.

It will happen, he's told her. Career back on track, debt settled, money for a down payment, there's a list of what needs to be checked off, though all Abby hears is that Robert needs to sell another script first—about as easy as winning the lottery. *Why rush? Let's do it right,* he's said, and Abby's begun to wonder if the course they're on was born strictly of convenience. *There's no freeway access to Abby's place,* she'd long ago heard him tell a friend. Could that be it? Was the exit simply not close enough? Four years later and here they are in a shared apart-ment, the freeway so close it sounds like rain.

This is not what she'd imagined would happen, not what her young, optimistic self had conjured in the Noxzema nights of her youth. Then what she'd pictured was the boy she'd had a crush on, Aidan Macken-zie, one day really seeing her and being hit with the knowledge they should be together, cheerleader girlfriend be damned. At that point, marriage was a given, a future she knew without question she'd have, and imaginings of a proposal soothed her back to sleep when she'd wake in the middle of the night. White tablecloths and candlelight, a bended knee in the fury of a New York crowd, an extended hand on the side of the road amid neat rows of corn like a world freshly combed. A romantic from day one. Now, in the car, Abby smiles at how ridiculous she was. Just yesterday she'd found a notice for her fifteen-year reunion, in only two weeks. Hidden between the glossy pages of a magazine, it sailed to the floor like an idea attempting to settle.

Tags of graffiti brighten walls and dozens of jagged bottles lie splin-tered against a building, broken as if someone had simply needed to hear the sound. The neighborhood is neglected, all of it, as if the whole place has just given up and is filled with women whose shifts at work are too long, men who pride themselves on the wrong things, and chil-dren who are told every day to go play at their friends' houses. Every-thing's coming apart at the seams.

They pull to a stoplight before the liquor store and Abby sees three guys with shaved heads and wife-beaters watching them from the cor-ner. It won't take long for them to cross the street, to be at the car, the Audi that was the one illogical thing Robert bought when he'd sold a script five years ago, a car that now might get them killed. Robert is more bookish than brawn, the one who stops fights, calming words and hands on shoulders, steering tempers away. Yet Abby can see it— one step in front of her, he'd be about to speak when the knife plunges into his side, tearing his shirt, scraping a rib.

Wait. A knife? Do gangs even carry knives?

"You okay?" he asks. They're parked. Robert's turned in his seat, watching her. It's one thing she loves about him; carried within him always is a barometer of her comfort. Though he's barely looked across the street, Abby knows he saw them and is aware they're raising her nerves. Because of this attentiveness, her fears have actually lessened since she met Robert, his presence like a hand that smooths the covers. *See? There's nothing there.*

They fly from the car to the store, Robert's steps spurred by heat and the time he sees on his watch, Abby's steps jet-fueled by fear. Still the guys are on the corner, locked in the reflection of the glass. Robert leads her to the counter, a dusty bottle of overpriced Cabernet in his hand, and Abby waits for the chime of the door, arms lifted, guns aimed—they don't have knives, she's decided—until she finally forces her gaze to the window in time to see the group boarding a bus.

The corner is a bus stop. They were standing there because they were waiting for the bus.

"What?" Robert asks, as if he feels the realization weight her, a shift in her muscles.

"Sometimes I disappoint myself." She glances back at the bus, its blinker a mere formality as it lurches into the lane.

It doesn't take long for the narrow, winding roads to lift them above the city. Parched chaparral and sage, houses with dry shingles and old wooden frames, everything just waiting for a spark, one bright orange inhalation. Abby spots a eucalyptus tree, dense branches reaching through telephone wires, bowing over the street. *Gasoline trees,* a firefighter she'd met had called them. *It's their sap. Incendiary. I even smell one of those fuckers, my heart slams into gear.*

She tries to peer around the corner. Blind. The drop-off a brace of blue to her left. One swerve, that's all it would take. A tire would miss the road, the tumble slow at first, an almost reluctant pull of gravity, then faster and faster, invigorated. The landing among trees, then silence. Nothing more than a broken glimmer from above. She can't look. "I bet the view is amazing."

"You're not even looking at it."

"That's why I said, 'I *bet* the view is amazing.'" She flashes him a quick smile before once again focusing on soil and plants, the solidity of the mountain. Agave plants line a driveway, arms twisting and reaching into the air like creatures from another world.

Then they arrive. A mid-century slab, geometric patterns in an iron gate. Hannah opens the door to cool air and the scent of pine trees, that "everyone's home" smell of Christmas. Abby finds it, a candle, glowing on an end table. Wood floors so dark they appear black, a worn Persian rug, burnt sienna and hydrangea blue. The brown leather couch is purposefully worn and the walls are bone-white. Abby hands her friend the bottle. "We forgot the real wine at home."

A quick glance at the label. "It's a good one," Hannah says. "But you got gouged if you got it from that place down the hill. I've got tons— you really didn't need to stop. But thank you."

Her lips are full and a bit upturned—Abby's convinced she sells wine just by drinking it—but her smile is wide and slightly goofy. *Too pretty*, Abby had thought in college when they first met, until Hannah smiled and the curtain drew back, revealing her as a girl Abby felt she'd known all her life, someone who had a Porsche key chain for the key to her Kia, who played the French horn when she was younger, and wore flip-flops in the rain. One in a long line of exquisite women, Hannah seemed to not even glimpse her own beauty, so accustomed was she to the sight.

Everything, as Abby expected it would be, is perfect. White snapdragons tower in a crystal vase by the window, and the view above the arrangement stretches from spotless panes of glass, a city tinged with evening.

"I know what you're thinking," Robert says, lips to her ear, as Hannah gets their drinks. "And I sell this script, that's all it takes."

Hannah returns with a frosted beer mug for Robert and a gleaming crystal glass for Abby, the wine poured only a third of the way up the basin. Abby swirls the wine. "I feel like I'm at a grown-ups' dinner party."

"You *are* a grown-up. Robert, can you help Ben? Our neighbor left a bunch of firewood by the driveway. Abby, this way."

A tiled patio is off the kitchen. Pots of rosemary, deep Adirondack chairs painted a slick poppy red, a copper fire pit in the center. A patio—what Abby would do for a patio, the simple ability to be home and outside. "You have a Cuisinart," she says as she sits, watching Robert in the kitchen window with Hannah's husband, Ben. "And trees."

"One little speck of earth is ours."

Abby turns, peering up at the wild hillside that ends at an old wood fence. Behind it all, a eucalyptus soars into the sky, white bark a ghostly skin. "I had one of my old nightmares last night."

Hannah's already reclined, legs stretched, ankles crossed. "The dream? The field one?"

"The meadow. The tree." A lizard darts into a crack in the retaining wall. "I found a reunion notice. June seventeenth. It's like my mind put me right back there, back in high school, afraid to sleep."

"Or too busy thinking of that guy to sleep." Another grin.

Aidan Mackenzie. *That guy.* Even now, years later, those words swim on the surface of what he'd meant to her.

"Maybe I *should* go," Abby says. "Robert's script is going out. I don't know if I want to be here for that."

"You don't think it will sell?"

"We've been through it. Close calls. Celebrating for nothing. Only now I know it decides my future as well."

Hannah tilts her face to the sky. "He is how he is, right? I hate it, but I guess try to see it as noble? He wants to be sure he can provide."

"Right. That's how I try to see it, because I love him and the alternative sucks—that he's waiting for *his* life to start. Not ours."

"Well, that's ridiculous. From the moment you met him, your life together started. You're not waiting for anything. You're in it."

Abby sets her wineglass on the ground beside her. The sky's begun to blush, trees darkened in silhouette, branches black and stretching. Again she sees the oak tree, the chandelier, the table set and waiting. *You're not waiting for anything.* And yet, since last night, she has the feeling that she is.

The way Aidan sees it, there are three types of people from Makade: those who left, those who never left, and those who left only to return. That last category—the ones who left only to return—is deemed the worst. A reveal of uppity presumption (*you think you're too good for here*) mixed with failure (*guess you're not*). Not only is Aidan in that category, but he's in a special offshoot. After all, he had the brazen gumption to leave for the Cities—albeit for college—and the sorry need to return, but as far as people could tell his choice to return was career-related, which spoke of failure as a man. *Line to make detective in St. Paul must've been around the block* was one of the first things said to him.

So in a way he understands: his third forgery case in only months. Dues to be paid, a pecking order to remind him that he's no better than the small-town guys. Forget that he went to high school here. Forget that he came back—over a year already—because he missed it. All that matters is that he'd left. Infuriating, but he gets it. What he doesn't get is why he was called in on his day off, for a forgery.

Dark shoe streaks on linoleum, Styrofoam cups on rookies' desks, chipped ceramic mugs on the old-timers'. Aidan looks at the clock on the wall and then back down to Sergeant Budd Schultz, whose gray hair is more of an idea than an actuality. "You called me in for a forgery?"

It's then that he sees them. Roses. On the edge of his desk, long-stemmed and red. The night, just started, goes from bad to worse. *Thinking of you—* Ashley. What girl sends a guy flowers? The same kind, he supposes, who mends his shirt on the third date. The kind who buys you a vitamin B complex because she thinks you're under too much stress. The kind you either marry or dump immediately. "I should've ended things a month ago," he says to no one in particular, and sets the vase on a cabinet in the corner.

"No, I didn't call you in for a forgery," Schultz says. "Rape, three AM this morning. Violent. Woman named Sarah Breining. In surgery now." He scratches his temple. "Mother was even there, heaviest sleeper in the state of Minnesota."

Detective Clive Harris—a know-it-all, a walking spoiler, the last guy you tell anything—nods to the coffee machine in the corner. "Got the good stuff. Gonna rock around the clock."

That's when Aidan sees it, a dark excitement. Officers with bags head straight to the secure evidence lockers; a few place hushed phone calls. Now he remembers another rape case. Just a couple of weeks ago. Lila McCale. "Serial rapist?"

Schultz nods. "But worse. Like in Marshall. And they didn't release key details then, so for it to happen the same way, I'm going with the 'not a coincidence' theory. Briefing in the morning."

Aidan says nothing, not about to give them the pleasure of him asking what happened there. He was in the Cities, not up on smaller town crimes, and they know it. "My old partner from SPPD is there now. If you want to talk to him."

"They'll collaborate, they'll send someone," Schultz says. "Same M.O. But we're keeping the details tight—no sense in a mass panic. Still gotta get fiber matches back, see if we get a positive link to Marshall, but meantime you might want to tell Miss Roses at the Station to keep her doors and windows locked. Double-bolted. Get a dog, set the alarm. I'm telling Carrie to skip her night class." Again he scratches his temple, a red mark left behind. "This guy's not done."

Aidan leans back in his chair. "Shit. What the hell happened in Marshall?"

Before Schultz answers, one of the rookies enters the room. "Sorry," he says to Aidan. "If you're not busy. Call from one of your cases. Rebecca Sullivan."

Aidan looks down and sees Rebecca Sullivan's name on the forgery file.

"Go," Schultz says. "Make it quick."

Rebecca's building is one of those mid-seventies contraptions with a long hallway of short green AstroTurf carpet and doors that lead to uniform apartments, each one with Navajo-white walls and Formica countertops. Everything smells musty, like a sweater from the Salvation Army. It's been almost ten minutes, and so far all Aidan can tell is that Rebecca's one of those women who need attention, who's had it all her life and patterns her days in ways to lessen its loss. She's late thirties in a way that tells you her twenties were the good years.

"And no one saw him try to run you over with the car?" Aidan asks.

Rebecca folds her bare legs on the couch, knobby knees extending a bit beyond the cushion. Smoker's lines splinter from her lips. "If a tree falls in a forest and no one hears it, does that mean it didn't fall?"

Aidan smiles. "You mean make a noise."

"Fuck you." Her mouth opens in something like a smile, and Aidan sees the pink of her tongue press against her upper molar in a strangely suggestive way. "No," she continues. "No one saw him try to do it. If someone was there, he wouldn't have done it."

"There a reason you and your brother been fighting?"

"Him forging my mom's will's not enough? You've got the file. Or maybe you don't have to read it." She pats the couch cushion beside her. "Come join me and I'll tell you a tale."

The officer standing by the door shifts his feet, staring at the rug. Beside him, on the wall, is a photo of two blond kids, the younger boy's hair sticking up as if amped by electricity.

Aidan doesn't move. "I know you're contesting your mother's will."

"I'm contesting what he *did* to my mother's will. Rick hated her, always did. And he hates me, because me and my mom were close. But now *he's* in her house—the one she wanted me and my family to have, that she told me we would have. My boys don't have a yard. Okay? I know that might not seem like a big deal, but boys need a yard. Used to be they could run around at her place, she even got a climbing structure for them, but now they can't do that. So that's one thing. That's the current thing. Then there's other factors, like he's a fucking asshole."

Aidan looks again to the picture on the wall.

"I had blond hair when I was a kid," she says, watching him. "My brother and I were towheads till my dad was killed. Then our hair went black."

"Killed?"

"Accident. Car accident. I say *killed* because it wasn't his fault."

"Your kids were asleep when this happened? Tonight, I mean."

"No, but they were inside. I was outside. Where the car is. Where cars tend to be. I might as well be talking to my husband."

"Your husband doesn't believe you?"

"You see him here?"

"I'm not ignoring you."

"You'd be the first."

Aidan glances at the officer by the door, who shrugs.

"You've been here, what," she says to the officer, "six times?" She looks back at Aidan. "I'm about ready to set a place at the table for Officer Hughes."

Officer Hughes shakes his head. "We've had no proof your brother's even been *near* here."

"Again," Rebecca says, "I'll bring up that tree in the fucking forest."

Aidan fills out the report on her kitchen counter. By the stove is a stack of mail, the top envelope with his high school's emblem. The reunion invite. He lifts it up, glances at the recipient's name. "I was in the same class as your husband."

"Really? Same as my brother then, too. Before he left, I mean."

Rick, her brother—Rick Sullivan. Now Aidan places him, remembers him from freshman year, studying the bulletin board at the end of the hall during breaks to make it seem as if he were alone for a reason. Pants that were always too short, the hazard of being tall in a life of hand-me-downs. Once he'd gotten in trouble for having a garter snake in his locker—whether he'd put it there or not, Aidan doesn't remember. Nor, he realizes, did he see him beyond that one year.

"Where'd Rick graduate?"

"He didn't. My uncle was a housepainter, gave him a job. He quit school."

"That's too bad."

"Yeah, well. He's the one with the house. For some reason."

Aidan just nods and goes back to filling out the report. But then he pauses and moves the stack of envelopes away from the stove, thinking of the silent, sleeping kids.

⤳

Three bottles of wine later and they're on the patio, the fire an orange plume between them. Rosemary and burning pine fill the air and the sky is mostly dark, though clouds closest to the moon are lit up, great swaggering tumbles of light. Hannah sets a tray of cheese and crackers on a stool, a bowl of grapes alongside.

"I have a Sauternes in the fridge," she says, and disappears back inside.

In the kitchen window, Abby sees her reaching for the appropriate glasses in a top cupboard. When did this happen? Gradually, of course, but with the house it's suddenly obvious. Gone are the years of late-night runs to Denny's, turkey sandwiches dipped in ranch dressing, sweatshirts over pajamas, counting out exact change. Replaced by sturdy patio furniture and a view of the city, weekends early to bed, podcast commutes and scripts that need to sell. On the other side of the fire pit Robert sits back in his chair, eyes closed, enjoying the moment.

"You okay?" Hannah asks when she returns, noticing Abby's distraction.

The glass of Sauternes gleams in the firelight. Abby smiles. "I'm good. Sometimes I just miss us."

"Me and you?" Hannah squeezes into the chair next to her. "We're still here. Evolving, but still here."

"We don't wear pajamas anymore to Denny's."

"No, that is true. We don't. Not for a long time."

Ben places another log on the fire, which sways, ducking and dancing. *Fire moves like a boxer,* Robert once said to her when they first met. Even that seems long ago. Then she saw her life so differently; never would she have guessed that nothing would change in four years. Again she thinks of Aidan Mackenzie, that sense she'd had when she was younger that they would be together. What does he look like now? Though Abby refuses to join Facebook—InYourFacebook, she calls it—she now thinks of registering just to see. She'd heard his parents moved back to Idaho when he was in college. Could he be there? A log cabin, a flannel shirt, thick, sturdy arms. Irish Spring soap and pine.

Hannah takes the cheese plate from the side table and holds it before Abby, who reaches toward the knife but stops when she sees the crackers. "Sesame seeds."

"Crap," Hannah says, leaning forward, squinting. "I didn't even check."

It's a little oversight, but a detail Hannah never would've missed before. There's no way around it, her best friend's life has changed, filled with so much that's wonderful, so much that Abby is thankful for, and yet she can't help but feel left behind, can't help but miss the days when Hannah stood beside her, studying ingredient lists, stocking up on Benadryl just in case, back in the days when it was just them and there were no expectations yet, no ways to fall behind.

"I'm fine," Abby says, trying to be. "This is perfect." She lifts her glass, the flare of light like a strike of happiness.

Later that night Abby lies in bed, eyes open. Will she have the dream again? *State of mind,* her mother used to say. *If you go to sleep thinking of the dreams, you're summoning them.* Partly true, she knows, but not thinking of something that worries her is almost impossible. Still, there's no reason to think the dreams are back. *One nightmare is one nightmare.* Think of something good: Robert selling his script, their future house, string lights and wind chimes, summer dinners in the garden with pots of lavender and fig trees, fruit like giant drops of purple.

Then her mind veers back to Aidan Mackenzie, the first day she'd met him, late in October of their freshman year, the world a torrent of orange and red. Even before he'd stepped on campus he'd been talked about—*Olympic developmental soccer team, only a freshman, six feet already.* There'd been a rain, one of those fall rains that take down leaves and moisten an already damp earth. Laundry steam a slow wisp from the side of a house. Streetlights still on. Even now Abby remembers the red of his mother's car in the gray morning as she idled two blocks from the school. *I'll be fine,* Abby heard him say before the car finally left. While he stood there, unmoving, facing the school and his unknown, Abby pretended to hunt for something in her backpack. That this athlete, handsome even from across the street, status already a given, would be nervous, would ask his mom to drop him off blocks away, was something that had never occurred to her, and immediately she was charmed. He was tense, uneasy. She could see it as she stepped onto the dark pavement.

The first thing she said to him as she approached: *Are you the one from Idaho?*

When he turned, everything changed. Untethered, an immediate severing from what had held her in place her whole life—she'd not even known it was possible, the feeling.

The second thing she said to him: *Wait, do I know you?* Because in that moment she knew she did.

And though he'd arrived in the state only two nights prior, he searched her eyes at the question. *I just got here,* he finally said—a reply

Abby would recall later that night and later many nights, because he'd not answered her, not really. They'd walked to school together, and when they arrived it took all of ten minutes for him to be claimed by a different crowd, their paths forever fissured.

The way he'd been pulled, she remembers. A glance back at her. *Thank you,* she thought she saw him say. Of course they'd had the following years of school together, but their paths crossed at most in halls or at desks not too far away but never close enough. For those minutes, however, in that gray morning with the devouring brilliance of turning leaves, he'd been just hers.

For a while longer she thinks of him, the thoughts a familiar fit and comfort, until at last the tangled beginnings of sleep weigh in, her eyes staying shut longer with every blink. Nonsensical thoughts and images sprout off wildly, transforming and merging.

Bougainvillea. Branches with thorns like fangs, petals thin and reddish pink, a fury of fevered skin. Abby's head is at its base, and as she looks up, the wood of the branches thicken and the petals begin to fall. Her eyes are closed as they drift onto her lids, brushing her lips. But the moment she sweeps them away, she sees that the branches are now that of the oak tree, limbs wise and twisting into a sky of burned-out gray. Beside her, the table and chairs wait, and the shimmering sounds of the meadow gather into whispers, whispers that begin to take shape just as the ground beneath her shifts and opens and her body starts to sink. It's when the dirt falls into her mouth that Robert shakes her awake, and it takes her a while to realize that the sounds she'd made in her dream must have filtered into the outside world. Something about that doesn't seem right, as if a thin layer has been pierced.

Her heart is wild. The back of her neck moist with sweat, hair damp. Three AM. The same time that used to jolt her awake, a chasm in the night. Robert watches her, the lights all now on. He tells her he had no idea.

But it wasn't just the dark meadow. It wasn't just that she couldn't breathe. This time the whispers gathered and became her own voice. And what she felt was fear. Pure, serrated, helpless fear, as over and again she said a name.

Claire Ballantine. Claire Ballantine. Claire Ballantine.

2

Then

SOMEONE'S CALLING HER NAME. Claire hears it three times, faint, like in a dream, a scream rendered nothing more than a whisper. Past the window, plunged into the black night, the lake water is dark as oil, slick and smooth. The parlor is empty. No one's there. She faces the door, convinced the voice will emerge again, but the only sound is the pace of the grandfather clock. She must've imagined it. It happens frequently in this house, the hope—or fear—that someone is there when they are not.

She turns back to the window. On the walnut table beside her is a silver tea set and Van Briggle's Despondency vase, a large vase with a man curled at the top, hands on his knees, head facing the opening, a seemingly endless void. The mulberry and blue matte glaze deepens toward the top, becoming almost black as the figure emerges, a form lifting from moroseness. When Claire first saw the vase in her early twenties, years had passed since her debutante ball, and she'd resigned herself to either a loveless arranged marriage or being alone. In preparation she steeled herself against either option with her pottery, and since she's fallen in love not just with the vase but with the man who created it, a man who could've understood the slight sadness she's always carried within her. Artus Van Briggle, dead from tuberculosis at only thirty-five years old. He knew he was dying when he created the piece, and after Claire learned this, she saw within it both love and mistrust of the human form, the fragility of such vessels, the emptiness we cling to. That first time, though, upon finding the piece, she'd seen only herself. Not dying from anything other than life.

Winter is what she wants, what she misses, which is not something people in Minnesota do. Trees outlined in white, ice skating, bursts of cloudy breaths, delicate chimes of ice. But especially the sweaters and long sleeves, able to disguise the fact that she's put on weight, not that anyone's said anything or even noticed, for all she knows.

Less than two years they've been married. Never tumultuous, never a voice raised in anger, and so it made sense that the change she'd noticed was civil as well. A look she'd caught almost eight months ago, on a beautiful fall afternoon, a look she's seen many times since. Distracted. He'd stopped before the window, smiling, a mosaic of brilliant leaves just beyond the glass—but she'd watched him and realized there was no focus to his gaze. What he saw was in his mind. And it was then she realized that the happiness she bore witness to had nothing to do with the color of the season, and nothing to do with her.

The next morning she took an extra slice of bread. From Wednesday to Saturday she's by herself, and the food that once had been a reward—*you've earned this, enduring this house all alone*—soon became a punishment. *You've never been good enough for him, and now it will show.* Entire lists of items she'll eat one by one, starting perhaps with the grasshopper pie or coconut cake, then leading to the zucchini bread baked fresh the other day. Only when she's physically, undeniably ill, will she stop. After that, later in the day or even during the next, her steps are slowed, the anticipation turned to dread, yet still she's compelled, her mind held hostage by the simple fact that eating like this is an option. On Fridays she's relieved, a flagellant whose whip is taken away. It will be over. Her husband will be back. Saturdays are the day of his return. Saturdays are when it stops.

After all these months of eating like this, her body has begun to change, her waist thick, the angles of her face no longer precise. When she works at the potter's wheel, her arms press against the protrusion of her stomach. All of her body is in the way, and she worries someone will ask her if she's with child—an embarrassment from which she might never recover.

Through the trees the water moves, doused in moonlight. What would it be like to drown? What would it feel like, water rushing into your lungs, every gulp for air heavy and weighted? Or maybe, just for a moment, your body would recall its inception, and perhaps there would be a feeling of recognition and peace?

This is how I started, this is how I end.

cl℧

The most radiant stars stay firm and fixed, but Eva's convinced the smaller ones are disappearing before her eyes, swallowed by the black sky just as she captures them in her gaze. A trick of vision, but maybe not. Maybe she *is* witnessing their disappearance. The thought gives new weight to staring at the sky, and she straightens as she takes the pastime more seriously.

It's the beginning of June, and the night air is scented with an awkward mixture of lilacs and morels, opened earth from nearby farms and the marshy scent of the settled lake. Rochester is less than two hours south of Minneapolis, yet she imagines the air up there to be completely different, a mesh of street smells and perfume curled with the heat of ambition. Time, too, would feel faster, she's sure, marked by the hands of a clock rather than the slant of the sun or the curl in certain leaves.

Though it's dark, anyone could see her, just sitting on the steps and staring at the stars, waiting. It's not a smart place for her to sit, being so visible, but the other option is the porch at the back of the house, and that faces the woods, woods that during the day are pretty and green and don't extend too far, but have multiplied and thickened in the falling darkness, have become an entire forest teeming with the hidden possibilities of night. No, she can't stare at the woods. Not by herself. She'd spend the whole time waiting for something to emerge. If he were with her, however, it would be different. Pulse-quickening in a delicious way.

He'd warned her he would be late, and then she lost her key. Worse, tonight's one of those romantic nights you don't need a sweater for, the kind that hangs on to the heat like someone too happy to stop smiling. No doubt he's strolling leisurely. Taking his time, admiring lawns and porches and tree houses.

At last there's a crunch on the gravel. Eva stands, excited, watching the moonlight release him one step at a time. Broad, straight shoulders— she hates sloping; a man with sloping shoulders is frail and too easily swayed, which is just no fun—dark, almost black hair, a strong, square jaw, and sturdy cheekbones. Really, everything about him is dark and unnervingly handsome.

He's got his keys ready by the time he reaches the steps. "Why are you outside?" Even when he's annoyed his voice is without edges, like Orson Welles or Gregory Peck.

"I must have left my key at home. But it's warm. I was all right."

As she steps past him, hoping he's not too mad, the night scent of flowers and earth and cooling water disappears, replaced by him and only him. Clean soapiness, a touch of musk, the slight scent of sawdust he can never shake from work—the smell of progress.

Inside, William closes the door. "That's the third key. And the weather's not the point. You were in view for all of Rochester to see."

"It was fine," she says. "I was—" but then she stops speaking, because he's pushed her up against the door, his end-of-the-day scruff against her skin, his determined and warm hand beneath her blouse.

There's not much food in the house, mostly canned goods, so as usual they'll start the next morning at the Princess Café and then head to the market for two days' worth of produce and another bottle of milk. The milk is for her, and because she is twenty-four years old it embarrasses her that she wants it, but she does. Milk and cows and youth and farms—all things best left behind, best forgotten.

But now, now they're on the back porch, the moon caught in the tips of the pine trees, tomato soup from a can in bowls they balance on their laps. The porch is painted green, like grass, and they each have their spot on the floor at the top of the stairs, her back against the left post, his against the right. In between them is a Monopoly game William found in a closet, prewar with metal pieces and nicely cut wooden hotels and houses. The porch light brightens as they play. Their drinks chime, shadows reach. Out here there's the faint scent of green onions that flower purple at the base of the wood railing. Out here they could do anything, their world without witness.

"Did you miss me?" she asks.

He smiles as he rolls the dice. "Always."

"I missed you, too."

"I know you did."

"You're arrogant."

"I know I am." He looks at her, his eyes devouring. "A new blouse. I like you in red."

She touches the buttons, carved Bakelite roses. "I only sewed these on this morning. One of which you knocked off. Ten minutes it took me to find it on the stairs."

He smiles. "Entirely worth it. Remind me to buy you a few sets."

When the moon is high, the bath is running and the soup bowls are stacked in the kitchen sink. The board game doesn't get put away. Everything is left in place, money and cards weighted down with rocks, tokens stilled in their journey, a continuation always imminent, concessions and defeat leading only to the start of a new game. She finds *The Voice of Frank Sinatra* and sets the needle. This is what they'll listen to the rest of the night, a long-playing record that will force him out of the tub only once to start the music again. Her clothes are on the floor by the bed, the loose button on the nightstand. The bathroom's begun to fog. She tests the water with her toe. When at last she hears the first few notes begin, Frank's slow, smooth voice sliding into the room, the candles are lit and she's sunk deep into the bubbles, one leg up, foot by the faucet. Pale skin and red nail polish. White, slick tiles. Her dark hair is wet at the ends. There are crickets through the open window.

He's got a brandy for himself, and for her a highball of whiskey and ginger ale. She takes it from him and presses the cold glass to her chest, against the heat of her skin. She watches him watch her. He swirls his drink. The world flickers.

"I'm sorry about the key," she says.

"I'm sorry I was late."

There's really not room for him, but it doesn't matter. The water rises with his weight. She leans back against the tiles, feeling a drop snake down her neck, and scoops up a handful of bubbles, admiring them in the light. Thousands of reflections. Colors swim and shine and burst.

"I saw a double rainbow as I drove down from Minneapolis," he says, watching her. "Just this morning."

"Aren't you lucky."

He nudges her with his foot. "I am."

She grins, then blows into her hand. A storm of bubbles rises into the air, a world of drifting light. He leans back, his smile that of a man entranced. One cluster has landed on a tile beside her. In it she sees herself, fractured and glassy, and tries, more than anything, not to think of where he was last night.

~

On Saturday morning, William searches for his belt. Behind the chair, by the bathroom, behind the door. Finally he looks up at the bed. Eva lies with one hand above her head on the pillow, the other absent-mindedly playing with the blanket, fingers kneading.

"Eva," he says, and watches her smile to the ceiling. Somehow she's positioned herself within a beam of sun from the window, and the light seems to lift her from the rest of the room.

She shakes her head, but then relents and pulls the belt from under her pillow. He leans down for a quick kiss and then forces himself away. Saturdays are when they say good-bye. Twisted sheets. Coffee in chipped porcelain. Pillow-whispered promises. The inevitable rush against the clock.

The bedroom, like the rest of the house, is small and decorated in the former owner's feminine Victorian style: crowds of tiny flowers on wallpaper, scattered pastel hand-hooked wool rugs. It was never supposed to be anything more than a rental—furnished, walking distance to downtown but also across from Silver Lake, function and pleasure. When he finally agreed to purchase it, the owner—an old woman with impatience in her eyes and a catch in her throat that chopped up everything she said—had been more than happy to leave all her former possessions, taste, and dreams exactly where they were.

It's 1948 and men have started wearing casual shirts without jackets, shirttails flapping even on the streets of New York, but William still loves his suits. Wool or tweed now that the war is over, the cuts wider, more generous with fabric. A good suit can do wonders, and the ones he has are some of the finest. At first he'd worn them to work as well—after all, he is the owner, and he'd thought that's what owners do—but Rochester, for all its big-belly growth, was still a small town and construction was still construction whether you're the owner or not. So now he wears a suit only while in Minneapolis and—because Eva loves them—when readying to return to Minneapolis, a sight to leave her with. She studies the lapels, the pleats of the trousers, stitching she says she could never duplicate.

Now he catches her watching him in the mirror. Their eyes lock and she smiles in a way that makes it hard to find his reflection again.

"I found a good spot for a picnic on the river," she says. "Not a person to be seen. We could pack an early dinner. It's warm enough. And I saw fish jumping—we could bring poles."

"You are the only woman I know who'd suggest fishing on a date."

"And *you* are the only man *I* know who must not be familiar with how long it takes to catch a fish. There's plenty of time for other things." One of her arms is above her on the pillow, and when she sighs, her chest rises. He forces himself to look away.

"Fishing it is," he says. "But, for now, my dear, we're late." He finishes his thought by motioning to her train case by the window, open and unpacked. Tucked inside the satin pouch that lines the lid is a note, something he knows she'll look for later when she's unpacking, wishing she weren't alone. Little thoughts scrawled on torn paper, sneaked into the case when she's not looking—though by now he suspects she looks away just to afford him the chance.

You sleep sideways and claim almost the entire bed . . . but I'm honored to be the one hanging on. —Me

The café is close and the menu never changes. His spoon's in hand as the waitress leaves the kitchen, and the second the oatmeal is placed in front of him he drizzles maple syrup on top in a perfect spiral. Then they're driving past the outer edges of Silver Lake Park, and more than anything he wishes he could stop the car, a Saturday for once luxurious with time. The lake gleams. The water at this time of day is the same shade as her eyes, a fresh, wicked blue.

"Miss me," she says quietly when they stand at the station. About a dozen other people are also waiting, scattered about as if directionless and ready to board whatever bus stops closest.

He puts his hand in his pocket and nods. "You'll get some chocolate if you're good."

"I'm always good."

His voice is low. "I can actually attest that you're not." He tips an imaginary hat.

Her train case hits the door as she boards the bus. Once he sees she's found her seat, he jiggles his car keys in his pocket and waits till the bus aches into gear and pulls away.

Truth be told, William likes to drive, and would like it even more if he had his other car, a Series 62 convertible, his buttercup-yellow dream. But the Cadillac draws looks. So he drives the Chevy Coupe, reliable and boring in beige. You have a *what* in Minneapolis? she'd asked when he'd told her, and he could see her mind juggling facts and statements. It's too flashy, he'd said. And it's not a car to visit sites in, not unless I want her dinged up and covered in dirt. Which I don't.

As he heads up the state, there are tumults of scenes, fast like passing, frantic thoughts. Dizzying corn, lakes, rivers, all part of the land he really doesn't know, as he's always lived in the Twin Cities. Sure, there are lakes there, but their banks are hemmed with roads, dotted with houses that seem to increase in number each year, growing thicker like something that's finally taken hold, a development started in part by his father's father, who'd seen the future, or so everyone said, and along with acres in scattered parts of the state had snatched up huge parcels of land at Lake Harriet, Lake Calhoun, and Lake of the Isles, the eventual sale of which amassed a fortune that spilled over and echoed clinking sounds in all of Minneapolis's ears. William's father, Irwin, a man whose humility challenged and confused everyone around him, had never joined in William's grandfather's business, but still was in part responsible for the change in landscape. As soon as he could, Irwin broke from his gilded life and joined in the Great War's fight, an impressive, unnecessary decision, only to return and shun his father's business. The fact that Irwin returned from the war at all, whole and generally the same, was seen as reward for being who he was, as the good are deserving. But that his own business then became successful— the inspired decision to pave the roads for the invasion of cars, followed by the magic wand of Coolidge's tax breaks—all that was simply proof that he was in fact a great man, as the righteous will shine like the sun.

It was not easy being the son of someone like this. Nor was it easy being his wife, William always heard. William's mother, Isadora, liked to joke that Irwin's existence counteracted her own, as if their lives were nullified by their differences. While every Thursday for twenty-five years Irwin went to Ray's Barber & Style Shop and listened, without the slightest impatience, to Ray talk of his sons, both killed in the Great War—the fog of which rolled from Ray's mind into Irwin's before being left again at the barbershop door—Isadora sought top stylists, Parisian men with long fingernails and snarled gazes. She was a woman used to life's finest, an unapologetic epicurean, but her generosity was lavish and her Christmas list pages long and specific to each person, drawing upon comments made throughout the year that no one thought she'd even heard. More than anything, however, she was fiercely loyal to her husband. *She will always be the seven-year-old who stole the candy canes off her parents' tree*, Irwin often said, *and gave them to me with a kiss.*

Eva, though, she knows the land. Prettier than a pinup girl, but her childhood as a tomboy comes through now and then, like a glimpse of burlap under a sea of lace. A confused, charming combination. She can name flowers and birds and weeds, an ability at which William marvels. That and her eagerness, her tourist-like excitement for things he finds mundane or has overlooked. The Zumbro River, for instance, which now sits languidly on his right. *Catfish and walleyes and saugers and smallmouth bass*, she'd rattled off the other day right before she'd leaned in to say, *I heard it was called the River of Obstruction.* She sat back. *That was its French name.* Her lower lip, slightly fuller than the top, drives him mad. *Rivière des Embarras, they called it*, he'd replied, and her mouth, with that ripe, plum-stained lip, had opened just a touch before she'd asked him to say it again and then again. That he could do that to her, with that one small phrase, brought him a pride he'd not felt the rest of the week.

When William reaches Minneapolis, there is the familiar collision of emotions. This is the day he doesn't like. Saturday. The edge of worlds, the border, the deep trench where there is nothing but a wish to be on the other side—either side. It's mostly just the first hours of being home, the adjustment from one life to the other, of going from a small clapboard house he's never cared for—pure function, a place to sleep—to his childhood home, which is sprawling and relates to function about as much as a chandelier in a barn. Brownish red stones, a red tile roof, a large turret, and a wrought-iron fence that lines the expansive lawn. There are nine bedrooms, five fireplaces, a den, a sunroom, a billiards room, and a library. There's even a tunnel that stretches from the basement to the carriage house, left over from Prohibition, when his parents' guests needed assurance of an exit. Not that anyone used it. As a child he'd loved it. Calls would sound from either entrance, the whole household searching for him as he sat in darkness, smiling at dirt he couldn't see.

It was a lot for an only child. And though his father claimed it was ridiculous to have this much house, he loved it for the glimmer it cast in his wife's eyes, and never, not once, thought of parting with it. Irwin and Isadora. Names like an opera, William always thought. *Step softly, a dream lies here* is the epitaph on their ivory headstone.

When he arrives, he turns off the car and waits, cherishing the seconds before the weekend twists to its other side. Through the distant dining room window, he sees a light blond curled head of hair. Ketty, the Danish housekeeper who joined his parents after the Great War. For a second she's gone, then appears in the next window. It's established what time he arrives on Saturdays, and he knows the table is set and the food will be hot, just as it was when his father pulled in the drive. In some ways William feels as if his life here, in his parents' house, is merely a skewed continuation of their lives. That is, with one dark-haired, blue-eyed, red-lipstick-wearing difference. He smiles just thinking of her, her infusion of life, like a black-and-white film blazing into Technicolor.

Ketty freezes when she sees him through the kitchen window. Within seconds she's at the car, pulling open the door. This is not an act of kindness. The Great Dane was the nickname he gave her when he was an adolescent and she was at her fiercest. For hours he could be in the tunnel, but all it took was one comment from Isadora that he'd gone missing and off stormed Ketty, straight into the tunnel and back out, dirt on her shoulder and him in tow.

She follows him into the house. "Salmon in dill sauce," she says. *Saman in deal sush.* Even after all this time, her accent is thick, her words hard to understand. She's in her fifties now, and her face is heavily lined. Seeing this, the progression, makes him uncomfortable, as if witnessing a starlet slowly smear the makeup from her face.

At the table, he sits with the napkin on his lap. Quickly he flakes a bit of salmon, just a small corner, eats it, and sets the fork back in its former position. He stares at the crystal chandelier, wishing he were back in Rochester, wishing it weren't Saturday.

There's a slight commotion in the other room and Ketty's voice shoots through the silence. Still he sits there. The mother-of-pearl knife rest gleams.

Finally the door swings open and he stands as Claire enters the room. She nods, her eyes immediately finding his plate, the place where a bit of salmon is missing. His wife's new ability to home in on transgressions is something that unnerves him more and more.

"You must be famished," she says.

"Not particularly." He sits again and waits till she starts eating.

"And your drive?"

"Fine. Road was silk. It's actually a very pretty time of year."

"You say that as if it shouldn't be." She smiles and picks up her fork.

He digs into his lunch, starving. Flaking fish, scooping pota-toes, swallowing and talking. "Dixon submitted our bid for a job on Elm. There's not a doubt in my mind, not one, that it was under Guy McPherson's bid. But at the end of the day, Jimmy claims *we're* the ones who are over, by three hundred dollars. *Three hundred dollars.* Hardly an accident. McPherson's Jimmy's second cousin. Crying collusion isn't much of an option."

He looks up as he reaches for his glass and sees that she's gone. Physically she's there, but he can see in her eyes that she's veered from the path of their conversation. He takes a sip of his water and watches her, not sure she's realized he stopped talking. She wanders frequently. This both annoys and intrigues him, as who or what captures her at-tention? Where does she go? Is she mixing glazes in her mind? A pot left in the kiln?

"Enough about my week," he finally says. "Tell me of yours."

She tilts her head. "Uneventful. Ketty's picked a fight with the butcher again, so I suspect we'll have fish for a while."

"Not surprising."

"I suppose not."

"Always on about something."

The tips of her blond eyelashes hold the light. She looks confused. Has she left again?

"What's the latest in the saga?" *A product of the war*, his mother used to say about Ketty, as if that explained the fights she picked with all the help and her simmering dislike of just about everything. And certainly it did bear some responsibility, as Ketty's father and two brothers—fishermen and not even a part of the Great War—were both killed on a boat in the North Sea, and only a year later her mother prepared and consumed a beautiful, lethal meal of foxglove and lily of the valley.

Ketty, having herself just barely survived an accident at the garment factory where she worked, had nothing left and came to the States. Who wouldn't be familiar with the failings of the world after such loss?

"Oh, William," Claire says, "I don't know. Elizabeth, Edith's sister, had twins last week. A girl and a boy."

He smiles. "One of each. Right off the bat."

"A lot of sleepless nights, is what it is."

"But *good* sleepless. Not bad."

"Well. That might depend on whose view you take."

They resume eating in silence. When his parents first brought up her name as someone he might like to take to dinner—the daughter of someone Irwin greatly respected—he hadn't known who she was. *You've met her,* his mother said. *Years ago, at her debut, at the Nicollet? And many times since then?* But it was only later, after his parents passed, when he sat across from her at Jax Café, halfway into his Tom Collins with fresh fruit and two jiggers of gin, that he really saw her. *You do ceramics?* he asked. As she spoke, he saw in her the love she had for what she did—a passion, really—and that in itself made him sit closer. Her hands moved in the restaurant's dim light, forming the clay as she spoke, and from her love for her craft emerged an exquisite heart-shaped face, startling peacock-blue eyes, a nicely shaped mouth, and a delicate nose—all such beautiful features on their own that somehow melded into one another and lost to the general appearance of someone faded and unremarkable.

Will you show me? he asked. And she did, letting him sit at the corner of the table as she jotted down notes on glazes, studying pieces until they silently spoke of their colors. But forming the clay, the actual work she did at the wheel—that he'd have only one glimpse of. Eyes closed, hands before her, she was a medium of sorts, responding to a command, before she stopped, embarrassed. A few months after they were married, he understood this shyness, this instinct to protect, when he overheard her mother reprimanding her for her "dabblings." *Only a fool would waste day after day hiding in a cave. Such unladylike endeavors.* Claire had said nothing, and so it was William who spoke, his voice startling them both from the hall. *Her* studio, he said. *Claire does her pottery in her studio.*

And though he loved her, he saw it then, in his wife's eyes, that what he felt for her could never equal what she felt for him. Love, a word with definition contingent upon experience. This was the closest he'd ever been, and he'd thought it real and magnificent until he glimpsed the height her own heart had achieved. So he'd told himself to be good to this woman with her fragile, reaching love, and yet he'd gone and done exactly the opposite.

Now Claire is back at the window, watching the dark lake, thinking of Artus Van Briggle, told by his doctor to take daily walks. She pictures him in the dry Colorado air, discovering feldspar and kaolin, so many things he'd use for his experiments with glaze. Then he stops to cough, and in her mind she holds the frailty of his shoulders.

The phone rings. She doesn't move. After a bit, she hears her name.

"Claire."

She doesn't move. Perhaps if she refuses to turn, no one will be there. It would be her name, again spoken by invisible lips. A simple manifestation of her recent loneliness, a distance she has felt for months that now makes sense.

"Claire," William says again.

Still she studies the dark water. "When?"

"Monday. I'm sorry to leave early, but there's an issue with the San-
dler job."

Her eyes refocus and the lake is gone, the image of the parlor snapped
into the glass. William stands in the doorway, and even in his faint reflection she can see and almost feel the excitement he tries to mask. It's
as if he's about to spring from himself, as if his body cannot contain
him. All to go back to Rochester, to leave her. And she knows why.
Once she'd seen it she couldn't work, her hands heavy, refusing to let up,
refusing to let the clay take shape, as again and again she saw him kissing another woman, a faceless, nameless woman who—unbeknownst
to William—had left a smudge of red lipstick by his ear. Not in the location of a polite kiss on the cheek.

Does he love this woman? Her William, her William whom she's
been trying, with every day, to love a little less? Granted it's for her
family's sake she needs him, but it was for herself, for her own eager
heart that she married him. Never in her life had she thought she'd get
exactly what she wanted, and yet there he'd been, on bended knee.

In the reflection she sees him nod, and wonders what he's affirming.
"I'm going to bed," he says. "Will you come up?"

She forces herself to smile. "I think I'll do a little work."

"How is that glaze you're creating?"

"I'm making it, not creating it. It's been done before."

He nods. She waits. Then he turns from the room and disappears.
She sits in silence, patient, until sure enough, there's the faint sound of
her husband making another call. Distant. She can't hear his voice, but
knows he's whispering.

Once more she turns to the window.

3

Now

FOR A MOMENT Abby thinks she hears them. Voices, footsteps in the hall. Sunlight through a stained-glass window hits the floor in jeweled tones, dust thick on every surface but the picture frames. The son reaches for another box. This ring, Victorian, rose gold with seed pearls and two bloodred garnets, comes with a story. As he conjures his memories, Abby takes notes, though after a moment she turns once more toward the hall, imagining the slow shuffle of the father before he died, slippered feet upon the rug, a heavy lean on the doorknob before he entered an empty room. Only empty rooms. His wife had passed just a year prior, after a marriage over seven decades long. *He'd bring a chair to her grave*, the son tells her, *and eat his dinner from their Tupperware.*

Later that morning, back at the jewelry store, Abby types up the memories, prints them on ecru paper, and cuts them into strips that are then folded into velvet boxes. Some customers won't care, won't even want them, but those who wish to see beyond this moment will appreciate the tales. *Kept for ten years in a biscuit tin in France, behind a fake wall*, she's written, or *Handed down over three generations, this ring has lived in ten states and seen twelve great-grandchildren.* She is, she understands, the last vestige of a great story no one may ever tell again, and it's this love of the past, the unseen fingerprints of long ago, that drove her into this field. All begun when she was a child with her grandmother's ring, but reignited in college when she first set foot into this shop, résumé in hand, the glint of diamonds like flashes of sun on a lake.

She's tired. Another dream last night, the fourth in a row. Mondays, however, leave little time to recover lost sleep, so the coffees she's been drinking are thick with sediment, acidic jolts that leave her tired yet antsy. That the dreams are worse than before and this frequent is like being dropped before a black tunnel in the mountain—there could be an end that's unseen, or maybe not. Maybe this is how it will always be.

The name, however, has not returned. Not since that Friday night, and for that she's thankful. Forgetting it, however, is not an option. Burned within her, branded in her mind. Claire Ballantine. Beautiful, really, nothing that should evoke fear. And yet it had.

"Sorry," a customer says. "You said there was a history? To the ring?"

The soon-to-be fiancé holds the doorknob, his desire to leave the store and be back in the safety of sunlight and cars and sidewalks so palpable that Abby almost feels angry. *Then don't talk about marriage,* she wants to scream, *don't make promises.* But then she sees his wrist, somehow too delicate for a man, and she thinks he could be a good man: He could let his girlfriend have first crack at the crossword puzzle when the paper arrives; he could run baths for her and call his mother without being reminded. She doesn't know. This could be a good man.

But then the man turns to his girlfriend. "Wasn't it you who said that's the problem? You don't want to wear someone's tragedy on your hand?"

On the underside of his wrist is a purple birthmark, like a thumb-print, and for a moment Abby pictures the doctor pulling him when he was born, a good grasp on the baby's arm that forever left a stain. Abby herself has a birthmark on her abdomen, near her lungs, but it's straight, a line, like a surgical scar. She was born via C-section and has always blamed the doctor, though her mother laughs at the thought. *As if I wouldn't have noticed that the doctor nicked my baby.*

Now the woman's mouth is opened like a bird's, about to protest, but Abby steps in. "Why would it be a tragedy? These rings were bought out of hope and love. That's what they hold. To me, at least." She smiles, a smile for the man, and continues: World War I and II, flashes of prayers that lengthened in the night, the Depression, the rings a re-minder of a better time, of hope, of love, of a moment when nothing mattered but beauty and promise. Children, even. "How often did you watch your mother's hand tucking you in, running a bath, making din-ner? People kissed these stones. There's life and emotion and love that you'll never find in a new ring."

The woman is nodding. Abby's made this speech a hundred times, its practiced intonations fluid, voice lower on *the Depression*, higher on *children*. Luckily, this is one of the rings that comes with a history Abby has documented, and as she recounts the story, she watches the wom-an's face, the slow grin of a decision made.

"I love that," the woman says, and the boyfriend nods in a way that Abby's seen before.

The door chimes as they leave. Abby puts the ring away and sits, needing a moment of nothing. The morning light is kind, submissive. She adjusts a couple of rings, angling them just so. The ring Abby wants was her grandmother Edith's; a platinum ring from before the First World War, a European-cut diamond with clarity completely unusual for the time, made by I&I, a small company that seems to have produced only a few other pieces. It carries a secret, the ring. At least according to her grandmother, who lied simply to witness confusion, who butted heads with just about everyone, especially Abby. But her grandmother hadn't wanted it and gave it to Abby's mother, then demanded it not be worn until she'd passed, and that detail, that denial of beauty, of luxury, lent credence to the story: There was a secret to this ring. As a child Abby wore it on her thumb. The bathroom light was best, and the second her mother's car left the driveway, Abby was in her dresser, feeling for the velvet, then standing beneath the fluorescents, washcloth covering the drain. An illicit meeting in the middle of the night, leaves crunching beneath feet, the ring in a pocket close against a racing heart—Abby's mind skipped from scene to scene. There was no limit to the unknown.

But when her grandmother passed during Abby's sophomore year in high school, Abby's mother left the ring where it was, hidden in her dresser. There was no reason for anyone to wear it, no pretense of romance or faith or shiny encouragement. The ring stayed dark, sandwiched between sweaters.

During a break, Abby retreats to the secret garden attached to the store. Long ago a narrow metal table had been shoved against a fence, and its base is now an explosion of orange and red nasturtiums that glow electric in the sunlight. To the right is a waist-high tree stump, all but lost beneath a curtain of black-eyed Susan vines, a thick yellow disordered gaze. A crow lands a few feet from the table, head cocked, studying Abby as though he sees her potential.

Claire Ballantine. The name sounds vaguely British. Ballantine. Ballantine. Mackenzie. Scottish. Was Aidan Scottish? Abby can't remember, but figures he must have been somewhere in his lineage. Even in high school he had the hulking presence of a Scot, with green eyes the same shade as a gardenia leaf. Aidan. Always more than just a crush, and yet even that had intensified when one night she had a dream—a nothing dream, pointless, just him in an old car—that days later she overheard him repeating, almost exactly, as something he'd dreamed just the night before. Everything changed. To Abby it was proof. Evidence of a future, a twining of fate that would bring them together. Roots stretched deeper, infatuation grown as if with the touch of sun. Right after school she went home and wrote down the dream with as much detail as she could—the tree branches splayed upon the hood of the car, a squirrel that crossed the road, the way he smiled and yet the conflicting sadness she felt from him, so strong it practically singed the day.

"Abby," Candace calls from the doorway. "Another estate trip. Now, though. You'll have to follow, but you can go home from there."

The heat presses and the pounding of a sledgehammer beats into the air. Abby waits at the crosswalk, her car parked in the small lot across the street. A few months prior, only a few feet away from this spot, a man had been standing looking at his phone when a car jumped the curb. Just like that, he was gone, and now she watches those who have no idea, their feet upon the exact spot of his last breath. The easily forgottens and the never knowns in life make her feel nervous, unsettled, a hazard in her line of work of extinguished lives. *Write it down, don't let them end.* And she did, even for that man, though all she knew of him was what a reporter managed to fit into a column. Still, she printed his name and taped the tiny strip to the nearest post, where it remained until water seeped into the paper and the ink ran, making it appear as if he mourned his own loss.

A block from her destination, Abby's phone rings, the chime she's assigned her mother. She presses Answer, switches to speaker, and balances the phone on her thigh. "I'm driving."

"Okay," Dorothy says, "but wait. Robert said you had one of those old nightmares."

Robert said. Her mother and Robert have a connection, a bond formed over *Jeopardy!*, battling from the couch when Dorothy's in town and sometimes from the phone when she's not. *Final Jeopardy's on, here's the question, what's your answer?* Most likely her mother had called the landline before trying Abby's cell, but in a way Abby feels told on, as if the return of the dreams is a weakness and a warning has been sounded.

"Not just one," Abby says. "Four nights of them. In a row. In one I heard a name over and over." Up ahead, Candace pulls to a stop in front of a large Craftsman house.

"A name?"

The curb Abby pulls alongside has no sidewalk, and bright fuchsia bougainvillea presses against the window, no doubt scratching the car. "Right as I started to choke. Claire Ballantine."

The moment she says this, she remembers the dream, the name spoken in her own voice—it started with bougainvillea. A fevered flush of petals, thorns like fangs. She looks away, a heat rising within the car.

"Claire Ballantine?" her mother repeats, with a short laugh. "You knew Claire."

"What?" Abby jerks up the brake, thrown. She wants out, to be in the open air—but she can't, or Candace will see her and the phone call will end.

"Well, you never *knew* her knew her. She was long gone before you were born. She was a friend of your grandmother's."

A friend. The idea that this Claire was real and not just a product of a rebellious and inventive mind has at first confused her, but is now curving into a comfort. An explanation. A chance to be understood. *This is good.*

"Your grandmother's best friend. Her neighbor. At that first house

I lived in, in Minneapolis, before my dad left—Lake of the Isles, right on the water. Mrs. Ballantine lived next door. Mother spent all her time with her. A ceramicist—not professionally, of course; those women didn't have jobs, they had hobbies. I have your grandmother's old letters. I know she's mentioned."

From inside her purse Abby takes out a pen and the little notebook in which she records the stories. "You have the letters?"

"With your grandmother's things. In the basement. I still haven't gone through it all, if you can believe that. And they had money then, my parents. At one point they were rich. I suppose that means the Ballantines were well-off, too. I always wondered where the money went, to the state?"

Candace is now out of her car, by the front path to the house, searching the street. A drape flutters in an upper window and Abby watches, waiting to see a face. "I thought the money went because your dad left."

"Not them. The Ballantines. Claire Ballantine disappeared, foul play. A robbery gone wrong."

Foul play. There it is. A feeling. The name a token, a link, a shining gleam above dark water—*there's more, keep looking.*

"Mr. Ballantine," her mother continues, "William, it was. He died a while after she disappeared. Suicide. Hanged himself in the basement. Devastated over the loss of his wife. The housekeeper found him on her day off."

Now Abby faces the bougainvillea, the piercing flame of color. *William, it was.*

"Your grandmother was a mess, yelling at a dead man. She was mad at him, I'll never forget that. Even later, when she was sick, she talked about it, Mrs. Ballantine's disappearance. Boy, did she still blame him."

"That's horrible. That he did that. I didn't know."

"Of course you didn't." But then a pause as her mother gathers her words, a churning of realization. "Abby, maybe you did. She *could've* said something to you. It makes sense. When you were young. Some horrible story about her friend. She talked about it all the time and she had no concept of what was appropriate, the things she'd say to a child. Remember when she had you keep the curtains shut?"

"No."

"The house was a cavern. She told you people were looking for her. This could be it," her mother says, her words rising with a glide of hope, "and now that you're having those dreams in L.A., there's no reason to stay away. Maybe you'll find something in your grandmother's things."

A scratching on the glass—the bougainvillea bush that's pressed against her window is shaking. Something's inside. Abby tries to see what through the glass, but all that's there is a dark tangle of woody limbs. Another beat and the branch goes still. Her eyes focus and there it is, a bird and its nest. A deep breath—*all is fine.*

"Maybe I will come home," she says. "If there's no reason not to." She grabs her purse and the notepad and it's then that she sees she'd been writing on the paper. The name, William Ballantine, surrounded by a gradient of ovals.

She looks up, and at last the door to the Craftsman house swings open. An old man's lined face peers into the afternoon. And though it makes no sense, Abby's struck with the irrational feeling that she'd been waiting for someone else.

℀

The river is a steady gleam. *Go, take a lunch,* Schultz had said. *Clear your head.* But Aidan went straight to the woods. His run was needed, missed in these last few days of recanvassing crime scenes, interviewing

friends at the ICU and neighbors on lawns, and developing a victimol-
ogy that's left him staring at emails and bank transactions until he actually felt the worry of Sarah Breining's bounced check, a deposit made
a hair too late. Sleep would be nice, on something other than one of the
cots in the station's lounge, but the run was what he needed.

Now he rests at the water, trying to hear only the sound—the har-
mony of a small portion of Makade Falls that hits a jut of rocks before
falling once again, almost lost to the muscled force that rounds the crest
and plummets fifty feet. Sprays of water, a roiling pool. The meshed
sound of those two currents is a soundtrack to the past. His old life,
easy.

St. Paul was where things changed. Everything had been taking
shape, honing, streamlining, leading to a point, the pinnacle that was
the future Aidan Mackenzie. He would be detective—under a year
away, if he'd had to guess—and he'd live in a little brick house with a
wife whose hips would take on a bit too much padding and whose
threshold for worry would be off the charts. They'd have kids, and now
and then he'd pull up a chair to help them with homework only to realize he'd forgotten just about everything from those pencil-scented years
of schooling. But for the present, his memory would be scalding and
accurate and he'd pour tall drinks to wash away the day's grit, and in no
time his wife would tire of waking him when he shook in his sleep. The
kids would grow up; he'd retire. Time-shares would be had. One of his
sons, he was sure, would end up a cop, and Aidan would then spend his
brittle years listening to how things had changed, how they'd morphed
from what he could never understand into something that was simply
unfathomable.

That was his life and it was as clear to him as if someone had shown
him the album. And most of that was fine—it went with the territory.

Until one day, a year and a half ago, the newspaper that covered a basement window in the Frogtown neighborhood in St. Paul came loose. The neighbor passing by couldn't resist a look—then stumbled back to his house, voice shaking as he called for help. Aidan was on patrol with his partner, Leon Haakstad, and when they arrived, he at first thought the walls of the basement were painted black. Despite the smell, his mind couldn't fathom that it was feces, smeared upon the ground as well.

No one who went into that room or saw the child came out the same. Aidan took leave. Haakstad took leave. Soon both had returned to their respective hometowns, each with his own excuses. Haakstad's wife was never happy in St. Paul, he complained to anyone who would listen, she missed her mother in Marshall. Aidan claimed he dated different versions of the same girls in the Cities and just wanted to settle down with someone nice back where he could buy a house near the river that he missed. No one questioned them. Good-bye parties were had. Fake gold watches as gag gifts.

Once in Makade, Aidan stuck to his story. It occurred to him he might not be cut out for what he wanted to do, but he told himself Makade was different. He wanted to be a detective, but he wanted to do so in a place lacking the kind of crime that could reduce a ten-year-old boy to twenty-four pounds, stuck in a room that was only dark. No, there was bad and then there was *bad*. Not being up for the latter meant nothing. Aidan still tells himself this. Doubt, however, is like an old injury, flaring and burdensome.

But now, here. Never did he think that violence in Makade could reach that level, and yet the briefing the other day has proven otherwise. It all started three and a half years ago in Marshall, with a young woman raped at home. Cut-and-dried. Woken from a dead sleep, gagged with a sock from her drawer, blindfolded, then bound. A good girl, managed a retail store, people liked her, even in a book club with her mother, whom she still lived with. An organized offender, Schultz said. Nothing this guy did was spontaneous. Gloves, felt like leather. Some trace evidence, fibers, car upholstery, rug. Six weeks later, another one. This one a student, worked in the college library, lived at home, blindfolded and gagged—this time only momentarily—then bound.

"Difference was," Schultz said, "he brought ketamine, what veterinarians use, gets stolen. Date-rape drug. Ketamine's got a quick onset, quick offset. He injected the muscle. She'd have been under in about forty-five seconds. Dissociated state. Dreamy, trancelike. People say it's like being out of body. And hallucinations can be intense, depending on dosage. A heavy dose, though, you can't move. So he does this on the second girl, and he sews her mouth shut." A pause. "Some theorized that with her mouth shut, her muffled screams sounded like moans."

Around Aidan, officers shifted in their chairs and a clock ticked louder than before. The linkage was strong, Schultz continued, definitely the same guy. And though Aidan listened, he couldn't stop his mind from returning to the fact that the woman was awake. Not able to move. Maybe not understanding, but eyes open as a needle hooked into her lips, skin pulled tight.

When Schultz stopped for a swig of water, Aidan raised his hand. "But she could scream? While under?"

"No. He waited till the drug wore off. About twenty minutes. *Then* he raped her." A pause. "The awareness, he wanted that. A few weeks later, another one. Forensic pathologist said the sewing was done while she was under, again—something about the way her lips tore when she could move."

Forensic pathologist said. No one in the room spoke.

"With that third victim," Schultz continued, "he cut out her tongue.

Severed her lingual artery. Then sewed her lips together. Technically she drowned."

For this now to be happening in Makade felt like rain from the sun. It just didn't make sense. Aidan listened to Schultz continue—going on to detail the first rape here in Makade, Lila McCale, cut-and-dried, and then the second, Sarah Breining, with ketamine and the sewn lips, the same pattern as in Marshall—and the entire time felt as if something fundamental had been broken. What waited for the third victim, as of yet unclaimed, was unspeakable.

"The store manager in Marshall," Schultz said, as he pinned photos up on the board. "She was the first one, that's often different. The other four were students, living at home to save money—not in campus housing, he didn't take that risk. Everything was planned out, most likely casing for a while, getting the lay of the land, noting sleep habits. All around two, three AM, most people are asleep anyhow, but these were heavy sleepers or long halls. He knew what he could get away with. All teens to early twenties, dark hair. In Marshall they had a theory he first saw them in the school library. Could be—these weren't partiers, they were homebodies. We obviously need to loop in nearby colleges, our community college, talk to employees, campus security. It's summer, but no telling when he found them, how long he's been watching. Profile from before said he was *not* a student, just that he's got a type. And that helps. Take a look."

Photos of the victims. One postmortem. Aidan studied the board, something within him stoked into a breath, taunted back to life. A tinge of his old intensity.

"So," Schultz said after a while, "the state's Bureau of Criminal Apprehension will provide help as needed from their nearest field office, and the BCA's crime lab in St. Paul's got everything on a rush, testing it against the Marshall evidence. Expect we'll get a hit, and Marshall will send someone. But this is us. So wrap up your cases or put 'em on hold. Everyone's on this now."

Now a movement catches Aidan's eye. A man he sees here all the time, fishing the eddy downriver, always with an orange tackle box on a rock beside him. The patience of a priest. His ability to sit still, to just watch his line, it's something admirable. These spots they're in—Aidan close to the falls, the man down by a bend in the river—this is where they always are. A shared routine, a common love of the water. River Man, Aidan's nicknamed the guy.

A wave, recognition—then they're back to themselves.

What he should do is end things with Ashley. Use this one moment of silence to sever ties. Tell her she'll make someone a great wife, just not him. Ultimately she's the current installation of the same girl he's always dated—so much for finding someone different—but still, when his phone rings, he glances at it to make sure it's not her before answering. Haakstad, from Marshall. "Was meaning to call you," Aidan says. "How's Marshall?"

"Crickets in the station. Guys have taken up knitting. Catch you at a bad time?"

"On a run. Taking a break."

"Surprised you have time."

"I don't. Sarge thought I needed a lunch."

"Your vic's still critical?"

"That she is."

A deep breath. "Heard you guys are bringing in help."

"We needed patrol. Got everyone in neighboring jurisdictions on extended shifts."

"And you got Hardt. Lucky you."

Detective Hardt, from Marshall. Arrived this morning when they got a positive link with fiber samples to the older cases. The second the man saw the chaos of the station—not one clear desk, stacks of paper by computer monitors, a printer on the floor—he determined his work would be better performed at his hotel. *Mark my words,* Harris said, *he's making calls from the pool.*

"Seems fine, from what I've seen of him. What's your gut on this?"

"Mine? No one cares what I think."

"Still."

There's a pause, a raspy breath, and Haakstad says, "This isn't Ted Bundy—not some good-looking guy with social skills. My guess is he makes people uneasy, spends time alone."

"Alone's okay."

"I know. You're at the river, alone. This is different. Guy probably lives outside town—couldn't handle neighbors. He'd be paranoid, convinced they're watching him."

Call-waiting clicks, and Aidan looks at the ID. Harris. A bad feeling just from the readout. He tells Haakstad he's gotta take this, and hits End.

"She didn't make it," Harris says. "Sarah Breining."

Somehow he'd thought this wouldn't happen. As if there should be a correlation between their efforts and her health, her ability to pull through.

On his phone he's got a list.

MARSHALL VICTIMS
1. Jessica Hall. Rape.
2. Megan Mitchell. Ketamine. Lips. Rape. 6 weeks later.
3. Courtney Thatcher. Ketamine. Tongue. Lips. Rape. 3 weeks later. X

Makade Victims
1. Lila McCale. Rape.
2. Sarah Breining. Ketamine. Lips. Rape. 2 weeks later.
3. ?

He stares at Sarah Breining's name for a moment and then adds an *X*.
Just like that.

Harris continues. "I'm waiting for the other call, you know, that it's
happened again. It's a lot faster than in Marshall. My bet's within the
week."

Aidan looks up at the falls, the crest of white water like a veil, plum-
meting into a dark, almost black shaded pool. *Makade*, the Ojibwe
word for this color: a starless night sky, a world of slate and coal. Now
he looks downriver, the shine of water gleaming like Saran Wrap in the
sun. River Man's got a fish struggling in a net but within seconds has it
by the gills and placed on a rock. Its body arcs into the air, scales shimmering in the sun.

Without even a pause, he bashes its head with his fist, and the fish
lies still.

4

Then

ON EVA'S DESK is a Singer Featherweight sewing machine, over ten years old, polished and sleek, the gold leaf on the edges complete, the most precious thing she's ever owned. The pattern for a "Siren Sundress"—a backless bodice and a full skirt she'll take up a few inches—sits alongside, a few notes written in pencil on potential fabric. The second she saw the pattern she'd actually felt William's hand on the small of her back, thumb on her bare skin as he'd lead her from his car into a cinema in Rochester, just as she then felt the stares of men in her hometown, the women clucking and fanning themselves a bit faster, gazes aimed skyward. It's amazing, she thinks, how one dress—or one person—can be received in different worlds, as if the very air changes what's seen.

There's a woman not far from Luven who has some nice feed sack fabric—flour, too, so close weaves, and since they'd been collected on a trip to Des Moines they come with the added bonus of not being easily recognizable as something recently on a shelf or piled in a corner. Though lately even feed sacks seem to be disappearing, replaced by paper bags that are apparently cheaper. The war's being over is a great thing, of course, but Eva misses the unity that blurred classes by turning basics into all the rage, everyone working for the same goals: conserve, ration, and repair. Now the lines are obvious once again, designers invigorated, Paris once more holding the reins. Now excess is celebrated in design and costs reflect the extravagance. Now it's obvious who is who.

As she debates on colors—blue backgrounds are best with her eyes—she paints her nails, one last stroke of red. The color merges and swims. William's favorite color. William's color. She smiles, seeing herself sleeping—taking up most of the bed, apparently—her hand upon his chest, rising and falling. The note he left her is with the others, placed inside the drawer of her nightstand. Each Saturday she must force herself to wait to read his words, their promise a treat after the long bus ride, then later a presence on nights when the stars barely light the sky and the silence of her room begins to blare.

The phone rings, muffled beneath carpet, flooring, walls. No one calls for her, so there's no need for the phone to be near her room, which is really the attic; hot, one window that blinks into an elm tree and at night is privy to sounds Eva bets the rest of the world is not.

The ringing's stopped. It was probably for her sister, Anna. Most likely it was Jim Dear—the term Eva hears all day long—calling just to hear Anna's voice, just to say he misses her, to give her more to talk about at the dinner table. It's always for Anna, whose friends have stayed many and the same. Eva envies her sister, the ease of her existence, the fact that people or moments don't shift or crack with other meanings, that things are simply what they are. Years ago, Eva and her sister were at Verly's Market and needed Pine-Sol, which was all the way up on the top shelf. As Eva reached for it, fingertips skimming the bottle, Mr. Verly stood by the coffee. *You almost have it*, he said a few times. Beside him Mrs. Verly's mouth became a straight, unforgiving line, and Eva's cheeks began to burn. Moments later Anna declared they needed a second bottle, and without giving it another thought, she'd gone to the same aisle and done exactly as Eva had, standing on the tips of her toes, fingers reaching. *Now, let me get that for you,* Mr. Verly said. And that was that. He handed her the bottle and Mrs. Verly never bothered to look up from her clipboard with all its lined papers and precise numbers. On the walk home Eva retraced the encounter in her mind to figure what she had done, as she must have done something. Did she smile at Mr. Verly and not Mrs. Verly when she walked in? Did she forget to tuck her blouse in tighter before reaching to the top shelf? The fault, she knew, came from within her, and with enough time she would find the source. Meanwhile, Anna's trip to the market had been nothing more than a trip to the market.

It wasn't always like this. When Eva was young, she was like everyone else, fishing with her cousins, waving to friends from the tops of trees, playing hopscotch on elm-shaded sidewalks. But then, overnight it seemed, the world shifted and people no longer said hello to her on the street. They stopped inviting her for sleepovers if there were older brothers in the house or fathers who lingered at the breakfast table. The looks from men and women became a tug-of-war, beckoning her closer or warning her to stay away. Nothing was simple. She was twelve years old and didn't understand why the word *pretty* was no longer a compliment, why her mother bought her dresses two sizes too big, or why some hugs were not just given at hello or good-bye.

Now that's changed. She makes her own clothes and they fit, an uncomfortable fit for many in the town, but to Eva, it no longer matters. Her mind is full of acceptance and the streets she walks along are only half anchored to the earth. Now she stands up straighter and lifts her chin, her sometimes forced confidence a thick pane of glass before her heart. Now the eye contact she makes might be a dare, and the sway of her hips a warning.

She glances at a magazine. She needs to do something with her hair. Styles are changing. She can't keep looking like a farm girl—not that she lives on a farm, but Luven is a farm town and it saturates, settles into your pores like a fine, clogging dust, carries on breezes and breaths, fabric and allegiances. Today, when she'd left William, the bus carried her into prairies and farmland, and she could've sworn as the highway went deeper into nothingness that she'd seen, actually seen the smooth sophistication of Rochester slipping from the people they passed. The farther south, then the farther west, the harder the faces. Weathered skin, bland clothes, everything in life for function, the word *fancy* an insult. It worries her that William will one day look at her and see a hint of this, that hundreds of years of farmhand genes will burst through. Clunky, she's always thought. Farm women are clunky and thick, sturdy and back-heavy as tractors.

Again the phone rings, but this time the sound is followed by a loud rap on the wall at the base of the stairs, and then the word *phone*. Eva steps down the stairs, confused. Her mother, Margaret, waits for her with one eyebrow lifted. Margaret hasn't lived on a farm for decades and yet the world has taken its toll on her as well, her beauty reduced to a faint echo, a whispered past evoked only by eyes the color of a June sky. *Your mother,* an aunt once said to Eva, *could've been your twin. But if left alone, grief is a tarnish that only gets darker.*

Now her mother slowly walks from the room, stopping to adjust a coaster on the sideboard. Above is a hole in the wall, left over from a nail. Years ago one of her aunts hung Jesus in the spot, but when Margaret saw the icon, Jesus came down and the nail was pried out with bare fingers. A bit of the wall came loose and Jesus went into a box in the basement.

Eva picks up the receiver. "Hello?"

"I have to go back on Monday," the voice quickly says.

It takes her a second. "William?" His voice without him. His voice from where his voice has never been.

"Can you be there?"

"I have shifts Monday and Tuesday," she says, and then adds, "but sure. Someone will cover."

This is the first time they've spoken on the phone. In nine months, the first time.

"Good," he says. "One more day."

She smiles. "Just one more."

She's about to tell him that she can't wait when he says good-bye and is gone. So quick, it might not have happened—but she's holding the phone receiver. Proof. He called. In another world she'd take her mother aside to ask her what she thought. *Could you tell? Could you tell how he looks at me? How he stands the moment I enter the room? How he hangs my dresses in the bathroom so the steam lets out the wrinkles?*

It occurs to her that he must've been calling from his house. Now and then she tries to picture it, weaving scraps of conversation with her mind's offerings, an ever-changing collage. A two-story house—after all, he is William Davis of Davis Construction; he can afford the extra space—a small lawn perhaps, neat, always tidy. The door, she's decided, is wide, with a wrought-iron peephole. But then she pictures the inside, and that's where the problem lies, as William, to her, is navy walls and deep leather chairs, brass frames and long heavy drapes—but he's not alone. There is a wife, one Eva tries not to think about, an often futile attempt. But in Minneapolis, his wife's presence would be unavoidable, and with this thought the long velvet drapes shorten and lighten and become choked with floral print, the walls turn cream, the crown moldings white, and ultimately Eva realizes she has no idea where he sits for his dinners or where he is when he dreams without her.

Just now, where was his wife when he called Eva? Is there a phone in the living room, a long hall that stole his words before they reached her ears? In her heart she knows he'll leave his wife—a jagged thought, as she knows that with her happiness will come another's sorrow. Mismatched. That's what she tells herself they are. After all, if everyone has one perfect person, as she believes they do, then the edges of his marriage simply don't fit, something both of them must feel.

"You know you've never even told me her name," Eva had said not long ago as they picnicked deep inside the park, a Friday afternoon freed when two of his meetings were canceled.

"Yes," he said. "I realize that."

She looked up at him. She herself was not sure she wanted to know the name, in fact had always been thankful it never came up—as in her conscience a nameless, faceless person's weight was considerably less— but learning the omission had been on purpose was something else entirely. "You're not going to tell me?"

To this he said no, and something came loose within her, so she asked why—coy, masking that fluttering, unhooked feeling with a smile.

"Because I don't want to hear you say it."

With those words, her life cracked open. The noises in the park sloshed over. Piercing geese. Insistent, lapping water. A dog's steps cracking leaves. She'd been sloughed away, left raw by the realization that he still, despite everything, wished to protect his wife. What did it mean?

Her mother returns with black coffee—the hour of the day or night never matters—and a deck of cards. On the table she lays the cards out one by one, her hands slender but wrinkled with abuse. "The doctor sure calls late."

The doctor. The doctor and the patient and the fake job, the supposed reasons for Eva's weekly Rochester visits. An imaginary life she's concocted that pales in comparison to the one she's actually living, the truth of which bunches beneath her skin: *I'm with someone who makes my insides leap—he may be married, but it's complicated. The money I bring home isn't from a patient but from the dresses I sell now and then in a little shop by the ice cream parlor. I have talent, the owner says. I have talent and a boyfriend and a stack of notes that make me cry because words, to me, have never been kind . . . until now.* But she can say none of this. Her mother might not believe in Jesus, but she still believes in sin.

"Iris needs to come in for testing on Monday," Eva says instead. "Her hip's giving her a lot of pain."

"You work on Monday."

Eva heads to the stairs. "Someone will cover."

"Like I said, it's late to make a call like this."

"He's known her family for years."

The lies are natural, fluid. Before she disappears, she turns and smiles, not caring that Margaret's eyebrow is once again lifted, not worried that it was Margaret who taught her to lie and like a teacher can spot what was passed along. She knows her mother won't say anything. Respective secrets are kept silent.

The next day, Sunday, is long and pointless now that Monday has meaning. Eva has the early shift, one that gets her there at the crack of dawn and lets her out a bit after noon. Not that many people come in, its being Sunday, but truth be told, this is Eva's favorite shift, as she gets to spend most of the time daydreaming, just standing at the counter and staring at the gas station across the street. Red pumps and bottle-brush grass that's tall at the base of the station, shooting out as if the building had been dropped onto a liquid that splashed. A Coca-Cola sign in the window: CONTINUOUS QUALITY IS QUALITY YOU TRUST.

She's slid the latest *Vogue Pattern Book* between some menus, and now and then opens to a page. "Make your buttons your most impor-tant spring accessory," a headline encourages. Buttons. *Remind me to buy you a few sets.* She smiles, then flips to the pattern she's going to send for, number 6358, a sundress with a camisole top.

Suddenly Eva's heart is racing and it takes her a moment to realize why: the smell, the cloying sweetness of alfalfa hay mixed with manure and crushed stalks of corn, all layered with something deeper, musky and damp, something that makes her breath come up short. She looks up. Uncle Lucas—one of her father's brothers—stands in front of her, his eyes on the *Vogue Pattern Book*. With one finger he presses on the sundress. "That's a nice one." Then he looks back up at her, a long look, and pulls on the brim of his hat before he turns to take his usual booth.

She finds Gerry refilling ketchup bottles. "Do you mind if I take my break now?"

He looks at the clock on the wall—it's too early for a break; she can see he's about to say no—but then looks out into the diner, at the four customers. Uncle Lucas sits in the back of the booth, arms spread on the table as he waits.

Gerry nods. "All right. I'll come get you when your break is over." He offers a small smile as she tucks her pattern book under her arm.

Once inside the break room, really just Gerry's office, walls deco-rated with calendars from past years, Eva opens the book to the sundress. A darkened print from Lucas's finger has smudged the bodice. Carefully she tears out the entire page, and tosses it in the trash.

On her way home, she passes the graveyard and blows a kiss in the direction of her father's stone. In the background the line of treetops swoops up and down like a crown, rendering the dead and their markers as subjects, colorless gems for a dreary royalty. She's made it to the corner of the street when she stops, closes her eyes for just a second, and then turns back. You can't ignore your father like that. Not when he's had so little.

White dandelion clocks are scattered like tiny spheres of light. The markers she winds through are all etched with names she knows. Lemahieu, Demuyt, Vershaeve, Verly, Bulcke, Doom. The town's ancestors, a history of troublesome names. Someone—she's not sure who, maybe a Bulcke—had long ago been from Leuven in Belgium, which worked its way into Luven by the time it got to Minnesota. Eva's own last name, Marten, is one of the simplest in Luven, though even that had been different. Before her family came to the States it'd had two a's, but, like so many other letters deemed unnecessary, that second a dropped deep into the waters at Ellis Island.

There's the pink granite stone of a boy Eva'd had a crush on in fourth grade, one who'd still had rounded cheeks and freckles when he'd been asked to be brave in the Netherlands. Just outside the town his family was from—generations and generations, all from Arnhem— was where he'd closed his eyes for the final time, his ancestors' September sky the last he ever saw. One of three boys from Luven who'd never returned from war. The second boy is by the elm at the back gate. He was a bit older and Eva didn't know him well, just remembers that before he'd been sent off, he'd arranged to buy a corn picker on the black market, a scandal that died down only when his first step onto the volcanic ash of Iwo Jima turned out to be his last. The people of Luven don't forget, but when you die, at least they turn it to a whisper.

It's the third boy whom she thinks of, though he's not here—missing, unaccounted for, dead or alive, he has never returned. Eddie Parks. The only one in Luven she saw herself with, a possible future the result of shared history and a pressing intuition. It was his grove of elms that had two perfect climbing trees, and while Eva scaled one, Eddie used to climb the other. They'd flash grins at each other over a canopy of green, the world around them spread in rows. During the winter they raced on frozen ice or balanced along the rafters in his barn, each taking careful steps as the other reached out a hand now and then. And when her world changed, he never did, though sometimes he aimed his smiles to the ground and eventually began opening doors for her, but never once did he reach for her. And now, she's thought with sorrow on more than one occasion, he never will.

At last she passes the worn slab that faintly reads *Baby Boy Verly*, and is then at her father's headstone. She was almost three when the tractor he was on tipped, and not one memory of him survives. In fact, she believes her first memory could be of the day he was killed, the moment her uncles—dusty from the fields, the corners of their eyes moist—stood in the kitchen and said words that slowly undid Margaret, pulling that one crucial string. In her mind Eva watched from the doorway, a red twilight burning through the window and touching her uncles' blond heads with fire, while her mother's dark hair spilled on the kitchen table, her tears silent. Though Eva thinks she remembers this, she can't be sure, as no one will talk about that day or about her father in general, other than a few scattered words here or there. If only she'd remembered that morning, if only her mind had kept even a faded glimpse of him leaving. At least she would've had that: a hand closing a door, a tall figure heading toward the barn. Tall. That's what everyone says about him. *Oh, he was tall.*

This granite slab with the mourning angel, this is the only way she's known him. His front is shiny, polished and with precisely chiseled lettering. His sides are rough-cut stone and he's got an eight-inch base on which he's perched. Sometimes he's dressed with geraniums, other times with lilies or irises. That's where she'd gotten the name Iris. She'd visited her father right before the lie dropped from her lips, and that day there'd been a string-tied bunch of vibrant purple irises. There was no need to worry her mother knew the source of inspiration, as Margaret does not visit the graveyard.

"I'm seeing him tomorrow," she tells her father, Joseph Marten, son of Mary and Remi Marten, husband to Margaret Marten. *The Lord gave, and the Lord hath taken away.*

There is, of course, no response. Nothing but the slight rasp of cottonwood leaves, the passing cars on the road. She lies on the grass alongside him, her head near his headstone. For a moment everything is still.

"I know it's not good to ask for what I've been asking for," she says, lips brushing the grass as she speaks. She rolls toward the sky, flat and empty as the plains. "I do. But I can't help feeling it's not my fault that I want it." These are things—with the infinite wisdom the dead possess—that he'd understand.

You give Dad God's power, Anna says, and Eva can never argue. Confessions, prayers, wishes, all are directed at her father, who she's convinced loves her unconditionally from his cloudy perch. Long ago their mother joined the wolves by turning away from God and keeping her daughters out of church, but the death of her husband somehow allowed this, providing something of a free pass. A drifted lamb. But Anna. Anna was the one who tried against all odds to fit in. Anna was the one who returned to church, who joined quilting bees, who hunched alongside other women over rows of strawberries and canned tomatoes in kitchens filled with late July heat. *It's Mary and Jesus you need to direct your prayers to,* is what Anna says. Anna, good Anna, who will marry Jim Dear the farmer and spend her days scrubbing the pig scent from his denim.

"There are reasons I'd like to not be here. In this town," Eva tells her father. She won't spell out those reasons for fear he doesn't know, though sometimes she thinks he does. Sometimes she thinks he had a hand in the punishing broken fence that kept her uncle searching through the night for his missing bull, or the gust of vengeful wind that dropped an elm branch atop his truck. Sometimes she thinks the reach of a father's love might be just this great.

Others enter the graveyard, so she turns to her father with a whisper. "I feel like I was put here by accident. With him, I don't feel that. I don't feel like I'm trying to go somewhere all the time—I feel like I've arrived. So, I'm sorry to ask again, but if you can help, I'd appreciate it."

From here she can see her house, bought by her father's brothers when he passed, a merciful way to get Margaret and two young kids off the farm and into town. White clapboard with black trim. In the winter, with the snow and the white sky, it's reduced to an outline. A pencil sketch of a house. An idea. The beginning of something, or maybe a faded end.

At home the table's set. Anna, who was two months old when their father died and rightly has no memories of him, is across from Eva, while their mother sits at the end. Macaroni and cheese in a Pyrex casserole, the edges burned onto the glass, and string beans baked with a can of mushroom soup. Everything their mother makes goes into the oven, while the stovetop remains sparkling white.

There is a glass of milk at each place setting, the bottle in the center of the table. Around it is a ring of moisture, catching the tablecloth's thatched fibers and spreading geometrically. Eva knows that if you lift the fabric, there is a stain in the wood, the finish worn in a circle from years of milk bottles, just as the floor is darker beneath the area rugs and the cherry end table would be spotted from the sun should you remove the empty vase and the broken music box, which you would not, because they belong right there.

There's a knock on the back door. Margaret scoots her chair from the table. Eva's and Anna's eyes meet. Soon there's the sound of boots stamping on the doormat, the kitchen floor creaking, and hushed voices. Then Uncle Lucas is standing in the dining room. He nods to each of the girls, then nods to the food. "Looks like a feast."

He's got overalls on, and even from across the room Eva catches that smell again. Though she hasn't eaten yet, something rises in her throat.

"We've got more," Margaret says, and tucks a short strand of hair behind her ear.

"Wish I could." He looks to Eva. "Had a good breakfast at Gerry's today."

Margaret scratches her neck, hard enough that red remains, and turns to Lucas. "Did you bring chicken?"

"Chicken? No. Got pork and beef. Didn't know you wanted chicken." He nods at the girls as Margaret disappears into the kitchen. "Enjoy your supper." His eyes linger on Eva, her hands on the table. "Pretty nails," he says, and looks back up, though his eyes never make it to her face.

When finally he's gone, Eva hears him tell her mother he'll meet her downstairs, and then hears the gate of his truck slam shut, then the back door to the house open once again, this time without shuffling and stamping his feet. After all, Margaret's in the basement already, with whatever she's canned this week, waiting. No need for niceties.

With their mother and uncle gone, Anna gets up and turns on the radio that sits on the sideboard. Nat King Cole's voice slides into the room. The volume is low, but enough. Both girls begin to eat. Their mother's food gets cold. They've learned there's no point in waiting. And the music, the music they like, as it helps to drown the sounds.

5

Now

AIDAN LOOKS TO THE NUMBER on the house before him. *Wrap it up or put it on hold*, Schultz had said about other cases, but after his run today Aidan went to talk to Sarah Breining's best friend—mascara a smear on her sleeve, tissues scattered like flowers—and realized he was two doors down from Rick Sullivan's house. In his mind he saw the photo of Rebecca Sullivan's young boys, the ones who'd lost their grandmother, who couldn't play in a yard anymore, and decided one quick visit on the forgery case was fine. In fact, he now realizes, he'll be in St. Cloud tomorrow, questioning Lila McCale's ex, a perfect time to drop off the handwriting samples to the examiner. Just those couple of things, that's all he has time for—and all his mind can handle. Fixated, that's how he feels about the rape cases. For almost ten minutes he'd looked through photos of Lila McCale, a cute girl with blue eyes and dark hair that fell in spirals to her shoulders, the face of someone open, an optimist who'd naturally see potential in a person and never think of ulterior motives. Until now, of course.

The house, the crux of what's being contested in the will, is a white single-story, with bushes that practically obscure the windows. It might as well have come out of a catalogue or been won on *The Price Is Right*, it's that basic. And it's across the street from Applebee's, the parking lot already full. As he steps up the front path, he figures he'll grab dinner when he leaves, take it to go.

The door swings open.

"Yup," Rick says. "I'm him. And yup, this is the house."

"Great. Detective Mackenzie."

"I know. I remember you." Rick swoops his arm toward the hall and turns back into the house, revealing, as he does, a scar along his neck. *Car accident*, Aidan always knew in that way that knowledge can be present and yet unexplored. What he now understands is that Rick must've been in the car wreck that killed his father.

A step inside. The place smells a bit like smoke and Aidan spots an ashtray on an end table, emptied but fragrant. He takes a seat on an old corduroy couch. "Nice that you're across from Applebee's."

Rick nods. "Haven't used the stove since I moved in."

"They got a big menu."

"I only get the ribs."

Every wall is covered with the whitened shapes of former paintings or prints. A few nails are left in place. Aidan sees the light shape of a cross near a door.

"You're a painter, right? Houses?"

Rick just blinks at him. Slowly. Calmly. "You think all maids have clean homes?"

"Fair enough." On the opposite side of the living room is a plasma TV. The mother passed away just a month ago and already the guy's packed up everything, moved in without bothering to paint, and hung a big-screen TV. Could be he's really motivated to move on, or could be he's not nearly as affected as a devoted son who inherited everything should be. If he won't talk about his family, he'll talk about his TV, Aidan knows. "What's that, fifty inches?"

"Forty-six."

"That's what I need. Perfect size."

"Get bigger. That's what I should've done, but they had a special."

A special that started the day after your mother died, Aidan thinks. We all got the flyer. "So Rebecca."

"Yeah. Sorry she's bugging you. She's got a history of it."

"Of what?"

"Bugging cops. Anyone who'll listen. Histrionic personality disorder. Ever since we were kids, she's telling lies. Sky's always on its way down."

Aidan makes a note, hating that he didn't know this. "So you weren't there the other night?"

"I was there. Trying to talk to her. But I didn't try to run her over."

"What made her think you did?"

"Hell if I know. Could've just been she was standing at the edge of the sidewalk when I pulled up. She's making a mess of things with this will contention. I wanted to talk to her."

Aidan spots today's paper on the table by a Barcalounger. SERIAL RAPIST STRIKES MAKADE FALLS. Serial Rapist. They couldn't have come up with a nickname, maybe? Meager details, he knows. The key ones haven't yet been given to the press, thankfully. Nothing will be the same when those come out.

"Nice house," Aidan says.

"It's a shithole. It's coming down."

Aidan looks back at him. "Once this is resolved. Not before then."

"Yeah."

In the distance a police siren starts up and a neighbor's dog begins a low howl. Through the window Aidan spots the climbing structure Rebecca's boys used to play on, tall weeds shrouding its base.

"You don't think it's odd that your mother gave you the house, when your sister's got two kids in an apartment?"

Rick smiles. "I think it's fucking perfect."

৶

Claire Ballantine. *You knew Claire.* After the estate visit this afternoon, Abby called her mother back. *I was hoping for this,* Dorothy said, voice unsteady. *If the dreams are there, you might as well come home, right?* Abby could feel her mother's happiness fanning across the country. No doubt she'd already started the grocery list, bed linens tumbling in the dryer.

Outside her apartment, Abby looks up and sees that their living room window has a crack. A bright line caught in the sun's last effort. Beautiful, really. Once inside, she studies it, traces her finger along its path. It's as if the world suddenly snapped with cold and one brilliant streak screamed into the air.

"What is it?"

She turns. Robert's sitting in the chair at the dining room table, watching her. She'd not even seen him when she'd walked in, so intent she'd been in examining the glass. "There's a crack in the glass."

"Well, don't touch it."

"Want to go to Minnesota?" she asks.

He looks surprised. "What?"

She tells him then about Claire Ballantine's connection to her family, the letters in her mother's basement that could hold an explanation for her dreams—the fact that she's not sleeping here, that there's no reason now not to go home. As she talks, an excitement builds within her. Already she's seeing the reflection of clouds in a lake. "It's my re-union. I have vacation time. Candace said I can go. Two weeks, even—it's slow and I'm useless. But you don't have to stay the whole time."

Guilty almost, she feels bad that her mind has already conjured scenarios and heard the comments at the reunion: *a few studios are in-terested; so much hinges on what actor can green-light a film; a lot of "hurry up and wait" is what it is.* A person she'd hate, that's who she'll be, ward-ing off her schoolmates' joy and green yards and houses and hallways lined with family photos, all with Hollywood bragging rights that here, in Los Angeles, wouldn't make the valet think twice.

"That's next week," he says. "I can't go. Not with the script go-ing out."

Her eyes find the line in the window. She can't look at him. The first time home in over a decade, her world a jagged spiral, and he won't be there with her. She feels off-balance; that's how convinced she'd been that there'd be nothing more important, nothing that could stop him. "You won't go," she says, a statement she's trying to understand.

"Abby," he says. "Not *won't*, can't."

"But I need you. I don't think I can do this alone."

"Three years it took to write this script. If it doesn't sell, I need to do something else with my life. Do you have any idea what that's like? I *want* to be there with you, but look at it from where I sit. And think of what it can bring. A wedding, a down payment."

"You could fly home. If there's a meeting. Easily."

"You know how this works. A call, an opening, I have to take it. I can't wait on a flight, I can't drive hours to get to the airport." A pause. "*You* have something you love. This is it for me. There's nothing else."

But a cloud has moved within her, blocking the pledge of his words. *You have something you love. This is it for me.* She understands, she does. Of course he only meant career, she knows this, and so with every minute the cloud slips a bit further and the light, diffused at first, is at last glimpsed. This is what they've been waiting for, as a couple. This is exciting, the moment, the turn. Feedback from this script has been great, and for the first time he has an A-list agent. This really could be it, just the beginning. She tells herself this over and over, though still the shaded, eclipsed part of her mind holds the response *What about me?*

In no time she's at the trip's precipice, staring down the night hours until the morning's flight, the return to Minnesota, what could be a mistake. Tomorrow marks two weeks since the first nightmare, and every night now the debate has been the same. Does she try to stay awake, to prolong these clear, dreamless hours, ignoring the dread that hems her thoughts, the anticipation that even a heavy eye blink might trap her once again in that meadow? Or does she rip the Band-Aid off, reach for a bottle of Ambien and swallow a pill that could inflame her dreams, but surely is the fastest way to the other side? One pill, no fighting it, she'll be asleep. But then she sees the sky above the oak tree, churning with what's yet to be unleashed, the table below set for a guest she's yet to encounter. No, she always decides, no Ambien if there's a chance the dream will be worse.

Makade. With Claire's name and the letters, Abby feels as though she's being led there—or, depending on her mood, chased right back into the lion's den. A lot will have changed, she knows. Her old friends, faces firmly tucked away in her past, are all adults now, most likely sleeping in sprawling houses with plush carpeting, the yards behind them wide and fenceless. At first there'd been efforts to stay in touch, emails and phone calls, but then the snowball of catching up loomed until calls just never happened and emails went unsent. The one time

Abby had gone back to visit during college, the nightmares started again, and from that point on it became easier, safer, for her mother to visit California, to spend time in the sun, bragging to her friends about the Hollywood sign that curved against a sky she only ever painted as blue.

Almost everyone Abby went to high school with will still be there, she's decided. Just about everyone came from generations born less than an hour away, and the few from out of state were considered exotic. Even Aidan Mackenzie, from Idaho, could stun the class with simple talk of mountains.

Marc Blanchard, the first boy she'd kissed, was from Louisiana. That was the detail she'd always start with when recounting the story, a fact she'd been strangely proud of. His accent was thick and draped over words that were slow and infrequent, but the tales he did tell made up for his silence, involving water with gators and catfish like nothing you'd ever seen, *nothin' like these northern cats*. He was short and had hair that always seemed flattened, as if every morning he emerged from a rainstorm. And actually, the night of the kiss did involve a rainstorm, one so bad the party was moved downstairs when the winds picked up and the walls pressed and creaked. Little basement windows flashed with light and the hostess whose parents weren't home suddenly became worried, perhaps picturing a tornado lifting the house away and revealing her disobedience. Abby, herself fifteen and guilty, was holding a warm beer in her hand when she saw Marc standing in an area sectioned off for laundry, smelling the fabric softener. *I prefer Downy*, he'd said. *It's what my mom uses.* She let him kiss her, the cap still in his hand. That's the part she loves, that the cap was still in his hand as the windows flashed and the rain pounded everything it could. End of story.

Though it wasn't, because then he reached into his shirt pocket and produced a joint, and with that offering, she felt adulthood crashing in on her, sex and drinking and drugs—nothing that she was really ready for, despite what she wanted her friends to think. It was too much. Never could she be unkissed—that girl was gone—and in that moment she missed her innocent self so much she had to walk away. When later asked what had happened, she'd said he had bad breath. Horrible, a lie. He was supposed to have been there for only a year, but his father, who set up grocery stores for a living, had had a stroke and suddenly travel was a problem, and so there was Marc in the halls every day, avoiding her eyes.

It makes her sick to think of this. Both because of what she'd done and because still, to this day, she misses herself.

And now she's thinking of another boy she'd been cruel to, one whom her mother, an English teacher, used to tutor. He'd bring her gifts, a little leather pouch filled with stones. Tourmaline. Obsidian. Jade. Pyrite. She'd loved them, the shine, the smoothness of the polished rocks, but she was young and what was she supposed to do with rocks? So she tossed them into her desk drawer. Shut away, forgotten.

She can't be awake with her failings, not now, not in the darkness of her room. Carefully she folds back the covers and goes to the hall, where she sees Robert's screen saver, a torrent of stars, soon gone with the jiggle of the mouse. She pulls on the chain of his desk lamp and the reflection of the room springs into the window before her. William Ballantine, his name as fixed within her as Claire's. She'll look him up, just to see. What had her mother said? Killed himself, in the basement, on the housekeeper's day off.

Hands on the keyboard, she pauses for just a moment and then types his first name. Then the last—how to spell? Ballantine. Ballentine. Ballintine. Ballantyne. She closes her eyes and types, her fingers selecting the first spelling for her. A slew of images come up, faces from today and yesterday and years and years ago, insurance salesmen and teachers and a man in the Navy and someone with spectacles. She scrolls down the page, not sure what she's looking for. Could she search by date? She's about to do this, but then stops.

Right there. A face. Dark hair, a strong jaw, heart-racingly handsome. Intense. More than anything, it's the intensity about him that makes her feel spent, unnerved, as if her gaze is returned and he, too, is studying her. But there's no name, just an image. This might not even be him, just a man she's drawn to. In a way she doesn't want to know. Wants to leave him here, anonymous, so in her mind he can always be William Ballantine. Ridiculous, she thinks, to protect an idea of someone you've never met. *Just look.*

At last she clicks on the picture and for a moment there's nothing, as if the power has been flipped, the screen black, though around her, lights blaze. A pulse and there he is, larger than before, staring at her, steady. A slight five o'clock shadow—she can almost feel the bristle on his cheek.

She looks at his name: William S. Ballantine, from Minneapolis, Minnesota.

His obituary.

At once her skin chills. Someone, she understands, is watching her. She looks up, but the window before her reflects only the room. Her own face stares back. Whatever it is must be kept at bay by the light, but can see her plain as day. Quickly she forces herself to stand and pulls the chain of the lamp, dousing the room in darkness, her steps hurried, the weight of someone's stare whooshing behind her, focused and intent.

6

Then

STANDING IN THE BEDROOM WINDOW, Claire looks into her neighbor's yard. Her friend Edith and her children live there, Dorothy and Teddy. While Teddy picks flowers and weeds, Dorothy plays with a large marble, attempting to roll it toward a glass vase set in the middle of the garden path. The arrangement within the vase is ungainly, an explosion of vegetation, but when Edith appears, she beams at the creation as if it were carved in ivory. Claire loves Edith, and in the last two years Edith has become her closest friend, a woman who would stand upon an etiquette book if it allowed her to see something she shouldn't.

She watches as Edith shows her wrist to the children, who quickly run to her side. At the base of her thumb is a monarch butterfly, and even from her second-story perch Claire can see the wings unfold and refold, unfold and refold. Last summer Claire watched as the weather warmed and Edith and her children searched beneath milkweed leaves in their yard and at the lake's edge, hunting for eggs and tiny striped caterpillars. Everything that's found is brought into Edith's parlor, kept in a large screened container, clippings of milkweed sprouting from crystal vases. Claire knows that this one upon Edith's wrist is feeling the sun for the first time. *Twenty-four hours after they hatch*, Edith once told her, *and then I let them out. Then they need to eat.* Though she added that in nature the time affords them the chance to find a nectar source, Claire preferred to think of it as a break—all that work they've done, the skin-splitting, magnificent change, and for one day they are simply able to exist, to take in the world with new eyes. She's thinking of this when suddenly the butterfly on Edith's wrist lifts into the air, wobbly at first, unsure of its flight, then soaring on a breeze. The children clap as it sails above the rooftop.

Claire turns from the window. She won't stay upstairs by herself, not if she can help it. The second William leaves, the house goes silent, as if he were the sole reason it was warm and welcoming, and now that he's gone, it lies still and sullen and cold till his return. It's like a living creature, Claire thinks as she makes her way down to her studio, a big unwieldy creature with deep aches and groans and a preference for one particular owner. Sleeping alone is the worst, because though she falls asleep easily, the hours at the end of the night come loose, unhooked by little sounds and distant noises, and for untold minutes she'll lie there, praying for the sun to rise, trying not to let her mind wander to the tunnel that starts just two floors below. If she thinks of that, the noises she hears clutch at her breath, taunting, until she feels the tunnel, humid and pounding.

It's silly, she knows, to be afraid of a tunnel. Only once has she gone in there, and that was when William was "introducing" her to the house, when she'd first moved in. Roots sprouted like claws into damp air, catching your hair or scraping your arm. And though both ends of the tunnel are now locked, the sheer existence of it unnerves her, like a man perched in a chair beside you, watching as you sleep.

It was months before she figured it out—the fear of the tunnel, the instinctive terror that went back years and years to an instance she's told no one, as it really seemed like nothing to tell. Claire's family did

not start off as William's had; the rise to wealth was made not by pre-
vious generations, but rather by her own father. She was five when her
parents bought a house they could barely afford, a house they would
grow into, her mother used to say, which really meant there was shopping in her future. A majestic Tudor with a round picture window on
the second floor. Up and down the street, velvet curtains opened and
closed as her family arrived, pale faces peering from windows. Her
mother, Charlotte, wore her best dress for the occasion and made wide,
swooping motions with her arms, trilling instructions into the gray
afternoon like someone orchestrating happiness. Off to the side was
Virginia, Claire's older sister, on a blanket on the lawn, writing a letter
to a friend in her tight, perfect cursive.

At one point, Claire followed her father inside the house, up the
dark stairs, and through the hall. What she'd wanted was to see the
picture window. The glass looked like candy, the hardened pieces of
sugar bark her grandmother made that turned her tongue colors and
dyed her fingertips, and she'd wanted to touch it, to see if it was sticky.
So strange, Claire thinks now, that it can all be traced back to that. The
desire to touch the glass.

When her father disappeared into a room, she did the same, but he
was gone. She was in a room with two doors. She picked one, went
through it, and was in a room with three doors. All were closed. She
knew she'd go through another and it would keep going, becoming
smaller and smaller like the many horrifying mirrors at the carnival.

The only reason she stayed calm was because she had her doll, a
Raggedy Ann she'd renamed Ellie, always held tight against her despite
the fact that her mother had recently tried to keep her on the bed and
only on the bed. As far as Claire knew, she had only ever existed with
Ellie; in her mind she and the doll came into the world at the same time,
joined from the start. Naturally, by this time Ellie was worn, her yarn

hair decorated with crumbled bits of leaves that never let go—becoming slightly smaller only if the effort was made—her white apron dingy and in no way white, her mouth unraveling, making it look as though she was talking, constantly chattering away.

So Claire stood in the silent, empty room and studied the doors, and as she did, she held Ellie, breathing in her earthy, peppery smell. Instantly she calmed. She forced herself back the way she thought she came, and when she finally found the hall with the stairs, she stumbled down toward the light, toward the wide-open front door.

Charlotte was on the narrow porch, beside her a tall, bony woman. Claire ran to her mother and wrapped her arms around her legs, her face in the fabric of her dress.

"My," her mother said with a laugh, and shook her leg slightly.

When Claire stepped back, the bony lady looked down at Claire, her eyes like a blackbird's. "How nice to meet you, Claire," the woman said. "I'm Mrs. Hadley. I have a daughter just your age. Ada. Won't that be nice, to have a friend just down the street." Then there was a pause, and the woman angled her head slightly. "How precious."

And that was when her mother saw the doll.

The next day Claire awoke to find her mother sitting on her bed. As usual, Claire reached for Ellie, a motion as habitual as pulling back the covers. But Ellie was gone.

"Come with me," Charlotte said, and Claire knew this meant she'd get Ellie, so she followed her into the kitchen, where her mother opened a door and led her down narrow stairs to the basement. The floor was dirt, the ceiling low, the smell like wash that refused to dry. In the center of the room a hole had been dug. Beside it was a box.

Charlotte led her to the hole in the ground and then turned to face her. "Claire, when someone dies, you have a funeral. This is Ellie's funeral. Ellie is dead."

Charlotte went to the box and opened it for her to see. Inside was Ellie, black eyes wide open and staring. She was fine. Relief fanned through Claire and she stretched her arms to take Ellie, but her mother took Ellie away. She smashed the lid on the box tight, covering Ellie's face, and dropped it in the hole in the ground. Claire didn't understand. With her foot, her mother swept at the mound of dirt, and it was as the clods pounded the box that Claire was hit with understanding so hard she couldn't find her breath. The rough dirt scraped her knee as she fell, and then there was dirt against her cheek, a small pebble pressed hard at her temple. When finally she found the ability to cry, her mother was already stomping on the dirt, packing it in tight.

That was the first night Claire had the dream. It stayed with her throughout her childhood, forcing her eyes open in the dark, making her afraid of sleep. The dream is not elaborate, but rather consistent in its simplicity. She's in a box. The smell of cardboard is suffocating. A soft, scattering sound; landing dirt. Then pounding, footsteps packing in soil, growing distant, filtered, as the pounding of her own heart grows louder and louder till it echoes furiously, frantically in her ears.

It used to be the basement in which she was buried, but now it's the tunnel, and she's angry at the house for giving new life to her night-mare, for unleashing it after years of peace. Some nights she wakes and William stirs, as if the outer edges of his mind had heard her breathing change. But she's never told him, as that would mean once there was a doll, and once it was ragged and old, and once her mother had had rea-son to be ashamed.

Now she wonders, if he's having an affair, could it be her fault? She kept her past wounds covered, sectioned off parts of herself she'd never show her own husband. Denied from the start, he was, warded off from her entirety. Did he do the same to her? Of course now she knows she has only part of him. But what has he given the other woman? Does he notice at night when her breathing changes? Does he wake to ask about her dreams?

ॐ

Monday evening. Set apart in its routine by the fact that they're together, a long week due to problems with a job that blessedly forced him back to Rochester early. This is what Monday looks like in Rochester, Eva thinks, with him. That feeling of the first, heart-leaping day of a childhood summer, when so much joy was simply from the promise of more. More days. More hours. The ambrosia of anticipation.

On the back porch, by the Monopoly game, she watches a moth fling itself repeatedly at the light, confused and manic. When William appears, changed from his work clothes, holding a plate of cookies, she's standing there, ready.

"Can you turn this off?" she asks. He flips the switch and the moth settles on the glass shade, a brief respite. Quickly she brushes it into her hand, then walks to the far end of the porch, away from the bright kitchen windows. Her hand is cupped and its wings beat against her palm. The moment she uncurls her fingers, the moth lifts into the air, finally released from its lure, able to join the dark.

When she turns, William is in his spot, watching her. She wipes her hand on her dress and flips the switch back on, the porch filling with light and shadows. He nods to the game, to a stretch of his hotels. "My dear, you've a rough road ahead of you."

She rolls the dice—seven—lands on a railroad, and smiles. "I do love trains."

"Keep in mind, our doors are always open."

It's when he reaches for the dice that they see it: his wedding ring.

Usually it's left on the dresser, never on his hand when he's with her. Quickly he rises. "I'm sorry."

When he returns, she's standing, watching the woods, and feels his hand on her shoulder. The frenzied song of a bird punctuates the night, and she places her hand atop his, letting her fingers glide against his skin. "When robins wake," she says, "they sing. Streetlights wake them, and loud sounds, like thunder. Someone told me that in London, during the war, the bombs would wake them."

"Everything destroyed, and yet a bird sings like it's a brand-new day."

"I can't imagine."

"My grandfather," he says, "had lovebirds. Always nestled together, practically one, these beautiful orange and green birds. After a while he kept them in separate cages, one room away from each other."

"What? Why? They must have been so lonely."

"They were," he says, brushing her hair from her shoulder, kissing the space he's cleared. "That was why he did it. They would call to each other, and the sound of their heartbreak was more beautiful than that of their happiness."

She turns to him, stricken.

"One day," he continues, "I opened a cage and a window to the yard. When I went to the next room, one bird had already seen the other in the tree. Their calls changed. Hope, maybe. It was different." Gently he traces the line of her neck with his hand. "It didn't take long, when I let the other one out, for them to find each other on the branch. And then, for the first time, they were silent."

He lowers his head and his lips brush hers, lightly.

"Did you get in trouble?" she whispers.

"I did."

She smiles, and once more hears the bird call into the night.

The week dips in temperature, and rain lets loose from thick, pigeon-gray clouds. No picnic, but a fire keeps them warm, the Monopoly game on the floor by its heat. Then Friday everything shifts and the temperature is back to warm, the air invigorated with the fresh scent of flowering trees: chokecherry, wild plum, and crab apple. Orange honeysuckle burns bright in the bush at the base of the drive, and sparrows shake the branches, the flowers quivering.

Eva is wearing a summer dress, one that hits a bit below her knees but has an enticing V neck she's extended by neglecting to button the top button. The air is a bit humid from the lake and the recent rain, and the revealed hollow of skin shines in certain lights. Now and then, as they walk through town, William glances at her and she smiles, her lips painted red, knowing full well what the oversight with the button has done. He can't do anything, not in public, but she can see in his eyes what he's thinking.

"Eva," he says as two men turn the corner, their heads tilted toward her chest. "Best care for that button."

Eva stops, turns toward him, and while looking him in the eye, very, very slowly hooks the button into the loop. William angles his smile toward the sidewalk, then follows her up the steps to the Drive-ette diner. She scans the luncheonette for only a moment before locating a couple of empty stools at the far corner.

"What can I get you?" the waitress asks. Her dress is stained with grease, her fingers puffy.

"You first," Eva says to William.

William looks from the waitress's hands to the soda fountain. "Just a turkey sandwich, no mayo or butter. Plain, really. And a Coke, please."

Eva nods to the counter behind the waitress. "Apple?"

"Apple, pecan, lemon meringue."

"Slice of apple and a root beer, please."

The waitress doesn't write their orders, just taps her pencil on the pad a couple of times as if beating the selections to memory, and then turns to the cook's counter.

"You're going to ruin your appetite with that pie," William says as he straightens the salt and pepper shakers, aligning them perpendicular to his napkins.

"Better that than I don't want dessert." She grins, and moves the saltshaker closer to her plate, and then the pepper, adjusting everything three inches to the left. "You know, I've never thought about that."

"About what?"

"You. Being jealous of me. I mean, *I* have reason to be jealous of you, but it never occurred to me that you might wonder about other men."

"I try not to think about it," he says as the waitress returns with their drinks. He nods a thank-you and turns to Eva, when suddenly there's a man with his hand on William's shoulder.

"Mr. Ballantine."

Eva looks back at the man—short, wire glasses, eyes like shiny brown pebbles—and is about to say *No, you must be mistaken, this is William Davis*, but William is already speaking, smiling and not confused.

"Dr. Adams. How nice to see you. Please, this is Mrs. Eva Marten. Mrs. Marten's just come into possession of some land I'm looking at. Mrs. Marten, this is Dr. Riley Adams."

Eva's heart is suddenly beating too fast. *Mrs. Eva Marten?*

"It's a pleasure," Dr. Adams says, reaching for her hand. "Be warned, my dear, he comes from a long line of real estate sharks."

William laughs. "You're in town visiting, then?"

"I've actually accepted a position at St. Mary's." He nods in the direction of the hospital across the street.

"You've left the Twin Cities?"

"Sold the house to a couple from Maine. Why you'd go from Maine to Minnesota is beyond me, though clearly they've an affinity for snow."

"Property value will be on the rise. You might have been wise to hold on to it."

"Well, now, depends on who you talk to and where that property is. You at Lake of the Isles, I would never sell. I unfortunately did not choose so wisely. Besides, there's something about being back in a small town I rather prefer."

Eva looks down at her hands. Small town. Rochester. She tries not to smile as she imagines this man in Luven with its one main street, called, creatively, Main Street.

Dr. Adams leans in conspiratorially. "It was one thing during the war—everyone banded together, you know. Comrades-in-arms." He straightens and shakes his head. "Now it's back to happy times, make money for yourself, forget your neighbor. Oh, the economy flourishes, but I think the cities suffer for it. The selfishness."

"Well," William says, "a tip from a neighbor, then. You should really try the Kahler. Avoid these crowds and eat some real food."

Eva glances at the waitress in her stained uniform. Not once have they gone to the Kahler. Not once has he even suggested it. When has he gone? *Ballantine.*

"Honestly," Dr. Adams says, "I did try it. I went in, took a seat, and learned they don't serve liquor. If I'm paying for a prime rib, I'd at least like the *option* of a glass of wine." He smiles at Eva. "One needn't be an oenophile to feel that, am I right?"

The flush in her face is hot. The word, one she's never heard, violently scoops out a place in her mind. She hates this word. She hates this man.

Dr. Adams continues. "*Every* fine restaurant should serve wine. But here," he says, gesturing to the long counter, the swiveling stools, the thick sturdy plates with blue rims, the signs advertising ice cream, "here

I don't quite feel the same craving. Ah, well. Tell me, how is Claire? Someone remarked not long ago that you two have an extraordinary wine cellar."

Claire. The name echoes with reverberations of a secret finally spoken. Eva catches William's eyes flickering toward her. She stares at him and refuses to look away, even when his gaze has returned to Dr. Adams.

"She's fine," William says quickly. "And yes, we do have a collection."

Claire, Eva thinks. Claire knows about wine. Claire would be a part of this conversation. Claire wouldn't need a dictionary. *You two*, Dr. Adams had said. *We*, William replied. Those phrases, small and yet dense with everything. Ballantine. *Mr. and Mrs. Ballantine.*

"And her father? I understand he prefers the indoors these days."

Now William laughs. "Yes, well. He's got what he needs."

"I imagine he does. That's quite a house he's holed up in." He smiles. "Good, good. Well, I think I see a man who has just reached for his wallet. I'm off to stand behind him and hopefully get a seat in this"— he looks around him—"train car." A laugh. "Mrs. Marten, pleasure to meet you. Mr. Ballantine, I'm sure we'll meet again."

With a nod William turns back to the counter. Their food is there, waiting. Eva stares at the crust of her apple pie, burned. "Ballantine?" she says quietly.

He shakes out some ketchup. "My company name is my mother's maiden name. People assume my last name is Davis, but it's not."

"You've lied to me."

"Eva, you're probably the one person I haven't lied to."

She's too angry to speak, too jealous, too *inferior*. But then suddenly the anger makes room for words.

"*Real* food, William? This *train* car, this is nothing? *Our* life is bottom rung?"

William glances over his shoulder. "Eva, let's talk about this later."

"Yes. Right before you return to your *real* life."

His words are calm. "Even if you don't see it, you are the most real part of my life."

She says nothing, just scrapes the burnt part of the crust until her plate is covered with black.

৩৮

Later she asks about his name, and William debates how much to tell, how much to reveal. In the end, he shares everything. The truth was, by the time the United States entered the war, William had a plan set in place. His graduate studies were nearing their end, and a switch to medical school became the answer. Ophthalmology, he'd declared, and began speaking of corneas and scleras and more grueling years. Some men were obvious in their methods of evasion—*if you have the dough, you don't have to go*—but William had a reputation to uphold, status in the community, so when the time came, he said the truth to no one and vowed he would turn this dishonesty into the truth: He *would* be a doctor. A lifetime doing something he was interested in—though perhaps not passionately—was certainly worth the ability to have that lifetime in the first place.

None of this could be said aloud, however, not even to his mother, who cared not for duty or morality but prestige and standing. Once the Markhams' son volunteered, that was all it took—the rest of the fur-clad circle practically anointed the couple, and before long, half of polite society lived in fear of telegrams, not quite sure why they'd allowed the men they loved to go off and fight beneath gray skies just because of the Markhams—whose son, incidentally, was shot in the hand months after shipping off and immediately returned home. And it had been the left hand, not even the right. But because William had just started medical school when Pearl Harbor was bombed, no one challenged his stateside footing or the fact that his arms were filled with textbooks rather than a carbine—though sometimes his father's eyes clouded with unspoken judgment, as well as a confliction of relief. After all, he knew what it was to go to war.

No, there was no telling anyone William's choice. He didn't want to die—was that so wrong?—but there was no reason to shame himself or his parents in the process. So he studied hard and surprised himself—he liked the work, a blessed coincidence that eased his conscience as the war continued and men who were lucky enough to return did so in tattered form only. He struck up romance after romance, some with women who had mourners' passions, sad women who clawed at him and clung to him and often called him by the wrong name. Marriage, despite his parents' pressures and the glittery Junes and Julys of debutante balls, was a concept that had settled on his skin like grit, something that could be sloughed off by the next eager hand. Love would come, he thought.

He was happy with his life; promised the distinction of a doctor and interested in his field. But then, during a cold, slate-gray December, right as the world was about to flip to 1945, he and a few students visited the Mayo Clinic. There he saw a growing hospital, the first of its kind with integrated health care, single medical records, and tremendous advances in aviation medicine—but it was the town itself that stuck with him, and it was a feeling he couldn't ignore, a splinter beneath a nail. Rochester was sewn to the hip of the hospital, and each step the hospital took, the town was forced to follow. Soon it would rise from the surrounding plains into a big city, William knew, and suddenly, quite unexpectedly, he felt a gnawing need to build, to stand before nothing and watch it rise into something. Maybe real estate and land development *were* in his blood. For the first time in his life he really wanted something, and it was a thrilling, desperate feeling.

"Development," he said to his father, less than a week later. They were in Irwin's den, all dark wood and power, while in the other room Isadora commandeered the placement of holly boughs. William spoke of real estate, of construction, of the clinic that was getting bigger every day. His father listened. "A parcel I looked at," William continued, "only three blocks from the Plummer Building. I buy it and even sit on it for a year and I make a profit. Watch the grass grow and make money."

Irwin simply stared at the pocket watch nestled in his palm, the gold fob draped over his hand. It was Tiffany with green enamel, inscribed inside with William's grandparents' initials and the sappy inscription *Time stands still when you are near*. Ironically it had stopped working long ago, but Irwin loved the watch and kept it on his desk, polished and always within reach. Palming it had become a nervous habit, something he did when he was in deep contemplation or too upset to speak. William stared at the fob, at the green ornaments along the chain. He was confused. He'd thought his father would agree with his proposal, had thought he'd be impressed that it was William who'd approached him with this, that for once his son was thinking as a Ballantine. Innovation. Progress. Advancement.

Eventually Irwin spoke. "James Guthrie lost his son," he said. "His only son. Their name stopped forever in some Dutch village no one can pronounce. And here the Allies finally cross the Rhine and suddenly your itch to be a doctor disappears." He looked straight into William's eyes. "No need for medical school if the war's about over, now is there?"

It threw William, being accused of the truth—though it had been the truth for only a while, then it changed. "I *was* planning on being a doctor. This—I didn't know I'd want this."

With one hand Irwin opened and closed the watch, again and again.

At last he nodded. "Only someone used to an easy life would think he could escape war and let others fight the battle. Your mother spoiled you. I worried what toll it would take, on the kind of man you'd become."

Then he set the watch on the desk, coiled in its chain, and said nothing more.

Davis. His mother's maiden name, taken in a fit of righteousness when William left medical school and ventured to Rochester, scalded by his father's words, determined to prove himself. He would not take the easy way. Not once did he enlist family connections or tell the investors who he was. Not once did he ask for help. Each month he sent his father checks to reimburse him for medical school, and each month the checks were cashed. Isadora tried in vain to bring William home—a dinner, a lunch, even just a meeting with his father: *he was just angry, he's softened—* and yet each time William recalled the look in his father's eyes and he refused, determined to prove himself more than a spoiled boy, determined to show he could be successful on his own. To do that, his anger, the great motivator, needed to be kept whole, shiny, and unscathed.

Within a year the company had grown, thanks in part to the end of the war and the return of servicemen who wanted nothing more than to settle down and raise a family, to quickly make themselves permanent on the earth after years of living with a toe on the other side. The Twin Cities were filling up, so people branched out into the country, and William's company was right there, assisting in the slide to the suburbs. It was then William bought the little house he'd been renting, nothing fancy. Once more Isadora tried, this time telling him it was his father who wanted to talk. And though William's anger had faded with the smoothing wash of a year, he wasn't ready. There was just one more deal he wanted, and then he would go to his father, a check with the balance owed in hand.

But before that could happen, there was a last snowfall at the end of

March 1946. A silent afternoon, a day of trapped, frozen trees and bone-white skies. A patch of black ice, William was told, blended right into the highway, a highway that long ago Irwin himself had had paved. For a moment his parents were in the air—a detail added by the stretch of smooth, untouched snow—and then, after what must have been a muffled landing, one tree was freed, released of all its ice and snow, a whole cascade of winter falling atop what was left of the car. The Bentley's silver grille, still shiny even with the bark it had claimed, sat alongside the backseat.

At this, William let his anger grow stronger. Now it was aimed at God, whom William had never had a need for and now had even less, and at Irwin, for leaving him like a child tangled in his father's clothing. The anger was sturdy and in place, denying grief, denying sorrow—until, that was, William went to his parents' house and saw the last check he'd written, not cashed, sitting on Irwin's desk alongside the pocket watch. And there, beside it, was a note, written in Irwin's own hand, a blank envelope beneath: *I am proud.* Suddenly all William's anger splintered into sadness, and before he could think he swept the note and the watch into the top drawer.

In six months he was married to Claire. A genuine, deep affection, the closest to love he'd ever known—in fact at the time he'd thought it love—but also a continuation of the track, another reason for his father to be proud.

⚭

"I wanted to build my company alone," William tells Eva that night in bed, after explaining everything. "That's why I took my mother's name. He always thought I had it easy."

"Did you?"

"I did. He was right. Everything had been handed to me."

"So what does it mean?" she asks. "That Dr. Adams knows her family?"

He brushes her hair off her shoulder and lets his hand linger there. "I don't know. Her family, and mine," he adds that last part almost reluctantly, "are who people talk about. I don't want rumors starting up. I guess it means what it does; we have to be careful, we might not want to go there again, we should stay away from St. Mary's."

"But he knew—" She stops. *Because I don't want to hear you say it.* "Her, and her father. Will tonight get back to them?"

He takes his hand from her shoulder, and she turns to him, watches him as he speaks. "Nothing happened tonight. As far as he knows, I was trying to convince someone to sell property. In public, in a diner. That's it."

Eva rolls onto her back, trying to understand. He comes from money. A lot, it sounds like. And she'd had no idea. And his wife? The picture Eva had of her, of this Claire, was average looking, maybe short and definitely dull. Now that's changed. People born into society are molded. They're never left average looking, and if they are, they're trained in the art of compensation, be it in grooming, conversation, or seduction. Now the imagined plain girl who was *lucky* to be married to William is suddenly beautiful, cultured, smart, wealthy—no doubt the envy of many. Why would William ever leave that?

She thinks of his parents, his story. "William, do you believe your father's watching you now?"

He glances at her, surprised. "No. That concept's just for us. To not feel alone."

"Your parents aren't in heaven?"

"The only thing I know for sure is that they're at the Lakewood Cemetery."

She smiles. "There's no name for our cemetery. It's the graveyard. That's it."

"The Lakewood is the place everyone wants to be when they're dead. Next to the lake, rolling hills, big trees. It's ridiculous. You're dead."

"So no life after death at all? We just cease to exist?"

He rolls onto his side and rests his head on her chest. Through the window the moon is bright and full and low in the sky, snagged in the top branches of a sugar maple. "How would I know? Though I doubt it's golden gates and fluffy clouds."

"I believe my father watches me."

"If you believe that," he says, "then he is." A smile before rolling over to turn off the light. After a moment, he goes on: "What I told you, tonight, I've never told anyone. That's what you do to me."

She smiles. "So I'm not your lesser half."

"You're my better half. In the cities, I'm who people think I should be. Here, with you, I can be me."

Eva lightly runs her fingertips up and down his arm. "You escaping Minneapolis, me escaping Luven."

"This is our spot. We can be us."

I've never told anyone. His words, fixed in her mind, set loose a night that is unforgiving, summoning her to shadowed corners, to the barn where light fell in stripes through old slats of wood. When finally she wakes, the satin of her nightgown is damp and the nape of her neck moist.

William, beside her, has been awake awhile, it appears, leaning against the pillows, with the newspaper in his hands. "I wanted to let you sleep. Are you sick?"

"Bad dream," she says, sitting up.

"About?"

He's silent, waiting for more, and in the wake of his truth last night, Eva feels her own pressing in her throat, and before she can think better of it, she's letting it spill forth. "My uncle. The things he did." He lowers the newspaper, surprised, and she realizes what she's done. "I'm not going to tell you this," she says.

"Eva, what happened? This wasn't just a dream, you mean?"

She looks away, toward the window. The day's not yet taken hold, clouds still braced in pink. *If I tell him he will go.* The thought rips through her, and in a beat she knows he will see her as others have, the decayed foundation upon which she stands. *But this is William.* He wouldn't, not him.

"Eva. What did he do?"

"Things. That was the dream. Him. His breath. His hands. The barn was always dark inside. These lines of light would come through. I used to try and count them."

The words, barbed, never spoken, catch on their way out. Incredulous. Did she just tell him? She looks up and sees the sickness swirling in his eyes, deep and muddy, and realizes her mistake. Never should she have said anything. Those words, those horrible words, should have stayed anchored to the pit of who she is, only glimpsed by those men who say things to her they'd never repeat to others, who feign a loss of balance to brush against her or stare at her unabashedly, when for another woman they'd avert their eyes. *Come sit by me, this seat is open.* But William, he'd never seen this within her. And now he does.

He's standing. Pacing. At the window, the light outlines his silhouette like an aura. "How old were you?"

He's focused outside, and the fact that he's not looking at her makes it easier to continue. "Thirteen. He stopped when I was fifteen. I don't think he'd try anything again."

William turns quickly. "He's still around? This man?"

"He's my uncle, where would he have gone? He helps run the farm, all of them do."

"And you see him?"

"William, he lives in Luven. I can't *not* see him. He visits work, he eats there. He's a paying customer." She pauses. "I just don't like the way he looks at me."

William's words are slow, even. "How is he looking at you?"

She shakes her head and then looks up at the ceiling as she speaks. "Like nothing's ever over."

When she looks back to him she sees it—it's not disgust that's in his eyes, it's frustration. An inability—from this little room in Rochester— to undo the past, to save her. He wants to protect her. She sees it, so clearly now. And never has she known a feeling like this; never has she felt worthy of another's worry.

He sits on the bed before her and takes both her hands in his. "No one," he says, "should ever hurt you. And I'm sorry that he did."

The tears are sudden. She doesn't know they're coming until in one swift second her eyes prick, her nose tightens, and her cheeks are suddenly wet. He wraps his arms around her. A beam of sun shoots across the floor, scattered particles that dance in the light's direction.

7

Now

PLANE RIDES: The notorious reason for overdue phone calls, professions of love, and apologies. The morning she's to leave for Minnesota, Abby wakes Robert with a kiss.

"You're not gonna die," he says, reaching for a glass of water on the nightstand.

"I know. But I could. So could you."

"I won't die. You won't die. But you will find what you're looking for."

"Hard when you don't know what it is."

"You know *where* to look. You'll know the rest when you see it. Then you come home, and I'll have sold the script. And we celebrate."

Today his script is going out, in time for weekend reads. Abby waits till he takes her suitcase to the car and then slips a couple of granola bars in his briefcase. Apple cinnamon, his favorite. He forgets to eat when he's nervous and meetings can go long—especially if it's a good meeting. She pictures him at the end of the day, getting back in the car, hungry, finding it there and thinking of her, how she'd just *known*.

At the airport she gives him a long curbside kiss as if the plane is taking her to war and not to her mother's house, and tries not to turn around when she leaves. But she does, once she's dragged her suitcase through the sliding doors, just in time to see Robert looking over his shoulder before pulling into the airport traffic. This one act, so typical, so basic, one in a million, unwitnessed and unimportant—a glance over a shoulder, head turned, blinker on—locks the entire day in the grip of sadness. Tragic, that's how it feels, though it makes no sense. *Before everything changes,* her mother used to say, *there is always a moment of nothing.* As Abby watches his car, now traveling alongside everyone else's, stopping when told, going when allowed, she strangely fears that this is that moment.

At Enterprise in Minneapolis, Abby initials in a million places, tosses the carbon copy in the glove compartment, then hits the highway— only to veer off quickly and stop for gas, pretzels, and a few protein bars to keep in her room, since her mother believes in meals, no snacks. Minutes later she's back on the road, air dazzled with a flurry of white cottonwood seeds like the beginnings of an errant snowstorm.

Minnesota. Great stretches of grassland, wildflowers like joy un- controlled, all the way to forests with ferns and emerald shafts of light. The sky above is bluer than seems possible, clouds wider, fuller, spread fat upon the horizon. It's been so long that the first glimpse of a red barn makes her feel undone, a sort of desperate homesickness, because everything—farms with their giant satellite dishes, endless miles of fences, even the whoosh and shake of passing semis—all of it is home. And most of her time here was fine, wonderful even, despite her run-of- the-mill nightmares and fears—it was only in high school when the dreams of the meadow began that the world went sour. But now she's remembering the good. Dirt roads stretch away into forever like veins she will always have within her, and already she's decided she wants to come back for winter. Little things, mundane, the crunch of snow. The way it outlines bare trees and settles in miniature drifts in window-panes. There's nothing so beautiful, she once told Hannah, as a parking lot late at night when the snow has just begun. It made no sense to her California-born friend, even when Abby described working late at the mall and waiting in the quiet hush as flurries drifted under lights, then the warmth of her mother's car and that sense that everyone had gone home, another day done. Though always, she added, there was one ve-hicle left behind, tucked off in a corner, being slowly covered in white.

The landscape changes, cleared stretches gripped by thickets of trees. She comes to a railroad. The crossing gates are small and will barely cover her lane, but she's seen them from a distance, their prac-ticed descent, and brings her car to a slow halt well before the tracks. *I am fine. All is okay.*

When she hears it, it's behind a wooded bend. The whistle sounds, and even though the sun is out, it feels like something emerging from the night, that noise, that approach, the rattling steel. The whistle be-comes louder, longer and angrier, and even from within her car Abby can hear the tracks begin to shake. When it rounds the corner, she's aware of her foot on the brake—that's it, all that keeps her from its path. One inch. If her foot eased up one inch. An eruption of fire, the screech of brakes, the wreckage of her car dragged alongside.

She throws the gear into park, but in her mind the train now jumps the track and barrels toward her, rails burning and alive with sparks. Her eyes are shut tight and her heart slams within her chest as the train pounds past. An eternity. The longest train known to man.

When it's gone, there is silence. The world unbothered. The crossing gates lift, and she puts her car in drive, breath catching as her tires hit the tracks.

A bit later and the scenery has once again soothed her. Makade. Entered from a stop sign on the highway, two gas stations and an American flag at its edge. Within minutes, her old high school is on her right, its name advertised by a sign with removable letters as if on the weekends it's something else entirely. She's thinking of what she planned on wearing to the reunion tomorrow night: a revealing red halter top and her tallest heels, heels that will immediately scream *I no longer live in Minnesota*. This trip, she understands, will make her question everything—she'll look at Sears photos stuffed in wallets, mottled blue backgrounds and kids with tiny-toothed grins, and hear all the stories of weddings and births and block parties, and she'll miss this life she could've had. All because she wanted a world opposite of what she'd known—sun instead of snow, mountains instead of plains. The differences were deep, entrenched even in the way directions were given at a gas station: *Take the 5 to the 134*. Unfamiliar, a place where she could be whoever she wanted to be, with no past, no one who remembered her as the awkward freshman or the girl whose father left without saying good-bye. A big place, anonymity. And then time in Los Angeles with her mother, visiting UCLA, and not one nightmare. The right track, it was clear, the correct direction. And so she broke from a perfectly fine and beautiful mold to live in a world of Not Yets, a world where price tags are high and milestones—marriage, houses, kids, retirement—are pushed to the edge of possibility. Now all she has is what the people here cannot: Hollywood and the ocean. If only she could say they lived in Malibu, *right on the water!* But that could easily be debunked by someone's asking her for an address. *For the newsletter,* they'd say, ready to google the street view and value and do all the horrible things that Abby herself has done whenever she's been given an address.

But she has changed, she knows. She looks better, and that's something. Tamed. Hair. Eyebrows. Waist. She's reined herself in, plucked, and conquered. But more than that, she'd ended up in a place where people were fascinated by her past, unfamiliar with her familiarities, and within a matter of time she embraced who she was. Even her morbid fascinations and often ridiculous fears were all stories to tell at a dinner table, the elements people remembered. Her confidence grew, the attentive curiosity of a new place like water on a stone, colors seen for the first time.

Up ahead, just around the bend, will be her house, but already visible is Brittany Deschamps's family's house, just across the street from Abby's, a yellow Cape Cod that once loomed over her childhood like a blazing sun. Friends would come over, excited to play in the pool she'd just set up in the backyard until they caught a glimpse of Brittany in a window. Then the front yard was more enticing, hopscotch on the sidewalk, faces angled toward Brittany's room. *Is that a canopy bed?* High school was worse, as Brittany and Aidan became a couple. The worst thing possible, played out right before Abby's house, good nights whispered to the wrong girl, car windows fogging. Divorced, though—this one rumor of Brittany's current state has given Abby a slight guilty comfort.

She can't think about it. She's regressing. It's just a visit, but it's only the second in fifteen years and thus it's so chock-full of familiarity and significance that her emotions, her thoughts, everything is making her feel precarious. On the verge. And the dreams. Already she's remembering high school nights spent with her Walkman, piano concertos that filled her mind with sunrises and beaches and soaring birds, efforts at relaxing, at falling asleep to beauty instead of fear. How bad could the dreams get, now that she's returned? But this, she reminds herself, is why she's here. A name, a sentence, something might explain, might undo a subconscious knot formed long ago.

Her mother is standing by the front path as Abby pulls into the driveway.

"It's like a vision," she says the minute Abby's out of the car, wrapping her in a swaying hug.

Nivea Creme lotion, the smell of Abby's childhood, a breath of history. Of course she's seen her mother in Los Angeles, but the scent combines with the scenery in a way she'd not expected, and at once Abby's dropped back in time. She finds what's new—a line of orange marigolds that traces the garden path, the welcome mat a tableau of sunflowers. The house itself looks as it did before, an old blue bungalow with a wide front door that's all glass panes and dark oak trim, though grown up, paint faded, its trees taller, everything a bit worn, a bit wiser.

Inside is the same—everything familiar, but aged. The same dark blue corduroy couch alongside an antique French maple table, a tacky glass coffee table atop an expensive Persian rug. A mixture of heritage and present circumstance, castle to cottage, a house that's never made sense. *When you come from money but have no money, things are either sold or illogical,* her mother used to say. *And despite being a teacher, I've never been a fan of logic.* The only change, as far as Abby can tell, is a flannel shirt that Tom—her mother's boyfriend of eleven years—has left on the bathroom door's hook.

"We're meeting Emilia at Applebee's," her mother says, with a glance at her watch. "But you've got a few minutes to freshen up."

Abby sets her suitcases in her bedroom, the corner of the house. At a certain time of day the light from the front and side windows meets, almost smack in the center of her rug, an intersection of brightness. As a child Abby would sit in the spot. There was something about that moment, an embrace from a place unseen.

"No Tom?" Abby asks when they're back in the car.

Dorothy adjusts her seat. "I saw him last night. We don't need to see each other all the time. A relationship is not a crutch."

"Mom, I know. I was just saying."

"Just something to remember. Did you call Beth?"

Beth, Abby's former best friend who'd gotten married and had children and a station wagon all while Abby was seeing lights flick on in bars, when she owned place settings for two only because the second set was half off. "Not yet. Tomorrow, maybe before the reunion."

On the way to Applebee's, Abby sees that Makade has grown up as well. Spaces filled, stands of poplars and pines lost to a Home Depot, an ExxonMobil station with six pumps. Where once there was a field of lupine and dogbane there's now a condo complex that overlooks the community college, itself only a decade old. A new grocery store replaces the one where a winter long ago Marc Blanchard's father had slumped to the floor, his son waiting in the parking lot, the car running, and Abby even notes more police, as if the town is determined to be ready for the violence of the world. In a way it makes Abby sad, that Makade has gone on without her, like someone wishing their ex *well* while actually hoping for *not as good as me*.

Right in front of Applebee's, along the street, Abby finds a parking spot. Inside, the ceiling fans blur and black-and-white photographs of long-ago Makade line the walls.

"What an event," a voice says, "two such beauties."

Aunt Emilia. Her mother's best friend. A fixture in their lives, the host of long-ago Thanksgivings, hot dishes in Pyrex, plates of lutefisk and gravlax. Everything about her is home and good, and as Abby stands for a hug she feels tears stinging at the corners of her eyes.

The usual catching up as booths around them fill and balloons from a birthday party sneak a few tables down before being caught. The reunion tomorrow night, whom she might see, who's still in town, names Abby's not heard in years.

"Not one suspect's been brought in," Aunt Emilia says suddenly. "Not that I've read."

"What are you talking about?"

Her mother is silent as Emilia's eyes flicker back to the TV in the corner. Abby turns, in time to catch the words *Serial Rapist*. Subtitles flash on the screen as the reporter questions young women: *Nowhere feels safe.*

"What is this?" Abby asks. "Is this in Minnesota?"

Still her mother says nothing, just stirs coffee that's most likely already gone cold, eyes on the spoon.

Abby turns to Aunt Emilia. "Close to here?"

"You should've told her," Emilia says to Dorothy.

At last Dorothy speaks. "I found out right after Abby booked her ticket. I really thought it would be settled by now."

"Settled?" Emilia asks. She's angry, and in this emotion Abby understands that whatever's gone on would've stopped her from boarding the plane.

"I'm sorry," Dorothy says to Abby. "All I could think was that you were coming home. After so long. And I *really* did think it would be solved by now, and saying anything would be pointless. A whole lot of worry for nothing."

"It's a serial rapist who apparently did the same thing in Marshall years back. Killed someone there, too."

"Killed someone," Abby repeats, feeling as though she's just been handed cards with strange words and told to put them in order. Plates are set on the table. A burger sliced down the middle, pink juice soaking into the bread. She pushes it to the side. "Here?"

"Sarah Breining," Aunt Emilia says quietly. "Died from complications, I heard."

Abby looks back at her mother. "I knew Sarah's older sister." A little girl in a red dress, that's how Abby remembers Sarah, the younger sister at a long-ago birthday party, distraught because her balloon had lifted into the air. The whole party seemed to stop in that moment. For a while Sarah's mother just rubbed her daughter's small back, circular motions until she caught her breath. In Abby's mind the little girl's lips deepen to blue and the red dress turns darker, a rusty, spreading hue.

"Blood loss," Aunt Emilia continues. "Or internal bleeding? Is it the same? I heard he drugged her and took her fingers."

"Enough," Dorothy says. "I'm sure none of that's true. They've been very vague about the whole thing, it's all a bunch of speculation."

"Except that she died," Abby says. "And you didn't tell me this."

"Abby, you have nothing to worry about. I already told Tom I'd be staying home with you. I'll get another lock if that helps. You need to believe me—I thought it would be done by now. Please know that."

Out of the corner of her eye Abby spots a man staring at them, a book held low on the table before him. Quickly she meets his gaze, wanting to convey the message that she's caught him staring, but he doesn't give. He keeps staring. With a slight roll of her eyes—just to let him know he should be ashamed—she turns away, back to the TV. *Nowhere feels safe*, the subtitles had said. She wants to duck out of the restaurant and call Robert and Hannah, but one glance at the parking lot, lit only with shallow pools of light, and the urge is gone.

"Abby," her mother says. "It's the job of the news to scare people.

Okay? You should see the amount of cops here. The guy would be crazy to do anything."

The cops. Now it makes sense, how many more she'd noticed. Across the room, the man is now reading his book, a damsel in distress on the cover, shoulders bared, hair flowing. A *romance?* For a moment something within her rises with a thrill of surprise—but then the man licks his index finger, turns the page, and abruptly lifts his gaze, locking eyes with Abby. Unnerved, she turns and sees the busboy on the other side of the room openly watching her. *What is going on?* A cold current passes through her.

Then the busboy is at their table, refilling their water. *Water.* That was all it was. Still, there's a nervous feeling that's settled in, a slight jitteriness. Closing her eyes, she takes a moment to reground herself, absorbing the sounds of the restaurant, life, everyone fine and healthy. "Happy Birthday" breaks out a couple of booths away. Nothing could be that bad. When at last she looks back, the man with the book is gone, a pile of change left on the edge of the table.

When they return home, Abby calls both Hannah and Robert. They each have their own slant. Hannah: *You should come home, I don't like this.* Robert: *I'm sure it's been blown out of proportion, but take precautions. That's all you can do.* His logic, for once, fails to comfort. Would it be too much for him to worry?

It's when she's gotten in bed that she thinks of the ring, and gets back up to ask her mother to see it. No need to specify which ring, it's the only one since Dorothy sold her own wedding band to help fund a cruise. *We had the best pickled herring,* she'd come back saying, still finding little ways to justify the sale. *Who knew they could do it better than Olsen's?* Abby barely remembers her mother's wedding ring, just that it was yellow gold, basic, and at last thrown at her father's car as he backed down the driveway. *You could wear it,* Abby once said, about her grandmother's ring, after her grandmother passed, *even on the right hand.* But Dorothy long ago took a vow not to go down that road again, and the ring stayed tucked away in her dresser.

As she did when she was little, Abby takes the ring and goes to the bathroom. Light switches flicked on, a washcloth over the drain. The black velvet box is stiff to open, but immediately the diamond's facets inhale the light in an explosion of brilliance. Close to two and a half carats, a G if Abby had to guess. Almost no inclusions, though she'd need her loop to verify. The flashes are stunning, bursts of violet, gold, green, and magenta.

The last time she was here she'd not known to do this, but now—having seen how many people tuck receipts under the velvet lining, the spot she herself chooses for her snippets of histories—she carefully wedges out the velvet cushion of the box.

And there it is.

Its presence is almost upsetting. All these years, unread, unthought of. A little piece of smooth paper, folded and resistant to coming undone, tight with its own secret. When finally it's opened, her heart is racing because it's not a receipt, she sees, it's a note. Just three lines written in graceful, precise, cursive.

Dearest Edith,
Right the wrong.
With love, always.

Abby flips it over, but the other side is blank—there's no name signed. What does that mean? *Right the wrong?* She'd always known it as her grandmother's engagement ring, a painful reminder kept sequestered from sight after her grandfather left, but now she wonders. *Right the wrong.* Run away with me? A suitor, perhaps, a man who'd pined away in the distance, waiting for the right time. But then Edith had insisted it not be worn until she passed. What did that mean? The ring too meaningful to part with, but too painful to hold.

She goes to find her mother, but the bedroom door is shut, the light off. Dorothy falls asleep easily, deeply, and enviably. *You were having a bad dream,* a saying uttered by TV moms throughout history, sitting on edges of beds. Never the case for Abby, who'd have to journey down a long, dark hall for comfort, her mother not having registered a thing.

In her room, torn between needing to sleep and wishing to stay awake, she places the black box on the nightstand, where it's barely a silhouette in the darkness. So much she doesn't know about her grandmother. For all these years her job, her passion, has been capturing other families' stories, efforts at sending bits of them into the future through notes and gathered tales, and yet this whole time she's not known the truth of her own, and never even thought to wonder. Had her grandmother spoken about another man? Someone who died, perhaps, a tragic story that twisted into the dream that's never let Abby go? Or perhaps there was someone *before* her grandfather. Perhaps her grandfather had written these words to convince her grandmother to leave? An original love, abandoned.

Across the street, a car starts. But what's odd, Abby understands moments later, is that she never heard a door close. Not a front door, not a car door. And that's what makes her heart begin to race. Nobody got in; they were already there.

Ridiculous. Late-night theatrics, she knows. She'd just not heard the door earlier. Her mind was elsewhere.

Now she tries not to think, to replace anxious thoughts with images—rubies, emeralds, diamonds, old mine or asscher cuts, the grace and mystery of all her favorite pieces, a parade of beauty. The weight of sleep pulls her. It takes a while, but at last she lets go.

Immediately, it seems, she's there, in the meadow, as if the dream had been lurking. The table is set for two and the crystal chandelier shivers on the oak tree's branch, sky gray with an impending storm. Shards of rainbows from the prisms flash across the white porcelain, and a wind begins to whistle in the leaves.

Dead center on her plate is a cluster of white chrysanthemums. She's reaching for the flowers when she feels something stuck in her teeth, and spots a toothpick alongside the knife. But it breaks, splinters in her mouth. Fragments scrape her tongue. She spits them out, but it's not wood. It's bone. Bone from the tip of a finger. In one heave she retches out a flood of red, and it's the sound of her teeth hitting the plate that wakes her. One by one, they clink against the porcelain.

8

Then

EACH MORNING, before going to her studio—really just one of the bedrooms, not used for children but for her pots and glazes and clay—Claire goes to the kitchen, the only place there are more than just fleeting footsteps, more than just aches or creaks in the wood or the distant sigh of a door. She can't be alone with her thoughts, her suspicions, and the kitchen is where even early in the morning there's life, sounds, voices, movements. Standing anywhere else in the house you could almost imagine you were alone in the neighborhood, the last vestige of residency, the only holdout in the face of vacation cottages or countries of cobblestones. Summer swipes half the neighborhood away, allowing them to trickle back in late August, children tanned and taller.

If it hadn't been for William's schedule, for the fact that he couldn't go and thus they'd be separated even longer, Claire would have liked to disappear as well, and even has the place in mind, one waiting and her own. Her family cottage, part of a cluster of cottages scattered along the edge of a lake, separated by pebble paths and wooden railings. Purchased when her mother was just learning to spend the money her father was just learning to make. *The price of friendship*, Claire's father had said, as the other cottages were bought by Charlotte's new friends, women with high voices and pointed gazes.

Brown clapboard with a screened-in porch. There wasn't much to it, and its simplicity was what Claire loved. Sometimes they'd bring Ada Hadley, Claire's best friend who lived down the street and would eventually become absorbed into marriage and children and a life that took her away and across the country. Still, Claire's times with her at the cabin comprise some of her fondest memories, even just the two of them on the porch, reading side by side until the night set in and they were forced to angle their books toward the moon's light. Back then, life was easy. Cries of loons carved into the evenings, the water more green than blue. All the families there were missing heads of households, fathers who sometimes made weekend trips but mostly stayed away, content to leave the older boys to take charge, the servants to help out, and the women to gossip. And the wives, they were fine with this. Different rules applied and they had one another, were united in their abandonment.

For years they went to the cottage, until one summer Claire's older sister complained. No longer did Virginia wish to be whisked away to the great outdoors. She was too old to spend time identifying birdcalls or canoeing along the edges of the lake in search of freshwater mussels. Reading on the porch was *dull*. One of Charlotte's friends had the same problem with her daughter—*a boyfriend*, the woman said, *that's why I think she wants to stay home*. And that was the end. The children grew up. Life was no longer easy.

For her wedding, her parents gave her the cottage. No one had been there in years, but Claire saw herself, now an adult, with William, sitting on the screened porch, watching the silver glint of fish on a line or the reflection of trees that laced the water's edge. But they've never gone. It's too far, he says. There's a lake across the street. And in truth she knows the memories are the appeal—the cottage itself is nothing spectacular—and they're her memories, not his. Sometimes she pictures it as it would be today, swallowed by the woods, lost in vines and leaves, and wonders if all of them have gone that way, a whole cluster of abandoned memories, water lapping against an empty shore.

Claire's been sitting at the kitchen table for about five minutes when Ketty enters, spots her, and without asking places a plate of scones, butter, and jam before her. Breakfast. Barely seven AM, but Ketty knows the routine. She lights the burner under the teakettle, picks a fork from a jumble of silverware, and starts to polish.

"It's so empty without him," Claire says to Ketty, whose furious polishing slows at the first sign of conversation, despite the fact that she's heard this countless times before. "If I didn't come in here I'd go for days without seeing anyone."

Ketty nods, her polishing now slowed to a crawl, her movements like the measured working of a violin's bow. "This house, maybe it just needs little feet."

Claire tears off a large chunk of scone. They're buttery—Ketty uses a lot of butter when she bakes—and yet still Claire slices off a soft pat, then slathers the chunk and takes a bite, trying to savor. She loves butter. It's something her mother never used to let them have—*the honey will do just fine*—and she's glad that Ketty's now at the stove, turning off the burner.

"Yes," Claire says, "but with him gone so much." A pause. *And perhaps with another woman.* "It wouldn't be fair."

"A baby does not notice."

"No, but *I* would. It wouldn't be fair to *me*."

She's snapped her response, and Ketty goes silent as she pours the tea. Claire feels bad, but the truth is, she doesn't want a baby. She's never wanted one and it's her greatest fear that she never will. Other people have that need to mother, that urge and instinct. But Claire never has. Even when her sister, Virginia, unveiled her last baby, the crowd of women who'd gathered became all arms, reaching, wanting to touch, to hold, cooing and crying and caught up in something that completely evaded Claire. She stood far back, hoping no one would hand her the baby. And then when he was—*your new nephew, look at those eyes*—she didn't know what to do. She held him stiffly and studied him, knowing any second he would start screeching and his cries would identify her as the failure she was.

At times she wonders if there's a gene missing, but then worries the problem wouldn't be a missing gene, but rather a faulty one that if passed down could tarnish the Ballantines forever. William, though, William wants children. At some point she'll face this, she'll have to—that relentless clock has been ticking for a while. And this house, the estate, it can't end here. The Ballantine name would be snuffed out, a flame done in by tired fingertips.

After the second scone, she takes the plate and the third scone to the trash bin and scrapes her knife to make some noise. The scone is still in her hand, hidden at her side, as she tells Ketty she's going out. Once she's in the living room she takes a huge bite, and then another. Does Ketty know she does this? She must, or she would stop giving her three, if she thought the third was being wasted. Best not to dwell. Ketty is the help. The only one who matters is William, whose mind may only have room for someone else.

It's a fifteen-minute drive to her parents' house in Loring Park, the three-story Tudor they moved into long ago. A high brick wall seemingly holds up their lawn and house, and a tall gate ascends above that. Trees are numerous and thick. A blockade, Claire has always thought. A stout defense. In the driveway, she parks the car next to her mother's— never used, always gleaming—and sees a curtain on the second floor flutter. The warning has been sounded.

Right as she reaches to the bell, the door swings open. The angle at which her mother tilts her head always conveys a sense of guarded apprehension. "Did I forget to write something down? You've just missed breakfast." Her hand is still on the doorknob.

"May I come in?"

"Virginia came by yesterday and it was exhausting. Best to set something for next week, get you all in and out on one afternoon."

Charlotte starts to close the door, but Claire pushes it back. "I won't be more than a few minutes."

"And then what's the point of that?"

"You'd rather I stayed longer?"

"I'd rather you attended to your *own* husband."

In one swift motion, Claire pushes the door back completely. Their shoulders collide as Claire strides past.

"Claire," her mother says angrily.

"I have a right to see him." Now she's in the foyer, listening for sounds, trying to determine which direction she should take.

"There's actually *no* law that says you have that right." Charlotte crosses her arms. "Is that clay on your dress? You don't even change when you do your crafts?"

"I wear a smock."

"Well, it's clearly not up to its job. Perhaps it's not *wide* enough." A pause. "I'll never understand you, wasting the makings of a good life. In a beautiful house but locked in a little room."

"I'm asking for five minutes and I'll go home." Claire hears a door shut, toward the back of the house, and heads in that direction.

"Do you know who we haven't heard from in years?" Charlotte asks, quickly following. "Dr. Adams. Your father's old physician."

Claire stops as she passes the study, and though she knows her father wouldn't be in there, hasn't been in there for years, memories of the past compel her to peer inside. A spotless partners' desk, a polished globe on a wood stand. Dust is not given a chance to settle and the maids know to make everything look normal should anyone drop by unannounced, even splaying a different book each week upon the upholstered arm of a wingback chair. Only once has she been here when someone dropped by, her father herded up the stairs to a room on the third floor. *You just missed him*, Charlotte had said, breathlessly to the visitor, a man who used to play tennis with her father.

"He called, only just minutes ago," her mother now continues.

"Did you tell him?"

"Of course not. Don't be ludicrous."

"He's a doctor."

"It's hard to believe you care at all about your father when all you can think of is airing his problems."

"Dr. Adams was *his* doctor. It wouldn't be gossip." Claire hears a cupboard slam in the kitchen, and quickens her pace.

"Do not preach to me. As long as he doesn't want to leave the property, we should thank our lucky stars he's as happy as he is."

The kitchen is empty. Claire goes to the window and searches the yard. There, on the far path, is her father, quickly walking toward the tennis court, white hair lit up in the sun. He stumbles and catches himself, his arm jutting out for balance, the drink in his hand shaking, red liquid spilling. At this he stops, composes himself, and studies the drink. Claire can see only the back of his head, but knows he's smiling as he lifts the glass toward the light. A Shirley Temple. It's the color he loves, the sound of the ice that enchants him.

"Well, the truth of the matter is that Dr. Adams and I wouldn't have had time to talk about your father. He'd actually run into William. Last night, in Rochester."

The way her mother said *Rochester*, like a distant and troublesome land, combined with the notes of joy in her voice and her earlier comment about attending to *your own husband*, everything holds Claire angled toward the window. She will not turn. She can't, because if she does her mother will see her face, will see that her mind has left Minneapolis and is now in Rochester as well, picturing red lips and evenings he leaves work early. She forces a smile, hoping it's found in her voice. "It's always nice to know it's a small world."

"He says William's doing well in Rochester."

"Of course he is. You knew that."

"Dr. Adams ran into him at a restaurant, with a striking young woman who apparently had something William wanted. A parcel he was interested in. Some land, though he didn't say where. Eva Marten, that was her name. Has he mentioned her?"

Eva Marten. Claire turns from the window, the name tucked within her mind. "If there's something you're trying to say, either say it or leave me be."

Her mother's face narrows. "Avoidance of any issues in your marriage will cost *this* family. Think of your sister. She married well, but not well enough. I don't have to tell you what a scandal would do to their children."

"There is *no* scandal, mother. You said it yourself, he was meeting with someone whose property he wanted to buy."

"Don't be naive. Dr. Adams is a very intelligent man. If he sensed something was off, which he clearly did, I would wager there's something to examine. We should be thankful he took the time out of his morning to call. That he agreed to pay William a visit." Claire begins to speak, but Charlotte holds up her hand and continues. "As a friend. I said nothing more."

"My marriage is *my* business."

"Oh don't be noble. I've done you a favor. And since you can address only what you know, you should start listening to everything, including the silences. Stop playing with your clay and start paying attention."

Retired is what they say about Frederick, Claire's father, the story they cling to. And it makes sense, as after all, he'd made a fortune from one of the most successful flour mills, and after a lifetime of working, if one has the means, why not enjoy an early retirement? But the mill, to him, does not exist, and has never existed. Neither do the past thirty-five years of his life. All those days are gone, like thousands of pages caught in the wind, lifted and carried away.

His mind is snagged in his early twenties, before the girls were born, before there was money. To him, the house they're living in is his wife's friend's, and they're simply watching it while the friend is away. Every morning he wakes and asks when *the owners* are coming back, giddy to learn he has another day in this place that is like nothing he has ever known. The width of the staircase is *extraordinary*, the size of the parlor is *magical*. Afternoons are spent waltzing with his wife or wading in the pond, rattling his Shirley Temples and humming tunes none of the family recognize. What began right around the time of Claire's wedding, with little things forgotten, a face no longer remembered—his toast, a long pause her mother stood to fill—has recently steamrolled, a fast and quick descent, but Charlotte is not bothered by it at all. After all, he thinks they're newlyweds. His heart is always on the brink of bursting. *I live with a man who loves me like the day we met,* Charlotte once said to Claire after she'd found a doctor in New York who'd see him. *And he's happy. It's as simple as that.*

"Hello," Frederick says when he spots Claire. He's sitting on the bench by the tennis courts, sipping his drink. "I'm not in your way, am I?"

"Not at all. Do you mind if I join you?"

"For a game?"

"No, just to sit."

"It's not my bench," he smiles.

Claire sits by him. Not too close though, as to Frederick they've just met. They've always just met. *It is your bench,* she would've said when the problem began. *It's all yours. This is what you worked for.* But she's given up correcting him, given up pointing out that something's wrong, that life is not the simple glory he's enjoying. The pain, she found, that his memory causes her is nothing compared to the pain she feels when suddenly he knows to be afraid.

Claire is never okay, leaving her father. But today the weight of two secrets are piled upon her. Perhaps she's fooling herself. William eating dinner with some woman in public, suspicious enough that Dr. Adams would call her mother, is not a secret. And her father: hair a bit too long, face far too tanned, of course people talk—though they've been protected, placed in the extravagant shade of the Ballantine name, and the comments have been kept as whispers in respect for William's parents. *I hear he's lost his mind,* she'd once overheard at a dinner party, quietly spoken around the corner. She'd stood frozen, next to a monstera plant, the wide tropical leaves. *That he howls at the moon.*

William is the only son, the only chance to carry the name. Her genes, her own composition, could be the end, the water splashed upon a perfect painting. Now she realizes there could be another child, born of a woman whose father doesn't laugh too loud and isn't mesmerized by the chiming of ice. William could take the opportunity to have what he's always wanted.

William could leave her.

9

Now

SATURDAY SHE SLEEPS. Heavy and dreamless, sunlight a slow chase upon the rug, a languid brightness. Though the hours feel wasted, the nightmares have always taken their name quite literally and never happen during the day, so the luxury of sleep, the safety of daylight, is irresistible. Now and then her mother opens the door to check on her and the edge of Abby's mind registers the attention, welcomed and appreciated. *Tomorrow,* she tells her at one point, *I want to look at those letters.* Her mother assures her they're not going anywhere, and softly closes the door.

When the alarm on her iPhone sounds, she eats a protein bar and goes through the routine of getting ready for the reunion, hair straightened, face powdered, sweeps of eye shadow with names that seem to promise a voyage—embark, jaunt, moonglow. Her red top plunges into territory guaranteed to freak out a few good Catholics and her high heels should give her another three inches at least. There, she thinks, I'm different. New and improved. She sets her perfume on the dresser, ready for a last-minute spritz.

A few texts with Hannah. *This lipstick? Or this?* she asks, firing off selfies. Will Aidan be there? The night spans with possibility. Her phone bings. *The brighter lipstick for sure,* Hannah writes, *but what's on your face?* Abby goes to the mirror, leans in. Hives. Four of them, smack on her forehead, front and center. She grabs the wrapper from the protein bar and sesame seeds taunt her from the ingredient list. Benadryl, the only thing that's worked for her, was shoved into her suitcase as an afterthought. Thankfully.

Her phone rings, lit up with Robert's face.

"Stephen called," he says immediately. "Left a message. A producer at Warner Brothers loves the script. Wants to meet."

"What? He called him on a Saturday?"

"I guess. That's all I know, he's not answering. Didn't even say which producer. I have to go, I'm running into a movie."

"Without me?"

"You only want to see comedies. I don't write comedies."

It's happening. The timing, news delivered right before the reunion, feels fated, and the evening is now one she enters with validity, an excitement she has every right to voice. *Warners wants to meet. The wedding should be soon.* But only minutes later, her positivity plummets. They've been through this. In her mind calendars of meetings tear past, pages and pages of notes given and contracts redlined only for an actor to back out or the executive to leave the studio: *This was my baby, I'll try to set it up when I land.* What then? A glimpse of herself at the next reunion, pride a crack she tries to cover, heartbreak something she skims with trite sayings. *The timing was off. Everything happens for a reason.*

Already she's spotted another patch of hives, sprung upon her neck like an invading army. Benadryl. The nap-inducing pink pill. It'll be an early evening for sure, but better that than being stuck here with her thoughts, second-guessing happiness.

The few signs he sees from his window drive him crazy. Demands for answers, for justice, for good from evil, as if inside the station were a closet with the solution they simply walked past each day, determined not to look. *Don't take it personal*, Schultz told them a few days ago when a friend of Sarah Breining's set up shop on the sidewalk with a sign of only tally marks—black, accusatory slashes, a running count-down. *I look at that*, Harris had said, *and see how many days since I slept in my own bed*. Hard, though, not to take it personally. Especially when leads are cooling.

Everything about the day has been one problem after another. A computer that continually froze. A printer that jammed every other minute. Even a false confession, the second one they've gotten since the media became involved, given by a nut job driven to take credit for a crime he didn't commit, discounted when his account conflicted with the details they've withheld. And the one time Aidan answered his office line without looking at the ID, it was Rebecca Sullivan, brim-ming with histrionics. Histrionic personality disorder. Aidan had looked it up when he left Rick Sullivan's house that day: a need for atten-tion, flirtatious behavior, casting blame on others—everything he read seemed to narrate the experience of his visit with her. Someone who'd contest a will for the attention? Something to look into later, when they've time for other cases, when nightfall isn't the backdrop of what feels like an overdue and impending certainty.

"Sarah Breining's uncle," Schultz says, taking the coffee filter from the machine and shaking the grounds into the trash, "that veterinar-ian, says he put the motel in Sioux Falls on a credit card the night Sarah was raped. Out there visiting his sister. Bank's verifying and the motel's pulling their footage, but they're having problems with it, got a tech guy involved. Gotta make sure it's him and he didn't check in and leave right away."

"What's the sister say?"

"Says she saw him the next morning around ten. Not that night. He could've hit the road early and made it to her by then. Checked in the night before as an alibi. I never liked him." He fills the coffee filter, shuts it back into place, and flips the switch.

"Dr. Breining once came to our house," Harris says, "to give vaccinations because he knew Onyx hated the car. Man's a good guy."

"Good guy who knew the victim and whose office had ketamine 'go missing.'"

"Hardt says he was retired then."

"Not according to employment records, he wasn't. Someone check that, what Breining's saying." A small trickle of black from the coffee machine. "The clock is ticking." Then, as if remembering something, a glance at Aidan. "Why are you still here? I told you, go. Have fun and get back here."

All Aidan wants is his couch, his beer, and that show with the guy who makes tree houses. Forget the reunion. Forget the case. Forget everything. Just one night off, away from the world, away from the station, away from people with a pathologic need for attention. And Brittany. Her voicemail announced her return to town like a game show host announcing *a brand-new car!* Then Ashley, the message right after: *If you're up for going tonight, I can go with you?*

He should take her. Even in sweats she'd impress, the gleam of her youth like a talisman. That's it. He needs to call her before he changes his mind. Quickly he reaches for his cell phone and knocks over a cup. A mass of water overtakes a folder. In a second he's tossed a sweatshirt on top of it all and Schultz is there with paper towels, but the ink is bleeding, the paper bulging and dipping with water. The clock on his computer says he's late and going to be later—getting Ashley would be ridiculous at this point. He gives in and sits, beginning to separate pages, blowing on the black contrails of ink.

Four police cars are parked by the high school, as if the event were to be attended by someone famous. Abby watches one from the parking lot, convinced the man's asleep, then tilts her head toward the building—brick, a red tile roof, yellow lights at either side of the door. The reunion should be in full swing by now. In one swoop she can go in, see everyone, and go home.

Stepping out of the car, she squints up at a light. Stars behind it blare in competition. There are stars here, she thinks, and leans against the car. Jewelry, she realizes, she'd forgotten to put on jewelry and her perfume—but who cares. She's too tired to care. That's what's best. Just go in, a red-clad disaster, and view the whole evening as a science experiment. The stories she'll later be able to tell will all be worth it—*then there was that time I fell asleep at my reunion.*

A passing couple pauses. "Do you need help?" the man asks.

Abby stares at them, familiarity glimpsed through the murk of age. "No, I'm good. Thought I saw a shooting star." They relax, nodding and approving, and then wave as they head toward the gymnasium. Abby follows a good pace behind so they don't feel the need to slow and introduce themselves.

Then she's inside, and it's like walking into a little room in her mind. Who knew she could do this? Everything is the same. The hay-yellow paint and the dark blue mats held to the walls, the water fountain by the double doors that lead to the lockers. She scans the room and finds a table with wine, then quickly downs a glass. Everyone seems to be a part of a couple: one with a name tag—the alum—and the other without, the spouse. Though some name tags are paired together and Abby wants to take them aside and ply them with questions. *Have you only ever been with each other? Is everything in life a given?*

A hand on her shoulder. She turns and looks into the face of her former best friend, Beth, and at once is hit with the toll of age—shapes that have lost their boundaries, focus slightly softened—that view that only a lapse in years provides. Still, the second Abby says Beth's name, there's a squealed greeting, a maelstrom of catch-up.

"When is everything ever all perfect?" Beth now asks, having heard the recap of Abby's relationship. "There's no such time."

"He's just very logical. Wants things in order first." A vicarious defense of herself.

"So he gets to decide?" Beth asks, then smiles, trying to soften her words. "Sorry, just hate stories like that. A good woman, waiting."

Harsh, a bitter first taste—this wasn't how the conversation was supposed to go, and yet the truth of it burns, a painful passage. She follows it with a healthy sip of wine. "It's weird that they're giving us alcohol in *school*. Like when we're all together we shouldn't be adults, like the collective *us* should always be sixteen." Silence. She points to her head. "Benadryl. Too tired to make sense."

Beth tucks a strand of hair behind her ear, and leans in toward Abby. "Did you hear they almost canceled the reunion? With what's going on."

"Abby Walters," a voice says.

Though the Louisiana drawl has lessened over the years, the languid, thick delivery remains. Marc Blanchard, her first kiss, a good foot taller than she'd remembered. His hair has thinned unevenly and already Abby can see that one day his face will sink into itself, folding as if cinched with a string.

"Marc, good to see you. You look great."

"You too," he says, with something like a smile. And then he's reaching out to her. "Tic Tac?"

Abby can't help it, the laughter has already flooded over. "Really?" she says. Had he been planning that all along, hoping she'd be here?

But he looks confused and glances at Beth before offering one to her as well, and it's at that point Abby realizes this had not been a joke. He must never have known what she'd said about his breath all those years ago—or if he had, it had affected him so little, was so minor, that his mind had filed it away as trivia, perhaps competing with names of babysitters or snacks served in preschool.

"Okay, yes," she says. "I'd like one."

He shakes one into her palm.

"Do you remember Mr. Rosenthal?" Beth asks. "The English teacher?"

"Sure, why?"

"Excuse me," Marc says, and pats his pocket. "Smoke break." He's making his exit, taking a couple of steps backward toward the door, but his eyes never leave Abby's—and in this she sees that he *had* remembered. The fact of the ruse, the denial, leaves her unsettled.

She looks to Beth, who noticed nothing. "Sorry. What? I need a nap."

And that's when she sees him. Aidan Mackenzie. He must have just arrived and yet is already surrounded by his old friends. Abby pictures them scattered, pulled in like magnets the second he walked in. "Aidan Mackenzie," she says, just to say his name.

Beth turns. "Where? Yeah, he's back. About a year. I see him at the Kroger."

"I don't think he's aged a day. He's immune."

Then she sees Brittany Deschamps walking toward him. Well, they didn't arrive together, but the flirtation in Brittany's loose-hipped stride and the mischievous tilt of her head all scream that the past is not just in the past. At least not if she can help it. Nothing's changed. The cheerleader still gets the athlete. "Oh, for fuck's sake," Abby says. "I'm not regressing back to high school, where I just watch those two and get sad and wish I was blond. I'm getting more wine and I'm going to find my locker."

Weaving down the empty hall, she stops now and then to check the announcements taped on walls or to admire banners for various drives. Tendons of fluorescent lights stretch along the ceiling and the air pulses with their slight flicker.

When she finds her locker, she crouches unsteadily to get to the dial and spills a bit of her drink before setting it on the floor. Whirl. Click. Her fingers remember the stops before her mind has chance to conjure them—42, 17, 38. A physical memory. Though of course the locker doesn't open; the combination would've been changed years ago.

Suddenly she's so tired she has to sit. Legs sticking into the hall, head against her locker. Yellow. The lockers are very yellow. "Yellow Submarine" yellow. Not that any of the kids here would even get that reference.

Then she hears his voice. The one she used to listen for, that got her heart beating as thoughts crammed in her mind, a great clogging of words that allowed for few to make it to her mouth. She turns her head, leaning forward a bit, unsteady. Aidan Mackenzie. Talking on his cell phone, one hand cupped to his ear as if the noise from the gymnasium travels alongside him. Crisp blue button-down. A black belt. Jeans, ends frayed in a way she knows was done by life, not machine. Black shoes. He's more filled out than he was in high school, taller, sturdier. There's a solidity to him, a feeling he could take care of any problem and that his body would never fail.

What strikes her is that she's not nervous. Rather, she's entertained, as if he's the first page of a book set before her, the opening line in a play. *Something is going to happen.* She feels it with every step he's taking, and like an audience member, she leans forward in anticipation.

Not far from her he stops, still holding one hand over his ear, still staring at the ground. "I know," he says. "Right. Well, if you need a sample, just get me the info. It's all on hold anyhow, we have time."

It's only when he slips his cell in his pocket that he looks up, almost surprised to find himself this far from the party. Then he spots her. "Hi." A moment. "You okay?"

Abby smiles. He *has* aged, the sharp bite of youth turned mellow and refined. "I've escaped. This is my locker, but it doesn't open."

"You remembered your combination?"

She nods. "It was a fear. That I'd forget it in front of everybody. So I'd repeat it at night. Over and over—42, 17, 38; 42, 17, 38. Like counting sheep."

He peers down the locker bank. *To the right,* she wants to say. *The upper corner, that was yours.*

"I actually have dreams *now*," he says, "where I don't know the combination."

"I have the ones where I forget my schedule and am wandering through the halls."

He smiles. "I've had that. Or the one where I've forgotten to go to a class all semester. Then it's the final and I'm cramming."

"*Me too.* And you know what the class is that I forget to go to? History. My mind is telling me I've forgotten *history*." She laughs, and though the thought occurs to her that tomorrow she'll replay this conversation and cringe, for now the moment feels like an ellipsis and all she wants to do is see what comes next.

But what comes next surprises her, a page swapped with one from someone else's life. *He sits.* Right next to her, in the hall, his black shoes extending about a foot past her heels.

"You've escaped, huh?"

"I have. I'm Abby. I'm on Benadryl." Out of habit she extends her hand and watches as his fingers curl around hers. Betrayal shoots through her, though it makes no sense. "Do you remember me?"

"You were the first person I met here."

This recognition, the memory shared after so long, somehow undoes years of his absence. Untethered. The feeling is there once more, and again she sees him that gray morning, the slight mist that pulled toward them as they neared the school. Suddenly the noise from the party grows louder, as if someone opened a door, and Abby turns in its direction. The song blared is familiar, but then the door swings shut, the beat dipped back into the chaos of the evening.

&cl;

The line of her cleavage has snagged his gaze. Beneath the red fabric of her shirt is the scalloped edge of white lace—and he's peeking at this, the lace and the hint of what's beneath, when she looks back. Quickly he averts his eyes but catches one corner of her mouth raise briefly. Busted.

"So Benadryl," he says. "Don't most people take Valium or painkillers for these things?"

"Absolutely. And if I'd had any of those I would've taken them, too. But I have hives." She turns to face him. "*Had* hives. I hope?"

He takes the moment to openly look at her, a normally forbidden act, but in the context it's allowed. Each feature—her lips, the curve of her neck, the dip in her collarbone. She's pretty—really pretty—and though he remembers this being the case long ago, he knows that somehow it's changed, as if over the years she's grown into a deeper beauty and what he'd seen before had been just a rendering. And she's petite. That's not changed, maybe five-three, red high heels that probably give her a few more inches when she stands, and though her hair is straight, there's one spiral by her ear. Strangely she reminds him of someone, though he can't remember who. Brown eyes with a ring of green. Her face is that of someone whose laughter is unrestrained, full and contagious, and for a moment he searches his mind for a joke just to see if he's right.

"No hives," he says at last. "You still live near here?"

"God no. I mean, do you?"

"About four blocks away."

"Oh. That's cool."

He smiles. "It's not for everyone. Where do you live?"

"Los Angeles."

"Ah," he says, thinking of brown mountains, graffitied walls, and the reservoir encased in concrete his friend from college had been so proud of, a ragged evidence of nature. A sign had been posted on the fence that caged in the water—MISSING: TWO BLUE HERONS. "I was there once."

"I'm sure you hated it."

"No," though he did. He breathes in—whatever she's wearing reminds him of rain on a hot sidewalk, but with something else, like a crush of flowers, a twist of sweetness.

"Liar," she says, and he smiles as she continues. "I spend my life in a car. Sitting in a car. Not even driving in a car, just sitting in a car.

Coasting if I'm lucky. I went to college there," she says, as if that explained it. "Easier to stay than leave."

"I know that feeling. So what do you do? For a living."

"Estate jewelry. Some reproductions, too, but mostly originals."

"History. That must add something."

She smiles. "For me, definitely. The stories. Or the imagined stories, depending on the case." A pause—she studies him as if suspecting she can find the answer for the question she's about to ask. At last, "You've never proposed?"

Though it makes little sense, a heat rises in his face. She sees it and her smile widens, a bit challenging, as if she's caught the edge of a truth she wishes to pull free. He can't help it; even though her eyes are steady on him, he glances at her hand. Ringless. Her smile, he notices when he looks back up, has grown.

"No, no proposals," he says. "Though to be honest, most women I've dated would have cared less about story, more about size."

In a beat she's laughing, and he hears what he just said. The reddening in his face deepens and he aims his smile to his feet, but then looks back at her and finds he can't look away, enthralled as she tries to settle herself, her shoulders still shaking—he was right about her laugh. To watch her entertained, he understands, is worth all the stupid things he could say.

"Aidan?"

Brittany. Heels clicking on the linoleum, a gold bangle on her wrist flashing like a warning. Irritatingly he feels caught, hurled back to the days when the discovery of him talking to another girl meant having to chase a hysterical Brittany down the street. Why he followed is beyond him.

"What the hell?" Brittany says, as if she suspected their laughter had been at her expense.

"I'm sitting." He can still see it so clearly, her eyes bright with anger, hair flying as she'd storm off, only to stop again and take off her heels, a move he knew was meant to allow him time to catch up. He smiles, which she reads as an insult.

"*Here?*"

"Yes."

Her gaze slides to Abby, then back to Aidan. "Well, there's a lot going on."

"Do you know Abby?"

Brittany again looks at her, though squints this time, as if Abby's a speck in the hall. "You were my neighbor. I didn't think you were ever coming back. I'm *Brit*-tany. Remember?"

"I do. I'm *Ab*-by."

Aidan stifles a laugh and Brittany spins back to him. "I'll be in with the others."

They watch in silence as she sweeps down the hall.

"*In with the others,*" Abby says. "She's still sixteen. It's amazing. I can't believe you went out with her. Completely hollow. You always had so much more going on."

"It was high school," he says. "I'm actually sure I didn't have much going on. So what she said, though, you haven't been back in a while?"

"Second time since graduation."

Now he's really surprised. "You don't have family here?"

"I do. That's why I came back—to look into family stuff." A pause. "Last night I found a ring with a note. My grandmother's ring. A mystery."

He watches her, apparently lost in thought, or maybe falling asleep. It hits him how close he came to bringing Ashley. Right this minute they'd be in the auditorium, guys winking at Aidan behind their wives' backs, Brittany combusting as she spotted him with a younger, kinder version of herself. He leans his head against the locker. Shit. A younger version of Brittany.

"So back at you," Abby says, "with *that* question. What do you do?"

"Cop."

"No you're not."

He smiles. "I am."

"I did not see that coming. Must be crazy, with what's going on."

"It is. I'm lucky I'm here."

A tilt of her head—she's trying to figure something out. "So you really remember that? Your first day, meeting me?"

"Of course I remember it," he says. Because he does. A twist of nerves and fear, a small thread of excitement. His mother watched him in the rearview mirror, but he wouldn't move until she'd rounded the corner—and then he heard a voice. "We walked to school together. You were the reason I knew it was going be okay."

To this, a flush lifts within her cheeks and she turns her head just slightly—and in this moment he also remembers her laughter in the hall, a sunlit sound he'd look for, and the way she'd hide her face when at last he found her.

10

Then

EVA'S BOUGHT A MAGAZINE for the bus, one she's tempted to dive into, but instead she watches William drizzle syrup in a spiral on his oatmeal, listening to the clang of silverware and dishes, the sizzle from the kitchen, the swoosh of waitresses' nyloned legs hurrying from table to table. He's got a meeting in Minneapolis he can't be late for, and has checked his watch six times since they arrived. But that doesn't bother her. Since her confession this morning she feels buoyant. A tangle has been undone, a long-tethered ribbon finally able to lift into the wind.

"You're not eating," he says, motioning to her eggs.

"Too much pepper. But it's okay, I'm not hungry."

"Guess what I found in the garage?"

"Snowshoes. A garden elf. A bird's nest. No, wait, a sled. A sled?"

He smiles. "Fishing poles, for our picnic. Next week."

"No rain," she says, crossing her fingers. Then, after a bit, she flips open the magazine—just for a second—to an ad of a couple picnicking on a blue blanket, trees stretched tall into a blue-white sky. *A diamond is forever.* All else can be forgotten, broken down, disintegrated, reclaimed by the earth, everything but this promise. She looks up at William. *I told him, and he is still here.*

Suddenly she remembers. "My work shoes. They're at the house."

He glances at his watch and then the clock on the wall, as if hoping it might disagree.

"I took them out when I was packing," she says. "I can see them now by the bed."

"Eva, we don't have time."

"I need them for work. Gerry won't let us wear anything else. I'll take the next bus. You go. I'll be fine."

Back at the house, she takes the stairs to the front porch two at a time. The next bus will get her to work late, so she first calls Gerry to let him know—Iris fell, she says, surprising herself with real tears—and then heads upstairs. Sure enough, there are her shoes, right by the bed. She stares at them, the incriminating size—not a child's, not a man's—and wishes for a moment she could leave them here, could leave anything here—a nightgown, a roller, an eyelash on the sink. Everything's been taken up a notch—that's how she feels. Now she wishes Claire would make a surprise visit to Rochester, that they'd be exposed, an impetus for change, for *more.*

Claire. Claire Ballantine. Elegant. Eva whispers it aloud a few times as she locks the door behind her, each utterance more fluid than the last, spoken with a mere flick of the tongue, versus Eva, all harshness and a bit too close to evil. She's heard it before. *Evil Eva,* whispered by Michael Knutson after she let him kiss her, his chapped lips mashing against hers. In her mind she saw him in the field, setting gopher traps, a trickle of sweat on the back of his neck settling and spreading in a fold of skin as he stopped to look up at the flat, open sky. It was then she felt him turn from tentative to confident and an instinct rose within her, a limit reached, *push away.* And so she did. A tease. That's what she'd been called, because though her want was genuine, the jolt of her memory was sudden and without warning, a reflex. Only she understood; it was hard to feel right after years of wrong. The difference was that Michael Knutson listened when she pushed him away. *Why?* he'd called as she strolled away. Of course she'd not answered, Evil Eva.

Maybe she is Evil Eva, she thinks as she closes the front door behind her. After all, it is someone else's husband she wants, a fact that's hard to get around. In the air is the scent of the neighbor's lilac bush, thick and provocative, and it's as she's breathing in the scent that she sees a car door, a couple of houses down, open and shut. That no one got in or out makes her look to the driver.

Dr. Adams.

Bees hover near the lilac blooms and the air buzzes, a hum of anxiety. As calmly as she can, she turns around and continues in the opposite direction, holding her train case in front of her legs so he might not see it as clearly—if he saw her at all. She listens, and not once does she hear the car door open again. Had he been there to visit William? Did he see her? And if he did, did he notice which driveway she'd emerged from? Might he assume that what she carried with her were documents, papers that needed to be signed?

Even with going a block out of her way, the bus station is a short walk from the house. When she gets there, she buys a ticket and takes a seat in the far corner. The magazine is forgotten, already a token from a carefree time—*when I bought this, everything was all right.* She stares at the scuffed wall, the pinprick of worry pressing deeper with every minute.

What she needs to do is warn William. Let him know she was spotted, afford him time to concoct an excuse, just in case. A little under two hours for him to get to Minneapolis, another hour and a half for his meeting, some time to drive to his house—Eva keeps a tally until she thinks he might be home, and then later, at work, asks Gerry if she can make a call, just to check on Iris.

"Quite a spill she must've had," he says, waving her to his office. "Never good at that age."

The phone number she's memorized, gotten from the operator hours ago. "PRospect 5-9833, please." As it rings, Eva pictures the signal traveling through miles and miles of black wire, bounding through hills and diving deep into forests, ending where? The imagined two-story house with the wide front door no longer rings true, and now she sees a long driveway flanked by daffodils, a fountain in the center of the lawn.

"Ballantine residence," announces a woman with a thick accent.

"Mr. Ballantine, please." She will call herself Iris if asked, he will know.

"One moment."

She waits. Where will he be? Does he have a den? Is he wearing slippers?

"Hello?" the woman says again.

"Yes, Mr. Ballantine, please," Eva repeats, and it's in the pause that follows that she realizes this was not the person who'd originally answered the phone. This was a different voice, without the accent, and as Eva realizes what she's done, Claire speaks again.

"I know who this is."

Eva hangs up.

A clock on the wall ticks, outpaced by the fury of her own heart. At first there's nothing, no thoughts, just a hum within her, a drone of panic. Then all at once her mind snags a theory—Claire could've been talking about someone else, had been waiting for a call, perhaps, and Eva misunderstood, her own guilt placing the accusatory intonation . . . or she really knew. *I know who this is.*

"You look worried sick," Gerry says when she returns to the kitchen.

"I'm fine, thank you. Iris is sore, that's all." *I know who this is.* If only she'd not hung up, if only she'd stayed on the line to hear what came next: *I know who this is, but he's not available. May I take a message?* Or *I know who this is, and he won't be donating more to the foundation.* There are so many ways the call could've gone, but Eva will never know.

"You're a good girl, Eva Marten," Gerry says, handing her a stack of menus. "She's lucky to have you."

I know who this is, and he is not yours.

લ્જ

Was it her? And if it was, what does it mean, that she's called the house? The sun is confident and blaring outside, and Claire's forced to shade her eyes as she steps down the path. In the side yard Ketty hangs linen napkins to dry on the clothesline, limp ivory squares like a string of white flags, a banner of surrender.

"Ketty," Claire says. "You put a woman on the phone with me who was calling for William."

"I could not understand her," she says, shaking out another napkin. "He will be home soon?"

"No, his meeting's been delayed." Claire knows full well that the woman spoke clearly. Did Ketty suspect as well? Notes found in trouser pockets, lipstick on a collar. "Did she by chance leave her name?"

Ketty shakes her head.

Next door, Edith grows geraniums like ground cover, red blooms haphazard along the brick path. Normally Claire takes her time, studying that startling, tempestuous red, wishing to capture it in a glaze, but now her steps are hurried and her knock on the door determined. She needs to voice her worries, hoping against hope she'll be told her suspicions are invented, wild ruminations from a mind that's never been easy on its owner. *A fear that's kept silent,* her father used to tell her when she was little, back when the wheels of his mind were not rusted, *grows like a weed. But a fear that's spoken is out in the open, and that can be yanked!* He'd snap the word *yanked,* his teeth clanking shut, his eyes wide as if to scare her, and she'd laugh until her mother told her to settle down.

Claire knocks again. The neighboring houses are mostly shut tight, curtains drawn, latches and locks secure. Vacationing time. *Was it her?*

At last there's Edith in an ivory silk robe and a full face of makeup.

Claire averts her eyes. "He's having an affair."

"Well, we can't do anything about it from the door."

"Did you need to change?" Claire asks as they enter the parlor.

"It doesn't bother me if it doesn't bother you. Mathilde was running me a bath. Though to be honest, I'll be wearing the same thing afterwards."

Atop the piano is the butterfly cage, placed on a crisp white sheet, and as usual Claire leans in to check on the inhabitants. At least a dozen jadeite-green chrysalises hang from the roof of the container, little dots like gold leaf on their crests. *Nature's jewelry,* Edith once said. Four small crystal vases are filled with milkweed and the leaves are bent with the weight of the caterpillars.

"Where are the children?" Claire asks, taking a seat.

Edith opens the cage. "Left just this morning with Frank. Learning to fish off in the wilds of North Dakota, as if they couldn't do it right here." Carefully she reaches in between the chrysalises and gently pulls a caterpillar off the screened top. "They can't fend for themselves," she says, motioning to the chrysalises. "Completely helpless inside their shells, sitting ducks for predators or troublemakers. This guy keeps bothering them." She holds the offender in the palm of her hand, its stripes expanding and contracting as it takes a few steps toward her thumb. "Last chance," she tells it, "and then it's solitary confinement." She places it back inside, in the far corner.

"I can come back later."

"Don't be ridiculous."

Edith is the one the neighbors keep an eye on, the unpredictable one. Oddly she's sheared off clumps of geraniums—not a typical cut flower—and stuck them in a crystal vase. Tall and wild. Claire sits by them, breathing in their peppery, lemony scent. It's actually extraordinary, the smell, and suddenly their placement in the parlor makes sense.

"So tell me," Edith says, and Claire begins the list—the lipstick, the call from Dr. Adams, the woman who just hung up.

"You're right," Edith says. "He's having an affair."

She was supposed to at least put up a fight, to insist that no, it can't be true, William would never do that, the lipstick could've been from anyone, the call perfectly innocent. That she's not protesting in the slightest makes this real. "I've sensed distance," Claire says. "For a while now."

"He always was popular with the ladies."

Claire looks up sharply, then back to the geraniums, their thick, awkward stems. "I thought he would change."

Edith shrugs. "Of course you did. Love's trickery. Love at first sight, destiny, all that—lies so we have children. Mother Nature's one shifty broad."

"When I met him at my deb, I fell for him. Wanted nothing more than to marry him. That it happened, even after all those years, felt as if the stars had finally aligned."

"Something feels like fate, you think it comes with immunity."

Edith stands, her robe gaping wildly, and heads in the direction of the piano. For a moment Claire thinks she's going to start playing, some

vaudevillian racy number to accompany the insanity of love, but instead
she passes the piano and reaches for a crystal decanter on a trolley. Ice
cubes tumble and snap with a hit of scotch.

Claire watches Edith's back. "For my deb, I had a Mainbocher gown
straight from Paris, did you know? Ivory lace over white silk organdy. A
full, sweeping skirt. He told me I was the most radiant girl at the ball—
which he had to say, of course. But then he mentioned he had a few
pieces of Rookwood, one decorated by Kataro Shirayamadani, my favorite of their painters. I'd just started collecting, wanting to do pottery. My father, I guess, had told him that. William, of course, knew
exactly what to say. I spent the rest of the night watching him."

There were other nights, too, more balls, more parties, all of them
leading nowhere. Claire remembers his quick breathless sips of water
between songs, flocks of women, bare throats exposed with laughter,
husbands pointing to their daughters across rooms. One night he disappeared around a corner. A sultry female voice: *The Markhams will
never hire me again.* Then William: *The band sounds just fine—besides,
don't singers need to rest their voices now and then?* Silence, followed by
the woman's laughter and her claim that *this is not resting.*

Claire was used to wanting and not receiving. Wanting real love and
romance instead of fantasies of longing and lust, wanting to spend her
days doing her pottery—a venture her mother had only at first in-
dulged her in thanks to a stray compliment from a friend of a friend,
someone from Paris who smelled like cigars and was close to Coco
Chanel—instead of attending teas or charities. Ultimately she'd known
her father would find someone for her, the son of a business associate,
someone polite with slicked hair and a job at a company with his last
name. Not arranged perhaps, but encouraged. Though neither she nor
the boy would fight it, both would spend the rest of their lives loving

sleep if only for the chance it gave them to be visited by a certain dream; the craved voice, the longed-for face, the lost chance.

"A person like him can't be had," Claire says, then takes a sip of her drink, actually enjoying the shot of pain that courses down her throat. "Or maybe it's that a person like me could never have him."

"Oh stop," Edith says. "You've read too many books. A romantic will always be disappointed, it has nothing to do with you."

Mathilde, the housekeeper, appears with tea, and sets the tray on the trolley by the window—but it won't sit flat. Awkwardly she feels for the cause, finally finding a round rock.

Edith reaches for it. "Please."

She holds it up as Mathilde hurries from the room. The rock is almost perfectly round and Claire recognizes it as what Dorothy played with the day Edith released the butterfly. She'd thought it was a marble.

"A geode," Edith says. "Teddy found it. Dorothy wants to bash it open, thinking there's diamonds inside, but I won't let her. Poor thing's yet to learn the value of a dream." She sets it on the table before them, next to the vase, her own diamond flashing on her hand. "So yes. Frank is a member of the cheater's club."

She's said it so nonchalantly, with such ease, that Claire takes a moment to retrace the conversation, to make sure they're talking about the same thing. "He's had an affair?"

"Four at least."

Claire looks down the hall, in the direction of Edith's husband, Frank's, study. He's rarely home. *A partner in a law firm,* Edith once told her, *would not be partner if he knew his way around his own house*— said after an evening when he'd sat in the parlor for a half an hour before realizing the scheduled card game with his family was actually taking place in the game room. Claire had watched from her own dining room window as Edith threw the cards at him, the children sinking into velvet chairs.

"I still remember when I found out, about the first one. I was more like you then. Worst day of my life. Dorothy came home from school with strep throat and I just held her and cried into her hair. Because it's not just your future, it's your past as well. It's everything. All your happiness gets rewritten." She takes a lengthy sip of her drink. "You've got to nip it in the bud. One will lead to another, you can be sure."

"What if he's been waiting for me to say something so he can go? I'd be nowhere."

"Oh, you'd still be somewhere." Edith stands, setting her drink on the leather-top coffee table. Ringed stains are scattered along the edge, as she refuses to use coasters.

"But how would it look? With him leaving me, and then my family."

Edith, other than William, is the only other person Claire has told about her father. That Edith says nothing makes it worse. Claire sits back, eyes on the geraniums on the table. Tiny roots stretch from the cuttings, curled at the bottom of the glass.

When William is at last home that evening, she can barely look at him. The threat of tears is too pressing, and every step she takes seems to skim the edge of a great and wide ravine. Even the next morning, while he sleeps, her back is to his steady breaths. This will make it worse, she knows, this distance she's allowing between them, and yet the way her heart contracts when she sees him, as if it were being squeezed by someone who could not stop, is simply too much.

Sundays are the day William spends at the Lafayette Club. Normally she tries to work, but today the pressure from her hands is too great. "Letting go" is what her teacher called it. Too much pressure forms a mound of clay—one must let go to let the form appear. But Claire's mind is stuck, consumed. The clay slips off center. What normally is a metamorphosis, a creation sliding from one form to the other, lifting, rising, bulging and expanding, becomes attempt after attempt until she herself caves and sits back from the wheel. After the clay is put away, she washes her hands, takes her wedding ring from its protected spot by the door, and slips it back on, a routine act that now seems foolish.

Less than two years they've been married. Did he ever love her? He seemed interested in her only after his parents' death, and the proposal came quickly after that, the wedding—a small September ceremony, a much-coveted invitation—so immediate her mother made it a point to inform every guest that there were no plans for children as of yet. Why her? She'd wondered even then. William's father had known her father for years and there was a mutual respect—both self-made men, one by choice and one by circumstance. Was it that? That his father would have approved? Had encouraged, even?

She feels sick, as if the world were tightening into a dark, humid tunnel. For fresh air she heads to the garden, and before she knows it, she's thinking of tulips and again feels the world narrow. William bought her bunches when they first met, huge clusters that wobbled and drooped when first placed in a vase but then stood up straight the next day and swayed with the light. The first was a red bouquet. When he discovered they were her favorite flower—*they dance,* she'd said, *what other flower looks anything else but dead?*—he'd returned the next day with a selection of yellow. By Wednesday he'd found pink. Thursday it was a game, and he appeared with white; Friday, purple. On Saturday he had his work cut out for him, but finally arrived with a delicate cluster of yellow tulips with fiery orange edges. And then came Sunday, and she'd woken exhilarated, wondering what he'd find, convinced his arms would be empty. But there he was, late in the afternoon with stark white petals placed inside Van Briggle's Lorelei vase, and all at once she'd realized this was about him, not her. He had to outdo himself every day, it was a game, and to end it on a Sunday with a repetition of white held inside a vase by her favorite potter could have been seen as cheating. Still, at this point she was in love. They brought all the flowers into her parlor and placed them on the large mahogany table by the window, then danced in their little field.

A nap. Sleep the only way to escape her life, if she can manage. When Ketty knocks on the door, Claire sees that already two hours have passed, and William should be home soon from the club.

"What is wrong with you," Ketty says the moment she enters the room. It's not a question, it's a statement as she approaches the bed and sits heavily.

Claire rolls over onto her side and moves her jaw to release some tension, the loneliness inside her a hot radiance that seems worse with every move. She can't say anything. Her life is secrets, symphonies of doors shutting and bolting. "I miss William," she finally says, the truth.

"But he's back soon, for dinner."

"It only reminds me he'll leave again. Over and over we do this. An endless loop."

Ketty frowns, an expression her face slips into easily. "He won't stay for even a day if this is what he finds."

"I wish he'd take a week off. Just one week, to stay with me."

"I'd like a week off, too," Ketty says, standing and facing the closet. "But it's not always roses."

"Did you want this week off?" Claire asks. Ketty's not taken more than a few days here and there since Claire moved in, and in her mind she sees Ketty on the street, dressed in normal clothes. Where would she be going?

"Not this week," Ketty says, draping a dress over a chair. "Maybe next. Maybe we'll get William to stay home this week." She smiles, tight-lipped. "Get dressed. Poppy-seed cake is almost done."

Claire nods and Ketty leaves the room. The dress that was chosen, out of a closet full of gowns and sundresses and skirts and blouses, is the blue one, the off-the-shoulder one she's been wearing a lot lately for its room in the waist. Ketty must have had it cleaned, for Claire had worn it just the other day. But now it's here, ready. Nothing, Claire knows, gets past those Danish eyes.

11

Now

JUST ABOUT TWO WEEKS, she said last night. That's how long she has. And now another day almost gone. Aidan should call her. Make sure she got her car back—an excuse for contact, he knows. He's at Sarah Breining's uncle's place, a large beige ranch house near the park with white trim. Out of the corner of his eye there's movement—at the neighbor's across the street, the curtain falls into place. He waits in the car, and sure enough, the curtain moves again. Someone has something to say.

"I have this feeling," Aidan says when the neighbor answers his door, "like you want to say something."

Aidan hands him his card and the guy's eyes flick to Alan Breining's house.

"Other than that he never takes the bins up? You know you're supposed to do that the next day, but they're right there till the end of the week. Right at the curb."

"That's annoying."

"Sometimes he never takes them up. Just brings the bags down."

"Other than that, you like him?"

"I don't know. I got issues with him."

"I would too, he keeps the cans on the curb."

Again the guy looks across the street. "I got your card. I'll think on it." The door closes.

Two newspapers are on Alan's front walk, and Aidan gathers them as he approaches the door. Right as he's about to knock, his phone rings. He takes a couple of steps back toward his car.

"My cat's missing," Rebecca Sullivan says.

"How'd you get this number?"

"My cat's missing. You didn't even notice we weren't at the reunion?"

Right, her husband, in Aidan's class, he'd forgotten. "Sorry— skipped training day on feline recovery."

"I'm not joking. She's gone. She's an indoor cat, that doesn't just happen."

"Rebecca, you want to talk about Rick and the forgery case I'm all ears, *even though I don't have time.* Your cat goes missing, you open a can outside, put up signs, I don't know. We got bigger fish to fry right now."

"How 'bout you come by to check my locks? See how easy they'd be to pick."

"You want I can send an officer there."

"I would like that, thank you."

He's surprised she took him up on the offer. "Okay. I'll call the station."

The second he hangs up, the door swings open. "Working on a Sunday?" Alan Breining asks. Balding. Thick black glasses.

"Weekends off are a thing of the past," Aidan says, handing him his card along with the newspapers, taking a glance inside the house. "You knew my parents, they lived a couple houses down from you back on Cherry Lane."

Alan glances at the card. "I remember your mother. She gardened. Best-looking peonies. I killed mine. A woman's touch, I guess. They left, didn't they?"

"They did. They're in Ketchum now. Listen, Aaron Hardt stopped by the other day. We were just wanting to clarify—when did you work at that vet on Euclid?"

"My vet. Not 'that' vet. I started it. It was mine. Until a year ago. I retired."

"Why'd you tell Hardt two years ago?"

"I didn't. I loved what I did, I waited to leave as long as I could."

"Okay, he noted you worked there till two years ago. Guess it was a mistake."

"It was. I had a party with about a hundred people. Why would I fudge it by a year? Because ketamine went missing? I was there when that happened, I'm not hiding that."

"We're just trying to get it right. You remember when it went missing?"

"Sure. He asked me this. We had a few things taken. I passed along names of employees." He pauses. "Usually I feel them coming."

"Excuse me?"

"Storm," Alan says, nodding to the horizon. "Not this one. Snuck right on up. Like a tiger."

Aidan turns. Sure enough, in the sky is a summer storm, haunches of rolling darkness edged with bands of lighter gray.

cℒb

What woke her was the feeling of real tears on her cheek. The pillow was wet, the windows dark. After a while her heart settled, the nightmare receding, then replaced with the recollection of Aidan and his words. For a while she was up with this, undisturbed with thoughts of him, a replay of everything he'd said. For once the early morning hours were kind in their solitude, a time blockaded from the rest of the world, cordoned off and hers alone, *he remembered that first day*. Then the sun warmed her bed and sleep was an eager friend, kind and waiting.

Now it's the afternoon.

"Your car," her mother says, sitting in the kitchen, newspaper in hand, "is still at the school. *Aidan* drove you home. *The* Aidan, I'm assuming? He was polite. Sober. Which was good. With what's going on, you need to be careful."

A memory skitters through her mind—being confused at his car, that it wasn't the old Bronco he used to drive, and then tuning the radio incessantly, looking for a song that most likely never existed. "I was really tired," she tells her mother. "And yes, *the* Aidan."

The coffeepot is full. She takes a mug from the cupboard and pours it to the edge. Aidan Mackenzie. The way he looked at her. *You were the reason I knew it was going to be okay.* A trapdoor in her mind. *Stop.* "I want to read those letters. Anything that might have to do with Claire."

"They're downstairs. There's a lot down there."

"So do you think your mom was having an affair? *Right the wrong,* the note with the ring, did that mean come with me? Leave Grandpa?"

Her mother lowers the paper. "I didn't even know it was there. I didn't really know her. No one did."

"That's sad."

"It is what it is, but thank you for saying that. I used to miss her, some made-up version of her I had in my head. Childhood longing is a powerful thing."

Abby's cell phone rings. Robert. "Hold on," she says as she answers, then steps outside. A wasp hovers near the roofline, so she walks onto the lawn. Bare feet, the blades soft. "What'd you find out? A call on a Saturday, that had to be good."

"The producer is friends with Stephen. I think they had plans anyhow."

"Come on. No downplaying it, this is huge."

"What it is, is the beginning. A first step. Don't go booking wedding venues."

Abby stops in the middle of the yard.

"Sorry," he says. "I didn't mean to snap. I'm stressed. I keep thinking of all I need this to do, how far it needs to stretch, and it just doesn't seem possible. But then I think of it not happening and—"

"I've never needed a wedding. What I've wanted was a marriage."

"I know. Abby, I wish—"

"*You're* the one with the list. I'd go to Vegas tomorrow."

"Abby, I know, and I wish this was just about that. But there's so much more riding . . ." He stops himself. Triangles of light spread through the top of the fence, reaching into new shapes. "Let's forget it. I don't want to do this. How was the reunion?"

Wonderful. I spent the entire night wanting to kiss another man. "It was fine."

"Reunions are usually a letdown."

"I wasn't let down. I was on Benadryl and wine."

"Not a good combo there. You know that."

Would it kill him to be concerned? Instead he immediately jumps to judgmental. And worse, she hears him typing on his keyboard, a patterned tapping that tells her she has only part of his attention. "Luckily this guy I know drove me home." A reaction, childish, but for even one second she wants him not to think of her as a given. She waits, silence.

"Good," he finally says. "I love you, I don't want you driving like that."

And though she hears the distraction in his voice, she now also hears the faith. Never would he think it anything other than good that Abby made it home safely. And this breaks something within her, because he has no idea.

Ghosts. The usual reason for fears of basements, attics, or closets at the ends of long halls. But Abby's never believed in ghosts. Nothing flits in the corner of her eye; her rocking chair never moved on its own. For her, the fear is suffocation, breath faster and shorter, world compressing, everything heavier and heavier till she's gasping, an openmouthed futile plea. Once, when hiking with some friends, she thought she actually tasted dirt in her mouth, though it could have been the iron in her blood from biting her cheek. She'd stood at the open mouth of the cave as she watched her friends go inside. Darkness. One look and she felt how easily the earth could shift and the dirt ceiling would no longer be a ceiling—just that was enough to unleash the panic. Still, it's accepted. That fear. *Claustrophobia*, Robert said when they searched for apartments and she'd requested *no ground floors*—a demand that made sense to him, in the land of earthquakes. But she's looked it up; usually people have a fear of restricted space as well as a fear of suffocation. She only fears suffocation. MRI tubes, small closets during hide-and-seek—nothing like that has bothered her. Her fear is a smothering collapse from above—dirt, floorboards, sand, there's a myriad of ways the world can come crashing down.

The day has gone dark, overcast. She stands at the top step of the basement, box cutter in hand. It's just a room. She takes a step. No earthquakes here, no sinkholes, no reason to be trapped. Another step. Tornadoes? The sky looked ominous. *No, it's fine.* Then another and another until she's hit with the smell. Must, a damp soil scent combined with the odor of old, hidden things. She feels faint. The blade of the box cutter, even sheathed, blooms with heat. *Just walk down the damn steps.*

She forces herself the rest of the way, the smell of dark earthy secrets caught in her throat. And there they are, at the far end of the basement. Just four boxes from her grandmother. Abby had thought there'd be more. House sold, belongings scattered, and all that remains is packed away into four little boxes, forgotten in a basement. But at least they were kept; someone had reason to store the boxes, tucked away though they may be. If Abby died today, who would keep her journals, her photo albums? Maybe Robert, for a bit, but he'd have no reason to mourn for long, no reason to be saddled with a dead woman's belongings, a dead woman who's not even his wife. Her mother would keep them, of course, but then what about when she passes? The sense of impermanence is overwhelming. This is why people have kids, Abby thinks, so someone keeps your boxes.

The first one is not very heavy, and Abby lowers it to the floor and presses the blade of the cutter into shiny beige tape. Dorothy and Ted's baby books, a few framed photos, a lot of stuff she'd like to go through at some point. Then she sees letters. Under old linens, dozens and dozens. And beneath them, a large velvet box. Pistachio green with swirled brass designs in the corners. At one point there was a lock and the indentation is still present, velvet missing where bolts had been, but now the lid opens easily. A sewing box, she sees, mother-of-pearl tools, scissors and hooks, all held in place on the inside of the green-satin-lined lid. In the box is a small cloisonné container—yellow and red flowers against a black background—a round rock, and a little glass vial, capped on either end with copper, a necklace chain melded onto the top. Beneath everything are more papers. She reaches for the necklace and holds it toward the light. The glass spins—within it a solitary monarch butterfly wing. Carefully she puts it on and the glass vial sits against her chest, making it appear as if the wing emerges from her skin.

The rock. It couldn't have belonged to her grandmother, who wouldn't have cared for something so bland and base, and she wonders why it was kept. And the cloisonné box—pennies inside, at least a dozen of them. The dates are all from the early 1900s, one even an Indian head. There's a smell, she notices, from the inside. That musty, out-of-sight smell combined with something else. A hint of jasmine? Just as she identifies it, it's gone, and for a moment she wonders if what she'd breathed in was the exact air from her mother's childhood.

The letters. The aged, gritty rubber band that holds them together gives up and snaps into fragments, the letters scattering as they hit the cement floor. One is left in her hand, addressed to her grandmother's sister, from her grandmother, returned with others after Edith's sister died. The date in the corner is from a time when Abby's mother was still a baby. Unable to resist, she opens the envelope, reads the first couple of paragraphs and is immediately struck by the fact that her grandmother was *happy*. Never did Abby know her as happy. Suspicious, paranoid, angry, always a victim in some way—but happy? Even her handwriting was different, soft swirls of *l*'s, smooth crescendos of *r*'s, everything rising and falling from some uplifted part of a young Edith's spirit that for some reason wouldn't last, that Abby now realizes was fragile and limited and would soon be gone. *When you wrote this, you didn't know who you'd be. Whatever happened was still to come.* The tragedy of hindsight, the anguish of knowledge, markers of meaning glimpsed only in the landscape of an entire lifetime.

Her cell phone rings, left at the top of the stairs where there's reception. Without thinking she stands too quickly and the basement splinters before her eyes. She lowers her head to her chest, but all at once being down there is too much. The smell, the feeling on her skin—

dank, clammy, pressing. Within seconds she's at the stairs and climbing. Go. Just go. Go fast.

Even as she grabs the phone she feels oddly disconnected, as if part of herself has been left behind, rifling through letters. Through the living room windows she sees dark gray clouds, fists of water not yet opened.

"It's Aidan Mackenzie. Did you get your car?"

She smiles, his voice winding her back in until she feels the walls of herself, the soles of her feet now upon the kitchen tiles. "I did *not* get it. It's a seriously ugly rental and there's a very good chance I may never get it."

Her mother, standing at the stove, turns when Abby walks in, but immediately freezes, her expression an odd mix of longing and alarm.

"What?" Abby asks, feeling someone behind her. In a flash she sees the way her flesh would split, the rise of red.

"What's wrong?" Aidan says, having caught the fear in her voice.

"That necklace," her mother's saying. She's reaching toward her, lifting the glass vial with the butterfly wing, studying it as if expecting it to quiver with life.

Abby sighs, relieved. "Jesus, Mom. Okay. So you remember it?"

"Butterflies. She raised them. I haven't thought of that till now."

"Abby?" Aidan says.

"Sorry. I found this necklace, these letters of my grandmother's. Family research. What were you saying?"

She takes a seat at the table and a crack of thunder shakes the house.

☙

He knows he shouldn't do this. Knows he should simply remind her where her car is, that he gave her mom the keys, maybe even suggest some Gatorade. That's it. He knows that. But he's seeing her legs in the hall, how she'd pried off her shoes and kicked them across the lino-leum, completely lacking an edit button and so unaffected by the usual female protocol he tends to encounter, agendas and games and suffo-cating ego. And the way she'd smelled, the whole time he wanted to lean closer. And that lace, just the edge.

Lightning flashes, the sky reverberating brightness, gradations of energy. "Do you need coffee? Because I do. Bring the letters."

Abby doesn't say anything, but he doesn't fill the silence. He's learned that if you do the talking, you never hear what you need. A glance outside. The storm is about to unleash.

Finally she speaks. "Why?"

More proof of who she is, refreshingly unfiltered—and he surprises himself by responding in turn, unfiltered. "Because I'd like to see you again." He quickly adds, "And because I need to eat. The coffee shop has red velvet cupcakes."

She laughs. "I can't deny an honest man a cupcake."

Halfway to Abby's house the sky gives up, rain hurled with the ferocity of something held back. Even with the wipers on high he can see only in second-long intervals, at one point even pulling to the curb to wait it out. Rain pummels his car, tall grass at the edge of the road bent in the force.

When at last he pulls into her driveway, he sees her in the window. A blue bandanna holds back a mass of curls, and in a crack of recognition he knows that this is how he will always remember her, this blurred image seen through a softened haze of rain, her face in the window, hair held in blue.

She spots him, but he motions her to stay there, then goes to the back of the sedan, finds the umbrella, and meets her at the door. Despite the little arc of shelter, the ends of her hair immediately bead with water, a sprinkling of light, and again he smells the perfume or shampoo she uses, that scent that pulls at something within him.

Inside the car he allows himself a moment to look at her. Curly hair. *That's* who she reminds him of—Lila McCale, the same spirals, the case never far from his mind. He pictures the other victims, all straight hair, but the photos he'd seen of the Marshall women were all driver's license photos, not truly representative of day to day. They need varied pictures, or they could be missing a key similarity.

"Your hair is curly," he says, because he's been staring.

"And you drive an unmarked Crown Vic. What are you, undercover?"

"Detective."

"You are not."

"I told you."

"You said *cop*."

"Detectives are cops."

Mouth open, she shakes her head. "You are so full of shit. You *know* how cool that is."

A little laugh. "I guess I forget." He looks over his shoulder as he reverses, taking the opportunity to glance at her again. Along with the bandanna she's wearing an oversize blue sweater, jeans, and white Converse sneakers. This, he decides, is his favorite look on a woman.

Within minutes they're at the café. He takes the umbrella to her side and holds it out to her, leaving himself exposed, pelted by the rain.

"Get in here," she says. "What are you *doing?*" She grabs a fistful of his shirt and pulls him toward her so they're both under the umbrella, pressed against each other. Instinctively he puts his arm around her and the action is so natural that for a moment he wants to stop, say good-bye, and head back to the station, where the only thing he must think of is not getting food on his keyboard. "On the count of three," he says, and they awkwardly run to the door.

The café is really a diner. Thick plates lined in blue, chipped coffee mugs. It's not a truck stop, but the truckers have discovered it, leaving their rigs in the vacant lot behind the building, and there's always at least three or four of them lined up along the counter. Thick backs, overgrown hair. A testament to good food, Aidan's always thought.

He points to a booth by the window and they ease their way in, the rain a gray curtain. She looks around the diner. "If we were in L.A. and you suggested coffee, we'd be in some place with retro couches and re-claimed wood walls and a dozen screenwriters on their laptops."

"Reclaimed wood walls?"

"Those are the places Robert—" she stops, and picks up the trifold advertisement for pies.

Aidan watches her. Instead of changing the subject, she simply chose to stop talking, as if perhaps he'd think he'd imagined her talking in the first place. He smiles as she concentrates on the dessert selection. "Robert?" he asks.

She doesn't look up. "My boyfriend."

There's no music in the diner, just the sound of rain. She has a boy-friend. He keeps going, thrown, though maybe he shouldn't be. The assumption was clearly just on his part—though he can tell by the way she keeps looking down that the attraction is mutual. "And he likes those coffee shops. With the walls."

Now she looks up, almost apologetically. "He's a screenwriter. No screenwriter can work at home—I don't know why. It's like they have to prove they're writing."

"How long have you been together?"

"Bit over four years."

He's surprised. "That's a long time. No ring?"

"No, the ultimate irony from the woman who sells rings. There's a list of things we need to get done first. Why rush."

"So he's not ready?"

Now it's she who's surprised. "It's that obvious?"

"That he's an idiot? Yes, very obvious. Clear right off the bat." He smiles. "At some point, though, you just want it and put the list away. *If you want it.*"

She bites her lip, as if deciding what to do with the comment.

"I know the routine," he says. "Excuses when you're not ready. You look beautiful like that, by the way."

Her flush is sudden and deep. "Like what?"

"Bandanna. Wet hair. Slightly accusatory stare."

"Thank you." As if needing to break the moment, she reaches into her bag and produces letters and an old green velvet box. "So. A little background."

Dreams that started long ago. The name Claire Ballantine a new addition. A woman who disappeared in 1948, an event that forever impacted her grandmother. He listens to her talk about the nightmares and sees she's trying to both summarize and minimize her experience. The tightening in her jaw and the way she swallows—with effort, as if something's caught in her throat—tells him the dreams are not something she talks about.

"So neither one of us is sleeping now," he says.

She smiles. "At least you can catch your reason. Make it go away."

"You've got potential here. Let's see," he says, motioning to the stack. She hands him half and he glances at the addresses. "How'd you get these? Most of these are *from* your grandmother."

"Her sister gave them to us. Or her kids did, when she died. I can't remember. Nobody wanted them."

"Afternoon," the waitress, Carol, says. Carol, who always gives him free dessert. Smoker's voice and orange nail polish. "Get you something to drink?"

"Beer?" Abby asks.

Carol cuts him a quick look. "Pabst, Michelob, or MGD."

"Oh," Abby says. "*Really?*"

Now he laughs, and Carol glares at him. A betrayal, he knows. A broken allegiance. As Abby asks for an MGD and a bowl of chicken soup, his eyes go to her lips.

"And you, Detective?"

He looks back to Carol. "Just the soup. And a cupcake. And coffee. Thanks, Carol."

Abby waits till they're alone again. "You don't have to read these. I don't know why I brought—" She stops as Carol returns with a coffee. Waiting, she looks down at the table. At last, "You don't want to do more work."

"*This*," he says, motioning to the letters, "is a welcome distraction, and something I like doing." He opens a letter, reads the first line, and pretends he doesn't feel her smiling from across the table.

What Aidan can tell is that Abby's family's past was different than anything he's known. Luster glares from the pages, a world of oyster shells and caviar, balls and country clubs and maids. But then, in 1949, something changed. The handwriting becomes starkly different, words sloping drastically, crowded.

"Look," he says, "this must be about Claire. 'I've lost everything. My best friend gone.' Even her spacing changes. She disappeared in '48, right? The lines are practically on top of each other. Confusion. Just two years prior and her writing's fluid, letters rounded. Lines straight."

Abby leans in, reading the older letter Aidan holds out. "It says Claire

had her appendix out. Where's your appendix? I have a birthmark on
my stomach that looks like a scar."

"Let me see."

"What?"

"Your scar."

"It's not a scar."

"Your birthmark."

"You just want me to lift up my shirt."

He grins, and she does something completely surprising, and stands.
The look on her face tells him this has surprised her, too, as if her mind
has just caught up to her actions. But there she is, raising her sweater as
he slowly lowers his gaze—a bit too slowly, but it seems he's allowed.
The eyes of the restaurant are on them, but he doesn't care, he's enjoying this, a public striptease meant only for him. Then he sees it. A
mark. A line in pale skin.

Behind Abby he catches Carol by the counter, watching them, hand
resting on a slung-out hip. Definitely no free dessert after today. But
then he sees River Man a few stools over, and it's so jarring to see him
here, so disorienting, that for a second he forgets Abby in front of him.
Then he realizes that River Man doesn't even see him—he's staring at
Abby's back, her exposed waist. Abby, noticing Aidan's distraction,
turns and quickly drops her sweater.

His phone rings, the station's number on the screen. The first
thought: it's happened. A third victim. But then Aidan remembers it's
just early evening and every incident occurred at that moment when
night hooks into early morning. *The witching hour*, he's heard it called.
"One minute," he says to Abby, and heads to the pay phones near the
restrooms, as if this is the only appropriate place to talk on the phone.
Still he sees the curve of her waist.

"It gets worse," Harris says. "Sarah Breining's mother attempted suicide."

"Fuck," Aidan says, realizing too late he spoke too loud. A mother and son pass by the men's room and the boy's eyes go bright. Aidan mouths an apology, then turns to the wall.

"She thinks it's her fault," Harris continues. "If she hadn't left Sarah's dad, this wouldn't have happened. He'd have busted in, saved the day."

"I remember him, he wasn't saving anything. Before I forget, the Marshall women, the pictures I saw of them were DMV. People look different for those. I want to see what they really looked like."

"Sure. Listen, the mother's attempt got people talking, and now we've got a reporter who's not so interested in the integrity of the case."

"When?"

"Tomorrow. Gonna go from bad to worse. Article gets graphic. Lips, tongue. All the details. Be warned. Nothing's gonna be the same."

Back at the table, their soup bowls are waiting and Abby's got the green box open, holding up what looks like a bank ledger. "They were paying money. Or she was. This account's in my grandmother's name. Must've been after my grandfather left."

"To who?"

"It's blank. Just dates and amounts. The whole thing. Every couple of months, for years. The same amount each time." She flips to the back, pages and pages filled. "It kept going. No wonder her money went." She looks up for a second, then quickly back down. "That guy creeps me out."

Aidan turns to see River Man, standing and unfolding his wallet. He selects one bill, lifts the corner of his empty plate, and wedges it beneath. Then he turns to the coat hooks on the far wall.

"I saw him once before," Abby says. "At Applebee's."

"He's okay," Aidan says, watching River Man slowly put on a dark green jacket. "I see him at the river."

"Oh. Well, if the river vouches for him." She smiles.

Through the window now River Man stops beneath the awning to light a cigarette. The ember burns as he leans against the wall. Aidan searches the lot. Which car is his?

"Look at this. My grandmother sold a house in 1996. Where's Morrow Lake?"

"You didn't know about the house?"

"Not a thing." She angles the paper toward him. *Warranty Deed*, written at the top in tall, ornate letters.

"Morrow Lake's north," he says. "Look at the sale price."

A wrinkle forms between her eyes, and she flips the page over as if an explanation could be on the back. "A dollar. She sold it for a dollar. This was years before she died. No dementia, not then. What the hell."

"The question is *who* she sold it to, and why. Who's Eleanor Hadley? Why does she get a house for a dollar?"

"Wait, I saw a letter," Abby says, and starts sifting through the pile. "Hold on. From Eleanor Hadley. Here. Same address. Morrow Lake." She scans the page. "'I'm sorry for what you've gone through. Some days are hard. I mourn Claire's loss as well.' She knew Claire."

"We should see if she's still around." He's about to say more—*to see why she got a cabin for a dollar*—but an old obituary, cut from a newspaper, has fallen out of an envelope and its photograph places a stillness within him. Pale hair that looks ivory in black and white. A young face, yet knowing. The page is cut from the newspaper and is missing the date.

Claire Ballantine, of 435 Lake of the Isles, has been declared death in absentia, having been missing since 1948. A victim of foul play from a robbery at the Ballantine estate, Mrs. Ballantine leaves behind no children. Her husband, William S. Ballantine, predeceased her legal death.

"Claire," he says. He hands Abby the obit, watching as she reads the words. The next envelope is blank, empty, and he's about to move on when he realizes there's actually something inside. A little note, jotted in penmanship he recognizes as Edith's, post-event, but even messier, as if she'd not had a firm grip on the pen.

"'Claire,'" he says again, reading the letter aloud. "'How I wish you were still with us. I stay on the left side of my house so I don't see yours. But still I see the basement, and still I remember. Out of sight is not out of mind, I can tell you that. Every day I fear the police will come. I can't live here. I can't live at all.' No address on the envelope. Written after Claire disappeared. More like a confessional."

"The basement," she says, processing something. "I've always—" She stops, pushing past whatever was in her mind. "My grandmother was paranoid. Always thinking someone was at the door, there to get her. There was a reason. I didn't know. Was Claire killed in her own basement? Could my grandmother have seen it?"

As she twists noodles from her soup around her spoon, Aidan holds back his smile. "We don't know what she's talking about, if what happened in the basement had to do with Claire's disappearance. Though the dates of the letters, the difference in her writing, all that coincides with her disappearance. I can look for the owner. Claire's house. Get a number. You could go inside. A lot has changed on our end, but I can also look for her file. Or his. And this Eleanor Hadley—if she got the cabin in '96 she might still be there."

Across the table, Abby sets her spoon down. "You would do that?"

He nods. "When I get a chance to do it, it'll only take minutes. I

might have to say Claire's your relative." He motions to the obituary
Abby still holds in her hand. "What happened to the husband, do you
know? It said he died. He must've been young."

Abby traces the type with her fingertip. "My mom said he hung
himself in the basement. He never got over Claire. Could that be what
my grandmother meant? What happened in the basement? Him?"

Suddenly the rain picks up, as if the sky's been angered. He has to
admit this is interesting. A house basically gifted to someone Abby's
never heard of, a woman gone missing, a robbery. Never will they find
the answers—the past is too layered, too thick and unreachable—but
perhaps that's the lure. No one's life hangs in the balance; people don't
need to lock their doors to ward off whatever happened all those years
ago. "I'll go with you to Claire's house. If I can."

For a moment she just looks at him steadily, and he knows she's
thinking of the boyfriend, if this is wise or fair. If she says no, that will
be it. They might exchange emails. See you at the next reunion. Give
me a call if you're in town for Christmas. "I used to live near there," he
adds, as if this offering tips it to an innocent slant.

Finally she says, "I'd like that."

"Okay. Haven't had a full day off in two weeks. They've got to start
staggering time off—not much, but our overtime cap's been gouged.
That and the only thing keeping guys awake is foul coffee and driving
with the windows down." He smiles. "So I can probably swing it."

Then he remembers River Man and turns back to the window, but
all that's left is the rain.

12

Then

I KNOW WHO THIS IS. Sunday, hot even during the early shift, was achingly slow. Every time Eva stepped outside, the air grabbed and tightened and clung. The farmers aren't happy and the litanies of complaints are endless—soybeans wilted, corn starting to curl, wheat crops maturing too quickly. All of Luven accepts it with guilt, as if the heat's been conjured just for them, the hot breath of God's anger.

Make it to Wednesday, that's it, she told herself throughout the day. Till then she knew William was inaccessible, captive with a wife who may or may not have discovered their affair. Hard to think of anything else until Gerry walked back inside, wiping the sweat from his face with a handkerchief he stuffed in his back pocket.

"I got news," he said. "Eddie Parks. They found him."

Eva's breath wedged, stuck somewhere by her heart. Eddie Parks, missing three years, found. Only then did she realize she'd still been holding out hope he was alive. The weight of what he once meant to her pressed deep. "His mother, she knows?"

"Sure, where do you think I heard it from? Are you crying?" He reached for the crumpled handkerchief, but Eva quickly shook her head and wiped the tears with her thumb. "Well," Gerry had continued, turning back to the kitchen, "I suspect he'll come in here as soon as he's back. That boy loved his chicken-fried steak."

Alive. Eddie Parks was alive.

At home now, Eva tries to distract herself with thoughts of Eddie. On the floor by her dresser is a decoupage box filled with class photos, notes from friends no longer, funeral cards, some in Flemish, others English. The repository of things hurt. She opens it and finds a photo of Eddie and his little sister on the day of her First Communion. The last Eva saw of him, right before he left. In the background is the grove of elm trees, and within a second she's found the one she used to climb. Would she still be able to? With age comes knowledge; with knowledge comes fear. Too much could go wrong.

But these thoughts are of no use. It's William who lives within her now, a sharp radiance that can't be ignored. Besides, it's been years since she's seen Eddie, and she's witnessed enough soldiers' return to know that he might come back in name only.

Just make it to Wednesday.

Sometimes she's convinced she feels it—a fight between him and Claire. She'll be working—scouring syrup from a plate, jotting an order that changes with every breath, or standing there, waiting for her food to be ready, always standing—when suddenly there it is, a shift in energy, a distant threat, a clamping on her throat. Of course there would be a fight. Every hour is a new possibility: him leaving his wife, his wife leaving him, him choosing Eva, him choosing his wife. Anything or nothing.

But by Wednesday it's changed. The feeling has lifted to desperate, everything edged with panic, each minute spring-loaded. *Today is the day*. And though all she has wanted is for him to leave his wife, now she just wants things to return to the way they were. In the face of nothing, she'll take something. Monopoly in the moonlight, hot, humid nights, dinners on the back porch. Bubbles and fogged mirrors. It was perfect, really, just subtract those days he's gone. Nothing matters but him.

The bus ride to Rochester takes longer than usual. Scenery creeps, reluctant to let her pass. It's getting dark by the time she unlocks the door to the little house and takes a seat in the living room. She'll see him the second he pulls in, be waiting when his key turns the lock. In one move she'll wrap her arms around his neck and her legs around his waist, throwing him off balance. *Whoa*, he'll say, and laugh and dump whatever briefcase or keys or newspapers he has in his hands. Then he'll swoop her up in his arms and kick the door closed. Never will seeing someone be such a relief.

She looks back at the clock. He should've been home by now. The yard has gone from dark brown to black, the driveway leading to nothing more than a faint trace of street. He's never gotten home this late. Something is wrong. Now she knows it. Feels it in every inch of her body, as if she's fluttering about inside herself. She won't make it through the night. So many hours—dark, unforgiving hours.

The stairs creak in the silence of the house, somehow louder, as if aware that only one person is home, as if able to concentrate their sound for one set of ears. From the threshold of the room she stares at the bed, sliced diagonally by a shaft of moonlight. Fully clothed, she lies down and curls on her side, arm stretched to where William used to be.

13

Now

DREAMLESS. FOR ONCE. A sleep that carried her from end to end, a solid raft in black waters.

"What'd you do different?" Robert asks. Monday morning, soft light in leaves, the distant hum of a plane. "Why last night?"

"I don't know. Maybe just lucky." Abby stretches on the couch, luxurious with rest, then curls and faces the wall, the window above brightening in dust motes like a sprinkling of mica—*fairy wishes*, Aunt Emilia used to say. Beautiful. Everything. Amazing what a real night of sleep can do. Though maybe it wasn't just the sleep, a thought tugging on her. "But I read some letters." *I spent the evening with a man who wasn't you.* "I have a game plan." *To see him again.* She hears Aidan: *You look beautiful like that.* The way her heart slammed against her chest, it seemed impossible that others weren't hearing it. "When's your meeting at Warners?"

He tells her Wednesday, though they're not meeting on the lot, but at a restaurant, and gives her the name of two producers, neither of which mean anything to her. "Look them up," he says. "They've done some great stuff." There's a pause. "Abby, I saw it on the news this morning."

For a moment she's confused—the producers were on the news?

Robert continues. "Have you read what they're saying? What he did?"

"Oh. No. I haven't looked."

"Well you might want to. They're even talking about it here."

But she doesn't want to. She wants to stay in her pajamas, stare at a blank wall, and replay yesterday. Which she does. Over and over again. It's strange, right alongside the heart-leaping feeling—that top-of-the-roller-coaster lift and flurry—there's also something calming about Aidan, as if for years her view had been uncertain but just now it's shifted to familiar. *You know this place.* She's fallen right through the rabbit hole and once more is consumed with him—though differently, not just a crush, not fraught with teenage lust and a need for vindication, but rather a whole body-and-mind craving, like someone compelled to eat a certain food, not consciously aware of the reason for the demand but wanting it all the same.

Reason, however, has wrapped yellow caution tape around him, but deemed that thoughts are fine. She can relish in thoughts, bathe in thoughts, sink her feet deep into them. We all want the house down the block; we all wish we were ten pounds lighter. It is human to want. The problem is that in her mind she has already kissed him. He has already unbuttoned her blouse and she's felt the warmth of his hand. They've gone grocery shopping and folded into each other watching marathons on Netflix, popcorn falling on the floor. Lust and life, all of it. And because her mind has taken her there, there is a part of her that understands she has already cheated.

And it makes her nervous, because this want is nothing like she's known.

To think of something else, she goes to her mother's computer and looks up the producers. A man with thick eyebrows and a woman, young, with sharp chin-length blond hair and pale skin, eyes lined in black. Sophia. A fitting name. Another picture is taken at an event, and a split in her dress reveals some of the longest legs Abby's ever seen. She clicks on Filmography and takes in the names of two of Robert's favorite movies. *Stop.* She closes the window and there, behind it, is an article her mother must've been reading just this morning. Abby sits back hard. The details, not just of the cases here, but also of the ones in Marshall—lips sewn, tongue cut out—are burned into her mind, and as she closes her eyes dark blood pools around twine, skin pulled taut. A knife sawing into a tongue. It's only when the room begins to splinter that she realizes she's not taken a breath.

Her phone rings, startling her. A Minnesota number. She recognizes it, though she hasn't yet programmed it into her phone. As if he had sensed her panic, there he is. A lifeline. Everything surges within her as she swivels in the chair and hits Answer.

"So I have a large pizza. Pepperoni," Aidan says. "Which is not how I start many conversations."

She smiles, still feeling the dark details behind her. "Sounds like you're really hungry."

"I've got about forty minutes. Working, but I'm close. We can go to the park. I have napkins."

"I just read the article."

There's a pause. "I know, it's graphic. I'm around the corner."

Within minutes the gray sedan turns onto her street, windshield catching a stray bit of light. When he pulls into her driveway, he smiles through the window. This moment, so simple, disarms her, and in an instant the world and everything bad within it is gone. She tucks herself against the wall, where he can't see, just to catch her breath.

Inside the car, she clicks her seat belt into place.

"Hi," he says.

"Hi."

She smiles to the window. Never has such a small word been so loaded.

He's just reversed and hit the street when Brittany appears in her driveway, a garbage bin wobbling behind her. For once her face is without makeup and is remarkable in its unremarkableness. When she sees them, she angles her face into the light and shoots them a smile that's in no way an indication of happiness. "Shouldn't you be working?" she says to Aidan.

"I am. Late lunch."

He's wearing cologne, a scent that takes Abby to a forest, the end of a long day camping, sun and pine and smoke. For a moment, a cruel moment, she wants to ask what it is so she can buy it for Robert. A many-tendriled guilt spreads within her.

Brittany's already started back up the driveway, but now pauses at the side gate and picks something up. She heads back to the trash bin. "My sister's smoking again. No money to pitch in, but apparently she can spend nine bucks on a pack of Reds. Wait till my mom hears that." She pauses, taking them both in. "I'm back to Chicago today. So. You two have fun. Don't do anything I wouldn't do." A wink at Abby.

"Wow," Abby says as Brittany disappears, the gate bouncing on its hinges. "She's truly delightful."

But Aidan doesn't move. Hand on the gearshift, he studies Abby's house. There's a space of skin on the back of his neck, a little smooth patch between his hair and his collar, and the swift impulse to run her tongue along it shames Abby to the point that she looks away. She'll think of something else. Inside her purse she finds a free-floating stick of bubble gum, the wrapper thankfully intact. She starts chewing.

Now he turns and looks past her, back to Brittany's side yard, where she'd found the cigarette butts.

"Aidan," Abby says, "the park is that way." She points straight ahead.

Then turns around, looking behind them. "No, wait. It's that way. Shit. I have no idea where it is, but it's not here." Settling back in her seat she blows a huge bubble, and then, from behind the bubble, glances at him.

"Did I tell you how pretty you look?" he asks.

Her heart flies. The bubble pops. "No. You didn't."

"Well, you look pretty."

She doesn't even try to hide her smile.

The article this morning unleashed a shitstorm, the street in front of the station clogged by news vans, the tip line blowing up. Everyone seemed to have someone they'd like thrown under the bus, and now leads splinter in all directions, fissures of mistrust. All Aidan planned to do was work, yet here he is.

Every once in a while he allows himself a detail, a component that forms her whole. When she turns her head he catches the freckles above her cheekbone. When he looks behind her, to the street, he sees her ears are double-pierced. She bites her lip when she's studying something, and her right eyebrow has a slightly higher arch, as if her natural state is to question. One look, then another. Only once does he allow himself to see the edge of lace just below the neckline of her shirt. The exact shade of white, like a ship's sail turned to the sun, warmed and breathing, stays in his mind. There's no way to explain it, except it feels that someplace within him is already inhabited by her.

What he has to do is be good. In the past he's crossed lines he shouldn't with people whose lives he complicated or worse, all for an evening, a night, a week in Mexico. He knew it wasn't right, and unfortunately that was what he'd liked about it. But he was young then. The guy women seemed to sense was the face to accompany the story they'd later tell, the one bachelorette parties immediately homed in on, minds of mischief. He didn't care. And even when he grew up enough to make better choices, he was still filled with ambition, working in the Cities, not yet ready for the distraction of anything real. Too many times he'd seen it, friends of his in serious relationships suddenly happy about a desk job or a teaching opportunity, anything that kept them off the street. *You love someone,* he was told, *you don't want them to wonder every day if it's your last.* So intended or not, he found himself in relationships where love wasn't a risk. Now he wonders if he's actually past that. Somewhere out there is Ashley, completely available to him even after weeks of putting her off for the case, and yet he'd be fine never seeing her again. Meanwhile there's a girl beside him he can't stop thinking about, a girl who lives with her boyfriend in another state, and yet everything tells him this is where he should be.

The park, usually filled with young mothers and kids, is abandoned, and the playground merry-go-round is bent beneath their weight, Aidan on the edge, Abby cross-legged in the center, the pizza between them. New trees have just been planted and are surrounded by chicken wire to protect against deer, and a plastic reindeer has been stuck in the mesh of the one closest to him. At least someone in the town still has a sense of humor.

"How's he getting in?" she asks.

"All different points of entry. Catered to the situation. Does his homework. By the way, Eleanor Hadley," he says. "Records show she's still up there, at Morrow Lake. I just had time for one call, though—no answer."

"You really don't have to do that. Today must've been insane."

"Honestly, it took two minutes. And I requested a copy of the report from when Claire went missing. That'll come from Minneapolis, in storage somewhere, if it still exists."

She eats a bit of mozzarella she's scooped off with her fingers. "Do you ever feel sad you can't live other lives?"

His mouth lifts in a smile and she continues.

"Like Connecticut, old houses, making applesauce. I will never have that. I can think about it, I can talk about moving, but I'm never gonna do it. Or the bayou. Little shacks and cattails and fireflies. Porches with rocking chairs and crickets. That will never be my life."

"Might be a good thing. Those crickets are the size of cats."

She leans back against a pole and straightens her legs toward him, bare foot an inch from his leg. The urge, the drive to touch her—even as an accident—gathers in his muscles, almost brutal, like the need to stretch while cramped in an airplane. Just slightly, he shifts in the other direction, away from her. He will be good.

"You know what it is?" she says. "Limitations. Every day I feel them, more and more. All the things I won't do. Who I won't be. I will never live in France, in a stone house. I will never be a big powerful CEO. Or a businesswoman who dresses in suits. Or a college professor in an East Coast town, with a Volvo—I would've liked that."

"I will never be a fisherman in New England."

She smiles. "You wanted that?"

"Not in a way I thought about, but I guess it's always been there."

"Old men with pipes and leathered faces?"

"Lobster traps and raincoats." The sound of gulls, bell buoys. The sea air. "When I was a kid," he says, "my parents said I'd look at people in magazines, just regular people across the world, and cry I'd never meet them."

"You did?"

"I guess. I don't remember. I was five. Apparently a very emotional five." With one foot on the ground, he pushes just slightly and the merry-go-round inches forward.

"I get it," she says. "I miss the things I know I'm never going to have."

They stop moving. The leaves in the park hold a sheen of yellow from the sinking day, and she's got her bare arms crossed, as if for warmth. "Are you cold?" he asks.

But before she can answer, his phone rings. The neighbor of Alan Breining.

"I couldn't keep my mouth shut," the guy says.

"About what?" Aidan asks.

"Surgeries. In his house."

Aidan shuts the pizza box and motions to Abby to follow him to the car. "On people?"

"Animals, they say. But I've seen the cans, there's blood in there. I don't know if it's animal blood. I saw the article this morning, I'm not taking chances."

It takes seconds to get there, a crowd already in front, filling the driveway and sidewalk. Mostly neighbors, Aidan guesses, but a news van as well, a female reporter with shiny blond hair and a dark blue scarf, despite the warmth. One sign spikes out from the crowd: FOR THE EVIL MAN HAS NO FUTURE; THE LAMP OF THE WICKED WILL BE PUT OUT.—PROVERBS 24:20.

"Stay here," he tells Abby.

Already she's stepping out of the car.

"Okay then. Come with me."

The one officer present is DeVinck—a man who owes him money from a poker night that didn't go as planned, unprepared and over-whelmed. "I will pay," DeVinck says to him. "I swear to God. Just don't leave me here."

"He home?" Aidan asks.

"Not yet. The lady who lives in the gray house says he's never home during happy hour."

"Really? Okay." He glances at his watch. "Gotta clear the driveway so Breining can pull in the garage. We can keep him out of this mess."

It doesn't take long for more officers to arrive, Harris as well, and the barricade to expand, the driveway now open. Aidan tries to keep an eye on Abby, who's talking to some of the nicer neighbors, but with the arrival of more cops, the crowd seems to agitate, as if given permission to be angry. When he looks for her again, she's at the edge of the group, keeping a safe distance, a bit pale. He should have taken her home before coming, but was hoping this would be nothing, was hoping for more time with her. A bad choice. His judgment, when it comes to her, is clouded.

"He's gotta come in for questioning," Harris says. "You know about this surgery thing?"

As Aidan explains, Harris looks through pictures in his phone. "Other pictures of the Marshall victims. Here."

He holds the display and immediately Aidan sees that though the last two victims had straight hair, the first had coiling brown strands that hit her shoulder blades. He looks at his list of the victims, and adds a *C next to the ones who had curly hair.

MARSHALL VICTIMS
1. Jessica Hall. Rape. *C
2. Megan Mitchell. Ketamine. Lips. Rape. 6 weeks later.
3. Courtney Thatcher. Ketamine. Tongue. Lips. Rape. 3 weeks later. X

MAKADE VICTIMS
1. Lila McCale. Rape. *C
2. Sarah Breining. Ketamine. Lips. Rape. 2 weeks later. X
3. ?

"Both sets, here and there, the first women had curly hair."

Harris takes his phone, scrolling through the pictures. "So two out of five victims had curly hair. I'm not sure where you're going with that."

"What if it sets him off, reminds him of someone?"

"Honestly, the real anger came out with the others. If I had straight hair, I'd be more worried." Then Harris motions to where Abby is, her back against an elm tree, watching the crowd. "You've looked at her eight times already. Carol told me about her."

"It's not getting in the—"

"I'm not saying that. Over two weeks we've been on this, you want to have a picnic in a bed of flowers I don't care, we need breaks. I'm saying I can see why you're worried about the curly hair thing. But to me it's a nonfactor. Also, the oldest victim was twenty-four. Whatever you do, don't tell her I said this, but she's a little old."

Aidan's phone rings. One last glance toward Abby as he answers, then takes a few steps onto the lawn, toward the house and away from the crowd.

"He was in my apartment," Rebecca Sullivan says.

"Come on. Call the station. If he's breaking in, you call the station. I'm off this right now."

"I called the station. They sent someone out, not even from Makade."

"Neighboring support's helping with lighter police work."

"Lighter? He was in my place. He moved stuff around. Rearranged my things."

"Like what?" One lower window of the house is shrouded with curtains that gape in the middle, the sharp point of a four-poster bed all that's visible from where he stands. Aidan takes a few steps closer.

"My shit. Jewelry box. Stuff on my dresser."

"So you put them back differently." A crocheted blanket on the bed, pillows fluffed. The top of the dresser is bare, save for a porcelain tray.

"No. It was exactly how I had it, only it was reversed. *Everything* reversed."

Aidan turns back, looking for Abby, who's now leaning against his car, watching as a second and third news van pull up. A quick glance back at the house and he catches Harris's eye. Harris looks to Abby and nods.

"I gotta call you back," he tells Rebecca.

At last, a moment when he can take Abby home. The drive is quick. Porch lights turn on and kitchen windows brighten. The air lacks the sweet barbecue of summer and streets are empty of children, bikes tucked away. Forever, Aidan knows, kids will remember this as the summer they were kept inside, trees unclimbed, fishing poles dusty in garages.

Abby, beside him, watches the houses they pass, doors and windows closed. "They were so angry. They don't even know if it was him."

"People get scared, they get angry."

"A woman I was talking to, she said Dr. Breining does surgeries on animals. For people who don't have money. That's why he does it at home."

"We'll look into it. Search his place, I'm betting there's ketamine."

"Which he'd use, on the animals."

"That's what he'll say."

"So you think it's him?"

"You know what? I don't. I saw the pictures," he pauses, choosing his words, seeing the way the lips bulged, swelling between the twine. "I saw what was done and it was crude. A doctor's got skills, even if in a hurry. But it's one lead."

"So you're not stopping."

"No. Far from stopping."

She smiles. "Good."

"Dinner tomorrow night?" No pretenses, no excuses, just the question. "I'm being given a shift off."

The streetlights wash over her as she says yes.

14

Then

THE NEXT MORNING, finality pervades the house. The pillow across from her is empty and even the light in the room is softer, as if already the world is cast in a haze of memory. Eva sees her train case on the floor below the window, still packed, and realizes there will be no new notes.

It's real. William has not come.

Claire, she decides, must have slid the pieces together, seen the picture, the truth of his betrayal, and convinced him to save their marriage. His clothing could be sent for, his meetings postponed, all else abandoned. Eva can't allow herself to feel—not fully, not yet. She must make it back to Luven, claim Iris didn't need her, and only then will she allow what's happened to sink in. Though there is one thing, one task she forces herself to do: a stop at his office. She'll leave him a message, a folded-up note with only three words. *I love you.* She's never said it before. Neither one has, obeying an unspoken rule, a silent recognition that these words would only make things that much harder. But now there's nothing to protect. Her heart is already shattered.

The building is three stories and brick, next to the park. Only once has she been here, with William, on a Friday night when he'd forgotten to sign checks that were needed on Monday. Standing in the hall, she'd caught a glimpse into the office as the door closed behind him, and even in that quickly diminishing slice of space she'd noticed the secretary watching her, as if having detected an intruder's scent in the air.

Now she stands before her, a little woman with dark hair and small dark eyes. Inexplicably, she wears a brooch on each shoulder. Eva tries to look into his office, but the door is mostly closed.

"He's sick," the secretary says.

The relief Eva feels is so sudden and overwhelming that she can't hold back her smile. The secretary looks confused and slightly angry.

"Did you hear me? I said he's sick. Can't even talk on the phone. I'm not sure he'll be here at all this week."

"Oh, yes, I'm sorry," Eva says. "My mind was elsewhere."

The secretary straightens some folders on her desk, then reaches into her purse for a stick of gum. Her eyes are steady on Eva as she folds the piece into her mouth.

"Thank you," Eva finally says. "I'll check back next week."

As she leaves the office, she tucks the note back into her dress pocket.

The bus is hot, and even the passing scenery appears scorched, water in a pond pale and caught in a lifeless noon sun. He's sick. He can't talk. Unless that's just what he's told his secretary, so as not to air his marital problems? Eva doesn't want to think that, but suddenly it's what makes sense. The truth would never be passed along, it being far too private.

The relief she'd felt is gone, and again she remembers the silence of the house, the softness of the light. Was that the last time she'll be there? What if she never hears from him again? Why would any of this have happened? So she falls in love, finds someone who accepts every inch of her mind and body and past and future only to say good-bye?

As fields give way to rows of corn, she thinks of their first meeting, back to her inexplicable interest in Michael Knutson, and his surprising announcement to his family that he wanted to be a firefighter and planned to interview in Rochester. She had decided to show up. *I love it here*, she'd say, and just like that, there'd be a connection between her and the city, a bit more enticement, another reason for him to leave Luven and venture off sideways. Over the years she'd learned that people need a lot of reason to leave, the strings that bind them to family farms so strong that any movement often snaps them back to fields where they remain until their knees give out and their shoulders permanently hunch. But if Michael was to see her in Rochester? If he knew she'd be interested in living there, well, that could be the release he needed, the scissors to the strings. And if he left Luven, if he fought fires, hell, if he did anything, she could learn to love him. He really wasn't all that bad, just a bit dull, a bit bland, like a healthy meal.

So she'd been in Rochester with plans to fix Michael in her head. A haircut. New shirts. ChapStick. But on her way to the Fourth Central Fire Station—where she knew he'd be spending the day—she spotted him on a far street corner, his shirt untucked as he stood on one leg, trying to scrape something off his shoe, and in a beat she understood that new shirts would never make a difference and that learning to love someone wasn't actually a plan but a surrender. And so she turned, quickly rounding the corner before he could see her, and in the swirl of her decision she tripped hard when her heel caught a groove in the sidewalk.

When she landed, there was no one around, and she'd looked up, relieved her fall had not been witnessed, yet also disturbed, like a child who needs a mother's gaze for comfort and a release of tears. She was alone, and the palms of her hands stung, pricked red. Blood on her knee soaked and smudged right through her ruined nylons, and her mind instantly conjured Mrs. Pinkston, a prim lady who during the war painted her legs with tea and drew a seam with eyeliner on the backs of her calves, though everyone else in town simply accepted ankle socks and slacks. Mrs. Pinkston's dresses were at least a decade old, the fabric worn and almost transparent in some places, yet she'd cared desperately about her nylons.

Eva was still thinking of Mrs. Pinkston when suddenly she saw the legs of a man squatted before her, and heard a deep, smooth voice asking if she was all right. She looked up slowly, so absorbed in Mrs. Pinkston she was confused as to where she was—the sidewalk was unfamiliar, the sounds different from those in Luven, the voice unfamiliar, a movie star's voice. When she saw the man's face, she was more confused. The man was *striking*.

He held her elbow to keep her steady as they walked. He'd studied to be a doctor, he said, and his house wasn't far. She nodded and glanced at him a couple of times, still feeling as though she were walking in someone else's life.

"I was across the street," he said, "leaving the watch shop, when I saw you. Forgive me for asking, but was someone chasing you?"

A small laugh, one she tried to hold back. "Only the life I didn't want."

To that he'd smiled. "I know that chase well. Here, just down this street."

When she saw the house he took her to, a feminine little place, she came back to herself. He had a wife. Of course he did. But there was no ring. And then he was dabbing a warm washcloth on her knee, slowly, delicately, gazing at her whole leg and not just the injury. If there was a wife or a girlfriend, the house was pretty silent and the husband's gaze mighty liberal.

"You've got a nice house," she said.

He laughed. "It came like this. Old-lady wallpaper and everything."

A shot of relief spiked her pulse. Suddenly she was nervous, realizing there was possibility. "So is this the life you're running from?"

He looked surprised but answered. "No. It might not look like it, but this is the one I've run *to*." He poured hydrogen peroxide on a cotton ball. "My life is complicated. Brace yourself, this might sting."

As he pressed the cotton ball to her knee she closed her eyes tight, trying to block the pain. "*Everyone's* life is complicated," she said. "If it's not, you're dead. So I can handle the complication. I don't know about you, but I've never even crossed the Mississippi."

When she opened her eyes, she saw he no longer had the cotton ball on her knee but was watching her. Normally she didn't like brown eyes, but his were a lure. A warm, captivating lure. He wasn't looking away either. He was staring into her eyes, and that's when she saw it—all that was to happen with them. Not only did she see it but she felt it; it struck her with such force it knocked out her thoughts and left her wondering what was just said. She finally looked down, to his wrist, a tear on the cuff of his sleeve.

"You have a tear."

He lifted his arm, examining the rip. "I caught my wrist on the gate. When I saw you falling, I reached out. Ridiculous, of course, you were so far away."

"Instinct." The press of his gaze was almost too much. "Do you have needle and thread?"

And so she sat at his kitchen table, mending the sleeve, while he stood at the stove in a different shirt, asking questions. She answered everything honestly, telling him about clothes she made and about Luven, how people could drive in and out of town with their breath held, it was that small. She told him about the trains that went through, always stopping even though no one ever boarded, no one thought to leave. And when she was done, she realized she had asked him nothing, yet there were so many questions, where to begin? "Did they fix your watch?"

He reached into his coat, which was hanging on the back of the chair, and handed her the most beautiful pocket watch she'd ever seen, with green, almost iridescent enamel. The back was inscribed: *Time stands still when you are near.* She looked up to find him still watching her.

"It was my grandfather's," he said. "Legend was it stopped working when my grandmother died. To the minute. But now it's working. Hasn't missed a beat yet."

"Do you believe that?"

"That the watch knew when she'd died? No. But he did, and he never fixed it."

"Well, the rest of his life would be about that time. Makes sense that the watch should be as well."

"A romantic, I see."

The heat in her cheeks must have entertained him, as his smile only grew. She looked out the window, to the long driveway. "Which hospital do you work at?"

"I don't. I found the healthy people in construction much more to my liking. I have a company, actually, right by the park."

In her mind a vague map of Rochester unfurled. His office had been much closer to where she'd fallen. Much closer, indeed. And yet he'd taken her to his house for a reason, she realized, and so when she handed him his shirt, she'd lifted her bare leg and pointed out a little scrape on her ankle. *Do you mind?*

She might have encouraged, but he initiated. And he, of course, was the one with the information, information he withheld until they'd had dinner and Eva was already caught in the warm snare of his brown eyes, was already rehearsing the stories he'd told so she could hear them again as she fell asleep. He knew what he was opening the door to, the labyrinth of his life. And though in the past she's seen that as proof of their overwhelming connection, now she sees differently. Now she sees it as cruel.

You made me love you.

15

Now

DRIVING BACK FROM DINNER with her mother, Abby passes the grocery store, a gas station, the bank. Reporters are poised anywhere they might encounter someone scared, someone with a story—which is just about everywhere.

"Looks like we're officially national news. Not that I think we need it," Dorothy says, "but I have someone coming to install another lock."

"Tonight?" Abby turns her phone on—it's close to nine PM.

"Three places, I called," Dorothy says. "All booked. This guy's a friend of Tom's; he's fitting us in after hours. Not for a friendly price, but such is life."

Though the media is a thick, undeniable force, the actual people of Makade are sparse, and their neighborhood is quiet, the lack of life a strange sort of presence itself. Noticeable. Curtains are drawn, windows shut tight. "You can see him still, you know," Abby says about Tom. "You don't have to stay home for me."

"I want to stay home for you." A pause, then a smile of admission. "That, and he's at a conference in Milwaukee till Thursday."

Back at the house, the sound of the drill, the whirring and shaking, the doorframe rattling the wall, only creates anxiety. Abby shuts the door to her room and calls Hannah.

"Okay, pizza," Hannah says after a while. "'Friends eating pizza. At a park."

"I think this is trouble."

"I know this is trouble."

"Do you still love me even if I want someone who's not my boyfriend? It feels weird to even say that."

"My love for you has nothing to do with who you want. I just don't want you to get hurt."

"But by who? The one who keeps putting his career before our relationship and wouldn't even come here? Or the guy I always felt I'd be with, for some crazy reason? The one who's going out of his way at the worst time to not only see me but help me?"

Hannah gives a little laugh. "When you put it like that, I want to smack Robert."

"Maybe this is all in my head. Maybe Aidan has a savior complex."

"Yeah, I'm sure that's it."

"I feel guilty, even though nothing's happened."

"Abby, you feel guilty because everything's happened. Listen, I don't want to defend Robert too much, but this is a four-year relationship you're talking about. And maybe it's not that he's putting his career ahead of you as much as it is that he's dealing with some pretty heavy career stuff and figures you'll be there. Maybe that's why it feels like he's taking you lightly, because he doesn't question you in his life. He assumes you'll always be there."

"But that's the problem, isn't it?"

Still, what Hannah said about what Robert's going through stays with her, and when she hangs up, she calls him. "We just had another lock installed," she tells him when he answers.

"That's good." There's a shadow in his voice, an edge of something. Bad news about the script? "I saw you on the news just now," he continues. "At a house."

"*Me?*"

"All those people who were there, they think he did it? That vet?"

"It was crazy. They were mostly his neighbors. All turned on him. A man who does surgeries for cheap for people who can't pay. A good guy, they all liked him till now. I can't imagine what happened when he came home."

"You didn't see it when he pulled in?"

"No, we'd left, why? What happened?"

There's a silence, and then "We?"

In this moment Abby realizes it wasn't the script that cast the shadow in his voice. What had he seen? Her standing with Aidan? Getting back in his car? That's all it could've been. "My friend Aidan, a detective," she says, and tells him about records he's looking up, the help she'd never get otherwise.

But Robert doesn't latch onto this, won't let what he'd seen slip beneath the conversation. "Aidan? That's the one you had a crush on, in high school."

"He's a detective," she says again, wondering what she'd told him. If only she'd known it would be used against her. "You'd like him. I'm just happy he's helping."

And eventually he accepts this, he has to. She's given him no reason not to.

Everything's happened.

Now the night hangs before Abby like a rope bridge spanning an abyss. There's a chance her sleep will again be dreamless, like last night, but nerves have already angled her toward a dark night. Once again, she's sure the table will be set, the sky a roiling dark.

Think of something pleasant. The moment she'd crossed her arms and Aidan had seen. *Are you cold?* A thrill that he'd noticed. That he was watching.

In bed, she thinks of Aidan at work, thinks of Robert thinking of her, and then thinks of the safety of the morning, the soothing daylight hours. It's too much. She could make coffee. Stay awake all night, plan on sleeping during the day. But last night was fine, she tells herself, there's a chance tonight will be as well. *Something pleasant, images, no thoughts.* In her mind she sees Ireland, a place she's always wanted to visit, and forces herself there, but still the dream is a presence behind her, staring at her back. *Stop.* Thatched cottages and red doors. A basket of flowers on a bike. *Everything is fine.* Soon she's falling asleep as castles rise from green pastures and roses climb stone walls. The Cliffs of Moher, a majestic, soaring expanse of rocks. White waves burst upon its base like a line of frosting on a cake. But then the earth begins to crumble into the ocean.

The dream—an ominous shape at first—descends, forming, gathering, and is then there, sudden and fast. For the first time there's a deer, a buck, scratching its antlers against the oak tree. She watches it, alone under the gray sky, and though it's far away, the sound grows louder and louder until suddenly she's tugging toward consciousness and then awake, the sound now a rustling by the fence on the side of the house. And though she doesn't trust herself, her mind still caught in the paranoia of her dream, she thinks she hears it—their gate's high-pitched squeal as it opens.

16

Then

THE DOOR SHUTS. William in the bathroom once more, sick. Claire feels bad, but she has her husband. Still with her, still in the house, still in her arms only. It feels like a holiday, like her childhood when her father was home for a few days because other people insisted on celebrating. Waking in a house where everyone was home, breathing beneath the same roof, set loose into the day with no expectations, no duties or obligations. A strange, delirious entrapment.

And like her father all those years ago, William, too, appears to be thinking of other things, her every word pulling him back in a reluctant return.

"I've missed work," he tells her Friday when she dabs a washcloth on his brow. "We may have lost a bid because I was too sick to speak. Again, I feel better in the evening. It makes no sense."

"You've spent an entire day getting everything out of your system. Of course you feel better in the evening. Ketty will be up with some soup. You don't have to eat it now, but try. At least the tea, to settle your stomach."

In the hall she runs into Ketty, who emerges from the staircase holding a tray, a bowl of soup crammed next to a cup and the silver teapot. Since Tuesday Ketty's made soups and ginger tea, both mixed with an old family recipe, a tincture her mother taught her to make. *Sip, you'll feel better.* Motherly, it would seem.

"It won't get any worse," Ketty says to Claire.

"I'd like it to stop. So we have a few healthy days before he leaves."

Ketty nods, and the two women head off in opposite directions in the hall.

The only thing Claire's not sure of is what they're really accomplishing. She's bought herself extra nights with her husband, one week in which he doesn't go to Rochester. That's all. At first she thought that by showing him she cares, nurturing him, dedicated and devoted, he'd remember that he loved her. Remember that this is his home.

But she can see it in his eyes—it's not just work he's missing.

ॐ

For days, Claire has sat on the edge of his bed, relaying his words to employees, pressing a cool cloth to his forehead, holding a large bowl if he couldn't make it to the bathroom—and yet all he's thought of is Eva. On Thursday he managed to call her, a quick phone call when Claire disappeared down the hall, but she'd not been home and he left a message that the doctor was sick with the man who answered. The uncle? The thought made the nausea stronger than before. Briefly he'd wondered if she'd been in the background when he left the message, angry and insolent and refusing to come to the phone. He thought of the jutting points of her elbows when she crosses her arms tight. Her ears, the shapes of her toes. The blue vein on the inside of her pale arm—the whole of her makes him happy.

On Friday he called her house again. Two more times, the line unanswered. He'd told himself he wanted only to be sure she got the message, but the truth, he realized, was that he needed to hear her voice. Just that, the word *hello*.

On Saturday, William begins to feel better. He doesn't understand, and figures his body has simply revolted and rebelled against his mind, the guilt of the affair he always justified and contained set loose by a mutinous physicality, legs that would not hold, arms too weak to function, and a stomach that refused to settle. This was just his body's way of forcing him to face that from which he'd always turned away.

Eva. Claire. His two compartmentalized, justified worlds. If the guilt and the need to be a better man made him physically ill, his mind was telling him something. It was time to decide.

At the beginning, Eva was a reward. A treat. Dessert, a hot bath. He married the person his parents had encouraged him to, he lived in their house and kept up their friendships and charities and agendas. An entire life—he only now realizes—woven with the cords of his guilt over his father. How could he not have seen that? At the time he thought everything logical. All his choices. And though early in his marriage to Claire he'd realized that what she felt for him trumped his feelings for her, it wasn't until Eva that he grasped how much more there was to love—a whole other layer, an entire world of other layers. Still, in his mind what mattered was that he did right by his wife: provide, listen, attend holidays and birthdays and Sunday dinners. As long as he did that, who was he hurting with a few days a week that belonged to just him? A ridiculously naive supposition, he now sees. Selfish, too.

He loves a woman who's not his wife, and that love has taken its toll. The ways in which he was good to his wife are no longer. He is not a good man. Claire is worthy of love. Worthy of an entirety of affection and devotion, not increments doled out on certain days. Really, he sees, he never gave his life with her a chance, had stacked the odds against her from the first day as a married man that he'd felt the road to Rochester beneath his tires, from the very moment he told himself that providing was the priority.

But he can't not be with Eva. He can't let another man's hand skim her waist or the rise of her hipbone, or let someone else hear the tales of her childhood, stories of fishing and forts and fields that are told as the bathwater grows cold and the sound of her voice and the life in her eyes slips the evening to night. Time with her, he's realized, obeys no clocks.

That night, Claire takes him to dinner at a restaurant they haven't been to in months and the maître d' spots them with a polite nod, knowing better than to comment on their absence, then leads them to the best table in the house, a corner by the window. The dark lake glitters in the distance. Candlelight and white linens. For a moment he pictures Eva sitting in Claire's seat, hair dark, alluring folds like a curtain asking to be pulled back.

He's sure Eva got the message, and all is fine. But what had Wednesday done to her? Thursday she probably went home, but Wednesday, Wednesday she wouldn't have known he was sick—she would've waited. Curled toward the window, her lake-blue eyes staring at nothing.

17

Now

THEY'VE GONE OVER IT a few times. What Abby heard, where she heard it, the dream that wove the sound into a fiction.

"We should've called the station's number," Dorothy says for the third time. "Let you sleep."

"Promise, I slept. It's all good."

He's done a preliminary look outside, but now needs to look a bit closer. Already the sky has lifted a few shades, the night losing its grip to early morning.

The lamp above the patio casts a weak arc of brightness over the concrete and does nothing to illuminate the rest of the yard, so with his Maglite he slowly traces the perimeter. Abby follows behind, and soon the ends of her pajama bottoms dampen from the grass's dew. "You should get inside, get warm," he says, but she just shakes her head and shoves her hands deep into the pockets of her sweatshirt, trailing him as he aims his smile to the shadows.

Now and then he looks back to the kitchen window, to where Abby's mother makes coffee. The house is easy to look into. No curtains in the kitchen, and it doesn't seem that she uses the ones in her bedroom. And that front door, all glass. Put as many locks on it as you want, breaking in would be simple. Again he thinks of Lila McCale and the first victim in Marshall, both with hair like Abby's, and again Aidan has the feeling that that one commonality set the guy off— though Harris was right, he tells himself, the real anger came out later. His worry over this is personal, not objective.

When Aidan gets to the side gate, he remembers where Brittany found the cigarette butts just yesterday—a hidden spot with a clear view to Abby's room. But none of the women reported smelling smoke. If the guy had been smoking, it would still be on him. Unless the women themselves smoked and therefore didn't notice. Quickly he texts Harris. *Any victims smoke? Cigarette butts from vantage points? Not just night of.* Brittany, he needs to call her later and see what her sister said, if she owned up to smoking.

The gate swings open when he pushes it, not latched. When he turns, Abby's right there, right behind him, mere inches away, and the fact that they're in this corner of darkness without one witness unleashes the need to hook his arms under hers and hoist her up, her back against the wall as he follows the line of her neck with his mouth—an urge that must somehow play on his face as she blushes, even in this darkness he can see it, and looks down at the grass. He turns back to the gate.

"Was this latched?"

"Maybe?"

He can barely look at her, the urge is that strong. Her lead—that's what he's taking. And she has to be sure, it can't just be the result of a few too many drinks or a current of rebellion.

"Maybe it wasn't," she says. "Maybe the wind blew it open."

"Could be," he says, though there's no breeze, nothing to make the gate move on its own. He'll put in a request that a patrol make stops here the rest of the week. DeVinck, he decides, he'll write off his debt, a clean slate for the next poker game—just make pit stops and keep an eye out, show your presence.

Back inside, her mother has gone back to bed, a full pot of coffee and a carton of half-and-half on the counter. They sit at the kitchen table as he fills out the report.

"Do you close your curtains?" he asks.

"Trying to decide what you're doing later?"

He smiles. "First, *we* have plans later. Second, you should. Your window's clear from the street."

"I hate the dark. The streetlights remind me there's a world outside."

The dark. That room, the newspaper undone on the window, a brightness the boy must have dreamt of seeing for so long, yet never saw. "I understand about the streetlight. But right now the world outside is something you need to keep out."

"Will do. Thank you for your concern, Detective."

And with her smile, the room with black walls and floor disappears.

18

Then

NO PHONE CALLS, no messages. Eva knows it's over. At work she feels her arms moving, her legs moving, her entirety existing and functioning without her mind. She pours coffee. Slides plates from her tray. Smiles half-smiles and pockets meager tips.

"They had girls in Europe," a voice says. "But none like you. And I even met Marlene Dietrich."

Eva looks up. Eddie Parks. A scar like a hook on his neck. Sitting there as if it were just another Tuesday morning. She breaks into a smile. "Where'd you come from?"

"A hospital in Belgium mostly."

"You met Marlene Dietrich?"

"Well, I was out when she visited. Sound asleep, or something like it. But she knew I'd wake up and she wrote me a note. Thought that was kind of her. I brought it home, too, if you want to see. Her name's all one word—she never lifted the pen, not once."

Behind her she hears Gerry ringing the bell and glances back at the kitchen, to the plates that are waiting. *I brought it home, too, if you want to see.* The sudden image of Eddie's hand in her own makes her feel as though she's sinking.

She's not given up on William.

As if having seen her thoughts play before him, Eddie says, "You got a guy?"

She can't help but laugh. "Right to the point now, aren't we, Mr. Parks?"

"You're not answering my question." His smile is challenging.

"Someone sure came back with confidence."

"Not confidence. Just figure if I'm alive, I might as well really live." She rises to the game in a reflex. "I'm not sure how *I* figure into that."

But he loses his smile. His eyes go to the table, to his folded hands, and Eva notices another scar that stretches the length of his wrist, disappearing into the cuff of his shirt. When he looks up, he sees the direction of her gaze and puts his hands beneath the table. "I thought of you. When I was there."

Sadness caves within her, because this moment, in the past, would've been exactly what she needed to slough away William's touch, to wear away the memory—but now she understands that her old rules no longer apply and in no way is this a game to the man who sits before her, whose skin maps a journey she can't fathom.

She glances back at Gerry, who stares angrily until he realizes she's talking to Eddie—Eddie the new hometown hero.

"Tell you what," Eddie says. "Maybe I'll stop in next week. Maybe I'll even be here this same time next week."

On her way to the kitchen she looks back once more at Eddie, whose eyes trace her every move.

❧

Wednesday morning they have breakfast in bed, yet all William wants to do is leave, despite the return of his appetite. The desire to act, to make a choice, to move forward, is so strong he feels it as a momentum, a gathering in his muscles that's hard to ignore. Eva. He'll try to cut his day at work short—though with so much piled up, that could be a challenge—and arrive at the house the second he thinks she's there. And if she's not, if she's decided to stay in Luven, he'll find her.

Finally breakfast is over. Just as he's unfolding the bedsheets Claire stands before him and drops the strap of her nightgown from her shoulder. The pain of this act, of this simple, desperate act, shoots through him. That she feels she has to do this. It's been a couple of months since they've been together, and then a while before that, something he'd thought she'd not minded. That she clearly has fills him with more regret. This gesture, the silk strap now looped down and brushing her elbow, is heartbreak. Pure, horrendous heartbreak.

He looks up into her eyes, and he sees that she's glimpsed this.

"I'm sorry," he says quickly.

But her back is already turned, the strap lifted once again onto her pale shoulder.

Eva's goal is to not feel. To not think. But rather to simply go. Just go to Rochester. Don't think about the fact that each mile is one closer to the answer, don't look to the horizon and see it as the sky above the conclusion. Just go.

When finally she's there, early evening has just begun to settle, the world like an aged painting. Even from the mouth of the drive she can tell he's not in the house. The windows are dark, his car nowhere to be seen. The one thing she knows for certain is she can't handle another night like last Wednesday. Maybe she should write a note. *Find me and I'll come back.* But how could she get back to Luven? The last bus left an hour ago. She thinks of the bottles of brandy and whiskey. If he's not here in a couple of hours, she'll drink just enough to sleep.

The porch steps creak and the door squeals. The place feels haunted, abandoned, even though the flip of the switch brightens the floral wallpaper. This is it, she thinks, and then takes a seat, staring at the windows until they fill with the reflection of her own eyes watching her, worried.

She must've fallen asleep, but the second she feels something on her shoulder, she's up in a flash, and in one swift move has her arms wrapped around William's neck, her check against his chest.

"William," she says, caught so off guard she's unable to hold back any emotion. "What happened? Why didn't you call?"

"I was sick," he says. "And I did call. Thursday. I left you a message the 'doctor' was sick. At your house, with a man. I even called again a few times, but no one answered."

"A man answered?" The only man who answers their phone, who should know better than to answer but does, is her uncle Lucas. He doesn't even say *Marten residence* or *Margaret's phone*, he simply grunts a hello—heavy on the *hell*. Uncle Lucas must have made a midweek visit.

"I couldn't talk without getting sick. Every time my head moved, it was like I came loose. And everyone was watching me, chasing after me with bowls and—" He stops. "It was hard to be alone, to make a call. Can I put my bag down?"

Claire never said anything to him. What does that mean? That she doesn't suspect? It must. *I know who this is*—she meant something else. And Dr. Adams must not have reported back, must not have read into what he'd seen. All this worry for nothing. And while there's something profoundly comforting about that, that they've not been discovered, at the same time there's a pull of disappointment. What now, they go back to how they'd been? The needle's at the start of the record?

"Were you very mad at me?" he asks, shrugging off his jacket.

"No." She doesn't move. "I was devastated."

He studies her from across the room, and then, with what seems like only a couple of steps, he's lifting her off her feet and carrying her upstairs.

19

Now

THERE ARE LINES ABBY'S DRAWN. Some sensible. Some arbitrary. These lines are the rail she clutches when she feels she might misstep. As long as they exist, as long as she continually checks them, everything is fine. And she does check them—though mostly to evaluate, smudge out, and move just a little. *We can talk on the phone, but we cannot laugh. We can plan to see each other, but not after the sun's down.* Then the border expands, territory within grown wilder. *We can go to dinner, we can laugh, the sun can be down—but there can be no candlelight.*

Dinner Tuesday night. A gathering long after sundown. Tables so small that legs are forced into each other, limbs threaded. Candlelight urging people to lean in—the line moved once more—an atmosphere unbearable if the person you're with is not the person you should be with. The final line, drawn in black Sharpie, thick and permanent and unmoving: *I can desperately want, but I cannot act.*

The restaurant is the original Makade firehouse and the bay door is now a wall of glass held in dark wood, the high ceiling lined in gold tin tiles that swirl to fleurs-de-lis. Only minutes after they're seated Aidan's forced to take a call, so Abby waits, looking back into the lounge area, a garnet-red Victorian sofa and richly patterned wallpaper, dark wood paneling and a door to the kitchen that's topped in etched glass. Beautiful. She had no idea. This building was vacant, boarded off and abandoned when she lived here, and as she wonders when this happened she notices one of the reporters from Alan Breining's house. Two tables over. Blond hair still perfectly in place, the heavy smear of makeup fit only for a camera. She's sitting with a man clearly on the other side of things, jeans and a navy blue fleece, a producer maybe. Discreetly a waiter lifts the black bill presenter from the corner of their table, and Abby prays they'll be gone by the time Aidan returns.

What is she doing? Even a month ago this would be unfathomable. *At some point, though,* Aidan had said, *you just want it and put the list away. If you want it.* Does she? For years it's been all about whether or not Robert was ready, whether he wanted to take that next step, her own feelings a given. Now she wonders. Certainty's undone. The realization is like the first step onto new ice, tentative and worried: though the final line has not been crossed—an innocence in thoughts alone—things may have already gone too far simply because a question exists where before there was none.

"You okay?"

He's pulling out the chair, sitting, watching her. The faint scruff on his face is darker in this light, and his cheekbones are flanked in shadow. Abby catches the flame of the candle lurch and dive, a reaction to the movement, the air between them rearranged as he draws closer. Then she sees the reporter, also watching, having seen him enter the room. Perhaps she saw him leave in the first place and has been waiting for his return.

As if on cue the reporter and her friend stand. "I don't mean to interrupt," she says, "but maybe a question outside after."

Aidan doesn't look surprised. "I'm not authorized."

"Okay. Didn't mean to interrupt. Have a good dinner."

Abby watches as they leave the restaurant. "That was easy."

"It won't be."

And sure enough, not ten minutes later Abby catches sight of a news van through the glass bay door, parked on the other side of the street.

"They didn't have their camera," Aidan explains. "Now they do. But there's also a back door and I know the owner. I'll have someone bring my car around. Let's just pretend they're not there."

Dinner continues and it's surprisingly easy to forget everything outside these walls, to feel only the heat of their own observation. The files of their lives are splayed open in a great fill-in of information, and gradually Aidan tells her what happened in St. Paul—a boy, a room. The entire time he speaks he looks only at the flame of the candle.

"I don't tell people that," he says at last, looking up. Dark green eyes that appear black.

"Because of what happened to the boy, or what happened to you after?"

A small smile. "Both. It's something with me, the fear of not making it in time. And I didn't make it in time."

"You couldn't have gotten there earlier. You didn't know."

"I was on that street at least a dozen times that month."

"That's guilt, toying with you. The newspaper was up. There was no way to know."

"That's what I tell myself. But I close my eyes and I see it down."

Behind Abby is the jangle of silverware as the waiter clears a table. Tray held high, he maneuvers to the kitchen right as a man stands directly in his path. A near collision. The energy, the slight chaos—a shadow of what this building has seen in its original life.

"Guilt is tricky," she says. "I know. My mom tutored this boy, mostly at the house. He was completely starved for attention—I mean, devastated when my mom sewed a button back on his shirt. And he liked me. Would bring me little gifts. Rocks, a tin angel. One day my mom told him he couldn't come anymore, said it was a liability and she had to tutor him only at the school. And it was fine till she saw us talking. That night she told me the truth. This poem he'd written. Something about his sister and his mom, and what he'd done or what he wanted to do. And she told me to stay away from him."

The waiter reappears and Abby pauses. A swirling rush of water, cracks of ice, a pour of more wine into Abby's glass. Then on to the next table.

She takes a sip. "One day some girls accused me of being with him. His girlfriend. It was a joke. Mean, you know, just one of those things to get a rise, but I fell for it and said no, that he was a freak and it wasn't me he wanted, that my mom had proof, it was his sister." She pauses. "It was a poem. None of it might've been true."

He sits back and looks at her evenly. "We say things without thinking. You were young."

"I broke their trust. My mom and his. She thought she was protecting me by telling me, but I used that information to hurt. I took her away from him."

"He found out?"

"He stopped tutoring. It could've had to do with me, or maybe not. I remember him, though, around the corner when I stormed off. Over the years the memory's changed. Now I think of it and he stares right at me. But sometimes I wonder if he was there at all."

"Guilt can rewrite history."

"That it does."

Again Abby thinks of Robert, his decision not to join her in Minnesota. He made a choice, and he didn't choose her. She knows there was more to it, but with every thought of Aidan, the facts of Robert settle, lost in cracks of conversations, spread too thin in the stretch between the states. Is it that she's choosing to consider only certain aspects of his choices to appease her own guilt, to form the toeholds that lift her past the next line she shouldn't cross? Or is it simply that being this happy has cast a light with which he can't compete?

She watches Aidan now, the shadowed dips below his cheekbones, the strong line of his jaw, and wants, more than anything, to taste the wine on his lips. Does Robert feel this? The sway of something amiss, a flicker of intuition as if she's just pulled back and the air between them has gone still.

20

Then

AT LAST they get their picnic. Four cottonwood trees are clustered near a bend in the river, right next to a rock that juts into the water, a perfect perch from which to cast their lines—though the fishing poles stay put, leaned against the tallest of the trees. A plaid blanket is spread upon a small grassy rise beneath the wide boughs, and in the basket are sandwiches and strawberries, biscuits from the diner they bought on their way out of town.

For a while they just lie upon the plaid, Eva curled into him, her arm across his chest, their food untouched. He stares up into a canopy that's constant movement, braced by clouds in a slow swirl. Leaves chime and a bird's call whittles through the air.

Soon the graceful rush of the river becomes a sound he mixes with the feel of her heart.

❧

After they've eaten, William leans against the tree as Eva sits in its lowest crook, one bare foot dangling by his shoulder. The leaves above her turn, angled and doused with the tint of fading sun. She'd not eaten the crusts of her sandwich, had in fact smiled, eyes upon him, as she ate right up to their edges—the most wonderful way he'd ever seen a woman eat, he informed her—and now and then he tosses a chunk of the leftover bread into the water. *You could be the worst fisherman ever,* she'd told him as the first bit was pulled under.

"Don't you think," he says after she's told him about Dr. Adams, "that if he had anything to report, I'd have heard by now? He didn't see you leave the house. Fact is, I wasn't home. Which is perfect, really. Maybe you needed a last-minute signature, and left when no one answered."

"But why was he there?" With her toes, she lightly touches the back of his neck, working her way up, then nudging him behind his ear till he grabs her foot.

"I have neighbors. I'm sure he has friends," he says, turning and kissing her toes. "He's nosy but not malicious."

She won't tell him about calling his house, about speaking to his wife. Reckless, she thinks. There was no excuse for that risk. And that Claire had not said anything to him the entire week proves that Eva *had* been mistaken with her fear. Claire had meant something else, so why bring it up to William? Paranoid, she thinks. This situation, my guilt, has made me paranoid. When will that ease? In her mind the years unroll with no change, the constant bus rides, glances over shoulders, a house where she can't leave a trace of herself behind.

But later that night—after such an absence—their routine is welcomed. Monopoly, the shadow of his drink spilled across Free Parking.

"Only second prize in a beauty contest?" she jokes as she places the Community Chest card at the bottom of the stack. The whole night the cards have been in his favor, the dice seemingly weighted toward his luck.

"Clearly I wasn't a judge," he says, and pulls on the metal lever in the ice cube tray. The cubes crack, then snap as they hit her drink. "I just started the water. Shall we?"

The bath, their Friday night of candles and bubbles and Sinatra. The second ice cube tray on a stool beside them, ready to save their drinks from the heat of the water.

Sunk deep into the bubbles, she watches him adjust the needle on the record. "William," she says, "I want to hold your hand on the street."

He turns to her, surprised.

She continues. "I don't want to live like this. The guilt, the fear. All I could think of was Dr. Adams seeing me. That I'd done something wrong."

He nods, then slowly gets in the water. The bubbles shift and shine.

"I feel the same," he says. "The guilt has taken its toll. I've been waiting to bring this up."

Her heart starts racing. As he leans back against the white tiles, her mind conjures his words: You're right, we should stop this. And despite the silence in the room or the fact that his lips are sealed, she hears those words so clearly that she drops her head and shuts her eyes.

"Listen," he says, "I don't know how this is going to go over."

He pauses, and Eva looks up, determined to make him say it to her, to look her in the eye as he speaks.

"But I think I'm going to leave Claire."

Her back slams into the metal faucet behind her.

"Eva." He laughs.

With one hand she reaches behind her to feel her skin, to make sure there's no blood. All she feels is the thinness of water and the dampened ends of her hair.

"I don't want to get your hopes up that this will be quick. I imagine it won't be. But I'm not being fair to her or to you. No one's getting what they deserve, and Claire"—he pauses briefly, as if the sound of his wife's name spoken before Eva, naked, her legs mashed against his hips, comes with an echo—"is being hurt. I'd thought it wasn't affecting her, but it is."

She doesn't break his gaze. More than anything she wants to hear him say the words. "And?" she says, daring, suddenly bold and wanting. "Why else do you want to be with me? Because . . ."

He doesn't look away. "Yes," he says. "More than anything."

Still she watches him, though one corner of her mouth betrays her, angling toward a smile.

"Those words, Eva. I will to say them to you. Because I do, I feel it every time I even think of you. But how can I say them and leave the next day?" He smiles. "So not yet. Not until I can hold your hand on the street."

☙

Claire has a plan. It's wicked, she knows, born from Edith's mind, the kind of plan other people have, not Claire. The way he'd looked at her. Just thinking of it makes her feel shamed. That unguarded, truthful, serrated moment.

She knows she's about to lose him.

On the dining room table are the usual china, crystal, silver, but also the Lorelei vase William gave to her when courting, usually kept on a table against the wall. Lilac-blue pottery, its entirety is the shape of a woman, her shoulder and arm resting atop the mouth of the vase. A feeling of sullen enclosure, of mystery, mixed with a touch of seduction. Lorelei, Claire has decided, was a woman underestimated.

It's Saturday and Claire's not wearing the blue dress. She's wearing a beige one, a dress that buttons up the front and was tight even when she was thinner. Now the buttons strain around her midsection, taut folds in the fabric like stripes across her waist. It's impossible not to notice.

For lunch they're having chicken and mashed potatoes and carrots. A huge meal, really, far too much for the middle of the day, but Claire requested the menu and is now actually craving it, hoping Ketty remembered to make gravy. She sits in her chair, hands folded on her stomach, her neck at a slightly awkward angle against the stiff wood back of the chair. All the yellow tulips she'd put in the vase this morning dip and lunge to the sides, not yet made sturdy by the intake of water.

A half an hour past when he usually arrives, Claire hears the front door open. "There you are," she says when he enters the room. "I was getting worried."

"I'm sorry. Sorry, sorry," he says, pulling out his chair. "There was a wreck."

She studies him, waiting for more, for details that might add truth to his statement. But he says nothing else, just glances behind her as the door swings open and Ketty enters with their dishes, steam swirling from the food. His eyes widen as Ketty places his lunch before him. "Thanksgiving already?"

She produces a laugh. "That's chicken, not turkey."

The fork's already in his hand. "Shall we?"

"Go ahead." She daintily cuts her chicken, thankful Ketty remembered the gravy, and carefully concocts the perfect bite: a small wedge of chicken atop a thin slice of carrot, all with just a dash of gravy. This is how she eats when she's with William—slowly, daintily, chewing her food contemplatively. She lifts her fork to her mouth and watches William eat like a man starved—or a man determined to not make conversation.

"So," she says after a while, her knife on the knife rest, "I've got some big news."

"What's that?"

He's still staring at his food, cutting another chunk of chicken. He doesn't see her. He never sees her. And if he did now, he'd see her take a big breath and visibly force a smile onto her face. But he doesn't. Claire holds the smile, her cheeks puffed and her eyes bright. This is the face of me joyous, she thinks.

"You're going to be a father."

Now William looks up at her, and as he does his arms lower to his sides, weighted with shock. He still holds the fork and knife and Claire knows bits of gravy are dripping onto the rug. She keeps her smile steady.

"A baby, we're having a baby."

She laughs, and for a second it feels real. The words, perhaps those particular words unlock some urge and instinct in all women, filling the body with euphoria, breathless delight. There are actual tears in her eyes. She'd not expected this, for it to feel so real, or for her to be happy about such a feeling. In a way, she wishes it were true. Maybe they should have a baby. Maybe she would learn to love it.

Though of course it's not real, and for that she is suddenly thankful, as William's face is still carved in shock, has not transitioned to happiness or anything else, for that matter.

"William?"

His mouth opens. He remembers the fork and knife and raises his arms, setting the silverware on his plate. His eyes go to the vase, the drooping tulips, and as he stands, the table shakes.

21

Now

THE OAK TREE HUMS, a low note of dread. One by one she sees them, bees emerging from a crack in the bark and settling on the plate before her like a thick, vibrating blanket. Suddenly the chair across from her moves, as if pulled from the table, but before she can see who's there, she's coughing, something caught in her throat, stabbing her tongue. Her mouth opens and a bee flies out.

At once, everything revolts. Gagging. Mouth swelling. More and more bees rise in her throat, clogging her mouth, trapped, buzzing louder and louder like screams she can't get out.

And then mercy. She's awake, ragged breath.

The room is black, it hurts to swallow. While asleep, she realizes, she'd been clutching at her throat, fingers deep into her own skin. Again the feeling that a thin layer has been pierced, that what her mind conjured should never have taken on a physicality. Lines are blurred, a barrier broken. But not only that. For the first time someone was there, the chair pulled out. She doesn't want to think it, but at three AM her mind knows only the wrappings of dark thoughts: Could she have ended up exactly where she's meant to be, the long-standing date about to appear?

From her bed she listens, the night quiet, but then she hears it, the sound of a car running, steady. She has to look. A peek through the window. Keeping her own lights off, she counts to three and then barely moves aside her drapes, just enough to see.

Headlights. Right there. Her eyes focus—it's a police car, parked by Brittany's driveway. Protection. And even though ten minutes later it's gone, still she feels it, an assurance, a presence. Sent by Aidan, she knows, and just the fact that he would do this, that he's thought of her enough to put in such a request is like resting beneath a watchful gaze, able to relax within the shelter of concern. Someone is looking out for her. Knowing this, feeling this, allows sleep to claim her once again, but this time her thoughts are of him, and even briefly she is unafraid.

One last box. The final possibility within her reach. In it she finds her mother's and uncle's childhood bits and pieces, report cards, drawings. Nothing helpful. Nothing that explains. Closing the lid, she feels anxiety pull within her. That was it. All she can do from here. Next would have to be a trip to Morrow Lake, if she can, to visit Eleanor Hadley, and then to Lake of the Isles, where her grandmother and Claire lived. Just the thought of visiting the Ballantine house unnerves her, a pin within her loosened, a creaking vibrato in her bones.

For a break she goes on a walk, hoping for some perspective. The dreams started long, long ago—they have nothing to do with the current situation in the town. She knows this now that the sun is out, now that the night hours don't hold her captive in a dark palm. But it's not just that. She's torn. Not only between wanting Aidan or wanting Robert, but between believing what she's feeling is right or wrong. Logically she understands she's in murky territory just by spending time with Aidan, just from her thoughts, but nothing about wanting him feels wrong. *Wrong* is a conceit that fits entirely differently.

Suddenly a bee shoots from a stalk of white flowers and the dream slams into the day. Without looking she backs into the street, and it's only when she feels her hand on the trunk of a parked car that she catches herself. *This is not the dream.* She stares up at the sun, the white burn of reminder. It has to stop. Somehow this has to stop.

There's a meadow a few blocks from her house. An open space that was never developed, a spot where kids collect wildflowers and lady-bugs, play games of tag after school. No one's there, and she takes a seat on a rock, still unnerved by the dream's insertion into her day. After a few minutes the quiet breaks with ringing—Robert. The list of all she wants to say is just as long as all she wishes to omit, and so far it's been easier to not pick up the phone. Yesterday, she realizes, was the first day they'd not heard each other's voices. An entire day, only text messages. She wonders if he noticed. The phone is still ringing. An entire day, that's never happened before. She hits Answer. "Getting ready for your meeting?"

"In the car now. Abby, the noise yesterday. Do you feel safe?"

"It's not—I swear, I'm just dramatic. The guy would be stupid to do anything now. There are cops everywhere."

The moment she says it, she hears her mistake.

He takes a moment. "Maybe you should come back."

"Early?"

"If it's not good for you to be there . . ."

He lets his words drift, and even though she knows he's talking about her report of the sound, her mind instead pictures Aidan.

"Robert, I was grabbing at my own throat last night. Everything I have here I've looked at, and nothing's stopped. But there are places to visit, something that might make a difference, and I can't do that from L.A."

"With him. You're doing all this with him."

There's nothing good to say. She pulls in justifications, holding them against her, a flimsy cover. "He's a cop—it might be the only way."

"Abby. It's not fair to do this to me when I'm not—" He stops.

"When you're not what?"

"When I'm not there to fight for you."

Everything in her sinks, a great collapse. "Robert, he's a friend." But even she doesn't believe her words.

"Abby."

"And you could've been here. I asked you to come. I needed you."

"Just like you need a house. What do you think I'm doing here?"

At this she finds her anger. "I don't need a house. Would one be nice? Yes, but is that a reason to stand still for the rest of our lives? No. It's you, you're the one who needs to have the impossible happen before you commit in any real way."

Silence as Abby realizes what she said. Through the phone, the ticking of his turn signal.

"The impossible?" he finally asks.

"I'm sorry. That's not what I meant."

"For you to say this, right before my meeting."

And though she apologizes again before hanging up, a thought snakes behind her words: What upset him wasn't that she felt their relationship was going nowhere, but that her saying so might impact his meeting.

For a while she sits with her eyes closed, the bright blaze of orange against her lids. When her phone rings she assumes it's him, calling to make things right. She looks down at the phone's display, the reflection of clouds behind Aidan's name.

"Hi," she says. A dragonfly lifts from the grass, turquoise on its tail. "You okay?"

"Better now."

"Good," Aidan says. "Little update. The owners of your grandparents' house are in Oregon—but we still have the Ballantine house to visit. I spoke to the owner, she's game, just gotta figure out a time."

"That's amazing."

"Here's the best part: I just got cleared for twenty-four hours."

"Off work? A whole day?"

"Starting today at two, then back tomorrow at two. Twenty-four amazing off-duty hours. It was supposed to be Harris, but he's got too many things lined up tomorrow, so it fell to me. Gotta get us recharged, no one's fresh."

"I bet. Just one day?"

"Ideally it would be two, but they can't swing them together, not yet. So off twenty-four, on a shift, off twenty-four. What I'm saying is we could fit in Morrow Lake. Leave today, back first in thing in the morning. Visit Eleanor tonight if we make good time, or first thing in the morning."

Abby's silent for a bit. "How far is it?"

"Almost five hours. I got us two hotel rooms in town. Fully cancelable if you don't want to go."

"You spoke to her?"

"No, but I got through to an owner of a house nearby. Guy said she's a hermit and never answers her phone. Worst-case scenario, we talk to neighbors, see if she's ever told stories. And I got the report on Claire. Not much we don't know, but I can show you." He pauses. "Honestly, the drive sounds good. Change of scenery. I could use a break."

Yes, she thinks. She should leave Minnesota. Everything here is dangerous. But then she stands up and asks what time to be ready.

༄

To think of something other than the trip with Abby, Aidan once more looks up the rapes in Marshall and vicinity, starting five years prior to the first linked case. Serial killers and rapists tend to start with one that's personal, one that gives an intense psychological arousal, as the victim is usually someone they know. However, that first foray is often different in countless ways, so Aidan isn't quite sure what he's looking for. Still, he's looking for something, anything to stand out. Schultz thinks the first was the store manager in Marshall, but instinct tells Aidan there was something before.

His phone rings—Brittany.

"You called my mom's house."

Shit. "Force of habit, I guess. The number just came back to me."

"Well, the message busted my sister, and yes, she is smoking again."

A deep breath. "Good. Okay. The same brand you found?"

"She smokes whatever her friends have because she's broke. And I don't know that any of that's *good*. This is seriously why you called? What's going on?"

"Just checking everything. She smokes on the side of the house?"

"That's her spot, so it doesn't get in the house. My mom would kill her."

Hanging up is a relief, both to be off the phone and for the easing of his mind. Though the worry is not completely gone, the explanation has rendered it faint, removed it from the spotlight.

Back to the older rape cases. They've pored through these before, but now, for some reason, one stands out. There's something about her face. He looks at the date—two years prior to the first serial rape in Marshall. He calls Haakstad, staring at the photo—nineteen years old, disordered brown hair, a short forehead, and arched eyebrows far too thin. Even in the photo, taken before the rape and provided by the family, she looks reluctantly wise, someone forced to make decisions and pay bills from a young age. "Tell me about Becky Cox."

"Who? No hello?"

"Sorry, cramming before I duck out for twenty-four."

"Good. You need it. You ask Hardt about her?"

"Hardt doesn't have a desk. Man works out of his hotel room— easier to call you. And nicer."

"Gimme a sec."

Rather than put the call on hold—a modern feature Haakstad has shunned—he sets the receiver on his desk, and Aidan listens to the sound of the Marshall station. Someone yells that the water tastes like dirt.

"This was long ago," Haakstad says as he picks up. "Got DNA, been running cold hits for years. No matches. You're liking her for the first?"

"I don't know. Just looking."

"Complete file's in storage—I'll get it pulled. I see her picture. She's cute. But man, who gave this girl tweezers? No one wants that. Or, well, I guess someone did." He laughs, then stops himself. "I shouldn't have said that. Now I feel bad."

Even after hanging up Aidan looks into her eyes. Blue eyes, almost aquamarine, he wonders if they're contacts.

Schultz is standing in the doorway. "Alan Breining's cleared. Motel footage. Definitely him there, definitely didn't leave."

"We need to revisit our lists," Aidan says. "Widen our vicinity."

Schultz nods, flipping the bottom of his tie over, pulling at a small thread. "Got police presence on our side now. But it's been too long. He's gonna get comfortable again."

"He's waiting. Some moment when we're not looking."

A knock on the doorframe, Schultz disappears back into his office.

"That's it," says an officer. "Finally. You didn't notice this smell?"

Aidan turns to him; in the man's hand is the vase of roses Ashley sent, when it all began. Leaves shatter with movement and the necks of the flowers are all broken, petals so faded they look burned.

22

Then

EVA RETURNS TO LUVEN as a visitor, her life here already long ago. Everything is different, brushed with nostalgia, seen with the careless freedom of a passerby. The town seems harmless, quaint almost. No longer is there threat in the patchwork fields that reach steadily and mercilessly to the horizon, or frustration in the undulations of the land, those shallow, desperate breaths. No longer is there danger in the thick stands of trees that hide houses and barns and old trucks with no tires, everything rusted. Rather, everything is touched with beautiful simplicity. Even the boring clusters of mailboxes at the base of roads shine like rows of silver teeth in smiling, laughing mouths.

Main Street, the graveyard, all the small houses filled with people Eva has known forever—it's all oddly pleasant in a way that only emotional detachment can provide. The world viewed in remembrance, train tracks gleaming with long-ago crushed pennies. Hudson's Pond, a world of white as she tests the ice with her friends, back in the days when she was young enough not to be excluded, when a reputation hadn't been crafted for her regardless of truth, and when fun was fun and it didn't matter with whom you had it. Flying across the frozen, bumpy ice. Cheeks red. On the count of three: *one, two, three.* Falling, sliding toward branches frozen at the edges. Another flip and the snow is gone. The pond now for Saturdays spent floating on their backs, staring at cloudless blue skies while their ears hummed with the sounds of the water and the earth and maybe even the whole universe.

Yes, everything is different now.

And she'll be the talk of the town, that's for sure. No longer will people be blabbering on about the new cribbed wooden grain elevator— *new*, despite the fact that it's been around for over a year. They'll be chattering about her, they'll fall silent when she passes, and at last she won't mind. The dresses she wears won't be questioned, no longer just Eva Marten putting on airs. They'll regret having said things they shouldn't have in the past. Maybe they'll be resentful, she thinks, maybe they still won't like her. But that's okay. People in Luven hating her even more will mean she's done all right.

She goes to her father and lies beside him in the grass. Everything's worked out, she tells him. They love each other, and that love has won. She'll be leaving. That's the only thing that upsets her, that her father stays here, anchored to the earth. No longer will she be able to drop by when she misses who she figures he would have been. No longer will all she's ever known of him be just down the street, always there, always listening.

After a while, when the temperature of the day begins to dip, she stands. It's time to go home, to tell her mother and her sister. Walking through the gates, she looks back once more, and realizes that when she's in the ground she'll be with William, in the Lakewood Cemetery with his parents. She'd never thought of that before, that she'd not get her chance to finally be nestled in beside her father and sister and mother, the family at last complete. And in a hundred years, people passing by this graveyard won't know. To them, it would be as if Eva just simply never existed.

"Well, I knew you were lying," Margaret says when Eva delightedly spills the news at supper.

"Yes, I was." Eva smiles.

Nothing will upset her. Never has she felt this happy, this justified and impenetrable. Let her mother try to ruin this, just let her try, because it won't work. The lines in Margaret's face all seem to droop downward as the conversation continues, and only Anna asks questions—when do we meet him, how tall is he, he's in construction?—as she herself is in love, and thus tolerant of its existence.

Only on Tuesday does she feel a slight yank of panic, a nauseating portent, a stabbing worry that thrusts her straight from sleep to consciousness. Her eyes open, vision clear, the sloped ceiling above her stable despite a feeling of pressure, of something terribly, terribly wrong. She lies there for a good ten minutes, waiting for her heart to settle, and it's from this position—in bed, still and struggling to be calm—that she hears his car pull up. She knows the sound. She's spent months learning to recognize it, waiting for it. Maybe, she thinks, maybe she'd even heard his car from a great distance, passing the Parkses' farm, then the Bulckes', then turning onto Main Street. He's here. William is here, in Luven, at her house.

It's nine AM. She has the late shift today. There are boxes by her door, packed with clothes and toiletries. She hears his car shut off. He must have left Minneapolis around six to be here now. The car door shuts. Four creaks on the front steps. Two raps on the door.

She's sitting up in bed when he knocks on her bedroom door, and that her mother must've let him in upsets her because Margaret would've known first. Eva calls to him to come in and hears him start up the attic stairs; then she sees the top of his head, then his face, then the whole of him, dressed in a suit, looking more handsome than she ever thought possible, the painful attraction of a last glimpse. He doesn't smile. Understanding is thick.

They say nothing. For a few moments he looks around the room and she feels shame—the ragged and stained hooked throw rug at the base of her bed, dingy walls, cracks spreading from the window like crow's-feet from the eyes of someone who's seen too much. Everything is cluttered and small and unnecessary—and yet she also feels pleasure. Let him see her life. Let him get a good look at where he's leaving her.

Then his eyes settle on her sewing machine, not yet packed, and the three batches of fabric she planned to use, feed sack fabric with blue and red and white flowers against a storm of blue dots. The labels, Johnson Flour, have not yet been removed. The fabric is bags, and he must be realizing that now. In their original form, not turned into a dress she'd wear to dinner, one he'd admire and compliment and ask about. This exposure grabs at something deep within her, a sharp yank, as with it comes a revisit of the past. How many of her dresses, he must wonder, once held flour or grain? How many times had she crossed her legs demurely, the fabric that draped gracefully actually from a bag of chicken feed? The beauty he'd seen, everything is undone, come loose by this one moment. She'd always been a farm girl. He was seeing that now. When at last he turns, she can't meet his eyes.

He moves to her bed, crouching beneath the gradual slope of the attic, and takes a seat on the corner. She stares at the space between them.

"Why," she finally says.

His hands are folded in his lap. "She's expecting."

His words are like a slap, her cheeks left red. "You were having sex with her."

"Eva," he says, surprised and uncomfortable, "she's my wife."

"But you love me."

He meets her gaze. "Yes."

"So that's it?"

"I can't leave her. Not when she's going to have a baby."

She nods. The whole of her is numb.

"Eva, the way things were, you couldn't live like that. It would be worse now. You'd have less of me. I'd have less of you. That's not right, not for you. Not for anyone."

She says nothing, because in her mind she's already wondering if this is the last time she'd ever hear him say her name.

He waits for a moment and then continues. "I won't be in Rochester anymore. I didn't want to say anything until it was settled, but I'm selling the company. Everything's arranged. The last two days have been—well, there are a lot of details I had to figure out. None of it is what I want. But there's no reason for her to raise a baby alone. Not when financially it's not necessary. The choices in my life—" He pauses. "It's not fair, what I've done to people. To you. To her. I need to be a better person. I need to be a good father."

No more Rochester. No more Eva. They love each other—it's ending and they love each other. Somehow she'd always thought that couldn't happen.

When he leaves, he doesn't kiss her. He stands at the top of her attic stairs and touches her cheek. "It's so we don't remember this as the last time," he says when she looks up at him expectantly.

She laughs, suddenly feeling everything inside her compress. "But I don't remember the last time."

And so he raises her hand instead, and presses it to his lips.

When at last he's gone, she opens the drawer to her nightstand, and quickly, before she can read the words, scoops up his notes and places them inside the decoupage box by her dresser, the repository of things that hurt.

At work Eva can barely move. Everyday objects no longer make sense. For a full minute she stares at a grease jar, trying to understand why she is where she is. "Roger Bulcke needs salt," Gerry says, nudging her from behind. "And his food's up."

Still she stares at the grease jar, and when at last she goes to Roger, she gives him the pepper instead, and has forgotten the food. As she promises him his food she turns and sees Eddie Parks.

"Same place, same time," he says with a smile.

It's too much. With her hand she signals him to wait, and then heads to the cook's counter and places Roger's food on her tray. She tries to breathe. William has left her. Eddie is here. Never before has she felt so strongly that she's at a crossroads, that this, this very moment is when she must pick a path. She grabs her tray and quickly slides the plates before Roger, who's got his fork in his hand, ready.

"You don't look happy," Eddie says, when at last she returns to him. "You look like you could use some cheering up."

"I might."

"What time are you free?"

She glances at the clock on the wall. "Not for a while."

"I can wait."

He'd ordered oatmeal and now drizzles maple syrup on top, just like William. "It'll be a long while."

He says nothing at first, as if hoping a few more seconds might sway her. Then finally, "Maybe next week then."

Eva nods and feels the weight of sadness, as if she indeed chose another path and already the sight of him is growing faint.

Days later, anger begins to spread its rays. Tentative at first, then stronger, shoving away sadness and casting her in an unsettling glow. Anger inspires action, and action is what will fix the situation. She's invigorated. There is no reason this needs to end. They can still be together, they can find a way. She never should've told him she couldn't live like that. She can move to Minneapolis. An apartment maybe, on a quiet block where he could come and go.

"You're looking better," Margaret says that Thursday, sitting at the breakfast table with a cup of coffee and a magazine.

Eva opens the refrigerator, finds the milk, and untwists the cap. She leans in to smell it, though she knows it's always fresh. "I have to go to him."

There's a silence, followed by the sound of her mother sitting back in her chair, a judgmental creak of wood.

"What he's got is a family now," Margaret says. "That's something you don't mess with. Fun and games is one thing, but it's a crime to take away a father."

Eva says nothing, just pours a tall glass of milk and drinks it quickly. It's cold, but feels as though it's burning her throat. "So that's the rule, is it?" She puts the milk back and picks up her glass, about to place it in the sink. "Because I seem to remember Uncle Lucas having a family, too. A baby as well."

Now there's the sound of the chair scraping against the linoleum, followed by the rough grab of Margaret's hand pulling Eva's chin toward her.

"Don't you *ever* think you have the right to tell me about my life." She drops her hand and steps back.

"What I don't understand is how you could do what you've been doing if you really loved my father." Eva watches her mother. "Or me."

There's a twitch in Margaret's right eye, as if her anger is coursing in clumps. "You're on thin ice when you tell another person how to love."

Eva can't stop. "Am I? I'm wondering, because maybe I need to learn. You've been playing mourner for twenty-two years, and best I can tell, almost ten of them were also spent with him."

Her mother's voice is steady as she picks up her purse. "Like I said."

"You've never visited my father's grave—that in itself I don't understand. His death is just another excuse for you to be angry, the only way you get sympathy from anyone, and you knew that and *you used that*. Sure is easy to say you loved someone once they're gone. But I don't think you did. Not the way you claim. Or you couldn't do what you've been doing."

The glass is still in her hand. Flimsy glass. Breakable. Just squeeze a little. She takes a deep breath and places it in the sink, and the glass just sits there, all by itself. Suddenly her ears hum with a surge of everything and she realizes she's going to cry—about William, her father, so many early endings.

But when she turns, she sees that it's her mother's eyes that have filled. Margaret's standing at the back door, her fingertips resting on the doorknob as if just feeling to make sure it's there.

"If you really must know," Margaret says quietly, "I'll tell you."

Eva doesn't move. She'd not expected anything.

Margaret hitches her purse up a bit on her shoulder and looks her daughter in the eye. "It's so he leaves you alone."

Eva says nothing. Just watches as her mother opens the door and steps into the searing light of a beautiful morning.

23

Now

GLACIAL LAKE COUNTRY. Past Lake Itasca, where the mighty Mississippi starts, headwaters as unflourishing and disappointing as an exposed magician's sleeve. A cooler of snacks is by Abby's feet and her carry-on bag is in the back of Aidan's Grand Cherokee with his duffel bag, a thrill even in the proximity of their belongings. There's a current she's feeling, the white heat of uncertainty. Both of them heading in the same direction, away from everything they know, only inches apart as the scenery changes, red and white pine, balsam fir and black spruce. The irony, she thinks, is that where they're going is safer than Makade, and yet more dangerous in so many ways.

In her hand she holds a copy of the report on Claire from the night she disappeared, a physical reminder of purpose, and now and then she glances at it: two shots heard by the neighbor, one bullet found, valuables missing. But what Abby keeps seeing is the "neighbor's" statement. Her grandmother. The officer remarked she was "tearful and distraught," and that she broke down as she described what looked like a man in the driveway dragging something. It was too dark to tell much, and the neighbor became "terrified and hid in the kitchen." Her best friend, taken.

"I never gave her credit," Abby says. "I remember my mom telling me once that when she was little she had strep throat, and my grandmother cried like she was dying. For days. We always thought she was just dramatic, wanting attention. Bit of a train wreck. But I never bothered to wonder why. I don't even think my mom knew, that she witnessed it."

"I'm sure. Why scare the kids? The officer noted her husband and children were out of town."

"She was alone, seeing that. I can't imagine."

The road dips into a town, a white church on cinder blocks, a man on its steps, leaned back and staring at the sky. When her phone rings she silences it without looking, but he tells her she should answer. "We'll be in the car for a while, go ahead."

Hannah. Abby slides it to answer and says her friend's name aloud, just so Aidan knows.

"Abby," Hannah says in return. "What are you doing?"

"I'm with my friend Aidan. We're heading up north to Morrow Lake. The house I didn't get. Eleanor Hadley."

There's a momentary silence and Abby can almost see Hannah calculating time differences and intentions. She rests her head on the glass of the window, watching clumps of prairie grass streak by. One tree by the road is bare of all its leaves, white arms that appear chilled in the late afternoon. As they pass it, she turns to watch it go.

"Right," Hannah at last says. "I know that involves spending the night. But I also know he's right next to you. So this will be a conversation for tomorrow. A long conversation. For now, I'm pregnant."

"*What?*"

"Pregnant. As in with child. As in about to become beastly."

"Holy crap. Do you know if it's a girl or a boy?" Beside her, she sees

Aidan smile. Robert, she thinks. She should be having this moment—learning that her best friend is pregnant—with Robert. Robert, who knows Hannah, who would feel the magnitude of the moment. For the first time she feels as though she's split from her life, is traveling along a rupture that snakes into a new direction. Tonight, she thinks, she'll call and tell him the news.

"Right now it's a bit tadpole-ish—so no. And I don't want to know. Which means Ben doesn't get to know. So you'll have to start thinking of names. For both."

"I'm going to be an aunt."

"You're going to be free babysitting, so brace yourself. And I'm emailing you the ultrasound photo. It's a thing pregnant women do."

"You have a sister?" Aidan asks when she hangs up.

As Abby checks her mail, she explains who Hannah is, how she keeps moving forward, marriage, house, and now baby, while Abby stands still. "Here it is." She waits for it to load and then shows him her phone, a fuzzy black-and-white picture with numbers on the side. "I see nothing."

Aidan pulls to the side of the road and puts the car in park. For a moment Abby thinks he's stopped to look at the picture. "Look up," he says. "Just look up."

Above them is a sunset that seems to rage, ripping through clouds, blazing so bright at the horizon it seems impossible the world still exists. Below, tips of trees are black, lost to the show, content to let the sky steal the glory. Then Abby sees, up ahead, a little green sign with white letters: MORROW LAKE.

"It's there," she says.

"I know. You ready? Or you want to do this in the morning?"

The turnoff is a dirt road, the forest thick on either side. If they get lost it will only be a matter of time till the woods lose to blackness, the road bursting only in increments from their headlights. But that sunset. "I want to see the water in this light," she says, and so Aidan puts the car in drive, and they pull onto the dirt road.

Water glows from between trees, little slices of brilliance. The houses are actually cabins, small and simple, each one painted a different masculine and bold color, combining to conjure a dark Scottish plaid or a Ralph Lauren paint collection: hunter green, navy blue, rich brick red. Some cabins are more neglected than others, though right away Abby can tell that most are lived in; thriving plants in pots by a door, a towel over a wooden railing, the recent trail of a canoe in the dirt, the canoe itself leaning against a birch tree.

When they find Eleanor's place, they park along the narrow drive, careful not to shine their headlights through her window. First they want to see the lake, and so they cut through the woods, steps shattering sticks and crushing leaves. The air is thick and humid, and when Abby pauses to look up, she sees red pines that seem to stretch forever, aged arms lifted to a darkening sky.

And then there it is, the water burnished gold and red, fading to the darkest purple at the edge, unbroken but for scatterings of shadowed black reeds. The only sound is the rhythmic kiss of waves against the shore. She wants to say something, a comment on the beauty of the lake, but knows her voice would splinter the moment, something Aidan must feel too as he quietly places his hand on the small of her back.

℘

The lights are on in the house, and Aidan has already seen a silhouette in one room, moving to the next. A television's blaring, a comedy, canned laughter through open windows. He looks to Abby before knocking, and then they wait.

The woman who answers the door is in her midforties with wide-set blue eyes. She's still laughing at something and doesn't bother to tuck away her smile when she sees them—a woman clearly unaccustomed to danger. "Car died?" she asks, her voice higher than Aidan had expected. "Heard you pull up a while ago."

"We're looking for Eleanor Hadley," he says, and too late hears, as she must, that the request sounded like a cop. Her smile is gone.

"Why?"

Abby steps in. "I'm Abby Walters. My grandmother used to own this cabin, way back when, and sold it to Eleanor. We just wanted to ask her about my grandmother, and a friend of theirs, Claire Ballantine?"

The woman nods, immediately softened. "Sure. I know Eleanor."

"Is she here?"

"No, honey, we rent from her. She's in a home."

"Do you know where?" Aidan asks.

"A few hours from here. We send her her mail when it comes in. She's not been the best about updating forms and such."

A few hours. The trip will end without finding her, without answers. Abby's disappointment is a marked shift in energy, he can feel it next to him, an absence that makes him aware of the power of her happiness. The woman must sense this as well, as she glances over her shoulder, then swings wide the door. "Come in. I'll get the address. So your car's fine, then?"

ℰℓ

Back on the road, the woods are pitch-black on either side and they've been driving for a while before Abby realizes she's not afraid. This darkness—a world of shadows and dirt roads and blind curves, some trees dead and skeletal in the night—is normally a prescription for fear, and yet all she's been thinking about is the woman who answered the door. "That never would've happened in L.A.," she says. "No one would answer the door like that."

"Maybe she saw us outside. Knew we were okay."

"Or maybe her husband was hiding in the other room with a shotgun."

"I'm sorry Eleanor wasn't there."

She nods as they pass an area cleared of trees, teeming with ferns like black spines. "I took it for granted she would be."

"We can try again. She's actually closer to Minneapolis."

"All this way, and on your day off."

"Where I'm from, you drive just to drive. This has been nice."

Aidan's phone rings through the speakers, the name *Harris* on the car's readout. Almost hesitantly, he hits Answer.

"Nothing bad, don't worry. This speakerphone?"

"Yes, it is," Aidan says.

"Right, I won't say anything embarrassing. Well, I will if I can think of something. Give me a sec."

In a beat Abby understands this means Harris knows they're together, which means Aidan's spoken of her. As a friend? As more?

Harris, apparently unable to think of anything embarrassing, continues. "Just wanted to let you know the second victim in Marshall, she remembered smoke. So smoking is something to look at—former smokers, too, because he could've quit. Lila McCale here doesn't recall smoke, but she's a smoker herself. Wouldn't have noticed. I got through to a couple neighbors who didn't find any butts, but there are a couple with good vantage points I didn't reach."

Neighbors. Cigarette butts. Now Abby turns to Aidan, who stares straight ahead.

"Good," Aidan says. "All quiet then?"

"Quiet. Sure. Tomorrow's my day off, that's all I keep telling myself. Bye, Abby."

Aidan hits End. Then looks to her. "I didn't want to worry you. That's why I didn't say anything—I was just checking. You heard him, though, nothing's been found in neighboring properties. And I asked, Brittany's sister is smoking again. I'm sure that was it. This is just me being paranoid because it's you."

A smile, no hiding it. The comment pushes back her nerves.

After a while, a figure looms from the dark, a Paul Bunyan statue. Hugely tall, wide straight shoulders. Lights illuminate him, tilting his shadow toward the trees, making it appear as if he's just emerged from the thicket. "I don't get the fascination," Abby says. "And I've never understood why his ox is blue."

"You've been away from Minnesota too long. We're getting close. I think Paul's the welcoming committee."

And sure enough, less than a mile away is the motel, small and basic; two stories, a long balcony that spans the width, green doors with black numbers, and a pool with dark clusters of what she hopes are leaves. A small diner is attached to the far end, with shiny orange booths and a waitress who leans back against the counter, eyes on a TV in the corner of the room.

The woman who checks them in assigns them rooms next to each other and tells them about pay-per-view and the breakfast in the lobby. But now all Abby can think of are the dreams, surely to be invigorated by the setting. "Can I get some coffee? Like five servings' worth?" She glances at Aidan. "Sleep will not be my friend tonight."

   Casually the woman's eyes graze their ring fingers. One corner of her mouth lifts, as if she's seen everything and already knows how the night will go. "Eight, nine," she says as she hands over the room keys, her voice lifting at the end, as if what she's said is just the beginning.

24

Then

ONLY ONCE has Eva been to Minneapolis, when she was ten years old. Her mother was selling the silverware she kept hidden in the basement, a wedding gift from a cousin who'd done well. *Won't get anything for it in Luven*, Margaret had said, piling them onto the bus with a dark burlap bag filled with a few pillows—as a disguise—and the mahogany chest of silver. *People here use utensils. Not silverware.*

On the bus to Minneapolis Eva tries not to think about her mother, but over and over again sees her walking out the door into the bright morning. *It's so he leaves you alone.* And he has. For almost ten years.

Now she remembers when they'd arrived in the city, all those years ago, Margaret had looked toward the tallest of all the buildings, a tower that pierced the sky, the very top with the name Foshay spelled in soaring, serious letters. "They had a *gala* not too long ago," she said. "When the building was done being built. Celebrities, fireworks. Mr. Foshay went all out. Then six weeks later was the crash and he lost it all, even his tower. He got indicted for mail fraud and received fifteen years in Leavenworth." She'd shaken her head. "Imagine having a building like that with your name on it and not being able to see it."

Eva wonders now how her mother had known this. She never saw her read society columns, has really never seen her read anything except a few books now and then. And why did it take her that long to sell the silverware? They'd needed the money from the day her father died, and before even that, Eva would venture to guess. Had she wanted a different life? Eva can't think about that. She can't think about her mother at all, not with her heart already so restless with loss.

The Northland Greyhound Bus Depot is a corner building with not one corner to be found. Rather, it's curved, and the rounded entrance sits diagonal to the intersection with a long awning that spans the length like the brim of a hat. Clusters of people stand alongside the building, eyes on watches or papers or shoes. When Eva steps onto the sidewalk, the sun's lower, the light becoming hesitant. Immediately she's hit with excitement—this is Minneapolis, William's city—but also with a pace-slowing insecurity. This is not her world. Her life is Rochester, a joke in the face of this, and Luven, not even worth the breath it would take to be said by any of these people, not that these people even know it exists. That corner of the state would be blank in their minds, just a space where farmers grow things they never stop to consider. Rice, wheat, corn. Nothing exciting. One of her cousins lost his wheat to Hessian flies, and his daughter found him hanging in the barn. Whole lives are built on ingredients, Eva knows.

Is budget a concern? the woman sitting next to her on the bus had asked when Eva mentioned she had no place to stay. The woman's hands were folded to cover the frayed cuffs of her sleeves, and when she asked the question, she was looking at Eva's train case, scuffed, a corner peeling. Without waiting for an answer, the woman told her about a lady she knew in the lake district who rented rooms by the night. Affordable, she said almost as an afterthought, as if it didn't matter, though clearly they both knew it did.

Now Eva has two addresses, both scrawled quickly on a piece of paper she holds in her hand. One is the place to stay for the night, and other is the address of Mr. William S. Ballantine, found in the bus depot's phone book. She takes a streetcar to Lake Calhoun and finds the little Victorian house first. The owner is gracious, talking freely as she leads Eva through a narrow hall lined with portraits. "Now where's home?" she asks. "Is it far?"

"I'm from Rochester," Eva says, and then keeps going. "Our house— my house with my husband—is similar to this, a little Victorian. It's right by the lake and there's a forest off our back porch. I may need more than one night. I don't know yet."

Maybe the owner sees the hope on Eva's face, despite the absence of a ring on her finger, but her smile is encouraging. "That's quite all right. And I might mention, my scones were written up in the *Tribune*, from a little contest. Be sure to stop in the kitchen before you start your day."

Soon Lake Calhoun is to her left. White triangles of sailboats glide on sunset-filled water. To her right is Lake of the Isles; smaller, more like the lakes she's known, with what look like islands in the middle, crowded with trees. Three people are in a canoe that seems barely above water, their movements methodical, practiced and smooth. Separating the two lakes is a lagoon lined with weeping willows. Such beautiful, romantic trees. If she lived here, she'd picnic beneath them. Every Sunday. With fruit in a basket, everything peeled and sliced and seeded.

What surprises her is how quickly she nears his house. So easy, everything's just come together, as if it were meant to happen.

The only thing that's not so easy is staying on the other side of the street, among trees, when more than anything Eva wants to get up close to these houses, the likes of which she's seen only in magazines or in films. Never would she have guessed this. At the most, even when she realized he came from money, her mind conjured a larger two-story house with a long drive, perhaps manicured hedges and a fountain. But these houses, they've got pillars and marble and gates.

Suddenly there it is, the number from the address she'd written down. She searches for a street sign nearby, double-checking, then triple-checking, actually hoping she's on the wrong block, in front of the wrong place, because this is not a house, it's a *mansion* of stones with a castle-like tower and a sloping, manicured green lawn. The fact that he grew up here, that he was a child running through that door, a kid looking through these grand windows, that now he's a man who calls this his home—all of it loosens the ground on which she stands. What does it mean, that she can't comprehend his life?

She leans into the tree, watching the house, the bark rough under her fingertips. So many rooms that must remain empty. So many places you could be, that are yours and no one else's.

And then she sees it, there in the driveway, just a bit to the left of the house and well beyond the wrought-iron gate: his Cadillac. Gleaming. Soft yellow. It literally hurts her, not only because it's beautiful and she could only dream of riding in such a car, but because she can *see* him in it, the sun on his face, happy. The way he talks about it, his voice lifts. And yet she was never a part of that happiness. Could never be. All she ever had, she sees now, was a small part of him, even if he claimed otherwise. A tiny, neglected corner, one not even missed by his wife.

She turns to face the lake. The water has filled with the last moments of the sun's retreat, darkened purple, deep and satiny. William is inside the house. He's there. Right behind her. Have they already eaten dinner? What did they have?

When she feels a bit stronger, she turns back to the house, and immediately her breath catches in her throat. There, in the lit downstairs window, is his wife. Claire. A beautiful off-the-shoulder beige dress— silk crepe if Eva had to guess—shoulder-length pale blond hair. When she turns, there's a quick flash at her wrist, a glimmer from what must be a diamond bracelet. All groomed edges and elegant demeanor. Sophistication. Even from here, Eva can see that her walk is like a waltz, like a starlet in a movie with gliding movements and a voice that's all sugar and honey. And Claire's not even aware she's being watched. This is who she is. Who Eva will never be.

When she takes a seat at the window, Eva waits for something to happen. But Claire does nothing, just stares at the window as if images danced on its surface, and suddenly it's Eva who feels watched. She tucks herself behind the tree. Could Claire see her? Why is she keeping watch? Eva sneaks another look, in time to see Claire's head turn just slightly, as if someone's entered the room. Another lamp switches on, the brightness greater. Eva presses into the tree—it will be William, she knows it will be. But it's a housekeeper holding a shining silver tea set. She places it on a table by the window and Claire nods a thank-you. That's what rich people do, Eva realizes, they nod. They don't even feel they have to speak.

The woman leaves and Claire again turns to the window. She never touches the tea. Even from here, without seeing its details and design, Eva can tell it's an expensive set, most likely worth more than she makes waiting tables and selling dresses in a whole year. All for a cup of tea that gets ignored.

And then he's there. William. Walking into the bright room. His dark hair and broad shoulders, a suit she thinks she recognizes. The fact of her longing for him combined with her inability to go to him renders her whole body weak, as if she's become a ghost watching her own life play on without her. He steps toward Claire, and Eva knows she should look away. She wants to, she *needs* to, but she can't. Never did she know this would hurt, but it does, an actual physical pain. Now he's behind Claire and Claire is saying something and William, so naturally, so fluidly, leans down just as she tilts her head, her pale skin exposed. His lips brush her neck. A practiced kiss. Something done a million times. It takes only seconds. The familiarity is like a paper cut, swift and searing.

When he leaves the room she looks away, back to the lake. In the distance is the faint refrain of water against the shore.

25

Now

THEY TOOK their time at dinner, not to savor the food, but to avoid this moment: silence, no witnesses, two doors. Every so often the whir of a generator kicks in and a cloud passes over the moon.

"I hope the TV works."

Aidan unlocks her door. "Cable's pretty much all they've got. They'd fix it before the plumbing."

They'll be sleeping only feet away from each other. In this quiet, you could probably hear the zipper of a suitcase, a shoe falling to the floor.

"See you tomorrow," Aidan finally says, which shakes them loose.

Inside, Abby waits, hand on the doorknob, until she hears his door shut as well. Then she turns to the wall and pictures him on the other side, facing her.

ℰℓ

He sits on a bed covered in a green blanket and listens for her. Inches of drywall, layers of paint. The closeness is like a hand hovering above your skin, a slight heat, almost an annoyance, like the last peel of an orange or the final steps of hot sand before water. He should've thought of this and asked for rooms at least down the hall. Instead he's left to wonder what she's doing, separated by so little; if her arms are crossed, lifting off her shirt; if she's running a bath, testing the water. If she's scared, her back to the window.

He can't do this. It's been a long day. A quick shower and he gets in bed. The sheets are clean but slightly rough, bleached to hell and back, which he's grateful for, and he sinks his arms into the cool under the pillow. Again he thinks of her, how easily he'd told her about finding the boy, a story he has never repeated—not because of its nature, but because he'd caved in afterward, and that fact was a window into something he'd rather people not see. A darkness he trusted no one with. But her.

At last he hears something from her room, the static buzz of a television. On the nightstand is his phone, and he thinks of calling her—*I know you're awake*—but doesn't, because he knows that's not all he'd say.

☙

At night you are you. Pure you. Nothing exists past your window. The world stops right there, caught in the reflection in the glass. A desperate time. Pure, inescapable self.

She needs to call Robert, to ask about his meeting, to tell him about Hannah, but just the thought of calling him with Aidan in the other room seems wrong. He would hear it in her voice, an edge of threat, a tone of want. He would know, more than he does. All he'd have to do is ask where she is and she couldn't lie. So instead she picks up her cell phone and sends a text, then sits by the window.

In the reflection of the glass she watches her own face, held in black.

Caught in an overlay of past and present. Not quite far enough down this new road that she doesn't ache for the ease of the life she knows so well and a love that used to feel like everything—and yet too far to call out, to stop what's happened, to not feel the verge of her own future, the scintilla of approach. In a way it's too late, she understands; she can't unknow this time with Aidan. Never would she be able to forget the sound of his voice, how just a glance at his wrist, those tiny golden hairs by his watch, how just that made her feel undone.

It's too much. What she's doing, what she's escaping or trying to avoid, and yet still she'd rather be awake, left with these jagged pieces, than asleep and in that meadow, at that table just in need of its guests. For the third time she washes her face, letting soap seep into the corner of her eye, anything to be less comfortable, to not slope toward sleep. She can't stomach more coffee, so she shakes sugar and creamer into hot water from the sink, hoping that will keep her awake. A mouthful. Horrible. Another one, and she sits in a green chair with a low back and pilled fabric. It forces her to sit up straight. On the television, Lucy smuggles cheese onto a plane. Abby turns up the volume.

Suddenly she takes a deep, frantic breath and sits up, a pounding in her ears. She was asleep—how long she doesn't know. Her heart is racing as if she's just run a great distance and she fights to catch her breath.

Once again the other chair was yanked from the table, but this time as it flew back, her own chair plummeted into the earth. *Buried alive.* Someone was pounding in the dirt, packing it. Over and over. She swallows, tasting the dirt that pushed away her breath. She can't be alone, not with this.

Now she's barefoot in front of Aidan's door, shoulders cold in the night. Softly, almost imperceptibly, she knocks. If he hears, she's meant to go in. If not, she goes back to her room, back to her late-night television and stiff green chair. She touches the 9 on the door, the swoop and curve of the plastic number. It's a beautiful number. She's never thought of it before, but it is.

Behind her the street is empty, the woods on the other side, dark. Too many stars. The night air is so fragrant with something it feels thick. She won't knock again.

But she doesn't have to, because there he is.

ॐ

He sees her mouth open, perhaps to apologize, to explain, to excuse, but without giving her a chance, he pulls her into him. Kisses her. Every bit of him pulses as if a switch was pulled, her touch charged. Almost unnerving, but not one bit of him wants to stop. His hand is in her hair, and her tongue soft, mouth like sugar and cream.

She's kissing him. At last. Every worry, every thought, everything is gone, and yet suddenly a lash of images whips through her mind—but just as fast they're gone, forgotten.

When at last he pulls back, he opens his eyes and sees the night behind her, a night she feels at her back along with everything else, the woods and the empty diner and a craving that's so deep within her it makes it hard to find her breath.

"I had a dream," she says, what she came to tell him. But her eyes are on his mouth. She wants him to kiss her again. When he stands aside, she pauses, only for a moment, and steps into his room.

The strap of her tank top has fallen, and as she sits on the bed every move is sketched into his mind. Eyes bright with anticipation, her hair loose. A blaze of memory, the first morning they met, autumn leaves in full fire—he'd turned around and there she was. A splice from that moment to this—unexpected, surreal how it's happened, and yet somehow it makes sense. She leans back onto her elbows, watching him. Shadowed dips of collarbone, a freckle on the swell of her chest, rising with a breath. All at once he scoops an arm beneath her legs, the other beneath her shoulders, and moves her further onto the bed. Pushing up her shirt, he kisses her side, tongue light along her ribs until he hears her laugh, phosphorescence upon a shore, and rises up to watch her, taking in her smile. Another laugh as she grabs his shirt, pulling him back to her. He cups her breast, trails his tongue along her skin. Her back arches, a bridge from one end of her to the other.

Skin against skin. It's magnificent, the weight of him. *Different*. She tries not to think of it, but it is, his body, so much taller, stronger than Robert's, she feels as if she could curl beneath his arm, her whole hand almost just the palm of his. *Don't think*. Roughened fingertips, the slight scratching of his hands against her, around her, over her and up her sends reverberations through every inch of her body. Her legs are on either side of him and she hooks her ankle against his calf. She wants him and the want is pure, flaring, and desperate. As he rises up ever so slightly, she feels the air between them and waits in excruciating expectation. When at last he lowers himself, she closes her eyes, no longer anywhere she's ever known.

26

Then

IT'S DARK WHEN CLAIRE WAKES; even the moon seems absent from the sky. Quietly she walks to the bathroom, then shuts the door as softly as she can. William had fallen asleep with his hand on her stomach, and in the night brought her water when he heard her cough. But though he's clearly determined to be a good father, she still sees a drag in his step and his eyes continue to look past her when she stands before him.

The lies are piling up within her. Stacking one by one into a column of tilting deceptions. All her life is fake. The marriage, the baby, the beautiful horror of a house. In a few months William will mourn a child who never was. He will actually ache for this child, and Claire will have caused that pain. Unnecessary. Cruel. What has she done?

❧

When she returns to the bedroom William has turned on the lamp and is sitting up. He couldn't sleep, hasn't slept for more than a few hours here and there since telling Eva it was over, for every time he closes his eyes he sees her face, her eyes, watching him break her heart.

"Were you sick?" he asks Claire. "Can I get you something?"

"I'm fine," she says, and gently lowers herself into bed.

He's trying, he really is. Already he's earmarked the pages of bassinets in the Sears, Roebuck and Company catalogue. Already he's bought her a present, a token of what's to come. If he just thinks of the baby, he might make it. His child is how he will be a better man.

"I have something for you," he says, getting out of bed. "Two things."

Inside the closet, the bag sits alongside his empty suitcase. He has to go to Rochester today to sign papers, and had been planning on taking the suitcase and spending the night, packing up clothes, his grandfather's pocket watch, just a few things. But even that he dreads, as he knows he'll hear her footsteps on the stairs, her laughter in the hall. Spending the night there would be too hard, he thinks now. If he can, he'll sign the papers and leave, pack things later—though perhaps he'll drive by the house, just to see if a light has been left on. And even that, that one image of a lamp bright in the window, is like a blast of oxygen to a fire, and he must force himself to look at the present he got for Claire. *No. No more.*

"I should've wrapped them," he says, back in the bedroom. "Sorry."

She takes the bag and looks inside.

"For a girl or a boy."

But her face has paled, and not from happiness. He's confused. He thought she'd like them, the encouragement, the optimism. Though maybe, he now realizes, maybe it's too optimistic. "Is it too soon?" he asks.

Without looking away from the bag, she nods. "Yes. Anything can still happen."

"I understand." He takes the bag from her and returns it to the closet, the Raggedy Ann and Andy dolls tucked away until a safer time.

Only the entryway lights are on, the rest of the house asleep, shut off
and unaware. Eva is determined to be there from the start of the day, to
not miss a chance. After all, it's only a matter of time until he leaves. A
small venture out, a tennis date, an afternoon golfing with a friend. Eva
will call to him from across the street and he'll nod discreetly, starting
his car and pulling down the block to wait for her, his brown eyes in the
rearview mirror. She'll talk with him. Face-to-face. She'll tell him about
the Victorian down the street, how easy it could be to stay here half the
week. Nothing needs to be over. When you love each other, you find
a way.

Fog rolls in great wispy tumbles across the lakes, the whole place
otherworldly. There's a perfect spot that she's found, adjacent to the
house, behind trees and a shrub so thick she literally must concentrate
on the one sliver of view to see the house. There's no way anyone would
see her. And not in this fog.

Suddenly she feels daring. A bolt of rebellion. She wants to be up
close to the house and now is her chance, when the house is sleeping.
She crosses, vulnerable, an animal entering a clearing. The base of the
iron gate is plain, just bars, but up at the very top there are scrolls that
swoop from spears of altering height. She holds on to two of the bars,
wraps her fingers around the cold metal, then looks at her pale hands,
so pale that for a second, in the fog, she herself could be a ghost. She
raises her gaze, peering through the bars, just as suddenly a light turns
on in an upstairs room.

A couple of hours later, the front door opens. *William.* In the threshold,
turning around and about to step outside. Eva's heart surges and she

stands—but then there's Claire. He's holding the door for her and she pauses so he can lean in and press a kiss against her cheek.

Eva ducks behind the tree and hears the approach of Claire's heels, the slower pace as she takes the steps down to the sidewalk followed by a pause at the gate and the creaking, heavy swing of iron and then more steps, slower now but more punctuated, heavier, as if she's heading up stairs. A quick peek. Claire's approaching the neighbor's door.

This is her chance, William alone in the house, even though Claire's just next door. It's all she's got. Quickly she looks back to William, but he's gone. The front door is closed. Where is he? The squeaking yawn of a car door opening—William's at the yellow Cadillac.

"Dinner when I get back?" he calls out as he lowers himself into his car.

"Do you have any idea of the time?"

"Lots of loose ends to tie up—I'd say late evening. If it's too late, please don't worry about me."

"Do you need anything from Bergdorf's?"

"Not a thing. You and Edith treat yourselves. I'll see you tonight."

Claire waits for the door to open. Hurry, Eva thinks, open the door. She needs to catch William. She needs Claire to disappear. William's pulling forward. Almost at the mouth of the drive—her chance slipping away. And yet Claire is *still* standing there, the beige silk of her hat lit up in the sun, ruining everything.

The neighbor's door swings open just as William's car touches the street. He's inching forward, looking at Claire and the neighbor woman. Eva smooths down her skirt and is ready to step out and get his attention the second he looks her way. But he glances to his left and back to his right. Not once does he look straight ahead. Not once do his eyes even pause at the lake, nor does he suspect, even for a second, that Eva, the one he loves, is standing there waiting for him, needing just a second-long glance, just one look, *just one*. Instead he looks back to the women and waves, shadows of tree branches splayed upon the hood of the car. There's a smile on his face, but it's sad—Eva catches it, she knows him that well. This isn't what he wants.

A flash of red brake lights—Eva stands taller, *this is it*—but then she sees the squirrel that had run before him, safely bounding to the other side. The car continues. She looks back up to the house and sees that Claire, too, has been watching him, must have seen the sadness, for she now aims her face to the path, a moment to compose herself before turning around. And Eva's so caught in this moment, in feeling that he's leading his life for someone else, that she barely notices how far he's gone until his back windshield brightens with light. A pause at a stop sign, already two blocks away.

At last the neighbor's front door closes, both women inside.

And it's then that his taillights round the bend, and he's gone.

❧

The one good thing about the farce is that suddenly the shame of Claire's recent weight gain has been lifted; the anger at her stomach, protrusive and constantly needing to be held in by girdles, has turned to a strange acceptance. No longer is she trying to escape her body, banging against the boundaries of her physical self, but she's almost— quite nearly—relishing in it, present in a new and liberating way. It's as if she's woken with a different face, smaller shoulders, daintier feet. And though she knows she has no right, for whole chunks of the day she feels beautiful.

"I wouldn't let him out of my sight," Edith says.

Claire leans in toward the butterfly cage. Ten chrysalises have changed from jadeite green to opaquely transparent, revealing folded orange-and-black wings, ready to emerge.

"Those loose ends?" Edith continues. "They might have red nails, if you get my drift."

"*Edith.*"

"What? I'd have gone with him."

Edith grabs her car keys from a table by the door, alongside a tiny cloisonné box enameled with garnet-red and golden flowers that Claire picks up.

"Dorothy's penny collection," Edith says. "She lost it before she left. I just found it in with the milkweed. Which made no sense, until I realized the flowers on the box are almost identical to the ones on the plants. Such an eye, to notice that."

They step out into the light of a sullen afternoon, muted and held back. "So, a few dresses," Edith says. "Loose, nothing tight. Just for a month, *nothing* can cling to you. Not even William. A pregnant stomach is hard. You don't want him too close, or he'll know."

Just one month, that's all she needs. The Rochester business and house sold, connections severed. Then a tragedy. In her mind he holds her, afternoon sunlight on the bed.

Edith leans over to unlock her door, and that's when—in a mere split-second glance, a most insignificant glimpse, one of millions per day—Claire sees a girl by the tree at the edge of the lake. Hidden but not completely. Easily within earshot. And though she has no way of being sure it's her, the instinct that this is *Eva,* that red spark of a name her mother handed to her, is swift and searing.

Claire forces herself to continue looking around the lake, smile still in place, as if she'd not just seen what she had. Then she gets inside, hand shaking as she pulls the door shut.

WHEN ABBY WAKES, she won't open her eyes, as if keeping them shut will prolong the night, prolong what happened without letting in daylight's inconsiderate edges. She pictures her body, starting with her head, feeling each part of her that's touching him, isolating those spots—her neck against his arm, her back against his ribs, toes against his shin—and only then does she know it's real, and only then does she open her eyes.

His arm is underneath her head and she's curled on her side. Before her is his hand, his watch, his wrist, those little hairs that catch gold in the light. A slight tan, veins that branch along his forearm—she studies the parts of him she can see till his fingers curl and his muscles tense. He's awake. This is that moment, a fold in time, consequences not yet gathered, repercussions too fine a mist. *Stay in this room.* If she could she would forever, safe from what's happening in Makade, safe from hard conversations. Reality waits across the threshold.

Still, she doesn't move, just lies there, picturing him beside her, staring up at the ceiling. He must think she's asleep.

"I know you're awake," he says, and she smiles and rolls over, legs threading into his, one of his hands already in her hair, the other on her back, pressing her into him. For one moment she opens her eyes, just long enough to see his eyelashes as he kisses her, a slight glisten in the morning light.

When she leaves to go to her own room she eyes the lobby and the parking lot and moves quickly. And though she makes it unseen, guilt is set loose by the green chair, the perfectly made bed. She stares at the pillow and for a moment wonders if maybe she can pretend that none of this happened. Tell her skin to forget that touch. His touch. She closes her eyes. The one thing in the world she wants is to never forget.

And that's when she sees her cell phone: Missed Call. Robert. Voicemail: *Warners wants the script. They have a director attached, he's got a deal at the studio. It's already green-lit. Abby, this is a whole new ball game—it's happening.*

Everything's collided. Robert, Aidan. Commitment and betrayal. She thinks of her life with marriage and a house and a husband who puts her first, but all without Aidan, and feels as if the air in the room has changed, a charge of panic. Just from the thought. So betrayal, yes, but which betrayal would be worse? Her own, by staying on a course she's wondering if she even wants? Wouldn't that be the greater falseness? A treachery of self?

What's confusing is that even though she feels guilty, she does not feel wrong. *Tomorrow we're going to wake up,* Aidan had said last night, *and not for a second do I want you to feel bad. Because nothing before has felt right, not like this.*

And she agreed. And still does. Everything was right. When she rolled over and met his gaze and felt his fingers on her shoulder blade. When the light fell steady on his chest and she felt her hand warm against his skin. She'd felt no need to look away.

28

Then

JUST FOR A MONTH. A month. The words somersault in Eva's mind. In a month William will have sold his company, the house in Rochester, given up every remnant of Eva and made a new start, a pledge to his wife. In a month the baby will suddenly disappear, a saddened wife in its wake.

She knew. This whole time, Claire *knew* about Eva. Had simply not said anything because she had a plan, and this revelation is shocking not just in its truth but in the fact that Claire is no longer whom Eva thought. She's underestimated her, a fatal mistake.

The walk around the lake passes in what seemed like only moments, and now she stands at a pay phone across from a delicatessen that's packed with people, arms lifting for attention whenever the clerk looks up. Eva knows Claire's not home, so she'll leave a message: *Iris called, it's urgent.* For the first time she feels real hope—what was in the way is no longer.

The phone rings several times before being answered by that maid with the heavy accent. Eva closes her eyes and says as smoothly, as liquidly as she can, "I'd like to leave a message for Mr. Ballantine, please."

She almost laughs at the sound of her own voice. This, she thinks, is something she'll tell William. *And I had to disguise my voice—like I was in a movie, some spy adventure with footsteps in the alley and silhouettes in the windows!*

But the maid falls for it, and says something quickly and unintelligibly in return. Eva apologizes and asks if she could repeat that, and the woman sighs. "He is not here." Each word is clipped with irritation.

"I understand. I'd like to leave him a message. But do you know when he'll return?" Again she tries to be that graceful woman, the Eva she could be at some point if only given the chance, but there's a long-drawn-out pause, and in contrast to the maid's earlier pace, Eva understands whatever message she leaves will not be given to William.

"He is not here," the maid says again.

"When will he be back?"

"Late, too late for phone calls. Especially from you."

Eva's thrown, all her words jostled loose. "Excuse me?" she finally manages. "This is—" But she stops, because she's heard the click.

"Ma'am," the operator says softly. "Ma'am, they disconnected. Would you like me to try again?"

There's no point, Eva knows. Instead she asks to be connected to his office in Rochester, and his secretary answers on the first ring. "I need to leave a message for William, for when you speak to him. Please tell him that Eva called. I'm in Minneapolis."

"Number, please."

Eva realizes she doesn't know the number at the Victorian where she's staying. "Never mind. Tell him I'll find him. Just tell him that."

"I don't understand, what—"

"Please write it like I said. I'm in Minneapolis and will find him. It's important."

"Yes, I'm putting the note on his desk right now."

When again she hears the click, Eva's about to hang up when the operator speaks. "I think he'll get the message." Her words are quiet but encouraging, and Eva's steps are lighter as she passes the delicatessen, the view just a throng of people, jostled purses and newspapers beneath arms.

∾

All their plans for the day were abandoned. Edith drove a few blocks and then turned around, declaring the street safe before returning home.

"I wouldn't have given her this much credit," Edith says to Claire as they wait for their lunch in Claire's parlor. Now and then they look to the street. "You know it was her?"

"I'm sure of it. She was *watching*, Edith. And the look on her face— she *heard* us." She takes her spot by the window, but scoots the chair back just a bit, as if seeking protection from the wall. "I feel hunted. Like she's hunting us. Or we're at war."

"Oh, we're at war, all right."

"Mr. Ballantine called," Ketty says as she appears with a tray and two plates mounded high with salad. "Meetings went long. He won't come back tonight."

Claire nods. One more night to figure out what to do. A small collection of hours before everything comes undone. She spreads her napkin on her lap. But Ketty doesn't leave. She stands there, tray empty.

"And a girl called for him. She didn't say her name."

Claire realizes she's still flattening the napkin on her lap. She stops, pressing the palm of her hand onto her thighs. "What did she say?"

"She wanted to know when he would be coming home. I said late, too late for phone calls."

"Ketty," Edith says, "now I know you're smart and you've got an inkling about what all's going on here. Maybe you know more than we do. I imagine that's entirely possible."

Ketty, at full attention, takes a deep, flattered breath.

"But what I'll say is, that girl you spoke to? On the phone? She's a threat. A real threat to Claire, to William, and to you. That's what you need to know."

Ketty glances at Claire for only a moment. "I am aware."

Through the window, Claire watches a woman with a pram stop to check on the baby. The baby must have cried. Clouds in the distance are ash gray, like smoldering remains. When the woman straightens again, she looks up at the house and sees Claire in the window. Claire smiles, but the woman startles and looks away and her pace quickens. The pram jostles over a crack in the sidewalk and Claire leans forward, watching them disappear. *It's my window,* she wants to say. *I'm doing nothing wrong.*

29

Now

RETURNING TO MAKADE has that end-of-vacation feel, the border between work and play, fantasy and reality. Shake the sand from your shoes, collect the mail, check to see if the car starts and if the plants are still alive. An inventory of potential damage, fallout from your fun. Real choices and real conversations.

And no longer are they safely tucked at the edge of the state, she sees that as they approach the town limits. A news van is parked right there, a woman in a red suit and perfect hair pointing to the sign as the camera rolls, an immediate reminder of what they return to. Aidan looks to his rearview mirror as they pass. "And back to work it is."

Another song on the radio and they're a block from her house. The drop-off. That moment when he pulls to the curb, the seconds before she pushes the door open. Will he lean over, will he kiss her? Or will their time be encapsulated, left in the woods by Morrow Lake? A kiss. A kiss in front of her house. She tells herself that's all she wants, but the truth is, it's just the start.

Just as he's shut off the car, his phone rings. She only half listens to his side of the call, still thinking about the kiss. When he hangs up, he smiles. "Tomorrow," he says, "we go into Claire Ballantine's house."

"You're serious?" Something within her lists, just slightly. Fear that this is it, one of the last chances.

"That was the owner. I may have told her Claire was your grandmother's sister."

"Tomorrow?"

"I'm off by six AM, hopefully. Gonna need some sleep, so I could get you at noon? Be in Minneapolis at two? I'll have the rest of the day off. Dinner?"

She nods. "Thank you," she says, still thinking of the house, and in a rush of nerves and hope, she forgets everything else and reaches for the handle. But he reaches further and pulls her door back shut, his seat belt stretching, his hand turning her face to his, his mouth soft and vaguely minty. Her heart races.

She opens her eyes just a bit to see her bedroom window behind him, the place she used to sit, chin on the sill, watching moments like this and wishing it were her. That now it is her is a great righting of wrong, the explanation at the end of a following chapter. But this feeling, as amazing as it is, opens to something else entirely: a circular roundness to life that suddenly unnerves as much as it comforts.

Her world is folding over, pieces of her old self meeting her new, ends coming together.

30

Then

IN THE SKY is an orange parrot. It finds a branch and lands, unaware of its magnificence. Claire wonders if it belongs to someone, if it escaped. It skips to a lower branch and then another, and finally, restless, jumps into gray air and arcs into another tree, bright wings like fire.

The storm clouds are rolling in, a great tumbling darkness that combines with the night. Soon Claire can no longer see outside, but realizes anyone could see in. The girl could be anywhere. Watching.

Suddenly every move she makes feels followed, tracked—and the realization that a window is open hits her with a crack of cold. Against the side of the house, a window that faces Edith's, the glass angled into the dark night. She's there in a moment and the metal of the crank is cold, the trees outside frozen in apprehension, all black silhouette.

One by one Claire turns off the lights. First the small one on the game table, closest to the window, the shade like dripping icicles. Then the lamp on the library table, stained glass with metalwork at the top like lace, a woman's draped shawl. Last by the chaise, her favorite, a Tiffany with bright yellow daffodils and vibrant green grass.

Now the only light is a small sconce by the door, but that is low and illuminates only a bit of the dark wood wall, just enough to see your way from the room. But she doesn't leave. Instead she goes back to her place at the game table by the window, and waits.

ℓ

From the second William enters into Rochester, he feels Eva's presence the same as if she stood behind him. Undeniable. She must be there, he knows. She's come to find him; he wouldn't feel this if she weren't here. He wants to sign the papers and be done with it, to see if there's a basis to his feeling. Already he's picturing her in the chair by the window, eyes closed, waiting.

What would one night do? What would be the point? He doesn't know, but he wants it.

His secretary has put the papers on her desk outside his office, and he sees them the moment he walks in. He sits in her chair, too high, as he looks them over. He wants to leave. To not bother going into his office, to sign everything quickly and take the steps of the Rochester house two at a time so he can find Eva sleeping, black eyelashes against her pale cheeks. He needs to get there. With a swoop he begins the *B* of his signature.

ℓ

When Eva arrives, William's car is still gone. The houses look shut off, darkened windows and drawn shades. Claire, though, Claire is in her spot by the window, looking out into the gray evening, shoulders still and straight. She must be waiting for William to come home, expecting the bright swoop of his headlights any moment.

Bundled up inside Eva's sweater is a towel she borrowed from the

Victorian, which she lays at the base of the hidden tree as if she's simply
there for a late-night picnic. It's cold. The sky slate and infuriated. She
closes her eyes and breathes in, hoping for a moment to feel her way
back to the day they ate alongside the Zumbro River, to feel William
beside her, that delirious confusion of time that certain scents create.
But all she smells is the storm. The moon, bold in the part of the sky
not yet drenched in dark, pushes its light in a halo, bright echoes of itself like something about to burst.

When she looks back to the window Claire is gone and the lights are
off. It's startling, the sudden absence, and for a second she looks to the
other windows as if her eyes had gone to the wrong spot. But no. The
glass reflects the moon, the trees, images like a world dipped in dark,
slick oil.

Claire must have gone upstairs. It must be after ten o'clock. Maybe
she takes a bath before bed. The thought reminds Eva of William, of
his legs pressed against hers, bubbles and Sinatra, and for a moment the
drive of her plan—to tell William—is forgotten as the pain of missing
him takes over. She misses him. There's nothing simpler than that.

And then she hears a car and steps out from behind the tree.

Claire doesn't know what she's waiting for, but feels it as a jagged edge
pressed against her, the tip of a bad thought. *Impending.* Something is
impending. Maybe it's just the storm. The energy, a gathering. She has,
for a moment, a thought that if she goes to sleep, it will be different. She
will deprive the night of its meal, steal the laughter from a joke. Things
will be different. Just sleep and tomorrow will come.

But then there's the sound of a car.

She turns to the street, the darkness of the room at her back, and sees the approaching headlights. Bit by bit the world is conjured and extinguished. Pavement. Elms. Cottonwoods. The car is getting closer. The black night bursts with images. Tangles of branches. Fallen leaves.

Then in a flash, a face. Staring right at her. Shocked white. Watching the house.

Claire backs from the window. Presses herself against the wall, then moves to the door, then into the bright hall, careful to avoid the windows, and backs into the depths of the house, toward the kitchen. In the maid's quarters she hears Ketty's music playing softly, Tommy Dorsey and his orchestra.

As she dials, she looks to the second floor of Edith's house, watching as Edith answers.

"She's outside."

31

Now

OUTSIDE, A WIND has picked up. Young trees bent, leaves gathering in a shifting pile by the station's front door. Within the last two hours the media presence all but disappeared, a train derailment in the corner of the state too enticing, and only one news van is left, its doors shut tight against the wind. Though they've wished for the glare of spotlights to be shut off and the microscope to be removed, there's also something disconcerting about it, as if with the shift is a recognition that they were getting no closer to catching their man, that there was no reason for the media to stay.

"You rested?" Schultz asks, emerging from his office. "Harris said you might not be rested." A wink.

Harris, the last person you tell anything to. "All good, Sarge."

"Great. These came in for you."

Notes from the handwriting examiner, for the forgery case. "Right, thanks."

"Just spoke to Lila McCale's neighbors. The ones across the street, good view to her room. They found cigarette butts the week before the rape."

"He was casing."

"Or it wasn't him. Unrelated. Could've been a gardener, a kid from down the street trying to not get caught."

"They remember brand?"

"Yep, because the neighbor used to smoke them. Reds."

Aidan pictures where Brittany stood, holding the cigarette butt—Abby's window directly across. *No money to pitch in, but apparently she can spend nine bucks on a pack of Reds.* Brittany's sister accepted blame, but for the location, for the assumption they were hers or her friends'. She could've been wrong. "They toss 'em?"

"Sure did. Didn't know to keep them, no reason then. Might not have gotten DNA off 'em anyhow if the guy doesn't get the butt wet. And again, might've been unrelated."

"The woman I'm seeing, her neighbor found Reds earlier this week. Perfect vantage point. But the sister smokes, could've been her. Or her friends."

Schultz takes this in. "Okay. I'm assuming you did already, but if not, get patrol on her street. And try not to worry—I get trash in my yard from kids driving by. I'm constantly picking it up. It happens. A good chance it's nothing."

"Thanks."

A good chance. But the detail clings to the edge of justification, refusing to let go.

When the night shift is in full swing he remembers the handwriting examiner's notes. "The 'a' of the questioned signature [Q1] does not exhibit the stinger formation consistent in the provided exemplars [K1, K2, K3]. Would request samples closer in date to the Last Will & Testament." A stinger—that's a new one for Aidan. He looks at the samples of Rick Sullivan's writing, and sure enough, a hook shoots off inside the circle of the *a*, reared back like a bee's stinger. Even this makes him think of Abby and the dream she'd told him about, and once again the replay of last night and this morning starts up. Her head on his chest while she slept. *Rewind, play.* Eyes shut tight, mouth open, a shiver below her skin.

Time to end things with Ashley. He knows it won't be a surprise to her, but as the phone rings, he thinks of the best way to say it—he doesn't have time, it's not fair to her. *You deserve someone better,* he pictures himself saying. But when she answers he's saying something else entirely: *I met someone.* Straight to the point, he's actually smiling as he says the words. *I know,* she responds. A little too straight to the point, perhaps. The phone goes dead.

Not even a minute later, it rings. Haakstad.

"One thing I just heard," he says, the second Aidan answers. "The mother of our last girl? She had this pillow crocheted with *Now I lay me down to sleep,* that saying? Kept it on her rocking chair by her bed. She said it was squashed, you know, not fluffed, even though she kept it fluffed all the time."

"He sat there. Watching her."

"That's what she thought."

"The daughter, that was the one who was in a book club with her mom, right? Real close?"

"No, that was our first victim."

"Her mom was home, too?"

"Dad as well. The rooms were spread out, sound was not a factor. She only noticed it a few days after the rape. Anyone could've sat there. But she thought it was something."

Schultz walks by and points to the coffee machine. "Used espresso."

Aidan looks at the clock and tells Haakstad he's got to go. A quick call to Abby. Through the station windows he sees the wind continues, the one remaining news van's satellite sitting in the sky like a moon, low and full.

"I hate this wind," Abby says when she answers. "I don't want to sleep."

"You can't say that to a man who's working till six AM."

"Sorry. I know. I'm thinking I'll try to stay awake myself. Coffee, whatever. Make it through the night and sleep when the sun rises, wake up for Lake of the Isles when you wake up."

He looks behind him to make sure no one's around. "Maybe I'll stop by later, we can keep each other awake."

She laughs. "I wish. My mom will be home. She's been a bit weird."

"Weird because of me?"

"She was home when you dropped me off. One glance out the window would've done it. By the way, I see a cop driving down the street. He was here earlier, too. Thank you."

The night continues. Red Bulls and strong coffee. Then, around two AM, they get a call. A young woman heard a noise, like someone trying to get in her window. The second Aidan gets there, she bursts into tears: There was no noise, her dog ran out the front door and the wind was loud and she was scared. Even when Aidan takes the leash from the hook on the wall, *Come on, let's get him*, she's crying.

"I just want this to be over," she says.

"Soon," he tells her, "we're almost there."

A white lie. The dog is found two blocks over. After he's dropped them back off, he decides to swing by Abby's, to finish filling out the report in front of her house. An excuse to keep watch.

A branch is down on her street and his headlights catch the leaves. When he looks up he sees two red lights and at first thinks they're a patrol's brake lights, but then he realizes what's odd—no other lights.

The street is dark. A car whose driver thought keeping the headlights off would make him invisible, forgetting entirely about the brakes.

He speeds up and is at the corner in seconds—but the road's empty. Three streets branch off within about fifty feet. The driver could've gone down any of them. He picks one, spots no one, flips around and tries another. Pointless. The car's gone. He makes another U-turn and heads back, trying to remember the exact distance he'd seen the red lights emerge in the dark. It would've been right around here, he thinks, as he pulls to the curb before Abby's house. He stares at her glass door. Then he puts the car in park.

At first the wind kept her awake. The world rustling outside her window like a persistent tide on a burning shore. Then a strong cup of coffee lent assistance. Pacing. A midnight snack, her face washed a few times. The branches in the yard moved steadily as the minutes crawled by and the sky deepened in the bend of night. Maybe she sat down on the bed for a minute, maybe it was longer.

Now it's dark. Darker than it usually is in the dreams, the storm about to break loose. Wind pushes against the oak tree, its branches somehow fluid, moving like snakes in the night, and the chandelier whips with every gust, clanking prisms that sound like a shower of glass. In the midst of the black meadow there is a clearing, the soil up-ended, clumps of grass tossed aside, twists of tiny roots left exposed. Abby sits on the ground, the palms of her hands pressed firm against the dirt as a worm brushes against her hand. At first just a touch, but then firmer as it weaves its way between her fingers, threading one by one, pinning her to the earth. Too late, she realizes she can't move.

A parrot shrieks alarm into the sky.

Then something works its way up her throat. Rising, shoving forth, forcing her to gag. Choking. Whatever it is, is stuck, and with her hand she reaches into her own mouth and grabs at it, gets ahold and pulls. The oak tree begins to quiver. It's a root, gnarled and bloody, never-ending. Coiled at her feet and yet still there's more; still she pulls and pulls until suddenly it snags, caught on something deep within her, a stabbing, searing pain in her side. Then she's sinking and there's nothing to do but hold her breath as the ground gives way and pushes into her mouth, filling her nose.

Too late she realizes she should've closed her eyes, as now they're fixed in place, open and filling with dirt.

32

Then

WILLIAM'S ABOUT TO TURN into the driveway but has already noted that there's no light between the trees. He takes his foot off the gas and the beginnings of disappointment bring him to a stop. But then he reaches for a dangling, frayed end: She could still be inside. She could be sleeping.

Inside he flicks on the light. The living room's empty. He takes the stairs two at a time. The bed is made, the room silent, save for the faint tick of the pocket watch. He sits on the bed, feeling foolish.

What did he think? He'd ended it. She listened. He gave her no reason to keep hoping, to try again. Downstairs he turns on the faucet to rinse a glass and the absence of human presence pours through the rusted pipes in a reddish spill. He lets the water run, swirls it from the glass and reaches for the brandy. Beside it is the bottle of ginger ale, bought for her. There are two glasses in the dish rack. Two. He'd forgotten to put them away, from the last time they were together. The last time? Though he was the one who said the words, who made the choice, the simplicity of these two glasses pulls at something deep within him. *He made a mistake.* He knows it. But how can he undo what's been done? He just needs to be strong. Stay on course. Wanting something doesn't mean he should have it. Willpower, that's what he needs. Life will go on. He'll have a son or a daughter. His Rochester days will be forgotten, sanded down by new memories. He thinks of his child's children, and their children, all of them, a whole future, no one realizing how close they'd come to not existing, how much he had longed to take the other path.

cloo

There's a rap on the glass and Claire startles.

"You didn't hear me at first," Edith says once inside. She's wearing a black mink coat on top of her silk pajamas, a black beaded evening bag in her hand. "Like my getup? It was the first black thing I could find."

"Did she see?"

"No. I'm like a prowler. And I went through the side gate, here in a jiff."

"Now what?"

Edith laughs. "I thought you had the plan."

Claire sits at the kitchen table. "The plan was not to be alone."

They say nothing for a bit, and in the silence are the faint, sparkling musical beginnings of "Marie." Edith taps her finger on the table. "Sounds like you got company. I didn't know the Great Dane was a Dorsey fan."

"I needed someone I can *talk* to."

"So let's talk." She nods toward the street. "A little conversation is in order."

cloo

Eva hears the front door shut. There, charging down the steps, are Claire and the neighbor, the woman William called Edith. Quickly Eva stands, grabs her towel, and hides behind the tree. Do they know she's here? They must. A creak of the gate. The swishing of a dress gets louder.

"All right," a voice says. "We know you're there."

Eva steps out from behind the tree and is about to play dumb, but there's Claire, up close, taller than Eva had realized, with pale skin and shiny, almost colorless hair.

The neighbor wears a black mink coat, holding what looks to be an evening bag.

She speaks again. "Let's be civilized. There's no sense in standing out here when right across the street is a very nice place to sit and a bottle of brandy, which I'm sure we could all well use. Especially with the sky about to open up. I'm Edith, by the way. You know Claire. Obviously."

Eva looks from Edith to Claire. Both are tall, intimidating. Yet the fact of their friendship softens them. They go to lunch together. They shop, they call each other when upset. Eva feels a tug of the impossible— if only things were different. Claire and Eva could slip aside and share what they love about William. Trade secrets. Laugh about his inability to make even a sandwich, his perfect handwriting, or the way he makes such a mess of the bed while sleeping that he must get up once or even twice to drag the sheets up off the floor.

Edith sighs. "It's almost eleven o'clock, and two residents"—she motions to herself and to Claire—"have seen you prowling around. As you can imagine, this area is taken quite seriously, especially when so many are vacationing, whole stretches of houses empty. All it takes is a call."

Claire's eyes shine with either the moonlight or tears. Without warning she turns back to the house, while Edith waits till Eva gathers her things and then walks so closely that Eva feels the brush of her fur-clad arm and smells the jasmine of her perfume.

33

Now

THE DREAM WAS the worst one yet. When she woke at three AM, the house was silent, terrifyingly so, the wind gone as if an intensity had been reached and it could do no more. A quick check on her mother, who was sleeping the sleep of the dead, one leg hooked outside the blanket, and then Abby was hopelessly awake, watching the window for the touch of brightness that signaled safety. She can't go on like this. Waiting for daylight to close her eyes, each night worse than the last. The house on Lake of the Isles—it has to help. How, she's not sure, but there's a feeling that something is there, waiting.

Could guilt be why the dream was worse? She's never cheated before. Never even close, dutiful as she is. *Was.* Though it didn't feel like cheating. Her night with Aidan felt like a moment in time completely separate from her world with Robert. And that's what worries her. Perhaps that's how all cheaters feel, clinging to some justification that makes them not like all cheaters. The common thread is that they feel they are not common.

Now she sits at the kitchen table. Earlier Aidan sent a text: *Any noises last night? All quiet?* She sees the message and replies: *All good except my dream.* Then he's responding, and even that, those silly dots that mean he's typing, makes her feel jittery. An extension of him, him who she wants. She sees his hands, his fingers. His response appears. *Want to hear when I pick you up.*

While she waits, she calls the nursing home where Eleanor Hadley lives and is told she can visit whenever she'd like. Another option, another chance. Even that, another possibility lined up, makes her feel better. But Robert. Yesterday she sent him a text. *I was sleeping. The dreams have been bad. Amazing news. You did it.* Some part of her knows this will be best for him, a burn that allows for new growth. With someone better suited, perhaps. Maybe this producer—Sophia—late-night note sessions, a bottle of wine, the assistant told he can go home. She would know the film world, conversations stretching hours about names that mean nothing to Abby. They'd see movies on the big screen—and not just comedies—and go to premieres, captioned together in pictures in *Variety* and *The Hollywood Reporter*, those magazines Abby uses as coasters. He deserves to be with someone like that. Justification, Abby knows. An excuse as she's caught holding a match to their lives.

As though her thoughts summoned him, Robert is calling. She stares at the phone, letting the call go to voicemail, then hits Play and pinches the bridge of her nose in order not to cry. The sight of his name makes her feel an internal collapse, but his voice is too much. *On my way to another meeting with the producers,* he says. *At Warners this time, they want to talk casting.* A pause. *Call me when you're ready. I love you.*

He knows. Not exactly, but enough. Abby sees him pulling onto the studio lot today, referring to a map the guard would give him, thin strips of sun between giant stages. He'd put the map away, his steps slow compared to those around him, eyes searching out building names, hoping he looks like he belongs. The granola bar is in his briefcase, she put it there before she left but never told him, and in her mind she pictures him hungry, back in the car, the door shut as he looks through his briefcase for something, anything, only to find it at the bottom, ruined, crushed. The thought of him hungry breaks something within her because she loves him, she does—just not enough.

Dorothy shoots Pledge onto the wood table, chasing it with a towel that's seen better days. A newspaper hits the front walk.

"Mom, you're getting it everywhere." She picks up her coffee, no doubt doused with chemicals.

Her mother stops, towel in hand, hands on her hips. "Abby, don't you remember what it was like, being left?"

Thrown. She doesn't understand at first—did someone not pick her mother up? Someone left her somewhere? But when she realizes what her mother means, the anger swells inside her. How dare Dorothy anchor Abby's situation to her own—Abby's father had a *family*, responsibilities, an actual marriage. "Mom, don't you remember what it was like, being with the wrong person?"

"Who, then? Who is the wrong person? The one who called me yesterday morning, asking for the ring so he could propose?"

Abby feels a tightening in her jaw. The timing, of course, lined up with the deal with Warners, but would he have asked for the ring if he didn't feel a distance? If he didn't think he was about to lose her?

"I was supposed to put it in your suitcase," her mother continues. "I didn't know what to tell him when he called."

"What did you say?"

"I said he could have it, of course. But what do *you* say?"

Without answering, Abby goes to her room to wait for Aidan. She calls Hannah, whose acceptance of what's gone on is tinged with fears of losing Abby. The words *long distance* punctuated conversations yesterday, the cost of round-trip tickets mentioned. *I don't know if he even wants a relationship,* she told Hannah. *I just know that I want him, and that changes everything.* Now she tells her about her mother's words, about the ring. The guilt.

"Listen," Hannah says, "you know what you want. What you've always wanted. You just need to make it right."

It's true. In a way she feels as though she'd given Aidan her heart first and has simply reclaimed it for him. The rightful owner. If he wants it.

"Maybe that's why it doesn't feel like cheating," she says. Through the window a slender branch of the maple trembles beneath the weight of a sparrow. The day is overcast. "In a way I feel like this is what's right. That everything else was wrong."

The ring is on her nightstand in its velvet box. She opens the lid and there it is, bursts of color unleashed, a spell of turquoise and lavender, wheat fields and a russet sky. She looks closer. The arctic hue of missed opportunity, the violet tinge of regret. But also the brazen red of truth.

What do you say?

In the two-hour drive to the Cities Abby leaves her mother and her words behind, and the weather swings into a summer day. When they reach Minneapolis it's sunny, even hot, and Abby takes off her cardigan, warmth on her shoulders. She studies Aidan's hand as he drives, tendons that fan to his fingers, and then places her own on top. She's so caught up with him when they're together, it's unnervingly easy to leave the rest behind.

"There's a great restaurant there," Aidan says when they pass the Nicollet Mall, the blocked-off street.

The tour: memory roads, side streets of recollection.

"And there, on the right," he says, motioning to the W Hotel. "That's the hotel I was telling you about."

The building is a tower that shoots into the air, the name Foshay at the top. Streaks of white clouds behind it, blue captured windows. How she wishes their day were different—that they could go to dinner, order a bottle of wine; she could slip her shoes off under the table and inch her toes up his leg. A walk beneath the glass awning of the hotel, through the double doors, gazes locked in the elevator's mirror as it soars. She wants to see the night's skyline in his eyes, her back pressed against the glass.

"The hotel sounds *really* good," she says.

He smiles. "Trust me, I almost swung into valet. Can you spend the night tonight? At my place? I have to be at work early in the morning, but you can lock up when you leave."

It seems impossible that after the trip to Morrow Lake there'd be any lines left to cross, but somehow this feels like one of them. His world. His bed. Where he hangs his shirts, his glass of water on the nightstand. Excitement pushes past guilt. "I get to see your place?"

"With the warning that I haven't exactly been around to make it look its best."

"No fresh flowers in the kitchen?"

"No food in the kitchen. Or, there might be, but best leave it where it is."

"In that case, I accept this super romantic invitation."

He laughs. "Good."

But a moment later he says it again. "Good." This time no smile.

She watches him. He's thinking about something, she can see. *Any noises last night? All quiet?* "Why?" she asks. "What are you worried about?"

It's clear he's debating over what to say. At last, "I drove by last night, saw a car by your house. Close to three AM. Could've been anyone, a neighbor, someone lost, but with the noise you heard the other night—"

"And the cigarette butts."

"Which were probably Brittany's sister or her friends—but still, since I'm off, I want you with me. That, and I just want you with me."

She laughs. "Straight to the point. I like it."

They turn onto North First Avenue and pass a curved black Art Deco building that seems to hug the corner, facing the intersection as if keeping an eye on the neighborhood. Silver stars are painted on its side, each with the name of a band.

"Used to be a Greyhound bus station," Aidan says, noting her attention. "Now it's a club. Was in *Purple Rain*—one of those stars has Prince's name on it. Okay, time to head to the house before I get too homesick. We'll get out at Lake Calhoun, walk around, sit in the sand, we have the time."

She watches him for a moment, framed by the city. He glances at her and their eyes meet. A quick smile before he turns back to the road. Homesick, Abby thinks, still watching him. That's how I feel when I look at you.

That deep blue of summer, endless and brilliant. The heat seems to come with a noise like insects, a noise that shimmers. Coolers hold down blankets and bees are gathered at trash cans. Abby sits in the sand at the lake's edge, happy, Aidan beside her, when suddenly she knows that if she closes her eyes she'll open them to a different world, the water gone, replaced by the dark meadow, tall, dying grass an undulating pulse. Her heart pounds. This is not a dream. The sun is real. But she has to do it, a compulsion, a test. Without thinking she clenches her eyes shut and begins a count, and by the time she gets to *seven* she

hears the whisper of the oak tree's leaves, the clinking of the chandelier's prisms. *Eight. Nine.* Just the beginning.

She opens her eyes. A sailboat slashes through the water, people
splayed on bright towels.

"You've never been here?" he asks.

She's still steadying her breath, watching a child with a red pail,
pounding in sand. "Once. Here, to Calhoun. With some friends in sev-
enth grade. I didn't remember my grandparents ever lived here. That
was way before I was born."

For a moment she closes her eyes, feeling the press of sun. Trying to
feel what's good. The fact that somehow life has delivered her here, to
this moment, with this man beside her, feels surreal, an about-face in
her life she never saw coming. "Thank you," she says. She opens her
eyes, squinting against the glare. "For everything. You've done so much,
all for some silly girl from L.A."

Gently he takes her chin in his hand, turning her toward him. The
reflection of the lake is bright in his eyes, patterns of shifting light.
"Abby. In no way are you just some 'silly girl from L.A.' But you are the
one who has deciding to do. I know what I want."

It almost hurts, how happy that makes her. And what she wants is
to remember everything. The way he said her name, the streak of sailboats, the green of his shirt and the blue of the water, the way he looked
at her with a certainty that completely disarmed her.

⸎

In the car, they have the air conditioner on. To the right are rolling
green hills. "I used to go there," he says about the hills. "The Lakewood
Cemetery."

"You have relatives there?"

"No. Everyone's in Idaho. Just a good place to think. People don't bother you."

It was his version of the river then, back when he lived in the Cities. A run around the lake, ending in the cemetery, catching his breath beneath the canopy of trees. Sometimes families would be there, clustered around a new headstone, clutches of fresh flowers scattered, a week, maybe two, after a funeral. It was then he felt he should leave. They were with their grief and he was using the calm to press his reset button, to start again. They were ending as he was beginning.

"That's Lake of the Isles," Abby says.

He follows her gaze to the smaller lake; darker, crowded with trees, an island in the middle. A couple is canoeing in the center, an old man on a bench at the shore.

Abruptly she sits back, face pale in the afternoon light.

"What? What's wrong?"

"That's it. The house."

They've just rounded a block and a dozen stately homes are perched with views to the water—not one address visible. But she's not looked away, pulled by whatever it is she's seeing. He follows her gaze. A large brown stone mansion, castle-like, with a rounded tower in front and tall, narrow windows. Overt, imposing grandeur. A green lawn held in place by a black wrought-iron gate.

"The stone one?"

She nods. Only when pulled to the curb does he compare the address to what he's written on a Post-it note: The numbers match. The Ballantine house.

Then he looks next door. "And your grandparents," he says, "that would be their place." Starkly different than the Ballantines', her grandparents' old house is grand and white, with arched Palladian windows and an immense front door flanked by double columns on either side.

It, too, is beautiful, though not as alluring as the stone house, which seems to beckon as much as repel.

"I can't see my mom living there," Abby says. "Playing on that lawn as a kid. Maybe kids don't play on lawns here."

He opens the car door for her. The lake water is glass-still and the heat of the day has intensified everything. Reflections. Sounds. Smells. There's a dark scent of the lake, a marshy, settled odor that hangs in the air. She steps onto the sidewalk, right between the two houses, and an elm leaf by her feet lifts into the air, skittering to the grass.

Strangely, the connection she feels is not to her family's old house, but to this other one. Fascination, she knows. Something happened to Claire in this house. Claire Ballantine, whose very name resonates simply because of its elegance. And Abby's grandmother. Something here left her grandmother distraught. *But still I see the basement, and still I remember.* "It's so sad," she says about the Ballantine house. "I've never seen such a sad house."

He takes a few steps up the path and she watches him, the house tall in the background, majestic and despairing. The stones soak in the sun, scorched, and in a split second the noise from the cars, the whirring, swift arcs of sound as they round the bend, everything slows down. Becomes clumsier. Rounder. Intensified. But then she blinks. The world straightens and the sun blazes in the glass of the windows.

"What's going on?" Aidan asks.

"I should've eaten breakfast."

Sun is strewn through the trees. She meets him on the path, her grandparents' house beside them, and for a moment she imagines them, Frank and Edith, as a young couple, standing on their own path, watching as Abby and Aidan take steps they used to climb. A night of gin rummy with the neighbors. Tweed suits and pearl earrings. The loose jangle of ice in a drink, a deck of cards shuffled and dealt. Now, standing at the door, Abby can almost feel their stare in the weight of the past.

And then the front door swings open, and Abby looks into a room that's all dark wood, crowned with the radiance of the chandelier she's always known, prisms burning with light, straight out of her dreams.

34

Then

EVA'S LOOKING UP, gaze fixed on the chandelier above her, as if with enough concentration she could possibly lower her eyes to find herself in the midst of a different night. A party. She'd be a guest; someone would take her coat. For a split second she feels it, really feels it, that she belongs, and in that moment she smiles—a smile that Claire catches seconds before she spins on her heel and heads into another room.

But then Eva looks down. The room is all wood, floor to ceiling, and it's crushing, a dark presence. As she follows Claire, she sees it's not just the foyer that feels wrong, but the whole house. Graceful, powerful, and elegant, yes. Alluring contradictions, the way a snowfall makes a room grow warm. But it's not William, and it's certainly not Claire. It seems to be no one's, belonging only to itself. This was William's childhood? Everything is hard edges and corners, shadows and echoes. She tries to imagine him as a young boy, running through the halls laughing, constructing a fort with furniture, or even making a random, rebellious mark on the wall, but can't. The inability puts something like mourning within her, for what he never had.

They turn the corner into the parlor, and as they enter, Claire flicks on a lamp with yellow flowers, then takes long, assured steps to a tray of crystal decanters. Ice cubes plucked with a silver tong. Eva's life with William in Rochester flashes in her mind, the metal ice cube tray, the crunch of the lever, cupped hands holding the frozen, slippery cubes on their way to a drink. The memory actually hurts, a life long ago.

"What's your name?" Edith says, voice inflecting just barely at the end, as if it were really more of an accusation.

Eva doesn't know whether to stand or sit. She looks behind her at a chair, but remains standing. She hates her confusion. Through the windows leaves have begun to move, thin branches caught in a low, aching sway. "Eva."

"Well, Eva, you can stop looking at the place as if you're about to inherit it."

"I'm *not*." She doesn't like Edith. Of course if she were her friend she'd love her—domineering, bossy, protective. But Edith is Claire's friend. Claire, who has now turned from them and is facing the window, perhaps waiting for William. What will he do, seeing her in here? She looks back at Claire. "He wants to be with me, you know."

Claire doesn't turn around.

"Right to the point, I see," Edith says, shrugging off her mink, letting it fall like a cotton sweater to a chair.

Eva will not lose her footing. "We all know why he chose to stay with Claire."

ↄlↄ

At this, her name spoken by the *mistress*, Claire turns. This, more than Eva's being in the house—*Eva*, how many times has her husband said that name, cried that name—is the invasion. "*You* do not get to say my name. I am *Mrs. Ballantine*."

"He's with you because of a lie."

Fury rises within Claire, her face flushing. Here, in her own parlor, is a girl telling her her worth, saying she's not enough, saying her husband does not love her, and it's so cruel and insolent and horrifying that in only steps she's before the girl, looking down at her. "He is my husband. *My* husband. Our marriage is none of your business."

"He was going to leave you. He told me that."

"This little—" Claire turns to Edith, but what she sees clutches at her throat. "*Edith.* Is that real?"

And now Eva turns and sees the pistol in Edith's hand.

Edith laughs. "It's Frank's. I don't much like holding this thing, and I don't want to use it. But I can." She looks to Eva. "My husband always liked to find activities I detest, and one of them was shooting. But we put an end to that, because nothing makes a man want to crawl under a rock more than his wife being a better shot."

"Edith," Claire says, and her own hand rises up.

Edith continues. "This area gets a lot of attention. Two residents say you broke in. Look at you, you're clearly the jilted lover." She waves her hand with the pistol, and both Claire and Eva follow it with their eyes. "You see how that would work out. So let's just call this over. You're young, you're not hard on the eyes, you'll find someone else, and we'll wish you the best of luck. We clear on the plan? William is *married*. William stays married."

Outside, at long last, the clouds open up. Claire turns to the sound. Columns of rain fall with such thickness and force they appear to be solid cords from above, great strands connecting heaven and earth.

35

Now

THERE ARE MOMENTS—a policeman spotted on the porch, a trail of smoke a block from home, the piercing, solid shriek of the flatlining of a heart—in which the inevitable approaches, just around the corner, and your steps slow. A few moments of prolongment. Tighten your robe, a longer pause at a stop sign, greet the nurse at the counter who can't hear your *hello* over the sound of your life changing. This is what it feels like as Abby finally looks away from the chandelier that seems to hang straight from her dreams. The rest is waiting.

"In here is the parlor," the owner, Cynthia VonDeffner, says. Prim. Sensible. A blouse buttoned to the top. As they enter the parlor she stays behind, like a Realtor just within reach but far enough to allow for discussion.

Abby stops in the doorframe, studying the white paint, and Aidan places his hand on the small of her back. "It should be illegal to paint wood like that," he says quietly.

There's a small nick in the paint, a faint crevice, a mere line. Almost imperceptible under the years of enamel, but she sees it.

"Oak, I bet," he continues.

Abby touches it, presses her fingertip into the slight groove, and nausea blooms within her. She yanks her hand back and closes her eyes, trying not to pass out.

"All right," he says. "Tell me. What's going on?"

"I really should have eaten."

"On the wall over there," Cynthia says from across the room, pointing to the corner, "is an actual bullet. Lodged in the wallpaper."

Aidan turns. "A bullet?"

"And a vase broke," Abby says.

Aidan looks back at her. "Abby, you're way too pale. Sit."

She does as she's told, and takes a seat on a dark red velvet sofa. Through the window, water shines between trees.

"Okay. Now what about a vase?"

He's watching her. She looks up at him. Such a concerned gaze.

You weren't here.

The words leave her mind as quickly as they came. Their trail deep. She blinks, and finally feels as if she's in the room. What had he just said? Something about a vase? "A vase?"

"What you just said. About a vase breaking."

"I said that?"

"You don't remember saying that, just now? When she told us about the bullet?"

"In the wall," Cynthia says, tiring of confusion. "The Stocktons, we bought the house from them. They left it and we left it. It gets people talking at parties—sometimes you need that." She pauses, as if just having made a connection. "I'm sorry by the way, for what happened. To your grandmother's sister. Your great-aunt, would it be?"

"You know about Claire?" Aidan asks.

"Just that she went missing that night."

"Nothing else?"

"No. An incomplete picture, at best, over the years. Rumors here and there. Excuse me," she says, stepping toward the hall, then motioning toward Abby. "She might need a moment."

Aidan puts his hand on Abby's shoulder. "Do you need to leave?"

She shakes her head. "No. I'm fine."

"Just tell me when you're ready to get up."

Abby does not go to the bullet, though Aidan does. Inspects it. She watches his back. The pull of his shirt as he lifts his arm. *This is the one, then*, she hears him say, *in the report. The night Claire went missing. Two shots fired, but one missed. Evidence just sitting here—my head would be on a plate if I left this behind.*

When they head upstairs, Cynthia lingers by the base of the banister, and Abby's thrown by how much better she feels. Whatever it is, now that she's no longer faint, she can grasp the beauty of the house. All the wood upstairs—everywhere else in the house, for that matter— is left unscathed, uncovered by paint. It was only the parlor that was white.

Eventually they stand at an upstairs window, facing Abby's grandparents' house. It's a concept she can't seem to hold. Such a different life. One she'd never known. What had Claire seen when looking through this window? Did she see a young Dorothy playing in the yard below, hopscotch in the garden? What would she have done if told that one day Dorothy's daughter would stand here, searching for her family in the way sunlight falls or the length of the garden path?

Aidan's fingers are soft on her collarbone, slowly moving a few strands of hair. He takes a step closer and is against her. Both arms wrap around her waist just as a sudden gust of air bursts through an open window and billows the curtain in a breath. They turn, watching it settle back against the wall.

36

Then

IF YOU ASKED CLAIRE, even minutes later, what it was that made them turn to the door to see Ketty standing there, she wouldn't have known. Maybe it was a dark shape where before there was none. Maybe Ketty made a sound or the floorboards groaned. Most likely it was the swing of Eva's shoulders, turning to try and run from the room. Whatever it was, everything then happened at once, as if some crucial tie came undone and the evening soared into the unthinkable. There were the sounds: Edith's startled cry and the blast of her gun, something breaking, and Claire's scream, which she became aware of only when Edith finally begged her to stop. But it was the sights that burned into her mind: the knife in Ketty's hand, flashing only for a second, then two bodies almost one, mere inches apart. The knife's handle, fingers strained white. Blood slowly catching the fibers of a dress, filling and spreading, filling and spreading.

Eva never saw it. What she sees are eyes. Cat's eyes, velvety deep and layered, and for a second the blue and yellow and tendrils of brown become mountains and rivers and valleys, edges of continents and vast, magnificent oceans. A map of the ancient world. The eye blinks, and Eva blinks, too. And looks down. Fingers let go of the handle. Rosewood, with three brass rivets. Eva blinks again and sees that though the fingers are gone, the knife's handle remains.

Outside the pounding in her head, voices squirm in the air, and she realizes she's in the summers of her youth, floating on her back in Hudson's Pond, surrounded by elm trees, clusters of black-eyed Susans, and roads that stretch forever. Her ears hum with the filtered sounds of the world. Somewhere a boy waves to her from a treetop, and colors burst from clouds, dry fields beneath a sunset, rolling and magnificent.

Claire watches the gun dangle from Edith's hand as if she can't let go, and when she finally shakes it off, it falls to a table and spins, the mouth turning, turning, turning, as in a game of spin the bottle. There'd been one shot and something broke, which she thinks means the bullet didn't hit anyone. She turns, identifying the sound. Shards of pottery are scattered. Lilac-blue shards. The Lorelei vase. A bullet hole in the wall behind it, dark metal caught in the floral print of the wallpaper.

"Oh, Jesus," Edith is saying over and over as Ketty reaches back to the knife.

There's a sound, a sound like nothing Claire's heard before, starting with the base of the blade's corner, caught on cotton. Ketty pulls the knife, slowly at first, the fabric snagging, until suddenly it's released with a single, solitary pluck. Then it all heaps together—the suck of steel from flesh and the swish of the blade pushing air, removed quickly, so quickly it hits the doorframe. *Chop.* The blade lodges in the wood.

Though Eva's ears still hum with underwater muddle, she now sees the knife in the doorframe. Slowly she turns her head. Blue splinters are on the floor, flowers scattered. Then Claire, eyes wide, hand pressed against her mouth. It takes a moment to realize that Claire is trying to hold it in but is screaming. And on her hand is a ring. Beautiful. Flashing, like a star. It twinkles in the night, beckoning, but then the night takes over. The world closes to black. Suddenly the star is gone, everything is gone, lost to darkness.

But Eva still feels. At first she's sinking, her body no longer weightless but heavy, so heavy. It's peaceful, giving in, this laden sleep, until she realizes there's no choice. She's loose inside herself. She has no control, she's tumbling, scrambling, trapped in darkness, hitting edges and corners and walls. The body she's had for a lifetime—the body that's been beautiful and amazing and always faithful—cannot be controlled, and in the darkness she understands that the last thing she saw is the last thing she will ever see. The star.

In her mind flashes an image of her sister, stomach large with child. The sound of her sister's voice, calling the baby *Eva*.

But it's the thought of him, as her knees buckle, that pulses and fills every space within her, a longing so powerful that borders and boundaries and lines should be rendered powerless and he should be conjured as a mist, a shimmer of particles her own body craves to join.

He never came.

Her kneecaps crack against the floor. A rush of air, silky apprehension. *Slam.* Her head hits the wood, and there is silence.

37

Now

HOMESICK. HEARTSICK. Whatever the feeling is, wherever it comes from, it grips Abby the second they step into the kitchen. Sadness spreads, aching even in the tips of her toes.

"The basement," Aidan says, turned to a closed door. And though it could be a pantry or any other kind of room, Abby knows he's right. The glass knob is beautiful, but not one she wants to touch.

"That's Claire," Cynthia says as she enters the room, "her and her neighbor and a woman who used to work here." She must see their confusion. "The picture? Sorry, I thought that's what you were looking at."

Now Abby sees the photo, hanging on the wall by the door to the basement. Her grandmother as a young woman and Claire and another woman, standing in the front yard, faces washed in sunlight.

"The woman on the right," Cynthia says, "was the housekeeper. When she died a while back, someone sent the Stocktons this picture. I feel bad. It's a nice frame and a nice picture, but I didn't want to put it in the living room. Neither did the Stocktons, apparently. It was in this spot when we moved in."

"Can I?" Aidan asks and unhooks the frame from the wall, turning it over to read what's on the back. "Claire Ballantine, mistress of the house; Edith Walters, neighbor." He pauses to look up at Abby. "And Ketty Rasmussen, employee of the Ballantine family since 1919.'" He hands her the picture. "Can we see the basement?"

"I'll let you explore," Cynthia says. "The basement's—well, it's not for me. But you should take that. The picture. It's yours, more than mine."

Abby nods, still studying the photo as Cynthia excuses herself, heels echoing, expansive, then fainter. The housekeeper's face. Claire's face. Her grandmother, so young and healthy. She puts the photo frame into her purse—an odd feeling, to be carrying them away like this—but then Aidan's got his hand on the glass doorknob and now all Abby can think of is the basement.

"We don't have to go down there," he says.

She lowers her head, still light-headed. "I should, so I never wonder if it would've made a difference." The strange thing is her feet look out of place, simply wrong, and everything's off-kilter—as if she's not standing flat on the ground but at a very slight, almost imperceptible angle. Lifted black-and-white linoleum—she sees it, right before the basement door, a slight gap, a raised bit of flooring. For some reason she can't look away, her gaze caught in that dark, exposed line.

"Okay, I don't know," she says. "I leave it up to you. Nothing about me is logical right now. Do with me as you will."

"Oh I will, Ms. Walters. Though maybe not in the basement. At least not this basement."

She smiles and looks up. Diffused sunlight is soft in the room, an even brightness. A neighbor's car door shuts and a dog barks. Life, common life, the sounds of days. Oddly comforting, in a way—the world continued right outside this door—and in an instant something within Abby lifts with hope. This is it, she knows it is, the beginning slide of a card obscured, a beam of radiance about to find its mark.

What she'll learn or how, she doesn't know, but the feeling that she's mere steps away makes her feel as though she's not the only one looking—something is looking for her. Something wants to be found.

"Ready?" Aidan asks, and steps forward. "I'll go first." In one swift motion he opens the door, reaches into the dark, and flicks on the light. For a second she wonders how he knew the switch was there, but then the basement is alive. Narrow stairs. Dusty walls. A splintered banister.

His first step on the old wood plank summons a deep wail.

38

Then

AT FIRST they didn't think she was alive. There was, when they lifted her shirt, a large gash inches below her breast. It continued to gush blood, scolding them, relentless. Her eyes were closed, her lips still, her pulse hidden somewhere deep inside her. A matter of time, it was clear.

"I have a mirror," Edith now announces.

Everything is slow, so slow, and sounds are amplified. Claire watches Edith's fingers, shaking too hard to undo the clasp on her evening bag. Claire is not inside herself, but rather hovering just above the person she understands is Claire. *That's Claire.* That's her arm, reaching for the bag. Those are her fingers, poised. Now they press the clasp. *Snap.* Loud, like another gunshot. She startles, though she herself caused the sound. Then her focus snags on the bag itself, a witness to martinis, gossip whispered by a coat closet, perhaps even fights in the car as headlights grew bolder. And now this. Whatever this is, there is no definition yet. Claire's mind is still in a disbelieving state and therefore, to her, it's entirely possible that nothing has happened, that what's seemed like a long-drawn-out horror is actually just a slender breath of time in one of those haphazard moments before sleep. Inside the bag there is a powder compact, silver with light blue enamel, and for a while Claire stares at it, wondering why they need to powder the girl's face.

Now Edith kneels on the floor, the compact open, rain outside a steady thrum. She holds the mirror an inch from the girl's mouth, but her hands are still shaking and bits of powder fall onto the girl's lips. Edith takes a shocked breath, then frantically tries to brush the powder away, but instead smears streaks of red across the girl's face.

A whistle shrieks into the room. Claire whips toward the sound.

"Tea," Ketty says, taking the compact. "To soothe our nerves."

Claire takes Edith's shoulder and leads her into the kitchen, where she shuts off the stove. Steam rises from the spout. Ketty has already filled the silver tea infuser with loose leaves and for a moment Claire wonders what's inside. *To soothe our nerves.* The idea that she might not wake from this tea strips through her mind and leaves a trail of laughter. She's laughing and she can't stop.

"Claire," Edith is saying over and over again until Claire takes a deep, stabilizing breath. "We call someone," Edith continues, "and she's passed when they get here. Then what?"

"We say the truth," Claire says. "It was an accident. She walked into a knife."

Edith raises an eyebrow, and Claire falls silent, having just heard her last sentence as Edith did. *Walked into a knife.* Though of course there was also the question of *was* it an accident? Why was the knife extended just so; why did Ketty not react, not try to remove the blade or herself or anything? Wasn't there time? Why didn't Ketty scream? Did she? The chronology of events jumbles in Claire's mind like photos strewn on a table. Which came first? No, Claire tells herself. If there had been time, then Eva herself would have moved out of the way—it was momentum, pure and simple, that drove her into the knife. Though even as she tells herself this, she isn't sure who took the last step, *whose mo-mentum* it was that drove the blade. A glimmer and then nothing. Two bodies almost one.

Edith closes her eyes and takes a deep breath, and when at last she looks at Claire, it's as if she's invoked a fragment of her former self. "Right," Edith says, voice now steady, though her eyes glance around the room, searching for something Claire realizes is not there. "So tell-ing the police that the woman your husband was having an affair with, who he was possibly going to leave you for, *walked into a knife* isn't the smartest of choices."

Ketty appears for a moment, then disappears down the hall into her room. Only when the music ceases does Claire realize it's been playing this entire time. When had Ketty heard them? There must have been a pause in the song for her to detect a different voice in the parlor. One fateful instant, a beat that allowed for recognition, a recognition that allowed for what should never have happened. A soft, orchestral moment. A pause before a gust of wind. Claire thinks of the song that was just playing and then rewinds the evening, hearing the soft, wavering beginning of "I'm Gettin' Sentimental Over You." That was it. That must have been it. If only a different song had been playing, something jam-packed with sound. One song could've changed the night entirely. Changed her life. William's life. This girl, whatever family she has. Claire thinks of her earlier feeling, that something was impending, and wishes more than anything in the world she'd just gone to bed. Or that the girl had just stayed hidden, had not been so bold, or so filled with youthful faith, as to come inside. What those choices have done. What that one pause in the music had allowed.

Ketty returns to the kitchen. "Nothing," she says, and tries to hand

Edith the compact. But Edith shakes her head, refusing to touch it, so Ketty drops it in the trash.

To remove her from the parlor, they roll her onto a large canvas bag Ketty had found and splayed open. The sound the girl's arm makes, lifelessly slapping the ground when they roll her over, takes them all by surprise. When finally she's laid by the stairs to the basement, right by the door, they sit once more and listen for sirens. But the neighborhood sleeps.

"If someone was coming," Edith says, "they'd have been here by now. The Carlyles are in Maine and the Grants are in London. If someone heard, they'd have been here by now."

Claire looks toward the stairs. Already she's become someone she never thought possible. Already her life has changed irrevocably, and for a moment she's mad, mad that this girl has done this, has made Claire leave herself forever.

She looks back to Ketty at the sink, washing the knife yet again. Her sleeves are rolled up, and for the first time Claire sees the long scar on Ketty's arm, the result of the factory accident. As if Ketty feels her staring, she switches off the water and unrolls her sleeve, then dries the blade. Claire pictures her later, cooking with this very knife, using it to slice onions for a stew. William would bring the spoon to his mouth. *William.* She closes her eyes tight, vision red with her eyelids. What will they tell him? Nothing? "Put it in a drawer," she says to Ketty, and then opens her eyes. "Take it out later." *Make it go away. Plant it so the handle crumbles in the earth and the blade scars with rust.*

Ketty nods and wraps the knife in cheesecloth, which just earlier today had been resting atop yogurt. Everything, everything has been tainted. Claire watches Ketty place the knife under the sink between the Maid of Honor rug foam, the Johnson's Glo-Coat floor polish, and the Last Lunch rat powder. A triangle of protection.

"If the police were coming," Edith says again after their third cup of tea, "they would've been here by now."

It's almost one o'clock. The rain has eased. They've had the same conversation a few times now.

"I don't think anyone heard," she continues. "I think it's best, this course of action. We never saw her. We make it so no one finds her. What's done is done. Why ruin more lives?"

"Yes. I agree."

"And she's from Rochester?"

"I believe so."

"And William didn't know she was here."

"Right," Claire says and then pauses, looking for Ketty, who's disappeared. The basement, she remembers Ketty having said. That's right. She's downstairs digging a hole in the tunnel, getting things ready. *Ready.* "Ketty never gave him the message. But Edith, where was she staying? A friend maybe, maybe they knew she was coming here."

"Intending to come here isn't the same as being seen here. People set out to go places all the time and get turned around or lost or—things happen. What matters is that no one *saw* her here, and won't if they pay us a visit. We deny. We don't even know who she is. You don't know who she is."

Back and forth they ask as many questions as they can until finally Ketty appears and requests help. At the top of the stairs, by the basement door, lies the girl. Claire stares at the face and vibrant blue eyes stare back, as if seeing, as if accusing, taking in Claire's face to remember later. Ketty steps in and closes the lids. The gaze is gone. Claire nods, thankful, and then sees the girl's eyelashes are dark and glistening. Was she crying? She looks away. Beside the arm the flooring is lifted, a little area at the top of the stairs where a dark line of blood has strayed and settled, slick in the space between the linoleum and the wall.

As Edith and Ketty carry the girl into the basement, Claire goes throughout the house and shuts off all the lights. There. Now the house is sleeping. Nothing happened here tonight.

39

Now

THE SMELL OF THE BASEMENT is at once sweet and musty, and in a beat Abby knows she'll forever associate this mix with the scent of secrets. The stairs are wooden and have more than a few loose planks, and the walls are old brick, punctuated with dark lines of missing mortar. On either end of the room are exposed lightbulbs, blaring from their sides but sinking the center into darkness, the territory of a mind prone to rebellion. But strangely, with every step the basement becomes less frightening, not more. For once Abby's not scared, not feeling the ceiling press or the walls tremble. Instead, it's wonder that holds her upright and calm, as if rather than an old room tucked into the earth she's standing in a cavern, walls of amethyst. She nods, feeling affirmed, though by what she couldn't say.

"Don't ask me what I'm feeling, because I don't think I could say."

Aidan goes straight to a trunk in the corner of the room, leather straps and brass rivets. Boxes of Christmas decorations line one wall, a collection of wreaths on the top shelf, plastic holly, glittering gold, pinecones dusted in white. By a boxed train set stands a giant nutcracker keeping sentry, angled eyebrows rendering his expression sheepish, as if he knows he's failed at his job. Without a doubt the VonDeffners have lavish holiday parties with passed silver trays and kids clad in velvet. Outside, the lake would dazzle in flashes of blue and white, the air an edge of cold.

But still I see the basement, and still I remember. What had her grandmother been trying to forget?

Aidan's kneeling at the trunk. "It's got stickers from all the countries it went through. Gemany, Norway. Can you read this date?"

Stepping toward him she gets a chill. Not slow, not gradual, but a full-force blast of cold air from a vent.

Aidan looks up at her. "What?"

"It just got really cold." Already she's looking for the vent, her mind replaying movies in which someone reaches inside, fingertips brushing an old cigar box, a stack of letters. She scans the walls, but there is no vent.

He steps toward her, arms out as if testing a radius of air. "I don't feel—" but then he stops. "Right here." He looks up at the corner of the wall, searching for an explanation. "Maybe there's something behind these shelves."

The shelving unit is bolted to the wall, crammed with boxes and buckets of paint. One at a time he grabs the items, setting them on the floor, revealing inch by inch more brick. With two more shelves to go, his cell phone rings. Just once, then silence. He holds the phone up, searching for reception.

Abby turns back to the wall. The revealed brick is brighter, having been shrouded in boxes, shielded from time. There's a tug within her, a shift in energy. Just two more shelves of boxes to go.

And there, about a foot above the ground, is a small spot in the wall without bricks. It's all mortar—and barely, just barely, she sees what she thinks is a handprint.

"Still nothing?" Aidan asks, giving up on a signal. But then he sees it and is kneeling beside Abby, looking closer. "Here." He turns on the flashlight on his phone.

The handprint is dark, almost like a shadow, and right above are initials, crudely imprinted into the mortar as if with a stick. *WB + EM.*

A tremble within her, something knocked loose. At once Abby knows she's where she needs to be.

"He was having an affair," Aidan says. "What was your grandmother's last name?"

"Walters. Same as me. When my dad left, we went back to it. I don't know who E.M. was. Someone else." She stares at the initials—a name that will remain a mystery—and feels her eyes sting with tears. *And still I remember.* A love affair? Why would her grandmother care about a neighbor's affair? She has the feeling that this is it—but how? A last testament to a love that will remain forever secret. "He must've loved her," she says, and as she says the words, something inside her splits, a pain so deep it oddly feels like relief.

But Aidan doesn't seem to notice. He's reaching forward and pressing his hand to the spot where long ago someone else had done the same. Fingertips slide into the grooves, the palm snug.

"He must've really loved her," Abby says again.

And though she thinks he heard, he keeps his hand in place, eyes closed, as if listening for a different voice.

40

Then

DEAD CENTER IN THE TUNNEL is the hole. Shallow, but deep enough. The girl is covered in the towel she'd had with her, a towel that's red now, near the abdomen, a few twigs and crumbs of leaves evidence that at one point it was laid on the ground. Scattered beams line the walls and ceiling of the tunnel. Roots jut like gnarled bird claws, and the light from the lanterns sends long shadows across the dirt floor. Claire remembers that it was William's father who'd insisted on the tunnel's existence, yet he himself had been reluctant to enter. *The War*, William once told her. *He was with the tunnelers in Belgium for a bit. They fought one another with explosions. To this day there are bodies in the earth.*

Another one now.

Claire looks for the purse the girl was carrying, and when she can't find it, the answer comes to her in a sudden recognition that the furnace is on. She glances back at the newly installed Homart Indestructo, currently sending heat and the pungent scent of a dead woman's possessions into the house.

She is dead, isn't she?

Claire doesn't want to, but forces herself to lift the towel. The girl's eyes are still closed. Her lips shut tight, never to open again. Someone has folded her hands atop her chest, a prayerful posture Claire has always associated with the dead.

"It'll disintegrate," Edith says, pointing to the towel that Claire lets fall. "With time. Just about everything will."

Claire just nods. Over the girl's body they say a few words, apologies, prayers for forgiveness, before Claire and Edith hurry from the tunnel, eyes to the basement floor as they hear the shovel's scraping scoops followed by the soft fall of dirt. Over and again.

When it's done, Ketty emerges and Claire sees what look like tears on her cheeks, though as soon as she speaks, Claire decides it's perspiration.

"Help me," Ketty says, motioning to the cabinet. "We use this tonight and then brick."

All three women push the cabinet to the opening of the tunnel, blocking it like a mouth silenced, words swallowed within. Then it's time for Edith to go home, time to pretend it's just another night of staying up a bit too late, gossip and bridge and brandy.

When the back door shuts, exhaustion coils around Claire, weighting her steps. She makes it upstairs and falls headlong onto the made bed. Too tired to stand up again, she grabs the blanket from the other side of the bed and pulls it over her, catching a glimpse of the clock in the process. It's almost three AM. She feels as though she's been awake for days. Illogically, the thought that she'll wake up tomorrow and none of this will have happened races through her mind. Is it possible? She's so tired, maybe her memories are not correct. Maybe she's remembering a nightmare. Maybe she's still asleep. The quilt is rough against her neck, her dress tight around her waist, but she feels nothing but unctuous delirium as finally, at long last, she sinks into sleep.

Minutes pass. Maybe minutes. She jerks awake. Heart pounding, she sits up in bed, the room still dark. Her breath is shallow. After a bit it steadies, and she listens to the silence. Yet seconds ago she heard it, she knows she did—the sound of a foot pounding in the dirt. Shuddering vibrations. That was what woke her.

Ketty checked, said the mirror no longer fogged, that there was no trace of a heartbeat, those blue eyes still closed. This—the panic—is what she's always gone through. The same noises in the night that have bumped her awake since she was a child, since her doll Ellie was buried in the basement. *Buried in the basement.* A foretelling, she sees now. She looks at the clock—only fifteen minutes have passed since she lay down, and yet she's wide awake, adrenaline coursing through her.

The truth will be her punishment, she decides. Tomorrow she will tell William. She has to. It will destroy her marriage, her life, but if the girl can't have him, neither can Claire. Penance. The slightest justice.

Again she tries to close her eyes, hopeful the plan of action might allow for some sleep—but there it is, waiting and relentless, the feeling that the ceiling is lowering. Faster and faster it descends till it's pressing, pushing her deep into the mattress and the floorboards and the basement and the soil, pressing harder and harder until she's so deep within the earth that no one could hear her scream.

The next morning, William wakes to a lifting dark. The space next to him is empty, the covers smooth. He reaches to the pocket watch on the nightstand and looks at the time. Just after three. But that can't be right. He brings it to his ear—the watch is silent. He winds it and winds it, but nothing happens. Once again it's stopped, a useless trinket.

Downstairs he sees the correct time and makes his oatmeal, planning on sitting on the porch, but pauses the moment he opens the door.

On the floor, exactly where they'd left it, is the Monopoly set. He stares at it, their metal tokens—him the race car, her the thimble—each carried and abandoned with a last touch.

Without disturbing the game he sits in his spot, back against his post, and balances the bowl on his lap. Across from him she does the same, then grins with the spoon in her mouth. He smiles in return till he realizes there's nothing there. The air is cool and a thick mist at the treetops thins as it reaches toward him. He looks down at the board, all the red hotels of his ambition. *Only second prize in a beauty contest?* she'd joked when they had last played, the night before Claire told him about the baby, the night before everything changed. *Clearly I wasn't a judge,* he'd replied, watching her slip the card back under the stack. With every move her nightgown's satin's sheen caught the light. Now he lifts the pile and there it is, at the bottom, the last card played.

He leaves it all in place, the rocks holding down the cards, their tokens in step. The thought of it existing, undisturbed, is a comfort, as if a part of them is still here, still playing beneath the porch light. Despite everything, he now realizes he's hopeful that the game can somehow be continued. But how? He broke her heart. And now there's the baby to think of. Even if he could find a way for them to be together, she would never want to. Not after what he's put her through. Not in the face of the complications that would await them.

Before he leaves, he pops into his office, sees yet another stack of paperwork on his desk, and decides he'll have to come back down to deal with it all. It will be a whole day's work, he knows. But then he sees something. By the phone, a little piece of paper. One word he recognizes immediately, even from a distance.

Eva.

He snatches up the message: *Eva called. She's in Minneapolis and needs to talk. Said she'll find you.* The message is dated yesterday. While

he stood in the other room, determined not to go into his office, wanting to leave, wanting to see her, not wanting to be delayed by any work
on his desk, this message sat there, unread.

Pulling out of the parking lot, he ignores the familiar, confused
faces gawking at the car they've never seen. There's no time for explana-
tions. No time for good-byes. He's back on the road. Flying up the state.
He'll figure something out. Eva's giving him another chance, and he's
going to take it.

When he arrives home, Ketty's cleaning in the kitchen, scouring the
sink with her usual ferocity. There's no sign of food or Claire. When he
asks where she is, Ketty doesn't turn around. "Missus in the parlor."

But he doesn't see her there. He's almost left the room, about to take
the stairs, when he realizes she's sitting in a chair in the far corner,
hands folded loosely, forgotten, on her lap. Fear blasts through him as
he sees she's been crying.

Within seconds he's crouched before her. She looks at him, straight
at him, her eyes unwavering as if she's trying to find her words within him.

And then she tells him, and he sits back hard on the floor.

The basement stairs aren't given a chance to creak before he's at
their base, staring at the metal cabinet shoved before the tunnel. Ketty
helps him move it as Claire sits on the top stair. He didn't believe her—
even when she said the name *Eva*, a name she hadn't known, even then
he hadn't believed. Harmless, stoic Claire. But then he learned that
Ketty had been involved—Ketty, who was fearless of the tunnel, who's
always had a European's unnerving acceptance of horror—and he knew
it was true.

He orders Ketty to help him dig, and she does. The tunnel is low
and he has to stoop, his movements awkward, his neck cramping. When

he sees the top of Eva's foot, her toes, her red nail polish—the nail polish she knows he loves—a numbness takes over. Her feet. That her feet are here in this tunnel makes no sense. The feet that she'd rest on the tiles above the tub, toes just touching the faucet. The feet that brushed him as she sat in the bough of the cottonwood. The feet that carried her into his arms. He starts to sweep away the dirt, faster, revealing a towel. She hadn't given up; she came to find him. Even as he thinks this, he's aware the thought is hollow, that only later will the words be assigned meaning, and that that meaning will crush him.

He pauses and has just barely lifted the towel when Ketty lurches back and hits the wall. It throws him, this reaction, and he watches her stumble through the mouth of the tunnel, past Claire, who appears at the entrance, curious. Claire takes a few more steps and suddenly her hand clamps to her mouth, her face white. She's saying something, over and again. *Oh, God, oh.*

But then he hears the words more clearly. *No God, no.*

He turns back, to the truth of the event before them.

Eva. Lips the color of a bruise, mouth open as if trying to call him. Her blue eyes open and fixed with fear.

41

Now

IT'S STRANGE to leave the house. The door closes behind them, and for a moment they stand on the front steps, blinking in the sun, adjusting to the sounds. Through the trees he sees the lake. Blue water mirrors the sky, clouds faded in the reflection. The world, it seems, exists as a fold of paper, an imprint left from one side to the other.

"I'm sorry," he tells her. He knows what it's like to need answers, to not get them. They leave the house with no new information, nothing about her grandmother, nothing about Claire, though her husband's assumed affair could perhaps explain his end.

"There *was* something," she says. "There weren't gonna be fireworks, I know, but something feels—dislodged. If that makes sense." She breathes in. "I think it'll make a difference."

His phone beeps with a voicemail. One glance and he sees them: six texts—*Report to station*—and more voicemails, all piled up from the time they were in the house. Sure enough, he takes a step back up the path, toward the front door, and the reception fades. "Shit," he says, heading back to the sidewalk. "I didn't get service, the entire time. Something happened."

Abby points to across the street, a shaded spot heavily overgrown. "I'll be there. Call."

Without playing the voicemails, he calls in, braced for the news.

"Finally," Harris says. "When can you get here?"

"Two hours. Sorry, I didn't— What happened?"

"You don't know? We got him."

Aidan turns toward the lake. "Him?"

"Not a done deal, of course, but damn, this is it. Name's Carl Sutton. Hardt got a tip this morning after you left. Some woman said this guy humiliated her during sex, tied her up, consensual, but she didn't like the direction it went. We look him up; *he worked in Marshall during those years.* Lived in Wilmer at the time, but that's an hour commute."

"High mileage on his vehicle?"

"Tons. You know that shit's consistent. So Hardt and I went to ask him some questions. Just questions. Until we saw the bones right inside the door, right fucking there, a partial skeleton, clearly human. Didn't even have to go in. This long table covered with an American flag with *bones* on top. Said they washed up onshore. Some crazy story, something about an insane asylum, a girl who escaped in a straitjacket and drowned, one bone washing up every year. The guy's nuts. Fits the profile to a tee. And get this, Lila McCale's here—just saw him. She's *met* him. A couple months ago in a parking lot when she had a flat. Remembered him because he hit on her. Now we're going over his lack of alibi, for here and Marshall. Says the nights of Lila and Sarah he was at home. He's about twenty minutes outside of town, no neighbor for three miles, so no one can back that. I gotta go. *You* gotta go. Hit the road, man, this thing could be over."

Over. Lives back to normal, sleeping in his own bed, people not afraid to walk on the street or look for lost dogs. He turns to the lake. Abby.

She's standing in a small clearing, the lake behind her. "They got him," he says as he approaches. "Not official, but it looks good. Abby, I think it's over."

When she turns he sees she's holding her arm, stunned.

"What happened?"

"A bee." A pause. "Aidan."

He's reaching for her wrist. Near her elbow is a red welt with a pinprick center. "You're not allergic, right?"

"Aidan," she says again, and this time he hears it. The air is vibrating. He turns, and there, less than ten feet away, is a swarm of bees. Clinging to a branch. Beautiful, really, the way they blanket the spot in the tree, dripping to a point.

He pulls her arm. "Come on."

She follows, reluctant to look away. The buzzing dims but can still be heard as they cross the street. From inside the Jeep he can see them, just visible if you know where to look.

"Are you okay?" he asks.

She nods, still looking in the direction of the swarm.

"We caught him," he says. "I have to go to work, so there goes our night, but life will change after this. For the better."

A deep, wavering breath, followed by a little smile. "I'll send my mom to Tom's tonight, he should be back. I need a break from her." She looks back to the spot by the lake. "My dream."

"Try not to go there," he says, though even he's never seen a swarm like that in person.

"It was like glass. Like being stabbed with a shard of glass."

"I know. But the worst is over. *And* we got him."

She turns to him, a small smile, but he sees in her eyes that she's not convinced anything is over.

42

Then

WILLIAM DOESN'T KNOW what to believe. His parents raised him Catholic, but when the choice was his, he stopped attending mass. Did he believe? Had he ever really, truly believed in the words he recited, the songs he sang? Religion was something he kept in his desk drawer, a forgotten note, found once or twice a year. It was only when his parents died that he'd really questioned and realized how little, if any of it, he believed. But his parents were good churchgoing people, and ultimately he'd decided that the strength of *their* faith would be their answer; they were in their heaven. Besides, what did the opinions of an unsure, privileged boy matter? What was the point of questioning? It was much better to decide they were where they thought they were, happiness and clouds and reward. But Eva. What does this mean for Eva, who was not religious, who had sinned? Yet another thing brought on by him.

The one debate he does allow himself is will he see her again. That, and *why*. Why did any of this happen? The beginning, the middle, the end.

Comprehension circles, twisting around him. Believing she's dead, actually lifeless and cold, knowing that the face he'd looked into, the face he'd dreamed of, knowing that that person is buried below him, forever and ever dirtied with mounds of dirt and captured in darkness, it's just not something he can understand. Though now and then it hits him with a running start, knocking away his breath. It's tricky, this comprehension. He's lost many people in his life; death is not new. But this is different. With her went his core, and the void left behind only gets bigger each day.

More than anything, he wishes he believed in something. Even if he's wrong, it wouldn't matter. It's the comfort of belief—stubborn, illogical belief—that he wants. The way a child believes he's safe because a light is left on.

After a week he makes it final. First he starts in the carriage house, continuing the cement over the space where once there was a trapdoor to the tunnel. And then in the basement, brick by brick a wall at the entrance grows higher—though in one spot, at the base, he sets the bricks back just an inch and covers the front with a thin layer of mortar. Their initials with a pencil. He places his hand below. No one will know, no one will see it as the futile reach of someone who came too late.

The bouquet of irises he lays by the newly constructed wall doesn't get touched, and soon the colors fade, the stems drying. Over and over he retraces his steps. Missing the message that she called, entering the diner at the same time as someone who'd known William and his real name, all the way back to stopping to help a beautiful girl who'd fallen on a sidewalk, and yet further, to the patch of ice that took his parents' car, to his need to please them, to redeem himself, to marry, and further still to not joining in the war, to taking his first breath in a gilded house. He can look at each of those footprints, those seemingly arbitrary steps, influenced by whims, by weather, by a glint in a glass window display that drew his eyes to the girl who turned the corner as if being chased,

he can reexamine all those tiny moments and feel the draft of the butterfly's wings, and yet he cannot change a thing.

He remembers that first day they'd met, how he'd reached for her
when she'd fallen. Instinctive, even then, to try and catch her. Helpless
to save her from the start. And not once, he realizes, did he tell her that
he loved her.

Everything led to this. All the little pieces. And it's that, that feeling
of intricate connection, of fate, that finally leads him to something to
believe: It's not over. It can't be.

43

Now

OVER. A possibility that's yet to settle, an idea that seems unreal in the swarm of media rejuvenated and returned, the jumble of the crowd that's gathered. Everything, to Aidan, seems as if it's just beginning.

At first he sees only a patch of Carl Sutton's shirt in the interrogation room. But then Schultz moves to the side and Aidan sees the rest of him: River Man.

Harris bangs out the door, beelining for the fridge.

"That's Carl Sutton?" Aidan asks. "I know him. From the river."

Harris's eyes widen. "You've been to his house?"

"No, I see him. On my runs, when I stop, he's downriver, fishing."

As Harris grabs water bottles, Aidan remembers River Man with the fish. Bashing its head with his fist. There was something artistic about it, something that embraced the violence of the act.

"We got a massive sweep going," Harris says. "I think BCA's sent half their agents. Already got control samples from his car and rugs to their lab in St. Paul, see if we can get matches. Got a rush on that. Somewhere in that forest is a goody bag with needles and ketamine and his prints. Man's creepy. That's what Lila McCale said, and she's right."

Harris starts back to the hall, Aidan alongside him. *That guy creeps me out.* That's what Abby had said when she caught River Man staring, when she'd shown Aidan her birthmark at the café. Then River Man stood under an awning in the rain, the ember of his cigarette burning through the gray evening. That was Sunday. The next morning Brittany found the cigarette butts, and later that night Abby'd heard the noise, the side gate unlatched. For the first time it hits Aidan: Abby really was being watched, targeted. A close call. He'd had no idea how close. Last night, the taillights he'd seen pull away from her house—he must've scared the guy off.

"Harris, this is good. Find out where he was last night."

"I know that. He was at that bar on Toland, the one with the red walls. Met a date. I know because she was at his place today. A little worse for the wear, both of them were."

Aidan stops walking. "She was with him all night? Last night. He never left?"

"We weren't verifying last night, but I can check. Oh, and he smokes. Got Marlboro Lights in his pocket."

A deep breath. "Not Reds?"

"I know. Reds were found near the McCale property, and across from Abby's. But come on, you can smoke other stuff. Maybe the store ran out. Maybe he's cutting back. Look, no one's head's in the sand here, we keep going, explore other leads till everything's nailed down. But we're gonna get a confession out of him, I know it. And we'll get matches to the fiber samples, pin him at the locations." He puts his hand on the door, a big smile. "My wife's gonna sleep tonight. Hell, I might even sleep tonight."

The door splays open as Harris goes in, long enough for Aidan to catch a glimpse of River Man staring at his handcuffed hands on the table. Again he remembers the man with the fish, bashing in its head, and for the first time he feels hope as he realizes this might be over.

"Everything good?" Abby asks when he calls.

"Chaos, but good chaos. You got the house to yourself tonight?"

"No." She laughs. "Tom picked tonight to get sick. My mom's currently in the other room, downing Airborne and judging me from a distance."

"That's good," he says. "That you're not alone."

"I *wanted* to be alone."

At the other end of the station he spots DeVinck. He tells Abby he has to go, says good night, and in seconds has caught the officer by the front door.

"I know we're even," Aidan says. "But I need you at a house tonight."

℃

She should be happy. The man's been caught, tickers with his information already streaming across newscasts, the word "alleged" tossed in as an afterthought. But the dreams. Being in that house, she felt something, like a scent that tugs on a memory not yet defined. A literal door opened, a step into her grandmother's world, and certainly one into Claire's; action after years of standing still.

But then she'd crossed to the lake. Without warning the air became electric, the buzzing so intense she'd thought it in her mind, a warning she was about to faint. By the time she understood the source, she'd already been stung. Then she knew—the dreams were not over. Nothing was fixed.

It's late, the moon a crescent. Windows holding black. Fear grows wild within her mind. What will happen, she wonders, if tonight is her worst dream yet, if it's been building? Would she silently stop breathing? Mouth open, arm off the bed. Fingers skimming the rug.

She needs to relax, something to soothe her nerves. Her desk drawer is a tousled mess, pencils with no point, a remote control from a long-gone stereo, pads of paper, a vintage Bakelite bracelet. And the Walkman. She finds it, the tape of piano concertos her mother made still inside. Surprisingly, when she hits Play, the wheels turn—but only for a moment, a last gasp, and then nothing. She yanks the desk drawer open further, searching for batteries, and it's then she sees the little leather pouch. Inside are the stones. Tourmaline, obsidian, jade, and pyrite. The long-ago gift from the boy she let like her, the ones she threw into the back of a drawer without a thought. The boy she ruined in the eyes of everyone.

An apology. It might mean nothing to him, but she can find out where he lives, if he's still in town, and pop it in the mail. She grabs a pad of paper and is turning to an empty page when she sees a paragraph written long ago. *The dream: AIDAN. Beautiful old butter-yellow car, shadows of tree branches on the hood, a tree-lined street. A squirrel ran in front of him. He waved, he smiled, but he looked sad. Really sad.* This, she knows, she'll have to keep, and tears it off the pad, weighting it with one of the stones on the desk. Obsidian, a captivating black luster, said to be strongly protective.

When she's done writing out the apology she finds some batteries, hits Play, and is immediately sucked back through the years. *No.* She wants sleep. Not a musical conjuring of the past. Everything tells her she's at the verge of another stage, some demarcation of selves. Too much has happened to be contained in who she's been. Robert's message from this morning: *Call me when you're ready.* She'd been avoiding him. Tomorrow. A conversation, the truth. Or as much as can be said over the phone, but a promise for more when she returns. Yes, she's certain, tomorrow she will not be who she is today. But here, in the night, unable to act, it's as though she's frozen in a runner's crouch, just waiting for the blast of the gun. Any sound could set her off.

But the only way to tomorrow is through the dark meadow.

From the hall she hears her mother snoring. They've barely spoken, words netted out of some sense of civility, to not spend the last days of Abby's visit fighting. So many conversations to be had, her mother the first installment. In her hand is a sleeping pill, which often makes the dreams worse. Already she's silenced her phone and shut the curtains, and now this, a possibly hazardous zip line to the morning. She turns on the light in the kitchen and sets a glass in the sink beneath the faucet. There's a feeling of inevitability—if she's going to have the dream, so be it, let it happen right away. She's angry at the dreams. It's a dare almost. A medicinal taunt.

The kitchen window is slick black, holding the room's reflection like an ebony cameo. In it she sees the stove. The microwave on the counter. The Felix the Cat clock on the wall, manic eyes darting. And beyond is the reflection of the front door—glass, hardly a barrier. Anyone could see her, from almost any direction.

Water overflows from her glass. She shuts off the tap and swallows down the pill. Again she looks to the yard. Her eyes try to refocus, to see past her world, but everything stops at the glass, at the frozen image of herself and the pounding of Felix's eyes.

⌒℧

In the sky hangs an earthshine moon, the dark side lit by the reflective blaze of the earth's oceans, braced and held in the crook of its own crescent. The old moon in the new moon's arms.

Carl Sutton's family is in the waiting room, and each time Aidan passes through he tries to avoid their eyes. They look normal, they look kind. They don't look like they would belong to a man who'd done this. Ridiculous, he knows, but the thought is there every time he sees the mother, a blue-beaded necklace that matches her sweater, her lipstick on but slightly uneven, as if she'd known it only proper to dress up, but the shake in her hand had been too great.

The night has been flying. Aidan steps out of the interrogation viewing room and takes a moment to breathe, standing by a far window. His workspace is a mess, he can't even be near it, overflowing with office supplies and folders as Hardt—wanting to be in the thick of things once an arrest was made—decided to set up shop in the station and jammed a table up against Aidan's desk. Now, in the reflection of the window, Aidan watches Schultz approach.

"Well, this isn't great," Schultz says. "Negative on the match to the upholstery fibers found at the scenes."

Aidan turns. "What? That's big."

"I know," Schultz says. "But maybe he uses a car that's not registered to him. Still got lots of other tests. BCA's crime lab is churning them out as fast as they can."

"Sorry," a young officer says. "Mackenzie, burger's on your desk. You guys hear about the kids at the Whiskey Barrel? Smashed some dude over the head with a pitcher when he heard it was last call. One even ran, too, DeVinck had to chase him three blocks."

"DeVinck?"

"Hey." The officer suddenly crosses the room as he shouts at a woman. "You gotta wait outside. I told you. We've been *through* this."

DeVinck. Not watching Abby's house. For how long? He looks to the interrogation room, the doors closed. Everything is fine. He'll grab

his food, get another officer out there, and camp out back in the viewing room.

Grease stains on the food bag, now smeared on his desk. Reaching
for Kleenex he sees it—a half-buried file with the name Becky Cox. He
grabs it. The young woman who'd been raped in Marshall two years
before the first serial rape. A note from Haakstad: *Might not need this
anymore, and it was ruled unrelated to our set, but have at it.* Aidan scans
the report. Becky Cox, nineteen, studying to be an architect, lived with
her mother in a house a block from the restaurant where she worked as
a waitress. The guy wore a mask. DNA from hair was found, but no
matches. Aidan sees more photos of her—curly hair just like Abby's.
He looks at her stats; even her build is about the same.

And then there are the reports of harassment. All taken from Susan
Cox, Becky's mother, four months prior to her daughter's rape. The
note from Haakstad: *They lived together. Who was the target?*

They lived together. Another mother who'd been home. How many
is that? In his mind flash reports, testimonies: *I was asleep, I had no
idea, I couldn't stop it.* Tonight, he realizes, Abby's mom will be home. A
feeling, immovable, he can't get around it. Something's not right.

And here they are, the whole station distracted, lulled.

He grabs the nearest officer. "Get Harris or Schultz. Hardt, I
don't care."

He keeps reading the harassment report, faster, adrenaline picking
up. Something's here, he feels it. Late-night hang-ups. Cat strangled,
left on their porch. Victim returning home to find furniture rearranged, exactly as it was, but reversed. Multiple flat tires. No known
enemies—though a customer, a regular, asked Becky out and got
shot down. Her boyfriend in the next booth. *You? You think she'd go
out with you?* No idea the guy's name, she never bothered to ask.

And he never came back. Included in the report is a copy of the restaurant's check. A burger, fries, two sodas, and instead of leaving a tip, he wrote the words *No tip for a bitch.* Payment in cash, to the penny.

Harris stands in front of him. "What's up?"

"How many had moms home? All of them?"

"Off the top of my head, two cases had both parents home, the other three were single moms. Why?"

Now I Lay Me Down to Sleep. The pillow. "Haakstad said one of the moms thought he watched her as she slept. Harris, *every time* a mother was home. These are girls in their twenties, too. That's odd. That's a thing. We thought the commonality was they were students, couldn't afford their own place, but what if that wasn't it? Here," he says, holding up the reports, "this woman, too, in Marshall, raped at home, mom down the hall."

"So you think this is him, too? We'll go in there, bring her up."

Aidan glances back down at the words written on the restaurant bill. *No tip for a bitch.* A pit opens within him. The *a.* Right there, a stinger-like formation. "No, I don't think it's him."

The forgery case. Within seconds he's got the samples in his hand. The *a*'s are almost identical to Rick's handwriting in the samples. A couple more letter comparisons—the *t*'s are the same, the bar of the *t* starting normally on the left, but becoming heavy on the right side, ending in an angry point. The *b*'s, the huge loop in the *o*. He's got his phone in his hand. *Answer.* But the call goes straight to Abby's voicemail.

Quickly he makes another call. As it rings, he shoves the rape report at Harris. "I think *this* was his first. And I think I know who this was."

Victim returning home to find furniture rearranged, the harassment report said, *exactly as it was, but reversed*. At last Rebecca Sullivan answers.

"Your brother ever live in Marshall? I didn't see it in his records."

"This is a middle of the night question?"

"*Rebecca*."

"Okay. Yes. With my cousin. Never paid taxes, never—"

"When?" A bolt of adrenaline.

"I guess it would've been six years ago? Lived above his garage, was there for a few years. Can we use the tax thing?"

Right there at the top of the harassment report is the date. Five and a half years ago. And the serial rape cases, all within the time he was there. "He smokes. What does he smoke?"

"Reds. Faster to hell if you ask me."

Reds. With a perfect view to Lila McCale's room. With a perfect view to Abby's room. One last thing—*say no*. "He ever know someone here named Abby Walters?"

Silence, then finally. "No."

And in this moment Aidan finds his breath.

But then she continues. "Mrs. Walters, though, he knew her— the teacher? His 'other mommy,' that's what we called her. They related?"

Facts hurl, crashing. He barely hears the rest of Rebecca's words— *he practically lived at their house till Mrs. Walters pissed him off somehow, everyone pisses him off somehow, I told you*—as he's moving out the door, Harris now alongside him. "Get units at Rick Sullivan's house on Tenth," Aidan says. "And at Dorothy Walters's—543 Acacia Street."

"Who the hell is Rick Sullivan?" Harris asks.

"*He's* the one. And he's been doing it when the moms are home—to punish *them*. Only feet away and they don't even know, they can't protect their daughters. We thought it was a twisted coincidence—*it was the goal.*"

&

A swift tumble of dark clouds, rolling at an impossible pace. Leaves of the oak tree twitch just as the chandelier begins to sway—but there's no sound, and the silence is what's worse. With silence comes vulnerability. No warning can be sounded. Turn around and someone is already there.

In the quiet she raises her face to the clouds, that great black surge, and the drops begin to fall. Sound returns. At last, the sky has opened up.

Her cheeks are wet and for a moment she rises to a light consciousness, her mind registering the pillowcase as damp. But she's caught in the Ambien's grip, tousled in the dream's wake, so tired that she sees only her chair at the table, pulled out, her place waiting, and just as she takes a seat something stings her arm. A bee, her mind tells her, and though for a moment she jerks toward wakefulness, there is suddenly something so calming, a sleep within a sleep, that she slides the other way.

The fleet of black-and-whites fan out, each on a different route to Abby's house.

Aidan punches through a red light. The reports were on his desk. Hours ago, had he just looked. And never did he fully look into Rick's background, the case he'd put on hold, so eager to prove himself. All

the missteps, each one lengthens blocks and slows time. Signs blur. A
startled man on the corner retracts his foot from the street, his face
open with surprise. Still Abby's house is distant, held at bay.

At last he hits her neighborhood.

A man is here. Finally the other guest has arrived. Only instead of sitting, he stands, seen through the blurred haze of rain, his head, hands,
and feet covered. He looks for something, and as he turns, the dream
world seems to meld with Abby's own, the table replaced by her bed,
her desk close by. He stops—the stones are there, the note. *Dear
Rick.* Then the rain becomes a veil, and the veil disintegrates to static.
If only she could see clearly—a thought already distant, a filament
snapped free. Wind passes through the meadow, she feels it even as
he traces her eyebrow with one gloved finger, and in this moment she
understands he could actually be real, that this is some intersection of
the dream and reality. But what is what? She can't shake the worlds
apart.

Then suddenly there's a shift and she's watching herself from the
corner of the room, as if perched in the rafters of a theater. Below are
threads of light that bend and weave with movement. A crimson ray
as the man reaches for the woman, holding her head with one hand as
the other holds the knife, blade angled toward her mouth.

Aidan pulls up as patrol cars tear onto the street. Haphazard parking,
doors open. The windows of Abby's house are dark. And for a moment
he thinks all is well—they're sleeping. This is a normal night.

But then he sees it: Rick's Buick. Two doors down.

They're out, guns drawn, splitting off and surrounding the house, then ready to break through the front door. *On three.*

Abby sees the man with the knife, but understanding is a slow saturation. The dream gets its grip once more and the oak tree's limbs shoot up and down the walls, growing, stretching, and thickening as great secrets are whispered in voices she knows—and she's so relaxed that the burst of the door is simply a part of a giant heartbeat, and the chaos in the room a mass of kinetic color.

And then the room fills with a green light as if filtered through a thousand leaves, and she realizes she was wrong before. Because this is who she's been waiting for. At last he's here.

The first thing Aidan sees is the knife, brought to her neck the second Rick sees them. Her eyes are half-open but flickering and Aidan wonders if she's coming to, if she will wake only to glimpse the end. A wretched last image. Fear on everyone's face, and Aidan, who didn't make it in time.

Too late Aidan realizes Abby's mom is in the hall. Someone, Harris it must be, is yelling *Get her out of here!* Cops holding her back, one strap of her nightgown off her shoulder, stretching, about to snap.

But Abby can't wake. Someone's left a television on and loud voices are yelling, banging. This can't be real. It's a dream, a dream that's flipped on its side, gills sizzling in the bright sun, mouth open, gasping. She wants out. Her worst nightmare, she never realized, is the one from which she cannot wake.

But then she lets go, drifting back into the dream she knows, an odd comfort. Dry grass waves and branches twist into the black sky.

Still Abby's mother is there, struggling and screaming, and that's when Aidan catches it: Rick watching Abby's mother, his face filling with something so far beyond hatred, so far beyond that it's joy. And he's so lost in this that he never sees Aidan raise his arm. Never sees the eye of the gun.

At the table he sits before her and reaches for her hand.

There's the sound of the shot, and the knife hits the bed.

44

Then

THE DAYS ARE SCOTCH MUDDLED. The house has Eva in its heart-beat. It's been only two weeks, but he knows he can't go on like this. He won't go on, not for long. The anger's begun to drip into singeing sadness. William created this. Claire, so desperate for his attention, so punctured by his betrayal, had been reduced to this deception. A baby she'd invented, a lie that undid everything. Ketty, decades of loyalty to his family brought to action by his behavior. Even Edith would be forever affected by his choices. The entire situation brought on by him. Everything. His father had been right, he was selfish. A spoiled boy who thought he could have it all. But when he thinks of never having pursued Eva, of her never being in his life, the emptiness he feels spreads to his entirety. She, he realizes, was the one true choice he made. The problem was years and years ago, when he first took his step on a trail of gilded tinder, never understanding what one truth could do. The destruction is his own.

It's late. The lamps are off, forgotten. He sits at his desk and swills his drink. Claire knocks on the door to the study, then pushes it open when he doesn't respond. He sees her absorb the darkness.

"I have to leave," she says, sitting across from him. "I can't sleep. I don't think I'll ever sleep again if I stay here."

William says nothing. He wants her gone. Her eyes are skittish, reminding him constantly of why. She says she's going. And he will let her. He points to the scotch in an offering. When she shakes her head he asks, "You'd leave, for good? What about your family?"

"I'm a guest to my father. A strange girl who visits now and then. My mother's happy to at last have him to herself. And my sister would miss me, I'm sure, but her inheritance would increase." She pauses. "It would be better if I disappeared. If it was a tragedy and not a divorce. Even if people learn about my father—it would be understandable. They'd assume it was my disappearance that undid him."

"It's drastic."

"It's not. It's simple. It makes things go away." After a moment, she continues. "You'd claim to miss me. That's all I ask. That you claim to have loved me and my family, because people will follow your lead. Even if you remarry, that wouldn't change."

"I couldn't remarry."

"You could. You'd declare me dead."

"No. Claire, I couldn't."

She says nothing, and in the quick averting of her eyes, he sees she understands. *I could never love anyone like I loved her.*

45

Now

EVERY MINUTE IS broken apart and spread out. Crammed with doctors, police, well-meaning friends—and Robert, who tries time and again to join her. *Not now. Please,* she finally had to say to him, and in the silence that followed, she heard the squeaking pivot of his desk chair and pictured him turning away from his computer, from his scripts, from all he has control over, facing an empty room. He relented, and she knows that his acceptance of this is an indication that he's aware of what's changed. But near death trumps betrayal. Conversations can wait—she's earned a bit of silence.

The hotel they check into—she and Aidan in one room, her mom in the other, grateful beyond words, the bearer of constant coffee or snacks for Aidan—is drab, with a door that sticks and needs to be yanked. Sunlight brightens a steady layer of dust, and the only way she can sleep is in his arms. The irony, she realizes, is that the nightmares have stopped. A promise made good? An immense relief, but one like the dull edge of a knife—there's something to be happy about, but it still hurts. Claire's name, however, remains a mystery.

Over and again she's told she's lucky. *Lucky.* A silver-tipped word, slippery. *So very lucky*, Aunt Emilia said, hot dish on the hotel-room credenza, her voice a whisper, as if someone keen to challenges could be listening. *Spared* is her other favorite. Yes, she was spared. But still her ears ring from the blast. Still she feels the wet that sprayed her face. Spared. People should keep their words to themselves. But a heartbeat later she hates herself for her anger.

Life and its patterns and paths and giant loops leave her dizzy. The world and all its faces. Every movement and every action and every re-action. It's too much. Time will help, Aidan tells her, but all she can think of is where she is now, her trip extended, the unknown return like a lull between words, the empty half page that precedes a new chapter. And she needs it, this space of nothing. Trying to decide any-thing right now is impossible. The only thing she wants to do is sit by the window and watch the water in the swimming pool, the way it catches the light, so different as the day goes on.

༂

Days pass and the hotel parking lot fills and empties with different cars, red brake lights a mere pause before turning onto the highway, people finally going home or venturing out further. Abby watches them come and go from the window. She's feeling better, she tells Aidan, and he sees it in her hesitant merge with life. One day he pulled up to find her in a lounge chair by the pool, fully dressed but feeling the sun, and the next day she'd walked to the store down the street by herself, the empty grocery bag in the trash like a token of improvement.

But she won't go to her house, her soon-to-be old house. Dorothy has put it on the market, with plans to live with her longtime boyfriend until it sells. *Strange*, Abby told Aidan, *what softens a person*. Aidan hadn't thought it strange at all. *When you almost lose everything, you sometimes find the most.*

Rick Sullivan. A copy of Sarah Breining's key made when he painted their house, almost a year ago. Was he holding on to it? Trying to resist? The only answers are now filtered through his sister, their childhood bright in the public's eye, tissues wadded in Rebecca's hand, mascara streaming in the heat of television spotlights. *Ever since we were kids,* Rick had said, *she's telling lies. Sky's always on its way down.* The truth, Aidan knows, sits off to the corner of their words. *Crazy is not created in a vacuum,* Dorothy said the other night. *I think I remember his sister used to mess with him, turned their mother against him.* She'd said this as she held pictures of the victims in her hand. *Yes, I think I remember that.*

Guilt, Aidan knows, can rewrite history.

He goes to collect the rest of her things, forgotten items she'd listed for him, a razor in the shower, a note on her desk, a pair of navy blue flip-flops on the back patio, everything written on a piece of hotel stationery. For a while he stares at the list, realizing it's the first time he's seen her handwriting, until he feels the noon sun, thick and urging, and goes inside, impressed with the job the cleaners did. The only giveaways are the broken yellow tape at her bedroom door like leftover streamers from a party and the missing bedding.

On her desk is a black stone that holds down the requested note. His name, the first thing he sees. *The dream: AIDAN. Beautiful old butter-yellow car, shadows of tree branches on the hood, a tree-lined street. A squirrel ran in front of him. He waved, he smiled, but he looked sad. Really sad.*

He remembers the dream. The car he'd loved so much he'd tried to find the name, the make, anything to match reality to what had been in his mind. He remembers telling his friends—could Abby have heard? He'd never brought up the sadness. It was felt so intensely, but he'd not known how to describe it. And yet she'd known. Strangely unsurprising.

Back at the hotel, he finds her on the bed, watching some daytime drama. She sits up when she sees him, eager. "I felt like they were betraying me," she says, explaining. "My flip-flops, how dare they stay in a place like that."

She laughs, just a little, and the sound—so wanted, so missed—at once changes everything. A hand wiping clean a surface. She's here, he can see her now.

Sitting beside her, he shows her the note she had him get, the dream. "You heard me talk about this?"

"No. I mean I did, but I'd had that dream before. That we'd both dreamt it, I thought it might've meant something." She smiles, and looks in the bag. Then stops. In her palm is the black ring box.

"It wasn't on the list," he says. "I know. But you can't leave something like that where people are in and out."

"This is the ring. This is the box where I found the note."

"Can I?" he asks.

She hands it to him and watches him take it in. "You were there," she says.

He smiles. "I made it just in time."

This affirmation has been repeated a few times, as if the concept still settles within her. He leans forward, a kiss. "Does it fit?" he finally asks.

It fits, but the wrong hand. "It's easy to size." She leaves it on, studying it under the light of a brass wall sconce. "It looks different now. Softer, in this light. It still makes no sense, this ring. The cabin." She turns to him. "Let's visit Eleanor. Something happened to my grandmother. My family. This is my story, I want to know."

The nursing home is a couple of hours away. White, slow clouds drift across the sky, the highway a dark band rolled upon the plains. Now and then they pass through small towns, painted business names faded on brick, half barrels filled with marigolds and geraniums. American flags and bait shops. Each town seems to have someone on a bench, watching the road.

Abby's got her seat reclined and is gazing out the window, though now and then she lifts her hand to the light to study the ring. *You might as well keep it,* Dorothy told her earlier. *I feel like it's always been yours.*

"You know what?" Abby suddenly asks as they pass a row of storefronts. "There's not a parking meter to be found."

"I think that's a good thing."

She nods. "I just saw a sign for chocolate zucchini cake."

"I know that's a good thing."

The home where Eleanor Hadley lives, Forest Glen Estates, is surprisingly nice, in a little town not too far outside Minneapolis. Aidan figures that families from the Cities must bring their parents here, pleased with the tranquil setting, the outdoor activities, the fact that it's away from big, confusing metropolises with mazes of streets and jumbled sidewalks. As they walk through the hall they pass gold names on doors—*Michael, Ed, Ray*—and he wonders how many of these men fought in wars. Trudged through waters off France, hid breathless and broken in someone's barn, German tanks rattling the rafters. And now here they are, bent over in wheelchairs or sitting on a floral couch, staring out a window, perhaps seeing the past, perhaps just seeing a parking lot.

"Belligerence is common in dementia," the nurse, Marjorie, says when they stop before a door. *Eleanor*, her gold plaque says. "She can be testy, depending on the day. And she's in the later stages, so you know the disorientation is pretty pronounced. But she has her moments."

"And she was living at Morrow Lake before she came here? Right up to a year ago?" Aidan asks.

The nurse nods. "Sure was. In a cabin all by herself. We forget— they come from a different era. Their parents used candles when they were younger, pumped their own water. Some, like her, don't even have birth records. We've got one gentleman who was born on the boat over, and since nothing official was drawn up, he tells people he's from the Atlantic." She knocks on Eleanor's door. "I'll go in first. Honey," she says loudly. "It's Marjorie."

There's a sound, a faint sound, which Marjorie interprets as a yes. She opens the door and goes in, leaving it ajar. When she calls to them, both Aidan and Abby step carefully inside, walking as if on glass. A little kitchen area sprouts to the right. A bowl of cereal, untouched, sits by the sink.

As they're about to enter the living room Aidan places his hand on the small of Abby's back and feels her take a deep breath. Some people aren't good with the elderly, and he remembers Abby mentioning she never got along with her grandmother. He's assuming that she'll freeze up, awkward, and so he steps into the room prepared to be the one to do most of the talking. Eleanor is by a large window, facing the other direction, talking to Marjorie, who's raced ahead to provide some warning, some information: *You're Eleanor, and there are people to see you, the people we talked about.* Eleanor's hair is swept up, loose, held by a mother-of-pearl clip, and her posture is that of someone made to balance books on their heads, trained to sit without slumping, someone taught poise.

But when Eleanor turns, facing them, it's Aidan who stiffens and holds back. There's something about her that suddenly makes him uncomfortable. He can't look at her. He feels exposed, as if with one glance she would see everything in him—though so far she's not even seen him, her gaze still fixed on Abby.

"No," Eleanor says, and then over and over again: "No. No, no, no."

She's agitated. Beside him Abby instinctively takes a few steps back, her face weighted with shock, mouth slightly open. For a moment he thinks she's about to leave, to hurry from the room and give up before a word is spoken.

In a beat Marjorie is there, holding on to Eleanor's thin shoulders. "Okay, Ellie, okay. They're just here to talk. Abby," she says, and reaches for Abby's hand, as if to prove she's friendly, "is your friend Edith's granddaughter. Do you remember Edith? Edith Walters?"

And Aidan sees it, words landing in a place of recognition. Eleanor's face softens as she searches Abby for her ancestry. Abby in return smiles hesitantly, as if trying to break from whatever it was that held her.

"My grandmother," she says, "sold you her cabin for a dollar. You must've been close?"

He can't tell if Eleanor's heard or not. She's smiling—dazed, it seems—and so he looks away, at the window, which is clouded and dirty, rendering the outside world faded, a memory gone to seed. "I'm glad you're okay," Eleanor says, still studying Abby. "After what happened."

Abby glances at him. It was in the paper, he remembers, and looks to the small dining room table, expecting to see one there. But there's just a wall calendar, lying open to a month long past.

"I'm fine, thank you," Abby says. "Well, thanks to him." She motions toward Aidan.

Eleanor must not have seen Aidan before, because when she does, she takes a sharp breath and suddenly her shoulders crumple, her head lowered.

Marjorie just nods, as if this is how it goes. "Like I said. She has good days, but this doesn't appear to be one of them. We had a big day today, a birthday party for her friend Virginia, who turned ninety-eight. *Someone* had three cupcakes," she adds, as if perhaps the sugar overdose explains the current confusion, as if Eleanor is a child who broke into the pantry. Then, with a lowered voice, she explains to Aidan, "Virginia mostly sleeps, so we let Ellie have her cupcake, since she's so good to her."

After a bit Eleanor looks back up, right into Aidan's eyes. He forces himself to hold her gaze. It's unnerving, those wet blue eyes. What they've seen, he thinks, no one will know. All those memories locked inside a mind that's collapsing.

Finally she looks away. "She was tough as nails."

"Who?" Abby asks quickly. "Edith?"

Eleanor nods. "Tough as nails."

Abby smiles. "I agree."

"Especially after."

"After . . . after Claire disappeared? Her neighbor?"

"No. No." She pauses, looking up at the light fixtures, eyes watering. "I couldn't sleep there. I'd never sleep again."

"Where? At Morrow Lake?"

But Eleanor's no longer listening, she's back to looking at Aidan. "You broke my heart." Tears silently fall, catching in the lines of her face.

"Okay," Marjorie says. "The confusion gets to her sometimes. Let's let her be."

Aidan takes Abby's hand, pulling her to him. He knows she's disappointed, knows there's an entire list of questions she's not able to ask, will never be able to ask. He squeezes her hand and then kisses the top of her head: *It'll be okay.*

He turns back to say good-bye, but the words catch in his throat as he sees Eleanor staring at their hands. Stricken.

Abby sees it, too, and pulls away, but Eleanor's eyes follow her ring, the lines in her face seeming to deepen. When at last she looks up, her gaze is slow, as if refocusing, adjusting the picture before her. The stricken expression smooths to understanding. She looks to Aidan. "I'm happy for you." Then to Abby: "I'm sorry. I'm so sorry."

Abby shrugs. "It's okay. I appreciate you trying. Thank you."

Eleanor's eyes fill again, the reflection of the lights like words just out of reach.

46

Then

ONLY HER CLOTHES ARE PACKED, some books. Claire is anxious to leave most everything behind, even her kiln, her wheel. She won't allow herself that love—any love—anymore. With the door to her studio shut, she stands in the hall, unable to let go of the glass doorknob. This is it, the last connection. But then a distant part of the house settles with a shriek, and quickly she lets go. It's been happening a lot, noises that Claire feels in her bones. As she turns, the floor wails.

The day before she's to leave, she steps onto the path and winds her way through the red grief of geraniums to Edith's house, the curtains all drawn. When Claire knocks, she sees a flutter in the fabric.

"I wanted to be sure it was you," Edith says, the door barely held ajar. Her eyes are beautifully made up, but her lips are naked and forgotten, and her chest is weighted with at least five necklaces. Claire follows her into the darkened parlor and thinks of her children, soon to return, children who will one day forget how their mother used to be.

"Take the tea set," Claire says, trying not to stare at Edith's tangled layer of necklaces. "And my jewelry. I'll get you everything. Sell what you can, and now and then I'd appreciate it if you could send me some money. William's giving me a sum, but I don't want to ask for more. I can't be in contact with him—he needs me gone." She touches her lips with her fingers. "I don't know how this works. How much I'll need."

"I'll give you the coat off my back," Edith says. "This is my fault."

"No. It's not. And I can't hear you say that."

"Your mother seems like an inventory taker. She'll notice what's missing."

Claire looks to the window, the curtain heavy, a split of light where the panels fail to meet. "Tomorrow night you call the police. Say you heard it. Two shots—one they'll see missed, a bullet in the wall. The other—they'll assume. William will be at a dinner, and when he comes home, the police will be in the house, and he'll tell them what's missing. My jewelry stolen. A few other things, his family's silverware." Then she looks down at her hand, fingers bare, and reaches into her pocket. The box, black velvet. "Edith. Please."

"No. Absolutely not. I've got so many rings." She flutters her bare fingers. "And I can't sell it. I can't wear it—people will recognize it. You keep it."

Claire keeps her hand out, the ring, the most beautiful ring she'd ever seen, braced silently in black. "I can't look at it. Give it to Dorothy when she's old enough. Or her daughter, when she has one. It's a promise, Edith. A promise of a life that never happened."

She goes to place the ring box atop the piano, and that's when she sees the butterfly container. Dried leaves, mostly bare sticks, the water in the vases clouded. A world already long ago. From the lid of the container hang a dozen empty chrysalises, which means the butterflies hatched. For a moment Claire feels a leap of hope—until she takes a step closer and sees the floor of the cage, littered with lifeless wings.

Early the next morning they left. It wasn't a long drive, and they took it
in silence. There was nothing to say. Their life together had gone hor-
ribly wrong, and though in a way that united them, bound them with
regret and sorrow, it also enhanced that which they would like to forget. Complementary cuts of misfortune that slid together to form a
whole clear, sad picture. No one could bring about the feeling of loss as
the other could. And so they faced forward, silently watching darkness
release the road in small stretches at a time.

At almost six AM they arrive, the landscape still dark. Black forms of
trees are just beginning to cut into a suddenly lightened orange sky. She
doesn't know what to expect of the cottage. No one in her family has
been here in years, and everyone else she knows stopped summering
there, choosing instead the view of expansive oceans or cities with
buildings that scrape the sky. And now the cottage has traded hands
again, from Claire to Edith, though Edith had protested. *If it makes you
feel better,* Claire had said, *one day you can sell it back to me. For a dollar.*
She'd laughed, though Edith stayed silent.

William stops the car, and that's when they hear the loons. Ghostly
cries. An eerie, haunting accompaniment to life on a lake. Every culture
has a tale of them. The Swedish family who lived in cottage number
three had said that in Norse myth the cries were riddles, chilling co-
nundrums that quickened a traveler's pace. And the old Cree man who
taught them to recognize birdcalls told them in scattered English that
the loons were messengers from the beyond. As a child, Claire had
heard their cries mostly as laughter, but now she agrees. Calls from the
other side, unsettling shrieks slicing through the silence. A life of this
will forever conjure faces in grains of wood, blinking eyes in darkness,
brushing fingertips in the wind. But this was also the sound of her
childhood, she reminds herself, and then it was graceful, majestic,

romantic even. And really, it's nothing more than the call of a bird, a bird that can barely walk on land.

The pebble path crunches beneath her feet. August, the month when each cottage teemed with children, small footprints in the sand, is not the same. Only a couple of cottages appear to be occupied, most likely locals whom Claire has never met, identical porch lights on, while the rest sit vacant or derelict. When she spots her family's, the last in the row, she refuses to look at William, afraid to agree with any expression he wears. The screen door is sealed with grime, the green paint all but missing, and years of leaves piled on every surface.

Thankfully, the inside fared better. Her first impression is that of dust, nothing a good cleaning won't fix, but then the world begins to brighten, and with it comes yellow stains on the walls and ceiling, a leaky roof's ominous watercolor. William does what he can, removing a squirrel's skeleton near the window—white, snagged streaks in the screen from its claw marks, desperate attempts for freedom—and knocking down the spiderwebs that shroud several corners.

"The roof, Claire," he says as he stands at the door, determined to disappear before the neighbors wake. "That's the first to address, before it rains. I'll find someone in the area, and call them—don't worry, I'll use the name Davis. Electricity, plumbing. The fireplace needs to be checked before you use it."

"Give me their name. I'll contact them. I don't want to be associated with anyone. Anyone real, that is. I'll have a new name."

"And that is?"

She pauses, almost not wanting him to have this, the extension to her new self. But at last she knows he must, if only for practical reasons. "Eleanor," she says. "Eleanor Hadley."

He nods, then looks around, one last time. "If you need anything, you should ask for it now. Soon I won't be able to help."

"I'll be fine. I have Edith. If something changes, she can let you know."

"No, Claire. I won't be around." He pauses, as if debating further explanation, but says nothing more.

She looks at him, William, her William, whom she's tried to love a little less with every day. She can't let him see her face, how she's failed. She turns toward the screened porch. Without looking at him again—a decision she'll often question later, as would one last steady look have hurt? One additional remembrance to carry her forever?—she steps away and onto the green-painted wood planks, the water before her overwhelmed with color, the sky burning orange and pink, a sky of day-dreams and desire. Out here the lake is full of life, splashing wings, cries and calls of birds whose names return to her. Loons, warblers, waterthrush. This will be her life. The sounds of her world.

And at night the noises will change, the beauty gone, and never will she forget why.

The morning air is cold despite the warm glow, and it's as she's watching the water that she hears the door close. Just like that, he's gone.

47

Now

HE WAS THERE. And still is. By her side as often as he can be.

But Robert. Things need to be settled between them, figured out and made clear. Best done in person, she's decided, and so the silences between them are long, words caught along the way.

"I had a strange dream last night," he says when he calls, as if hoping that treading on her territory will engage her.

"What was it?"

"It was one of those dreams where I was me, but I wasn't me. And I guess I'd been in a hospital for a while, because I woke up and found out Marlene Dietrich had visited. While I was asleep. I was so pissed. But then I wanted to go home. I remember that. Just to be home. Someone asked me where that was and I said 'lovin'.' Maybe I was from the South. I don't know."

"Marlene Dietrich?"

"I watched *Judgment at Nuremberg* a couple nights ago, I guess she was on my mind."

Acquiescing, that's how he's been. Walking softly, afraid to wake the sleeping giant. At least this is what she thinks, until he continues.

"Abby. I fucked up. If I'd gotten on that plane with you none of this would've happened. I think about that every day."

"Robert, that's not—"

"I know. My idea of being ready for marriage, I thought I was doing that. But I wasn't. I see that now. But I think we can get back. Can you just remember how we used to be?"

"I remember. And I'll come home soon, I promise."

And she will. Even if it's simply to have a face-to-face conversation, to move her things from one side of the dresser to a box on the floor.

Outside, kids jump into the hotel pool and a car door slams. Summer is almost back to normal. Bikes tear down streets, soccer balls are kicked into nets, the scent of charcoal again warming the evenings. Little feet once more find toeholds in the bases of trees, the world seen as if through green glass, leaves bright with sun. But mothers watch a bit closer from porches, and locks click shut in the evening. Almost back to normal.

"I've been thinking of going to the Cities," Aidan tells her. "Moving back. I want you to come with me."

"Us," she says, running her fingertips along his wrist, then up his arm, "in Minneapolis together. Maybe near the lakes. A little place."

"Just ours."

This, she knows, is right. She could work in estate jewelry here, maybe start her own business. Perhaps one day she'd come across more pieces by I&I, learn their stories. *Write it down, don't let them end.* The ring is still on her hand, and in its flash she once again sees the brazen red of truth. What would she write? What would be the words she'd print for this, her own story?

With this ring, a wrong was made right.

Pulling away from Makade, she feels as though she's leaving a piece of herself, convinced she could turn around and see the former Abby, left behind. Yet strangely the one that's replaced her feels more innocent—trusting—as if a reset button has been pressed. *They don't call it "a new lease on life" for nothing,* her mother said. But it's more than this.

Return the car. Return to life. Hard conversations. Movement. Though part of her wants to stay in limbo, maybe in Minneapolis, where only Aidan would know to find her, where she'd not be forced to face anything. Her hands are on the steering wheel, eyes steady on the distant silhouette of the airport. And then, in one smooth motion, she veers off the highway and toward the lake district, knowing she'll cut her flight close, but deciding to leave things up to chance, to offer her day, her life, like a petal in her palm. If it catches a breeze, so be it.

Water blinks with light and the cottonwood trees shimmer. When she's finally there, parked alongside the house, she shuts off the car. Through the open window she hears the faint kiss of waves and sees a sailboat, tilted on the water in a turn. She looks to the spot where the bees had gathered, but they're gone. It's just a tree, nothing more.

Especially after. The dividing line in Abby's grandmother's life, something that changed her forever. Claire, Abby had assumed, yet Eleanor said *no*—a product of her confusion? A moment of clarity? A mystery, that's all Abby knows. There's no one left to tell her grandmother's story, no one left to tell Claire's. And it makes Abby sad. People will pass by these beautiful, grand houses and admire them, never knowing who cried in the bedrooms, who danced in the parlor, or who said good-bye, perhaps for the last time, at the door, watching from the threshold as someone left.

But everywhere is like that, she knows. How many fields, houses, street corners are filled with invisible meaning? She thinks of the man killed near her work, how for a while people spoke of him, their eyes upon the spot of his last breath. But time passes. Soon no one will know, though maybe one or two will pause inexplicably, lingering a second longer than usual before turning the corner. And now her mother's house will be like that. One day a little girl will have trouble sleeping in the bedroom. Her parents will add a night-light, thinking that will help.

People stop telling stories. They forget. They don't know there was a story to tell.

Her phone chimes with a voicemail. Hannah, thankful Abby's coming back, even for a bit, says she has a distraction for her. *Write these down.* Abby does as instructed and grabs a piece of paper and a pen from the glove compartment. *You ready? These are the girl names so far. Madeleine—just pretty, right? Natasha—great name, but would people think she's Russian? And Eva.*

Abby's hand stops, pen frozen.

I've always loved that one. Do you like it?

In a flash Abby hears her call the baby Eva. The whoosh of a passing car startles her. She looks up, catching a bit of white in the trees that line the lake, and turns in that direction, searching until she sees it again—the sailboat slicing through the water.

Now she rings the bell and waits. Through the small window by the door she sees the inside of the house, wood walls that shoot up from the wood floor as if the entire room exists in the dark split of a tree, the chandelier above like an opening to the sky. One last time she looks at the photograph, taken on these front steps. There's something about these three women being here, returned to their watchful perch, that makes her feel glad. Gratified. A small sense of permanence in a world that's anything but.

Carefully she leans the picture frame against the front door and walks back down the path. She feels them behind her, their faces tilted toward the sun.

At the street she stops and turns back to the stone house, the iron gate before her. The lawn is pale with the caught sun. The lower windows mirror the trees, the water. The upper ones hold the sky. Some of the stones are darkened with time, and streaks that look like soot stretch along the top of the turret.

She lifts her hand to the ironwork gate and wraps her fingers around the bar, the diamond of the ring flashing in the light. The world slows down. Takes a breath. Shapes dart in the windows, the air thick like fog.

But then she blinks and lets go, and life returns.

ACKNOWLEDGMENTS

So many people to thank.

This story's journey from my computer to the world began with my agent, Lucy Carson. "Thank you" does not begin to tell the enormity of my gratitude. Your notes, your dedication, your support. You are a writer's dream. And never would I have met you if it weren't for Kaitlyn Wylde, who selflessly took the time to reach out on my behalf. Kaitlyn, thank you.

To everyone at Putnam, and especially my editor, Tara Singh Carlson. Your eye, your instinct, your wisdom. These pages would not be here if it weren't for you. I thank you. This story thanks you. Eva, William, Claire, Robert, Abby . . . they are eternally grateful, as am I.

In addition, I want to thank Detective Sergeant Brian McCabe, to whom I owe much for his patience, kindness, and generosity. You are nothing short of a hero. And former police officer Devin No, thank you. Devin, the fact that your wife, Cindy, read one of my first (awful) stories before I knew I wanted to be a writer, and that now you are one of my first readers for my novel makes me feel there is some beautiful magic in the world. And I'm so grateful to Lieutenant Michael J. Zorena, retired, for his assistance, and on his vacation no less. To Julia Cole, thank you for hearing my plea for help and helping. Jeffrey Berger, MD, MBA, you are a lifesaver, literally and figuratively. Thank you, thank you, thank you.

In no particular order, and always treasured for reading draft after draft and/or providing other invaluable support: Suzanne Unrein, Becarren Schultz, Stephanie "Seshi" Stephens, Bryony Atkinson, Judith Cohen, and Dianne Schwehr.

Forever will I be grateful to my writing professor at Loyola Marymount University, Dr. Chuck Rosenthal. Chuck, you one day said to me, "I hate to tell you this, but I think you could be a writer." The best bad news ever. Thank you for everything you taught me, most of which I've forgotten—but I remember your saying that was okay, because at some point it just comes out your hands (and it does).

To my parents, Addi Sardar and Zuhdi Sardar. Mom, you taught me to work hard. Dad, you taught me to dream. A great combination for a writer. I love you both.

Most important, none of this would be possible without the love and support of my husband, Joe Schwehr. Thank you for who you are—I love you. And last but in no way least, my son, Maximiliaen. You put the drive back into my world. Everything I do, I do for you.